The Yellowstone, Forever!

David M. Delo

Kingfisher Books
Helena, Montana

David M. Delo

The Yellowstone, Forever!

ISBN: 0-9662218-0-X
Library of Congress card catalog number: 97-92846

This book is published by

Kingfisher Books
P. O. Box 4628
Helena, MT 59604

PRINTING HISTORY
FIRST PRINTING 1998

PRINTED IN THE UNITED STATES
10 9 8 7 6 5 4 3 2 1

The Yellowstone, Forever!

To Mike,
who has been hanging tough all these years,
waiting to be heard.

David M. Delo

Preface and Acknowledgments

The events that led to the creation of America's first national park, the Yellowstone, have been well documented by historians like Aubrey Haines and Richard Bartlett. Yet many people like to receive their history lessons through the novel. In this one, the reader will find considerable research and truth in the tale, because the author, like historical biographer Irving Stone, believes that history is often more fascinating than fiction.

Nearly all of the characters in the book lived in the second half of the nineteenth century and performed roles similar to those I describe. I have by necessity filled gaps in the historical record by creating personality profiles, scenes, and the majority of the dialogue. On occasion I lifted paragraphs from historical letters and telegrams and converted the contents into dialogue.

I offer my thanks to the many individuals across the country who assisted me in my four years of effort. Authors, historians, friends and associates read portions of the manuscript and provided me with superb feedback, including numerous corrections to fact. Extra heart-felt smiles go to Iloilo Jones for her support and to Erica S. Olsen for her superb editing.

Historical Characters

Associated with Western exploration

Nathaniel P. Langford
frontiersman, politician, and banker
Ferdinand V. Hayden
geologist, naturalist, explorer, and promoter of the West
James Stevenson
Hayden's operations manager and companion
Thomas Moran
engraver and first painter of the Yellowstone
William Henry Jackson
the Hayden survey photographer
Emma Woodruff
a Philadelphian who became Mrs. Ferdinand Hayden

Associated with the Northern Pacific Railroad

Jay Cooke
Philadelphia's richest private banker
Harris C. Fahnestock
Jay Cooke's partner and manager of the New York office
William D. Kelly
a Pennsylvania congressman with a love of railroads
General Ab Nettleton
confidant and employee of Jay Cooke

David M. Delo

An Introduction to
Yellowstone National Park

Yellowstone National Park is a 3,450-square-mile region of mountainous terrain in the northwest corner of Wyoming. Within it, the visitor will see active hot springs, geysers, and mud volcanoes, all remnants of the park's volcanic past.

The evolution of the Yellowstone landscape began sixty-five million years ago, during the Rocky Mountain Revolution, the extended geological period when the Rocky Mountains were formed. As the mountain range developed, the Yellowstone region experienced a series of violent volcanic episodes.

The first volcanic eruptions occurred during the Eocene period, ten million years *after* dinosaurs became extinct. For thousands of years, the Yellowstone was a landscape of lava flows and volcanic ash whose air was gray with noxious gases and caustic particles.

For forty million years, the Yellowstone was relatively stable. Then, twelve million years ago, the Yellowstone landscape was raised thousands of feet. By the end of the Pliocene period, the general elevation of the Yellowstone was eight thousand feet above sea level.

Two million years ago, the Yellowstone underwent more volcanic violence when a gigantic explosion tore an enormous hole in the heart of the Yellowstone country. This event was repeated 600,000 years ago. When this last volcanic explosion breached the surface, it was as though a thousand Mount St. Helens had exploded all at once. Cubic miles of earth literally evaporated. The explosion left a huge scar, a crater thirty miles wide by forty-five miles long. Today, much of that caldera is filled by the waters of Yellowstone Lake.

No one knows who first encountered a geyser or touched the waters of a hot spring. When you consider that man has occupied the North American continent for perhaps 25,000 years, the first encounter probably took place thousands of years ago. The first person to see the Yellowstone may have been an ancestor of the Blackfoot or Shoshone Indians.

The first white man to witness the phenomena may have been John Colter, a member of the Lewis and Clark Expedition. During his return trip through the Rocky Mountains, Colter teamed up with Manuel Lisa, a trapper from St. Louis, to trap beaver. Speculation as to where Colter wandered in the Rocky Mountains has given rise to several books about his life. He is thought to have passed through the Yellowstone on his journey to contact various Indian tribes, but Colter left no written account.

One of the earliest written descriptions of the Yellowstone came from a Black Robe, a Jesuit priest named Father Pierre Jean De Smet who spent decades in the West. In his journal for the year 1852, he wrote: *I think the most extraordinary spot and perhaps the most marvelous of all the northern half of this continent is in the very heart of the Rocky Mountains . . . between the sources of the Madison and Yellowstone. It contains boiling springs that contain calcareous matter and resemble the springs of Asia Minor described by* [English archeologist] *Richard Chandle (1738-1810). The earth takes fantastic shapes . . . gas, vapor and smoke escape from a thousand openings and the noise resembles that of a steam boat.*

De Smet never visited the Yellowstone; he only heard about it from local Indians who, he said, spoke of the area with fear in their hearts. To them, according to De Smet, the underground noises were the sounds of the forging of weapons, and the eruptions were combats between infernal spirits.

The Yellowstone remained shielded from easy discovery by its protective circle of mountains. To a westward-stretching America, the Yellowstone became a realm of rumor and mystery. The few men who spoke or wrote of their experiences in that country, like mountain man Jim Bridger, were considered tall tale-tellers.

After the Civil War, three expeditions entered the Yellowstone by following the Yellowstone River. Three men explored in 1869, eighteen in 1870, and more than forty in 1871. The last two expeditions were widely publicized, so the public finally read and heard details of the Yellowstone's volcanic nature. Once Congress was made to understand the uniqueness and fragility of its surface formations, the Yellowstone was set aside for the public, forever.

The birth of our first national park did not occur by chance or popular demand. Five men unveiled her mysteries and converted superstition into science. The most influential of the five was Ferdinand V. Hayden, a government geologist. Another was Montana banker and politician Nathaniel Langford. A third was one of Pennsylvania's richest financiers, Jay Cooke.

The last two men were artists. They owe their fame in great part to their work, which captured the beauty and essence of the Yellowstone. One was William Henry Jackson, who took the first photographs of the Yellowstone. The other was Thomas Moran, an artist to whom the Yellowstone represented "grand nature." His paintings awed the public and critics alike, and made him equal in reputation to the greatest artists of the time.

This is their story—and that of our first national park.

PROLOGUE

"The story of the creation of Yellowstone National Park," said
Walter Trumbull in a voice laced with pride, "is a classic example
of Adam Smith's thesis that self-seeking men are guided by an
'invisible hand' to advance the cause of society."

The notes in Trumbull's hand fluttered in the light afternoon
breeze. As he looked over the audience gathered near the podium,
he wondered how many people knew what he was talking about.
Not that it mattered, for even if no one understood him, Trumbull
wouldn't have changed his presentation. He wanted to make a point,
and his reference to Adam Smith was the best way he knew.

"The men responsible for this park were part of that period of
high speculation after the Civil War, when bold men explored the
West and built railroads. They were part of the beginning of our
Industrial Age."

The occasion that had brought so many people to the little
town of Livingston, Montana Territory, was the celebration of
completion of the Northern Pacific line—the linkage of Puget Sound
in Washington Territory to Lake Superior, Minnesota. The construction of the 1,900-mile Northern Pacific Railroad had taken thirteen years. The line ran through Livingston.

The most important speeches had been given earlier in the
day by Northern Pacific Railroad President Henry Villard, Secretary of the Interior Henry M. Teller, former Secretary of the Interior
William Evarts, and former Northern Pacific Railroad Company
President Frederick Billings. Trumbull's task was to dedicate the
opening of the fifty-one-mile spur that ran from the main line into
the Yellowstone National Park. Trumbull had been a member of

the Washburn Expedition which penetrated the Yellowstone two years before Congress made it a public park. A few others from that 1870 journey were in the audience: Gustavus Doane, Nathaniel Langford, and Samuel Hauser. Above the evergreens that decorated the dirt streets, a banner proclaimed: *Livingston, the Gate to Wonderland.*

"Most of us were a part of America's rush to settle the West. Few of us knew that it was also a time when America was searching for its own cultural symbols. We won our political and economic freedom more than one hundred years ago, but our cultural standards remained European. Even when we described our own national wonders like Niagara Falls and the redwoods, we compared them against the splendors of Europe."

Trumbull caught the eye of artist Thomas Moran in the front row. Where were the others? He looked for photographer William Henry Jackson. Instead, he found the dark eyes and pointed beard of geologist and explorer Ferdinand V. Hayden, a man without whom the Yellowstone might have been lost to private interests.

"But new, American schools of thought and expression in science and in art were born while our settlers moved west. Joseph Leidy, Edward D. Cope, and Othniel Marsh, for example, gave life to vertebrate paleontology, a field whose development has greatly accelerated the understanding of Darwin's theory of evolution. America's Hudson River and Rocky Mountain schools of art also emerged as we moved west. American photographers like Brady, Jackson, Hillers, and Sullivan revealed the harsh reality of the human drama as well as the splendor and wonder of American scenery." As Walter Trumbull gestured toward the snow-capped mountains to the west, heads in the audience followed.

"During this momentous era, two individuals rose above the ranks of ordinary men. One was private banker Jay Cooke, a promotional genius who, in 1870, announced his intention to underwrite the development of the Northern Pacific Railroad. A second was government geologist Ferdinand Vandeveer Hayden, an explorer who, a year later, with his cadre of specialists, unveiled the mysteries of the Yellowstone.

"Neither Jay Cooke nor Ferdinand Hayden were altruists,"

said Trumbull. "They were simply energetic men of vision who embraced new challenges. Yet, through the synergism of their efforts, our country acquired the symbol it had sought for decades. Now, America has its own icon of incredible beauty and grandeur unique—the Yellowstone."

Trumbull's audience was becoming impatient. When his speech was over, officials would cut the ribbon strung across the track, and everyone could enter the park. Twenty feet from the podium, Northern Pacific Railroad Company President Henry Villard, former president of the United States Ulysses Grant, ex-governor William Marshall of Minnesota, and several congressmen conversed in quiet voices. In the background, a solitary railroad engine smoked and made steamy noises.

"Thus, led by Adam Smith's 'invisible hand,'" concluded Trumbull, "did Dr. Hayden and Mr. Cooke serve as unconscious agents of society. I hope they will be well remembered for their contributions. Thank you."

Amid scattered applause, the Fifth Infantry band struck up a hearty tune. President Villard cut the ribbon, and the crowd rushed into the passenger cars of the waiting train. Trumbull moved across the current of the throng. He found and shook Professor Hayden's hand. While they chatted, Thomas Moran, Gustavus Doane, and Nathaniel Langford drifted toward them.

Suddenly, a stentorian whistle echoed across the mountains. Snorting steam, the loaded locomotive began its short, scenic journey toward Mammoth Hot Springs. The first passengers who stepped off the train would create the final bond between the Northern Pacific Railroad and Yellowstone National Park.

The day was September 6, 1883.

BOOK I: SELF-SEEKING MEN

PART 1: HAYDEN'S VOW, 1860

Captain William Franklin Raynolds of the U.S. Army's Corps of Topographic Engineers stared at the volcanic ridge that blocked his way. The band of rock extended right and left without interruption. It was black, close to one hundred feet thick, and showed not as much as a crack.

Raynolds stretched his legs against the Spanish stirrups. His body told him that he'd been in the saddle too long. As he settled back in the saddle, an icy wind rushed down the hill. Trees high on the slope began to sway and snow dust was lifted from the slopes. The air mass chilled him. It shook ice-covered bushes around him and made his horse paw the ground. As the wind died, the last rays of the sun disappeared into a swirl of clouds. The snow turned gray, and the air held the promise of heavy frost.

Raynolds leaned to one side, placed a gloved finger on one nostril and casually blew through the other. Well, he thought, if this is the head of the Wind River Valley, it is supposed to lead to the Upper Yellowstone, so we'll find a way across or, by God, there will be hell to pay.

The officer turned his horse around and stared without pleasure at the men of his expedition. The majority of the men were soldiers. They waited silently for his word. Raynolds didn't need to make a head count: all forty were there, including his little, *scabby* band of civilians. They sit there, thought Raynolds disdainfully, each with his own unspoken opinion about the wisdom of everything. They were his pet peeve.

Raynolds closed his mind against the nagging question of why his expedition was not evolving as he'd intended. He was about to issue instructions, when Jim Bridger broke from the civilian group, and rode toward him. Raynolds waited for the frontiersman. The old guide moved as though the horse and saddle were a part of him. Raynolds wondered whether the mountain man had spent more time on horseback than he had on the ground.

Bridger was not bundled up as were all of the others. At first glance he appeared poorly prepared for the cold. But he showed no discomfort either from the weather or from the long ride up the Wind River Valley. He stopped his horse, pulled a corncob pipe from his mouth, and rested both hands on the pommel. The skin on the back of his hands and on his face resembled well-rubbed leather. It verified Bridger's claim that he'd weathered decades of dust storms and blizzards, dry winds born in mountain passes, and the flames of a thousand campfires.

Beneath a narrow-brimmed hat, the lines in his wrinkled face aligned themselves in a wry, knowing smile. "I told you there was no way you would ever get across at this time of year, Captain. Not after a winter like this," said Bridger softly. He let his eyes drift up the mountainside with its protruding band of black lava. "Them volcanics is a good two thousand feet below the crest. Even a bird can't get across without taking along a supply of grub."

Raynolds followed Bridger's stare, then gave a grudging nod. "All right, we'll camp here for the night," he said. Then he raised his voice to a shout. "I said, we'll camp here for the night!"

Here was a Y-shaped, flat-bottomed valley at the head of the Big Wind River. The valley was hemmed in by steep, forested hills. At nearly eight thousand feet above sea level, only snow-covered ridge lines and the sinuous ridge of lava appeared above the trees. The little valley was the last flat spot before their ascent into the Shoshone Mountains.

It was a poor place to spend the night: there were no trees to cut the wind and the earth was sodden from hummocks of melted snow. No one, however, risked offense or rebuke by suggesting an alternative. At least drinking water was close at hand. The de Noir, or Black Fork, emerged from its lava-rimmed valley to the north and joined the Wind River at the edge of camp. Beneath a partial covering of ice, the Wind River then made a few last meanders before it rushed down the slope into the Wind River Valley.

The men of Raynolds's expedition, civilians and soldiers alike, hurried to assemble fires. All they had was willow, which did poorly to stay the cold. Occasionally a soldier would look up at the black belt of rock. When a hole appeared in the cloud cover, the men could glimpse snow-clad peaks, distant and proud. The peaks shimmered. They were the kind artists painted.

The snow and the wind told the men to come back later; winter was not over. Captain Raynolds had no such intention. He stood slightly apart from his men with a posture that conveyed his disdain of the elements. His pose suggested that he was accustomed to the wilderness. On the contrary, Captain Raynolds was an inexperienced traveler in the West. This was his ground-breaking journey, and he revealed himself as a sour, egocentric man, irritated because nature might cause him to alter his plans.

As the officer pondered his next move, one of the soldiers muttered, "If the Indians call this the Warm Valley, why do I feel like someone has shoved an icicle up my bum?" His friends snickered.

"They say that wind like this always comes before a blizzard," said a private. "Can you see us scaling that cliff with horses while it's snowing?"

"It's the end of the line, and not a moment too soon for me," whispered a third in a cautious voice.

Raynolds scanned the huddles of his uniformed men with half-shut eyes, then walked a few paces toward the loose cluster of civilians. He had chosen the disciplined life of an army officer, so to him, civilians were a sorry lot. Yet each man had a specialty he needed to fulfill his scientific mandate, so he suffered their presence.

A diminutive form wrapped in a wool blanket moved slightly. Raynolds took two steps toward the man. A gust of wind whipped his long coat against his legs as he spoke. "Did you hear what that soldier said, Doctor?" said Raynolds, loud enough for everyone to hear. "He said that this is the end of the line. He believes that the

Rockies have defeated us." The captain raised one bushy eyebrow, leaned forward slightly, and hissed, "You haven't caused God to abandon us, have you, Doctor?"

The "doctor" in question raised his head. The motion revealed a wiry gentleman in his early thirties. He had thin, black, swept-back hair, and a thick, curly black beard. "Doctor" was a true title, not a sobriquet. Ferdinand Hayden was a medical doctor, even if his skills in that department had nothing to do with his presence in the Wind River Mountains. He had been hired as the expedition's naturalist. It was a position he might have enjoyed had Raynolds left him alone.

Dr. Hayden took a moment to adjust his woolen wrap. One hand held a notebook, the other a pencil stub. It was evident that, rather than simply huddling against the cold, he had been writing. The thick, worn notebook was the size one could slip in and out of a coat or jacket pocket. The brown leather cover protected sketches of rock formations and plants, and shorthand commentary on local geology, topography, fauna, and flora.

Hayden's pensive expression included hesitance. Nothing diffident, just simple wariness. More than a year ago, he had eagerly accepted the assignment Captain Raynolds offered him. The two men had shared one another's company continuously since their rendezvous on the Missouri steamer, the *Spread Eagle*, in April of 1859. Today was the last day of May, 1860.

It was a mismatch made in hell.

The past four months had been the worst. The Raynolds party had made temporary quarters on the Oregon Trail near Fort Caspar, but one of the worst winters on record had held the men captive in rough-hewn longhouses for six months. In addition to Hayden, the civilian contingent included two young geologists, an artist, a me-teorologist, guide Jim Bridger, and a young assistant named James Stevenson. It nonetheless seemed to Hayden as though he and Raynolds had been alone in a one-room cabin, jousting, bickering, picking on one another, and squabbling like vultures over carrion. When the expedition broke camp nineteen days ago, Hayden's ha-tred for Raynolds had been honed to a fine edge.

Ferdinand Hayden had known next to nothing of Captain

William Raynolds before he joined his expedition. He assumed only that Raynolds had to be a better person to work for than his previous exploration commander, Gouverneur K. Warren. Hayden was convinced that Warren—another officer from the Army's map-making Corps of Topographic Engineers—was the epitome of the stereotypical condescending officer. He would never forget that Warren had screamed at him, called him a dog and a liar, and accused him of shirking his duties.

This year, Warren had opted to remain in the East, so the assignment to lead the Corps' last expedition was given to Captain Raynolds. In retrospect, Hayden would gladly return the thousand dollars he had been paid, and would be delighted, almost ecstatic, if he could convince Warren to resume command. In Hayden's eyes, Raynolds had proven himself less experienced, more unpredictable, and more impossible than Warren. Hayden had found Raynolds to be outrageously pompous, a self-righteous ass, a proselytizing religious fanatic, and a martinet!

Small darts of orange flame from the willow fires reflected in Hayden's eyes like flashes of anger. At an earlier point of this exploration, he had vowed to himself to never again take to the field under the command of an officer of the United States Army. Now, from his blanket-shrouded position, he examined the commanding officer. "I'm sorry, Captain, I don't know what you're talking about," he said in a tone devoid of emotion.

"Oh, sure you do, Hayden," prompted Raynolds discourteously. "Didn't you hear my men? Or were you too wrapped up in your little book? They believe we're at the end of our journey. They have no hope. They imply that God has abandoned us."

Raynolds straightened and his tone adopted the chill of the air as he added, "But then I forget, God is not a topic to which you give much thought, is it, sir? You are fundamentally a godless man, are you not, Professor? One of those who believes that mankind is always alone, who believes that death is forever, and that this," he gestured to the frozen country with an open hand, "is the only reality in the universe."

Hayden gazed momentarily into the sky where the stars glistened like diamonds on black velvet. He returned his gaze to his employer, but having nothing he wished to say, his eyes softened as though contemplating a distant thought. He broke eye contact, resettled the blanket across his shoulders, and returned to his note writing.

The man sitting next to Hayden, Anton Schonborn, said, "You did well not to answer that fool, Herr Hayden. He may be in charge, but he is a unworthy of respect."

Hayden heard a good deal of anger in his companion's voice. Schonborn was Raynolds's artist and topographer. He was also German, and looked often to Hayden for conversation. They were the only two men of German extraction on the expedition.

The following morning, an early sun cast deep blue shadows on crystal-white snowbanks. Hayden pulled on his boots and listened to the calls of sandhill cranes in the distance. Jim Bridger, coffee cup in hand, looked into Hayden's tent. "Sun's up," said Bridger, with a twinkle. "Looks like God's returned."

A shadow appeared behind Bridger, then the voice of Captain Raynolds said, "As soon as you're ready, Doctor, you, me, Mr. Bridger, and a few others are going to look for a way over the top." Without waiting for a response, the shadow disappeared. One side of Mr. Bridger's mouth lifted a quarter of an inch. Then he walked away.

An hour later, with Raynolds orchestrating everyone in general and no one in particular, the party examined the exposed rim of the volcanic ridge. They found traces of an old lodge trail and hundreds of lodge poles, evidence that the Crow Indians had often used the upper valley to trap buffalo, but they found no pass. It appeared that the high, volcanic ridge stretched across the head of the valley without a break.

Raynolds pointed to the strata that sealed the heights against access and asked with exasperation, "What *is* that stuff, Doctor?"

"Basalt," said Hayden. "It's possible that this ridge links the dividing crest of the Rocky Mountains to the Big Horn range."

"Outstanding. Is the stuff good for anything?"

"No."

"Marvelous," said Raynolds sarcastically.

Raynolds's wanted to get across the Shoshone Mountains not

only to penetrate the Yellowstone, but because he had to rendezvous with the expedition's other half. When his expedition party
started out in the summer of 1859, it had been twice its current
size. At Fort Randall, not far from the great bend of the Missouri,
Raynolds divided his men. He instructed First Lieutenant Henry
E. Maynadier to take half of the men and follow the Missouri to
Three Forks, where the Jefferson, Madison, and Gallatin rivers
converged. Raynolds would lead the other half due west, past Devils Tower, to Fort Sarpy where the Yellowstone and Big Horn merged.
After having solved the problem of how the mountains and rivers
merged above the Shoshone Mountains, he would meet Maynadier
the following summer in the Yellowstone.

At Fort Sarpy, with winter dogging his heels, Raynolds turned
south toward the Oregon Trail. From where they camped, it was an
easy ride to Fort Laramie. There, the men could enjoy the warmth
of barracks and the camaraderie of other soldiers. Raynolds told
his men he had no intention of returning to the "States" for the
winter. He then ordered them to build longhouses—multi-cham-
bered cabins with earthen floors, log walls, and a two-foot-thick
roof made of logs, brush, and clay mortar, topped by a foot of well-
packed earth. While the soldiers were building, Raynolds ordered
the civilians to redraw their maps and rewrite their notes.

Temperatures remained mild until the sixth of December. Then
the temperature plummeted to minus twenty-five and the wind filled
the air with minute particles of snow and ice. White crystals penetrated every building crack including an undiscovered crevice in
Raynolds's quarters. The storm left snowdrifts as high as the roof.
Raynolds's room had sprouted a bank of snow two feet high.

Raynolds decided that his task for the rest of the winter was
to keep the men warm and provide them a firm code of moral authority. He found the latter task difficult, because time and again
the soldiers managed to locate whiskey and get drunk. When
Raynolds was not ranting against his men or taking out his frustration on the "godless" Dr. Hayden, peace reigned. Then the men
listened to Jim Bridger tell stories.

"This winter reminds me of a nasty blow we had back in the
thirties," said Bridger one evening as he packed his pipe. "Me and

a few of the boys were headed out to Jackson's Hole when we ran into a fellow we'd never seed before. The winter had gotten the best of him, poor soul. Said he was on his way back from a land of fossils when a late spring storm made him hole up. Don't think any of us was listening too careful until he showed us a petrified grasshopper. This fellow declared that in the valley he'd taken shelter in, everything had been turned to stone—rabbits, sagebrush, snakes, and grasshoppers. He sat up once, shivering, with fire in his eyes, and described bushes whose berries were made of raw diamonds, rubies, and sapphires."

Bridger glanced around the room. "Now I ain't said I've ever seed this valley, 'cause where exactly it is was never determined. The fellow died of fever the next morning. Me and the boys took a few days to backtrack his trail, but didn't find nothin'. I've seed whole petrifacted trees, so I don't squint at a man who's said he's seed more than me."

Bridger had been playing raconteur since his first days in the Rockies when he trapped beaver. He was now into his fourth decade of spreading Rocky Mountain lore, so his tales flowed with frontier flair. The line between fact, exaggeration, and fabrication had blurred long ago. In some cases, Bridger realized that the truth of an issue was no longer within his reach, so when someone had the gumption to question him, Bridger replied that it was rude and uncivilized to question a man's word. "Besides," he would add, "that isn't part of the game."

To Bridger's mind, those who wanted to listen, would listen; those who did not, well, that was their business. When the winter weather had been mild, he'd remained a listener, partly because he was always on the lookout for a new tale. But after a month of map talk, military jabber, and religious hokeypokey, Bridger decided it was up to him to make the passing of chilled, winter nights a mite more interesting.

The old mountain man had a simple philosophy of life: work all day when and if you have to, but once the campfire is lit, pipes are hot, and stars fill the sky, it's best to listen to the coyotes and get on with a tale or two. He'd let the men in the long houses know his creed. He'd also informed them that his experiences in the

Upper Yellowstone might be worth listening to.

Not long after Bridger's first night of tales, Captain Raynolds asked him to comment on the character of the land they would encounter in the Yellowstone. Jim Bridger took the request as a sign that he could set back a bit and let the words flow. He barely got started: Raynolds interrupted him three times in as many minutes. Ole Gabe stuck his pipe firmly in his mouth and returned to his leather mending. After several proddings—which were returned with frosty silence—Raynolds took the hint and got as close to an apology as anyone had ever heard. "I have nothing more to ask, Mr. Bridger. We'd be happy to hear you tell it your way."

"The only way I know," said Bridger, still miffed. "If I miss a fact or two, I'll be happy to fill in at the end." No one could determine exactly when or where his story began. but the mountain man took his audience on a trapper's journey up the Green River into Jackson's Hole. From there no one could discern how he found his way to the Yellowstone. Bridger's reference points were familiar only to him, and no maps of the area existed.

"Never mind all this map and route stuff," said Bridger as he scraped his pipe bowl with obvious irritation. "We'll get there, and when we do, you best watch where you put your feet, 'cause sometimes the earth ain't too solid. When you walk, smoke and steam may suddenly fill your path, or the land might start shaking and spout water where there had been nothing before, or a trail might lead to a canyon that's deep enough to swallow an echo."

No one wanted to ask where the smoke came from, how high the water spurted, or how deep that canyon was. The image sufficed, and wasn't that the point of it all anyway, to listen to a tale and let your imagination run?

"Once in the Yellowstone," said Bridger, pausing to spit, "I crossed a spring that gushed from a hillside. Nothin' special there. There was hundreds of springs, all cold enough to numb a bullet wound. But this one run so fast and so far downhill that by the time the water hit the bottom it was hot. Yes, sir. I nearly blistered my toes when I mistook it for a place to cool my heels."

"You spoke earlier of hot springs and jets of water," said Ferdinand Hayden one evening. "Would you expand a bit on their character?"

"Glad to. What you got is a valley big enough for a two-thousand-lodgepole camp, a land filled with smoking holes and water-filled pools hot enough to cook in. Most o' them pools are round and smell like sulfur and the water in 'em tastes bitter. Some are close enough to the river so that after you catch yerself a trout, you can toss him over your head without taking him off the line and boil him for dinner." Bridger's eyes flitted across the faces of his audience, but no one blinked nor did anyone don a sheepish smile.

"Now them water jets are harder to come across, because they just up and spout or they don't, and there's no tellin' when or where. But I once seed a body of water as thick as a man throwed higher than the flagpole in Virginia City. And it weren't no single squirt neither, but a whale's blowhole that never did stop."

"And where did all that water go, Mr. Bridger?" asked Raynolds.

"Well, it naturally jes' come back to earth and ran down the hill. But it weren't good water. You could tell right off, 'cause nothin' growed around any of those holes till you walked beyond the size took by a forty-wagon-train circle."

The long winter depleted Bridger's array of favorite recountables. Towards spring, he was forced to recall a few he hadn't told in years. The ones he was asked to repeat or expound on he didn't much mind retelling because they all dealt with the Yellowstone country and that was the land they were headed for.

Hayden noted that Captain Raynolds took private delight in Bridger's stories. To others, Raynolds dismissed Bridger's stories as "Munchhausen tales." He confessed only that he was impressed that a man could carry such an array of entertainment in his mind and tell such incredible stories without having to pause to think or swallow. But when Raynolds and Hayden were alone, they discussed the probable scientific character of the phenomena. Raynolds agreed with Hayden that Bridger's descriptions matched the hot springs and geysers of Iceland.

Nothing more of the Yellowstone had been said since the expedition broke winter camp and crossed the Big Horns into the Wind River Valley. Now, on this earliest day of June, Raynolds was discovering the truth of Bridger's prediction that they could never cross the head of the Wind Rivers at this time of year.

"Then we'll find a way around," said Raynolds flatly. "We're not going back. Lead on."

Jim Bridger knew a hard-headed person when he saw one, so he took Captain Raynolds to the foot of a pass high in the Wind Rivers. From horseback, Bridger pointed to the top of the snowy slope. "This route was always the easiest way to Jackson's Hole from the Wind," he said. "And from Jackson's Hole you can git to the Yellowstone. I jes' wouldn't advise trying it now."

"But it will take us to the Yellowstone, will it not?" asked Raynolds.

Bridger scratched his head. "Well, you can get anywhere you want to by following the right path, but you ain't gonna slog your way to the Yellowstone through this."

"No? Well, let's see."

With a party of nine that included Ferdinand Hayden and Jim Bridger, Raynolds pushed his horse through nearly three feet of snow toward the Continental Divide. The sun was up, but the land still slept under its winter blanket. The air that flowed down the mountain was heavy and cold. Half-way up the slope, the horses encountered a crust on the snow. Each time they stepped forward, the crust broke. Icy edges dug into their fetlocks and shins. They shied and floundered.

Raynolds dismounted and tied his horse to a scrub pine. He examined the slope before him, kicked at the snow in frustration, then pushed himself through hip-deep powder. No one else moved. After about ten paces, Raynolds turned with an angry eye. "Well," he growled, "are you coming or not?"

Nine men waded up the slope. They discovered that fallen trees buried in the snow were to be avoided. The snow around the tree trunks was softer so it was easier to fall through. The first time Raynolds sank to his waist, it took several minutes of short-tempered shouting before everyone discovered that the trapped person had to go it alone. Like thin ice, anyone who got too close to the edge broke through, too.

The higher they went, the thinner the crust. Men were heard

to exclaim "Damn!" or worse as they disappeared, sometimes to the neck. After two successive disasters, Raynolds began to crawl on his belly. Jim Bridger stared in disbelief until he saw several others do likewise. With the thought that he'd done sillier things in his life, Bridger shrugged and got down on his belly. A snowshoe hare peered at him from the shadow of a pine log. Bridger stared back. "Don't you say a damn word," he muttered to the hare.

Near the top, the snow was nowhere as deep as it had been on the shoulder, but tree cover was sparse, and the wind was a gale. Wind chill became dangerous to those who were wet with perspiration. Two men built a fire at the base of a tree. The others stomped to stay warm. Raynolds stood at the summit and shouted into the wind: "This is the heart of the Wind River Mountains, and the Wind River Mountains is the heart of the Rockies. I name this *Union Pass* in the name of the United States."

Exhilarated, he turned to Jim Bridger. "Now, Mr. Bridger, *if* you know where we are, you will *please* point out the Yellowstone."

Ferdinand Hayden stood with his back to a lodgepole pine in a small hollow just below the summit. He looked north and west toward the land of mysterious happenings and bizarre formations of which Jim Bridger often had spoken. It was Hayden's first glimpse of the horizon that marked the Yellowstone. The sun was high. The sky was a deep blue. The wind that numbed his cheeks carried the redolence of pine and frigid earth.

When Raynolds asked his question, Hayden was holding up a hand to cut the sun's glare. The wind had pushed tears into the corners of his eyes. The droplets were seeping down his cheeks. Without the wind and cold they might have been signs of deep emotion.

"Do you really believe that stuff that Mr. Bridger's been saying about the Yellowstone, Doc?" Jim Stevenson had asked a few nights earlier. Hayden had been writing notes about a new plant at the time.

"Yes, Jim, I do, all of it," he'd responded. "Nature works miracles; man remains ignorant of her ways and her powers." In the ensuing silence, he put his pencil down. "The only way we'll ever learn is to explore and document. Our work will help others to understand this country. I've told you that this is how I intend to spend my life, unveiling the West. If you work with me, that will be your life, too."

Stevenson had said nothing. "Someday," said Hayden, returning to his notes, "we will walk the Yellowstone. We'll breach her mountain passes, taste her waters, listen to her sounds, and watch her water jets rise from the ground." He looked up and smiled.

Stevenson turned away with the same skeptical expression Hayden had seen in the faces of his friends at college. At Oberlin, dirt-poor Hayden had been the butt of jokes. His classmates were forever snickering to one another, "There goes Hayden, the dreamer. He'll never amount to anything."

Hayden's reverie was broken by the sound of Bridger's harsh voice. "Damn right I know where we are, Captain. We're on top of the divide between the Wind River Mountains and Jackson's Hole. The Yellowstone is off that way." Bridger pointed north-northwest into a world of featureless snowdrifts and frozen peaks.

Hayden followed Bridger's finger to a jagged, blue-white horizon. He focused on the distant mountains, and his expression hardened. Suddenly, the view became crystal clear, and he was gripped by a certainty, as though tumblers had suddenly clicked into place, or as if a door had automatically been shut and locked in one motion.

It was obvious that any attempt to enter the Yellowstone this early in the year would invite disaster. The snow was so deep that the forests on the hillsides had lost all definition. Winter held all the cards this time, but in the long run it did not matter. Hayden could no longer feel his face. His fingers had lost the ability to hold anything. He found that he was shivering—not from the cold but from fear. He wasn't certain whether he feared what he might have to endure to reach the Yellowstone, or whether he feared arriving there only to discover that the Yellowstone was a trapper's fabrication.

Either way, Ferdinand Hayden vowed to conquer his fear and to put the mysteries of the Yellowstone to rest forever. And with that thought, he stopped shivering.

PART 2: NEW TRACKS, 1869

1) A Brief Railroad Survey

St. Cloud, Minnesota, was a lousy place to be on the afternoon of the second of July, 1869. The temperature was a steamy mid-eighties, and a thin farmer's rain was falling from a gray, seamless sky.

Nathaniel P. Langford stood under the roof of a covered walkway that fronted the last store on the western edge of town. He'd been standing there for fifteen minutes. During that time, the harsh drumming of rain on the tin roof had been drowned out by the splatter of runoff onto the street.

Langford was six-foot-two, made six-foot-four by new boot heels. His prominent forehead, devoid of hair, contrasted with the bristle of his full, black beard. Over casual clothes, he wore a rain slicker, riding chaps that reached his pointed boots, and a wide-brim hat. Standing in the shadow, partially obscured by the rain, the tall frontiersman looked a bit fierce. In truth, he was a well-mannered frontier banker.

Langford shook raindrops from his slicker, glanced at his pocket watch, then looked over his shoulder hoping to see his brother-in-law emerge from the store. No one could go anywhere without him; he was their leader. Langford was certain that he was talking politics again.

It will not do well to wait much longer, Langford thought. He tucked a small wad of tobacco into his cheek and surveyed the line of spring wagons across the street. Each had a hump of tarp-covered supplies, a four-horse team, and four passengers. Every horse faced the rain, so it stood with its head down. The majority of the men in the four wagons looked as downcast as the horses. Langford doubted that there was a dry bone among them. He expected that any minute one of the men would stand up, say "This is bullshit!" and walk into the nearest bar. And that would be it. Even if everyone toughed it out, he was ready to take odds that the group wouldn't hold together long enough to see the Fourth of July.

The men in the wagons were tenderfooted, soft-palmed Easterners: congressmen, reporters, and a few prominent businessmen. Langford could hear their joyless mutterings. He figured they were probably asking one another what the hell they were doing here. They were not used to waiting, especially in the rain. Langford doubted they were used to any of what awaited them in the coming weeks. But who went on this expedition, what each man expected, and how well each put up with unfulfilled expectations, was not his concern. This was Marshall's party. Marshall had simply asked him to come along. The telegram he sent to Langford in Helena a week ago had ended with "Come on, Tan; I need a good man."

Tan was Nathaniel Langford's nickname of long ago, one that only relatives and close friends used. Langford was between jobs, and Marshall said he'd pay for his travel, so he telegraphed Marshall that he'd come. He had to admit that he was curious. Marshall's telegram implied that somewhere down the line, the trip might pay off for him, and Marshall's word was usually good. It should be; after all, he was the governor of Minnesota.

Langford heard Marshall's voice and the door of the store slam, then felt a hand on his shoulder. "All right, let's go!" shouted Marshall to the pack train leader. He clambered into the lead spring wagon and made gestures for the party to move out.

Langford wiped rain from his saddle, mounted his horse, and fell into line. His butt was wet, his beard was wet, and he was positive that each space between raindrops was occupied by a mosquito. Sitting on a wagon seat all day in eighty-five-degree heat with a day-long drizzle might push even a peaceful man to the edge. It was a lousy day to start anything, much less a railroad survey across Minnesota.

Langford brushed a mosquito from his nose and saw water squirt from beneath a wagon wheel. Well, he thought, they could all get drunk; they certainly didn't lack for anything in the way of comfort. Marshall had thought of everything. And why not; he didn't have to pay for it. That rich Philadelphian, Jay Cooke, was footing the bill.

The old fellow in the warehouse who called himself Rudy, said the whole business looked a bit phony. Langford had helped Rudy load supplies that morning. Marshall had asked him to help because Langford wasn't a congressman, a reporter, or a member of the Northern Pacific Railroad Company.

Rudy couldn't work when it was quiet. "Who all's going on this so-called hunting trip?" he asked. "General Grant? And where in the hell do they think they're agoing? The Rocky Mountains?"

Langford checked off eight wall tents and two hospital tents. He wasn't sure the old fellow wanted answers, not when he supplied his own as he went along. But when Rudy stopped working and stared at him, Langford responded that hunting was secondary to the real purpose of the trip. "It's a survey," said Langford. "A survey for a railroad."

"Bosh! Could've fooled me," said the packer, eyeing a half dozen expensive fishing rods Langford had passed to him.

"Yeah, well, the governor is trying to accommodate a few congressmen."

"Oh," said Rudy. "Then I guess you're still waiting."

"Waiting for what?" asked Langford. "The congressmen? No, they're all here."

"I meant the stagecoaches," offered the old-timer. He spat, then rolled a dozen rifles into a large tarp. "You ain't tellin' me that them congressmen are gonna ride spring wagons, are ya? They're gonna get wet, sore butted, and all bit up this time of year."

"I guess that stranger things have happened," said Langford with a smile.

"Not in St. Cloud, they haven't," said Rudy with finality and another good spit for punctuation.

After two wet days and thirty miles into no-man's land, the weather cleared. The survey party took half a day to dry out. When they got underway again, Langford tied his horse to the back of the wagon and rode on the seat next to his brother-in-law. He liked

Marshall; the man was interesting and enterprising. Before the Civil War, Marshall had used his influence to get Langford into the banking business in St. Paul.

"Whose stupid idea was this, Governor?" Langford asked with a grin.

"An engineer named Roberts," said Marshall, laughing, because every time his brother-in-law called him "Governor," he knew he was being jerked a little.

Marshall shared his laugh with a dapper fellow on his right named J. Gregory Smith. Smith was president of the board of directors of the Northern Pacific Railroad Company. "Roberts is a trusted friend of Jay Cooke," added Marshall.

Langford gestured towards the empty road. "And this is where you plan to run a line between St. Paul and the Pacific Ocean?"

Marshall nodded. "This is it."

"Well, hell, Governor, from here to there must be more than two thousand miles. You said we were only going as far as the Missouri," said Langford. "Are you planning a second, slightly longer leg?"

"That's being taken care of as we speak," said Smith, leaning forward to be polite. "Mr. Roberts divided the reconnaissance into two parts. He took the other party to Puget Sound. He plans to explore all the routes through the Cascades and the Rockies. We're supposed to check out the country between St. Paul and the Yellowstone River."

"Allegedly. I'm not sure we'll make it *that* far," said Marshall, completing Langford's thoughts.

"Roberts's party is about the same size as ours," said Smith. "He's got Thomas Canfield, who's a member of our board; Samuel Wilkeson, a journalist who writes for the *New York Tribune*. . . ."

". . . and William Moorhead," interjected Marshall. "He's a partner and brother-in-law of Cooke's."

"And the son of Edwin Johnson, plus several congressmen," added Smith, not to be left out.

"Who's Edwin Johnson, another politician?" asked Langford.

"No, he's the engineer who conducted the first Northern Pacific survey several years ago."

"So why is Roberts repeating what Johnson has already done, or should I ask?"

"Oh no; that's all right. Cooke specifically asked Roberts to conduct his own survey of the line. He has not yet made a firm commitment to the Northern Pacific. He wants information from his own people before he associates his name publicly with any project."

Marshall nodded. "Cooke is a touchy fellow when it comes to confidence and good image, and all that."

"So Roberts has special credentials," said Langford thoughtfully. He didn't have to ask about Jay Cooke. Marshall had mentioned the man often. Even in Helena, Langford had heard of him. Cooke's name brought to mind money and power, especially on the East Coast. It was a good name to be associated with, and according to Marshall, Cooke was a good friend.

"You're right," said Marshall. "He's the former chief engineer of the Lancaster and Harrisburg. He was the first to design and build a two-level, lattice-truss bridge across the Susquehanna River, and he's just returned from spending eight years in South America, where he constructed a major railroad in Brazil."

Langford, lost in his own thoughts, heard Marshall tell Smith, "I think it's exciting to contemplate the opportunities for Minnesota from having a railroad that connects East and West—running right along where we're traveling now." Marshall tapped Langford on the shoulder. "Tan, if I seem a bit excited, it's because I know Cooke is going to do it, and your brother-in-law is going to help it happen." He raised a finger for all to see and shook it. "But I'm not doing it for nothing."

"Naturally," added Smith. "None of us are."

Langford had a feeling that he'd missed something important. The state of Minnesota was entering its eleventh year. Nearly all of its four hundred thousand souls were still jammed into communities that lined Lake Superior and the barge rivers that led south. The mosquitoes owned ninety percent of the state. As hard as he tried, Langford couldn't picture a railroad line running to the western horizon of Minnesota.

"Marshall, for the love of God, no one lives out here. Hell, no one lives between here and Helena, and that's more than a thousand miles west. And Helena doesn't have more than three to four thousand people. Once west of Helena, all anyone will find is mountains, Indians, rivers, and confusion. No white folk. Who's going to ride this train?"

"Settlers."

When Marshall saw the look of incredulity on Langford's face, he laughed. "That's part of the plan, Tan. Oh, I know, it won't happen tomorrow or next month. Perhaps not even next year, but it will happen. It's a big project, one on which to test your belief in the future of the country." He nodded to Smith with a matter-of-fact glance. "To do something on this scale, you need optimism, capital, and a hell of a lot of perseverance, right, Smith?"

While Smith spoke philosophically about the Manifest Destiny of America and the place of the great Northwest in the scheme of things, Langford sought new ways to discourage mosquitoes. He wanted to ask what fool would want to spend his life on the plains of Minnesota, but he kept the thought to himself. The governor was a Minnesotan of long standing, and he sang the state's praises loud and clear whenever possible. Besides, it was clear that Marshall believed in this railroad. To him, it was one more project in a long line of entrepreneurial opportunities.

Marshall had arrived in Minnesota in the late 1840s, when the country was occupied by Indians and pine trees. To a man of energy and vision, the opportunities were unlimited. Marshall spent a decade experimenting in merchandising, banking, and dairy farming. Then he became a newspaper man and merged the *St. Paul Times* and *Minnesotan* into the *St. Paul Press*, which quickly became the state's leading Republican newspaper.

When the Civil War broke out, a politically-aware William Marshall organized a local brigade and returned as a breveted brigadier general. "Nothing like a good military record for a man taken with politics," he told Langford with a wink before he was sworn in as the fifth governor of Minnesota.

Six months from now, Marshall's second term would come to an end. It was pretty clear to Langford that his brother-in-law had decided to place his future in the hands of Jay Cooke and the Northern Pacific Railroad Company. Langford started thinking about his own future. He had done well as collector of internal revenue for the territory of Montana, but in 1868, President Johnson had given him his walking papers. The Senate refused to go along with Johnson and reinstated him. Predictably, Johnson fired him a second time. Once again the Senate reinstated him. Then Montana Territory Governor G. C. Smith resigned, and Langford was appointed in his place. This time the Senate turned against him: Langford was not a union man, and the Republican radicals would not have him.

So he was between jobs. He knew he could always return to Minnesota and go back into banking. Marshall would find him a position. But the frontier had gotten under his skin. Marshall said that he might find something of value in this railroad project for himself. Langford wondered how.

"First you see nothing. Right?" said Marshall, with a sweeping gesture toward the plains. "I agree. Empty as a closed bank account. Now try to picture the entire Northwest open to settlement. Tracks are laid. Immigrants from the East Coast and Europe buy land from our land grant and build their homes. Letters from enthusiastic settlers bring more immigrants. The Northern Pacific Railroad helps them with easy credit terms. In ten years, you won't recognize a foot of this land we're crossing, Tan. This is probably the biggest project of the decade." He looked towards Smith for confirmation.

"Century," said Smith, "biggest project of the century. It's bigger and more complicated than the Union Pacific. This railroad will change the entire country. If I didn't believe that, Mr. Langford, I never would have spent the time and effort I have on the board." Smith leaned forward so he could better see Langford's face. "Every idea has its time. This one is long overdue." He nodded for emphasis.

The evening fire flashed orange until someone stuck another green branch in it to generate smoke to combat the bugs. Holding a short glass of whiskey that had been cooled in a creek, Langford listened while his brother-in-law led several others in a discussion about the character of the Northwest, its suitability for development, and the most probable sequence of events between now and

the completion of the railroad. The words flowed in visions, for
Marshall was comfortable with himself and his topic.

The group with whom he exchanged thoughts included Vice
President of the Northern Pacific Railroad Board of Directors J. D.
Rice, Philip W. Holmes of Jay Cooke and Company of Philadelphia, Congressman A. B. Bayless of New York, and two Vermont
congressmen, Worthington C. Smith and Frederick Woodridge. Sitting off to one side was Boston journalist Carlton "C. C." Coffin,
who, between longer and longer sips of whiskey, took copious notes.

When the conversation broke up, Langford replenished his
drink and waited until Marshall was alone. "What did Smith mean
when he said this project was overdue?" he asked.

"He probably meant that the idea for a railroad line across
the Northwest has been around a long time," said Marshall. "Hell,
it antedates the railroad surveys of the fifties. Unfortunately, after
the South Pass route was adopted, the northern line was dropped.
From time to time, someone has tried to revive it." Marshall laughed
in a deprecating way.

"Which means?" asked Langford.

"Most recently, it means that a Vermont politician named
Perham tried to sell the project to Congress as a vital link between
Boston and the Pacific. Congress told him it couldn't help. There
was no precedent to charter a railroad company and then grant it
public lands. States' rights Democrats have long held the position
that Congress has no authority to create a corporation. You probably know that Congress assigns all railroad construction grants-
in-aid directly to the states. Perham was energetic, but naive."

J. D. Rice sauntered over from the fire. "Did I hear Perham's
name mentioned? The man was a fool; he should have asked Congress for money, but he thought the American public would fund
him."

"I take it he was wrong," said Langford, sipping his whiskey.

Rice moved closer. He was a short man, dressed much too
fastidiously for the Plains, but he was never seen without his bowler
because it added three inches to his height. "Hell, no. The poor
sod only sold twenty thousand shares at one hundred dollars each.
Cost him more than that to promote the effort, see? Capitalists turned

it down because the land grant he had was worthless until the venture was a success. Congress never bets on a self-fulfilling prophesy, see? And the general public ignored him because there were millions of acres available to choose from in Iowa, Missouri, Kansas, and Nebraska. Why bother to open new territory, see?"

Langford wondered if the man had vision problems or was just stuck on the one word. "It's always a question of seed money," continued Rice. "Now, the figures that Edwin Johnson gave Cooke said that seventeen hundred and fifty-five miles of track will cost one hundred forty million dollars. Those figures don't compare well with those of the Union and Central Pacific roads, see, so Cooke wanted another survey done."

"Congress extended our deadline to begin work," said Marshall. "At the moment, we can sell bonds, just not against the value of the land grant."

"Then against what?"

"Against the value of the railroad and telegraph line."

"What line?" asked Langford quickly.

"Well, that's why we're here," said Marshall, with an expression to discourage Langford from asking many more questions.

The evening wore on. The whiskey flowed. Langford sipped and listened. "C. C." Coffin stood uncertainly at Langford's elbow, swaying a little now and then. His notebook and pen were no longer in sight, but every time he exhaled, swarms of mosquitoes disappeared.

Conversation around the campfire touched on railroad bonds, how to sell them, how much money was needed, and the tremendous size of the project. If the key man behind the venture is Jay Cooke, thought Langford, why isn't he here? He had the impression that the man was far from committed.

"This Jay Cooke of Philadelphia," he finally said to Rice, "is he the same fella who sold all those bonds during the war?"

"That's right. He's the one," said Rice emphatically. "He's the greatest promoter the country has ever known. When General Cass of the Pennsylvania Railroad joined our board, he took one look at the figures and said, 'Only a vigorous financial campaign will keep our enterprise alive, boys. We're going to have to strike a bargain with a promoter.' And I said, 'You mean Jay Cooke, don't you?'"

Marshall poured another two fingers of whiskey into Langford's cup. "I met Cooke when he was touring Minnesota on a timber-buying spree about two years ago," he said. "We got to talking railroads, so I set up a meeting between Cooke and Cass."

"And?"

"Cooke's coming in," said Marshall.

"You think he's committed?"

"I wouldn't be here if I thought otherwise."

"I hear hedging."

"Well, he has yet to sign the contractual agreement," said Marshall, "but . . ."

"Is this fellow paying the cost of the whole line out of his own pocket?"

"No, no, no," said Smith, joining them. "Cooke's worth millions, but not that much. The contract says that he will *raise* all the money necessary for construction—at least we hope he will."

"One hundred million dollars—in bonds," said Marshall slowly, emphasizing each word. He spoke with a straight face except for one raised eyebrow.

One hundred million dollars. Langford dipped into his drink to keep the smile from his face. No wonder Marshall was eager to have the railroad project take off; with that much money floating around, anyone with any intelligence could set himself up in a number of ways.

When the line of wagons returned early to St. Cloud, Langford chided Marshall that the explorers had lacked heart. Marshall said that at least they had traversed Minnesota to Fort Abercrombie and had seen the Red River. Langford observed aloud that the Red River was hundreds of miles from where the Missouri River cut into the heart of Sioux country.

"Yes, yes, I know," said Marshall testily, "but these fellows are politicians and administrators, not explorers. And the Northern Pacific needs their support. So the prairie still belongs to the mosquitoes; so what. Let the engineers work out the details. This group has seen enough. Besides," said Marshall with a little shrug, "General Sherman has already advised Cooke about the country between Fort Abercrombie on the Red River of the North and Fort Stevenson on the Missouri."

"Yeah? What did he say?" asked Langford.

Marshall laughed out loud. "He said it was 'god-awful.'"

Langford laughed freely with him. "Governor, I've known a few places that were rougher, a few places that were uglier, and a few places that everyone had left for one reason or another," said Langford, still laughing, "but I don't believe I've ever seen a place that 'god-awful' suited better."

"Never mind, Jay Cooke got his money's worth," said Marshall, adopting a serious tone. "'C. C.' must have sent back a dozen notices to the Boston area newspapers. I read a few of them. All his paragraphs are peppered with phrases like 'independence in the highest sense,' 'freedom of mind,' and 'all the comforts and luxuries of home.' He's a great writer."

Langford groaned.

"Hey, come on!" said Marshall, as he nudged his brother-in-law with an elbow. "This is publicity. It's for the future of the country! Coffin referred to our railroad corridor as the Seat of Empire. He stole the phrase from the Union Pacific boys who once used the term for Omaha, which was their base of operations."

Then Marshall gestured toward the plains behind them. "So there's nothing out there: just wait, soon there will be, and that's what counts. Hell, while we're bumping along this old trail, a whole passel of rich Philadelphians and their wives are being entertained on a look-see trip to the end-of-track near St. Paul."

"To see what?" asked Langford.

"The future," said Marshall. He clapped Langford on the shoulder. "Cooke's paying for the whole thing. It's called promotion, Tan. Promotion. People go somewhere, see something interesting, then they return home and tell everyone about what they saw and did. Right?"

Not always, said Langford to himself.

2) No Flight of Fancy

On a late November morning in 1869, David Folsom walked up Helena's original roadway, Bridge Street. The rutted roadway was full of scattered horse droppings, broken tool parts, and debris from packing cases. The obstacle course was a sure sign that the town was still growing. David once told his friend, Charles Cook, that the thoroughfare resembled the aftermath of a battlefield. All it needed was a few lifeless bodies. Charles responded that if David got up a little earlier than usual, he would find those missing items sprawled up and down the street most any day.

David Folsom was thirty years old. He had spent the past five years of his life in Helena. God had given him an intelligent face with deep-set eyes and a long, straight nose. He was somewhat taller than average, slender, and showed lots of length in leg and arm. Most of the time he wore a wide-brim hat because it covered his thinning hair. In his daily dust-colored clothes and hat, David was a typical frontier figure. In fact, if a bunch of locals including David were assembled for a group picture, David would have to be identified by his height.

Today, David wore clean clothes including a fresh shirt, string bow tie, and wool jacket. He normally took an interest in what was going on about him, but today he was grappling with a problem. His preoccupation made his gait a bit mechanical, and his eyes remained on the horizon like those of someone who'd been drinking. David was as sober as they come, but he was haunted by the incredible images he'd seen in the Yellowstone. The visions, complete with sound, color, and scent, mesmerized him still. Shaking the visions were not the problem; it was how to tell his friends about them without looking like a fool.

The unpaved streets of Helena were cut wide enough for two Shuttler and Bain wagon teams. Ahead of him was an exception to the rule, a bullwhacker's six-ox team with double-hitched wagons that took up more than half the street. A couple of unattended mules stood alongside the wagons, and, a mite too close behind them, to David's way of thinking, four fellows unloaded crates.

David angled across the street and stepped up onto the wooden walkway that fronted the stores. The walkways permitted a man and a woman to pass without the need to get acquainted, but most of the time, when David encountered a woman—which wasn't too often—he stepped into the street. It was easier than waiting to get past the barrels, and stacks of boxes, shovels, hose, and dynamite along the walkway.

Still, the hazards on the boardwalk were fewer than those in the street. And the boardwalks were more comfortable, especially where store owners had set four-by-fours in the ground and rigged a slanted tin roof. The fancier storefronts used lathed posts for supports. They were round, slender, and grooved. David had seen men in town caress them when they walked by. They would pat and rub the curves and grooves, and make references to the town's sporting women. Then they'd laugh and roll their eyes.

The men unloading the wagon were making a good time of the work. Like David, they enjoyed the freedom of living on the frontier. He heard the men shout "good morning," but he just kept walking. He knew he should have said something, but his mind had slipped back to the Yellowstone, so he walked on.

Today was warmer than the average November day. They'd had a good frost in September, but an Indian summer had hung on and carried the colors with it. Clusters of aspen tucked up in the high mountain valleys had turned after the first frost. Broad bands of saplings, sometimes whole groves turned the same color at the same time. Last year winter had pounced quickly. It started with a good hard frost, so the aspen were brilliant but faded quickly. This year the color came slowly, so citizens looked for patches of aspen that showed not just yellow, but a lusty mix of color from green to red.

David walked under the tin roofs. They weren't perfect, but they kept out the summer sun, some of the dust, and the occasional rain shower. The customers appreciated it, and customers were what Helena had a lot of—close to thirty-seven hundred souls at last count. That was ten times the population of Bannack, Bozeman, or Missoula.

Helena had successfully passed its boom or bust phase, and was on the verge of becoming a Rocky Mountain metropolis. Newspapers said her location had a lot to do with it, but the nearest city was a thousand miles, and the Union Pacific line in Utah was five hundred miles. David had taken the stage trip to the railroad line more than once. It took four to five days by Halladay coach, depending on the season. Any way you cut it, the trip south was a bone-jarring experience. David swore it was not worth sixty-six dollars, especially when you were told that as passenger number fifteen or sixteen you had to stand outside and hang on to the top rail for the duration.

As David approached the intersection of Bridge and Main, he encountered six men standing by an open wagon. Each wore long dark pants, a long-sleeved shirt, and a hat with low a crown. And each had a dragoon pistol strapped to his waist. Three were loading the wagon with mining tools while two more stood and argued. The sixth man watched the others five.

As David got closer, the altercation between the two men got louder. Leaning towards one another like fighting cocks, they broke into a foreign language David had never heard before. The sixth man—who happened to be the largest—picked up a shovel. He struck the loudest of the arguing men on the head, tossed the limp body into the wagon, and motioned the others to get in. As the horses pulled the wagon down the street past David, the driver, who was the other man in the argument, was now shouting at the man with the shovel and gesticulating to the unconscious man in the wagon.

Gold miners, thought David: miners headed back to camp. That's why everyone is here. His friend, Charles, said that gold might not be the only reason, but no one had ever suggested another to David that made sense, except maybe health. He knew of a few fellows who had come west because their doctors told them that western dryness was good for chest ailments.

It was dry; at least, rain was never a problem. Most of the ten inches Helena received every year came in the late spring. Once in a great while, a real summer downpour passed overhead. Swift erosion by sheet runoff often exposed small gold nuggets in the streets. More than once, David had watched Chinese boys scramble to pick up the shinies. The lads couldn't get rich on 'em, but it said something special about the place.

David had been in Virginia City when the stampede to Helena started in '63 and '64. Back then, Helena was called Last Chance Gulch. David was certain the discovery of gold had been a fluke. No one could would ever look at the land around Helena and say, "Yup, looks like gold country." The terrain was hardscrabble: rocky, dry, and full of horseflies, mosquitoes, and rattlesnakes. But for centuries, the streambeds flowing down the east side of the Continental Divide near Helena had been stockpiling placer gold. In 1863, four men dipped their pans into a stream and discovered the gold. By the end of the year, the quartet netted one hundred seventy thousand dollars.

In those early days, gold was the first and last topic, the first and last profession, and the first and last reason men came and left Helena. David didn't think much had changed, except that this year Helena laid claim to more millionaires than any other mining town in the West. And while everyone agreed that panning gold was a fool's errand, 'cause the odds so against a strike, the slim chance of finding big pay dirt made everyone a little feverish and a little foolish.

No one counted on Helena becoming another New Orleans with its fancy women and paddleboats, or another gateway to the West like St. Louis, but the town offered more than other frontier places of similar promise. Bannack, the first big strike in the Northern Rockies, was down to three, maybe four hundred people. As for Virginia City, six years ago she was the most successful town around. No less than ten thousand souls had walked or ridden across the plains to get there. Now she wasn't more than a fourth the size of Helena, even if she was the capital of the territory.

To date, Helena's mines had produced nearly twenty million dollars in gold. David remembered when miners uncovered the nugget that weighed one hundred sixteen ounces. One chunk that weighed more than seven pounds! When they put it on display at the assay office, it got more traffic than Miss Candy's parlor on Saturday night. At seventeen dollars an ounce, that hunk was worth more than two thousand dollars—three years' wages.

All of the gold around Helena was assayed at the First National Bank and Assay Office at 32 Main. That was David's destination this morning. He'd promised two friends to talk about his journey to the Yellowstone. He didn't fancy going through with it, but he'd given his word. One of the men was Samuel T. Hauser. He'd built the bank. While it was going up, he told David he was going to have a big sign hanging just below the roof. David knew that half the town couldn't read. He didn't say so, but he thought the best thing to do might have been just to draw a picture of a man assaying.

David didn't spend much time in banks. He was a surveyor. Like most men on the frontier, he was also adept at a lot of other jobs. He could pass for a freighter, guide, miner, hunter, or bullwhacker, and he was ahead of most others, because he could read and write.

David brushed his jacket, checked his hat again, then walked north on Main. He remembered to wave back to Mr. Rea who ran the grocery on the corner. For some reason, he started thinking of the way sulfur smelled, sulfur so thick it flavored the air and water and permeated his clothes. He was so preoccupied that he didn't hear the horse until it galloped right past him. The clatter of hooves drowned out the shouts of workers and the sounds of their tools, but the vibrations sent David back to the thumping land of earthquakes and boiling cauldrons. He could still hear the roar of the cataracts, see the rush of steaming gas as it roared from the holes in the ground, and smell the sulfur in the steam-charged air. From where he and his friends had camped, David had heard the thuds of a bubbling mud spring a half mile away. Nothing in his future would ever match the sights or sounds. Ah, what an incredible place, that Yellowstone!

David turned his shoulders to avoid brushing a deer carcass hanging outside the butcher shop, then nodded to Jack Neary, the blacksmith, who shouted "Ho, David" while he annealed a hot shoe. David signaled "hello," and remembered working hand in hand with Neary to help put out the big fire last April.

A stream of memories led David back to September sixth, just a few weeks ago, when he, Charles Cook, and Bill Peterson had gotten it in their minds to go see what was behind the rumors about

the Yellowstone. No one had asked them why they'd risked their
lives that way. If they had, they might have mumbled something
like, "seemed to be a good idea at the time." But aside from having
lived in the West a few years, none of the three had special skills
that made them well-suited for such an undertaking.

David East Folsom was a New Hampshire Quaker. He had
been in St. Paul, Minnesota, when Jim Fisk's Expedition was being
formed. He heard that Fisk planned to cross the Plains and head
for the gold fields of Idaho, so he joined up. After spending the
winter of 1862 in Bannack, he wandered into Virginia City, learned
surveying, and joined Charles Cook's ditch company.

David was a confident man who, in spite of his religious up-
bringing, did not find it necessary to back up when he faced trouble.
One time in Virginia City, in response to a threat from outlaw George
Ives, Folsom cold-cocked the man with a billiard ball. Friends
rushed him out of town before the killer regained consciousness.

Charles W. Cook was a transplant from Maine. His salient
features included clear eyes and a long face hidden by a thick mat
of mustache and beard. He'd arrived in Montana in 1864, herded
cattle. He managed water for the miners.

As for Bill Peterson, he'd been raised on a farm in Idaho Territory. He ran off to the Pacific coast to explore San Francisco. In
1862, he was among the thousands who tipped Idaho upside down
for gold. Peterson was a skilled packer, adept with cloth and cord-
age, and was known to throw one hell of a diamond hitch. Since he
had the best set of frontiersman skills and a good sense of humor,
David and Charles thought he would make a good third for their
journey.

As the three departed Helena, pulling a string of pack animals, friends shook their heads, fully expecting that if their hair
didn't decorate a Blackfoot or Sioux lodge pole, some satanic force
in Colter's Hell would sweep them from the face of the earth. A few
days later, the trio waved a second good-bye, this time to soldiers
at Fort Ellis. They had stopped there for a breather, but no one
offered to escort them. The three never knew that right after they
left, the Army had rushed five hundred reinforcements to that post
in response to the sudden increase in Indian raids. It was enough

that the three were venturing forth into a land of rumor; if they'd known there was a good chance of running into a war party, they would have stayed home.

David could now see the bank on Main Street. Once inside, David would have to talk about his trip. He'd agreed only because Sam Hauser and his mercantile neighbor, Warren Gillette, had asked. David and Charles had talked about writing some kind of article, but neither had planned on talking. The distance between pen and the written word, including the time it allowed one to find the right word, made writing easier than talking. The plain truth was that talking, especially about what he had seen in the Yellowstone, made David damn nervous.

David lit a rolled cigarette and let the smoke curl from his nose. The smoke reminded him of sulfuretted steam, the kind he'd seen rising above the treetops from hundreds of acres of hot springs. The vaporous clouds had been so dense they had obscured the sun. David frowned and put out the cigarette. How could he describe that? Who was going to believe boiling pools of water fifteen to fifty feet in diameter, or superheated pots of yellow and black mud? Would even Hauser or Gillette believe him when he spoke about the canyon of dread where wolves howled and the light grew dim because the trees were so crowded together? Would they laugh if he mentioned that the horses acted nervous all the time, and that some nights were filled with the screams of mountain lions?

As David hesitated on the bank steps, Nathaniel Langford walked up behind him. "Hello, David. Good to see you," he said.

David had known Langford since the two were part of the Fisk Expedition. The two had also spent their first two years in the territory together. Langford, like Sam Hauser, had been a vigilante, one of the men to rid the town of the damned Plummer gang back in sixty-four.

"I didn't get back until after you headed out. How was your trip?" Langford asked.

David said that he'd planned to oblige Hauser and Gillette with a short description.

"I'd like to listen in if I could."

David nodded. Langford was a friend, and he didn't spill at

the mouth. Might as well make it three to listen. The two men walked into the bank. Hauser and Gillette were waiting. Hauser led them toward his office. As he opened the door, David saw that the room was full of townsmen. He knew a few by sight, but many faces he'd never seen before. He couldn't call one man in the room by his name. As Hauser beckoned David to the front of the room, several men got up and shook his hand and told him they were delighted to have the chance to hear his story.

David couldn't believe what he was seeing! He thought Sam Hauser must have lost his mind. Sam knew the difference between a private chat and giving a talk. Scenes from the Yellowstone flashed through his mind. How could he expect him to talk about gorges thousands of feet deep, deafening waterfalls, and scores of hot springs, in front of strangers? Who ever heard of petrified grasshoppers, fountains that shot thousands of gallons of water hundreds of feet into the air for forty-five to seventy-five minutes at a time? By what means would he ever convince these strangers that he had witnessed a column of steam which rose with such a roar that it maintained its shape for forty feet in the air before it rolled away into the heavens? These men didn't know his reputation. They'd laugh him out of the room.

David felt betrayed. He sure as hell hadn't counted on talking to a group. He also knew that he was not the first to have explored the Yellowstone, nor the first to be asked to talk about what he'd found. And what had happened to those who had tried to describe their experiences? David knew: they were accused of indulging in *flights of fancy*. Flights of fancy!

As Hauser introduced him, David looked at the faces in the room. This was a nightmare! If he had been in the audience and heard a fellow talk about his ventures into the Yellowstone, would he believe the wild descriptions? David knew the answer.

Nathaniel Langford watched as Sam introduced David. It was obvious that David was very disturbed by the presence of so many people. He had not expected a crowd. What was it he'd said? "Oblige two friends with a short description."

Langford knew the importance of a man's reputation on the frontier. In Helena, if a man did not have gold, he'd best have a reputation for being honest. From what Langford had heard of the Yellowstone, he pretty well knew David's predicament. If David shared his experiences with strangers, he might set himself up to be called a fool, or worse—a liar.

Fifteen minutes later, Nathaniel Langford and David Folsom walked down the street together. David was still upset. "Sam must not have been thinking clearly," he said, with a pained expression. He glanced at Langford for confirmation. "Had I told those men what really happened, what I really saw and heard, I might as well have left town."

Langford was itching to ask David for an example, but he nodded.

"No one's going to put a 'flight of fancy' label on me," growled David. "No sir. If anyone wants to know the truth, they'll just have to go see for themselves."

Well, now, thought Langford; that's not a bad idea.

3) General Hancock

Inside the blocky limestone building in downtown St. Paul, Minnesota, Nathaniel Langford smelled an odor he couldn't recognize. He thought he knew what it was, but the name eluded him. He glanced around, looking for an obvious source. It had nothing to do with the smell from the wood stove, and it was too faint to come from the damp greatcoat that hung on the door. Perhaps, he thought, it had something to do with the fact that all the rooms in the building were occupied by military officers. The outer door opened and General Hancock marched across the room toward him. Nathaniel Langford cleared his mind of scents.

"Mr. Langford." General Winfield Scott Hancock reached out a hand as Langford stood. "Happy New Year to you. sir. Sorry to have kept you waiting." Hancock gestured toward the outer room and started to provide Langford with more of an explanation, then decided it was inappropriate. He seated himself behind his desk and said conversationally: "I don't believe our governor writes letters of introduction in an offhand manner, so you have my attention—at least for a few minutes."

Hancock's directness told Langford that he'd best make his case without a lot of chatter. The general's response might be a fast "No," but at least he'd know.

"General, I'm doing some advance planning for a group of men from Helena—myself included—who intend to mount an extensive exploration of the region known as the Upper Yellowstone." Langford stood, pointed to the map that covered most of the wall, and walked to it without pause. "If I may. . .?"

"Certainly." General Hancock nodded and turned his chair. He commanded the Department of the Dakota; his superior, General Philip Sheridan, commanded the Department of the Missouri. One of Sheridan's directives to Hancock was to keep the peace because Sheridan's superior, President Grant, had ordered peace initiatives with the Indian tribes. In January 1870, however, peace was a tentative thing, especially in the Department of the Dakota.

The parchment on the wall bristled with colored pins that carried the names of military posts. Thin black lines connected one post to another. The huge grid showed the dominant influence of the military in the inchoate West. That the West was still in its early period of formation was evident by the map: the names of Indian tribes in the Dakota Territory were more prominent and their locations more specific than the names of entire mountain ranges and the courses of major rivers.

Langford placed the palm of his hand on a blank area between Fort Ellis, near the Yellowstone River, and Fort Washakie in the Wind River Mountains to the south. "Are you familiar with this region, General?"

Hancock frowned and shook his head. "Not in any detail. I don't think anyone is."

"I agree," said Langford. "It's mountainous and complex, and to date it has been little explored. It remains the subject of rumors which have lasted for decades."

"Such as?" asked the general.

"Trappers' tales of burning valleys, pools of boiling water, bottomless caverns, bizarre petrifactions, deposits of pure sulfur."

Hancock smiled. "Oh, yes, I do recall hearing of that region. And, as you say, 'trapper's stories.'"

"Last year, General, some friends of mine traveled through this region." He tapped the area on the map. "They had a number of extremely strange encounters. Upon their return they drew a map, but they've said nothing publicly about their experiences. In time, I was able to get them to describe what they saw and what happened."

"What were they afraid of?"

"Beg your pardon?"

"Why didn't they speak out?"

"They feared that if they shared their experiences in public, they would ruin their reputations," said Langford solemnly.

Hancock nodded and offered Langford a cigar. Through a thin cloud of smoke, Langford continued. "The region may have precious metals. No one has mentioned any to date, but a lot of discoveries are still being made in the Rockies. More important to our group, which has no miners in it, is to verify the findings of my friends and to lay to rest these rumors about the Yellowstone."

"Do you believe there is a basis to the fanciful tales?"

"Yes, sir, I do, for several reasons. First, I believe in my friends. They are intelligent men of integrity, and conservative in their values. And secondly, what they told me reinforces the storied I heard several years ago from Jim Bridger."

Hancock didn't hear Langford's last comment; he was looking at the clock on the wall. "What is it you need from me, Mr. Langford?"

"Approval for a small military escort to accompany our party into the Yellowstone."

General Hancock stood and walked to the map. Langford was the same height as the general, but Hancock looked taller. There was something about the way in which he held himself, as though he willed himself to see over the heads of other men. Hancock the Superb, they had tagged him for his deeds during the Civil War. He had selected the site on which the battle of Gettysburg was fought. He had been responsible for thwarting the Confederate attempt to turn the Federal flank and for having defeated their all-out attack on the center of the lines. Hero was a short word for such a tall man.

"I assume you are worried about attacks by hostile Indians. At the moment my concern with raiding parties is directed at an area south of the Yellowstone." Hancock was referring to the continued attacks of Sioux, Northern Arapahoe, and Cheyenne on the settlements of South Pass City and Atlantic City. At least fifty citizens had lost their lives to Indian raids in the past two years. Camp Brown on the Shoshone Indian Reservation was too far away to deter future attacks. If the situation did not change, he would have to order the establishment of a second post in the area. He wondered where he would find the men.

"Of course," he added, "you will be traveling through Crow territory, and the Crow are highly mischievous." Hancock looked out the window. To himself as much as to Langford he added: "And the need to explore the West is always a significant priority."

He turned back to Langford and nodded. "I believe it would be good for all concerned if you had a military escort. Contact me when you are ready. We can detach a few men from Fort Ellis."

As Langford left the room, he recognized the odor that had escaped identification. It was the same smell found in libraries: stale air and books—the smell of history. He smiled to himself, shut the door, and walked into the frozen landscape of St. Paul, Minnesota.

A few blocks down the street, Langford related his talk with Hancock to William Marshall. Marshall waited politely with a twinkle in his eyes. Langford finished what he had to say and waited for a reaction. What he got was a question.

"Did I tell you my bit of news?" asked Marshall.

"I don't think so."

"Jay Cooke signed the agreement," said Marshall with a delighted expression.

"Hmm?"

"The railroad contract. Cooke accepted the job as the financial agent for the Northern Pacific Railroad."

"Oh. No, you hadn't mentioned it," said Langford, still trying to make the leap from the Yellowstone to Cooke. "Is this a surprise?"

"Not really. I mention it now for an important and related reason. The tracks of the Northern Pacific will go through Bozeman, which is quite near your mysterious Yellowstone. So, laddie, the next time you go east, I suggest you stop in Philadelphia and talk to Jay Cooke about your trip."

Marshall winked at him, a confidential signal. "If you find half of what you think you are going to find when you enter the Yellowstone, Jay Cooke will be most interested."

4) Lieutenant Gustavus Doane

Fort Ellis was a crisp-looking territorial fort that occupied a terrace three miles east of Bozeman. In keeping with uniform field procedures, the army had positioned the post on the bank of a creek, one of several sources of the East Fork of the Gallatin River. The post was flanked on the north and east sides by ranges and hills that formed the divide between the Yellowstone and Missouri rivers.

The primary colors at Fort Ellis included the sun-bleached lodgepole logs of the buildings, the brilliant whitewash of those walls the commanding officer did not want brown, and the green of local foliage. The colors formed a solid background for the red and blue accents of the American flag that flew in the center of the parade ground. The enlisted men lived in barracks; the officers resided in a small village of neat rows of log homes, where every house had a porch and two chimneys.

Nathaniel P. Langford tied his horse to a hitching rail and climbed the wooden steps of the building marked Post Commandant. As he entered, the Fort Ellis bugler played a brief, short, spirited tune to announce the hour of rest.

The orderly showed Langford to the C.O.'s office and announced his presence. Langford stood, hesitant, while the commanding officer, Major Eugene M. Baker, remained bent over his desk. Langford noted that the commandant was scribbling on a document. The officer's tunic was open at the throat and both forearms were on the table. The desktop looked cluttered. Langford heard Baker mutter to himself.

The officer looked up at his calendar for a split second, then wrote the date, August 20, 1870. When he was done, he looked up and past Langford. "Orderly!" he shouted.

In one motion, Baker handed the document to the orderly and looked at Langford with a puzzled expression. Langford had remained standing, as anyone might—civilian or not—in the presence of a ranking military officer. Baker brusquely motioned to three chairs scattered around the office. "Have a chair, Langford. It's too damn hot to stand." The official post temperature at four o'clock that day was ninety-two degrees.

Baker slumped back in his chair. "What do you need, sir?" He knew that Langford hadn't ridden all the way from Helena to begin a social acquaintance, and he was loose enough to be very direct. He interrupted Langford's first words with another question. "Shot of whiskey to settle the dust?"

Langford pulled a chair closer to the major's desk and said, "I . . . no thank you, Major. Bit too hot. Thank you anyway."

Major Baker eyed his visitor hesitantly, as though to assure himself it was all right to care for his own needs. He coughed slightly and poured three fingers of the dark liquid into his glass. Langford noticed several rings on the desk from the glass.

While the officer poured, Langford said, "I'm what you might call an advance scout for an expedition into the Yellowstone, Major. The rest of my party is about a day behind. I thought I would help get a few things arranged before they arrived."

Baker took a long swallow of the brown liquid. If he had any idea what Langford was talking about, neither his eyes nor his gestures disclosed it. "That is, with Lieutenant Doane's assistance, of course," added Langford with a slight shrug of his shoulders.

"Lieutenant Doane," said Major Baker slowly as he examined his nearly empty glass. "Yes, well, I wouldn't anticipate any assistance from Lieutenant Doane, Mr. Langford." He set the glass on the desk and tried to focus on Langford's lanky, bearded form. "Lieutenant Doane is preoccupied with military duties."

"I understand perfectly," said Langford. He sat up a little straighter. "I certainly did not expect him to drop what he was doing, but I anticipated from General Washburn that Lieutenant Doane offered to . . ."

"Who?"

"Breveted Major General Washburn, I should say. He's the Surveyor General for Montana."

"Hmmff," said Baker with a small, irreverent belch. "And he's coming to see me."

"I'm certain he will want to deliver his respects, sir." Langford was rapidly coming to the conclusion that Major Baker's one-third full bottle had been full earlier in the day and that their conversation was going nowhere. Nonetheless, he added, "I believe that Lieutenant Doane knows that General Washburn is on his way. As Commanding Officer, I'm sure your communications officer notified you."

"Oh, you are, are you? And if they did?"

"Then I could let the major get on with his business and I could attend to mine with the lieutenant."

Major Baker pushed back his chair and stood. He corrected his stance and fumbled with the buttons on his tunic. "Let me enlighten you on a few things, Mr. Langford. Did you know that Fort Ellis is located in the overlapping territories of six of the most hostile Indian tribes in the country—that our post is one of a series of critical links that form a military circle around hostile Sioux, and that without this post, the villages of Bozeman and Livingston would most likely cease to exist?" Baker stifled a belch.

"Do you know that last year, Indian attacks and atrocities were triple those of the year before, and that this year we expect at least as much trouble from those bloodthirsty bastards?"

Langford held his tongue, but he glanced quickly through the open door into the hall in the hope that someone would interrupt before Baker became too tightly wound.

The Major clasped his hands behind him and walked towards the window with his back to Langford. "Do you perhaps also know that this post has been at half strength since February? Down to eight officers and one hundred thirty-two men? And were you aware that two hundred fifty lodges of the Crow tribe deserted their reservation earlier this summer? Hmm?"

"Major Baker, I . . ."

Baker continued to look out the window. "Lieutenant Doane

has been in command of Company F since the beginning of the year, and the month of August is the middle of the Indian's open season on whites. Now, as commanding officer I should think that I have a right to count on my officers and men to be available to do their duty." He turned around to look at Langford, but he spun too quickly and had to reach out and touch the wall to steady himself. With a slower step and slight curl of the lip, he added, "But then, as a soldier I know it would hardly behoove me to interfere with a civilian jaunt into the woods, especially one under the command of a former general officer—especially an expedition approved and sanctioned by General Hancock . . ." He suddenly yelled, "Isn't that so, Lieutenant Doane?" and looked towards the open doorway.

"Yes, sir, I agree, *sir*," said Lieutenant Doane. The officer snapped his six-foot-one-inch, one-hundred-ninety-pound frame to attention. Aside from the inevitable sweat stains from a day's work in ninety-degree heat, Doane's countenance was neat and fully military, from his boots to the insignia on the hat tucked deftly under his arm. He stood stiffly, eyes straight ahead, without a quiver in his dark complexion, hair, or sweeping mustache.

If ever a man was designed, trained for, and at home on the frontier, it was Second Lieutenant Gustavus Cheney Doane, and Major Baker knew it. It was one of several reasons he despised the man. He knew Doane was well thought of by his men and had a reputation for being fearless. His record as an excellent hunter and a dead shot validated those rumors. The man was a thorough plainsman and an exemplary officer.

Baker also knew that Lieutenant Doane was bullheaded and sneaky. He'd gone directly to General Hancock and had promised material assistance to a civilian expedition without Baker's approval. From the very first, he'd planned to accompany Langford's civilian force into the Yellowstone. Never mind that Fort Ellis was understaffed, that the Sioux were restless, and that Doane had bypassed him in the chain of command.

"Come in, Lieutenant," said Baker with a deprecating slur, "and say hello to Mr. Langford."

Baker glanced at a small document that lay on one corner of

his desk. Doane caught the major's move so he knew what was coming. The paper was a telegram from General Hancock that ordered Baker to allow Doane and a few soldiers to escort the Helena expedition.

While Langford and Doane shook hands, Baker said loudly, "Mr. Langford is under the assumption that you have some supplies for his expedition, Lieutenant. Did I approve that order?"

"The material referred to, sir, is a pile of extra gear we acquired last year but have no use for. I thought the expedition could use the tents, and since our post will be participating . . ."

"Not with my approval!" shouted Baker in a drunken roar. "And you foresaw that coming, did you not, Lieutenant Doane?"

"Sir!"

"Sir, my ass." Baker held the now crumpled telegram from General Hancock and walked to where Lieutenant Doane stood. When Baker had asked Doane earlier how that telegram had come to be sent, Doane had denied responsibility. But once before, Doane had tried to get assigned to a group for the purpose of exploring. Baker had stopped him cold. Baker knew Doane was behind the telegram and Doane knew that Baker knew.

Baker tapped Doane on the chest with the telegram. "You try this again, soldier, and I will make you wish you had never returned from the Marias."

"Yes, *sir*." Lieutenant Doane came to attention again. Langford rose, and the two men left the room without a further word. Langford heard the ring of glass on glass in the major's office as they hit the doorway.

On the steps, the orderly handed Lieutenant Doane Special Order No. 100 dated August 21, 1870, which authorized him and four men from Company F to escort the Washburn Expedition to the source of the Yellowstone River. Major Baker had been forced to issue the order to acknowledge General Hancock's week-old telegram.

"He's been in a vile humor ever since," the orderly said with a weak grin. "Good luck, sir. I wish I was going with you."

A yell of "Orderly!" broke the stillness. The soldier flinched, turned, and disappeared inside.

5) The Washburn Expedition

Five cavalrymen from Fort Ellis escorted nine curious men from Helena down the trail. The contingent included two black cooks, three packers (who led their own procession of five mules), twelve pack animals, and several extra saddle horses. It took three days for the expedition to settle down. The last jocular farewells had been said to friends in Bozeman, and the majority of the pack animals had kicked their final kicks before accepting their role as beasts of burden. Slowly, the snarls untangled, and a single-file pecking order was established on the trail for both man and beast.

The expedition traveled south, climbing slowly against the flow of the Madison River, then angled southeast along Trail Creek, a deep cut in the north-south trending Gallatin Range. Once on the east side of the Gallatin Mountains, the party descended towards the Yellowstone River Valley.

Winding down the eastern slopes of the mountains, their horseback vantage gave them an unobstructed view. The Yellowstone valley floor was flat and empty save for foliage that lined the river. Wild cherry and cottonwood competed for space on both banks. Beyond that, there was only short, brown grass.

The Yellowstone flowed towards the riders from the southwest in a shallow trench. It was a smooth, black snake of a river, one hundred yards wide, a rippling creature that shimmered as it slithered behind the folds of the mountains to the northeast. The eastern edge of the valley ended abruptly at the foot of a range of snowcapped mountains. From a distance they looked monolithic, impregnable.

The riders stuck to the well-used Indian trail. The sun was hot; there were no shade trees. The grass that surrounded the men of the expedition added a pungent odor to the air that made breathing a task for some and made others cough. Beaver, coyote, and deer watched the dusty parade from a safe distance.

The first night in the valley, the expedition made camp near the Bottler brothers' homestead. The ranch was owned by three young Germans, each a competent hunter and trapper. Theirs was the last outpost of civilization before entering the Yellowstone.

Company was always welcome.

"You want to keep a sharp eye out, I think," said Hank, the eldest Bottler. "A few days ago twenty-five lodges of Crow went up the valley. They caught a fella by himself, so of course they stripped him and set him afoot without horse or gun."

The men looked at one another. After a few words, they asked General Washburn to take over the expedition. He made three suggested: that they be underway by eight every morning, that Lieutenant Doane should spread his men fore and aft while they traveled, and that the group halt by three in the afternoon.

Three hunters and several of Doane's men rode well ahead of the main body. No one spotted Indians, but the hunters brought back antelope, grouse, duck, rabbit, and tasty two- to three-pound trout from the river. On the third night, the adventurers found a dry, comfortable site on a terrace close to the river. Nute and Johnny, the two cooks General Washburn had hired in Helena, gathered driftwood for cooking fires while the packers picketed the non-military horses and cared for the packs and saddles.

Lieutenant Doane had requisitioned much of the expedition's supplies from Fort Ellis stores. In addition to forty days' rations per person and one hundred rounds of ammunition for each of his men, he'd managed to acquire an aneroid barometer, a thermometer, and several pocket compasses.

Jake Ward Smith stripped and picketed his horse, then sat on his butt. He watched several privates and a few of the Helena expeditionaires clear areas for tents and evening campfires. "Watch out that you remove that root, soldier," advised Smith. "You wouldn't want to cause anyone like Mr. Langford discomfort, would you?" He chuckled at his cleverness. The soldier paid him no attention.

Jake Smith wasn't afraid of work; he'd simply decided that he was on vacation, and on vacation, he could afford to be lazy. As owner and manager of the now defunct Montana Hide and Fur Company, he'd worked hard enough. "Don't you fellows ever get tired of people telling you what to do?" inquired Smith idly to no one soldier in particular. "When I left home, I was fifteen but I'd already decided I would never work for anyone again."

From his horizontal position, he scanned the volcanic ridges and wondered about the prospects of hidden mineral resources. Not that Smith was a miner; he was a stockbroker who had moved to Virginia City, Nevada, in 1859, speculated on silver, and made a fortune. But his money went as quickly as it had appeared, so Smith wandered into Montana and started a tanning and butchering business in Helena. Poor management—which Smith defined as sour investments—caused him to lose everything again. This trip into the Yellowstone was his idea of a change of pace, a "time out" before he tackled his next scheme.

The thick shadow of Sergeant Barker interrupted Smith's reverie. Barker was a no-nonsense Irishman in his mid-thirties who'd earned his stripes during the Civil War. As Smith shaded his eyes and looked up, Barker leaned down far enough to make his words personal. "Do yourself a favor, Mr. Smith," he said in a low monotone. "Find a friend to chat with. My men are busy."

As the evening fire blazed, Langford heard Nute bang a couple of tin cups together to signal dinner. Langford scraped his dish clean, poured himself some coffee, and stretched out against a log. Lieutenant Doane wandered over and sat next to him. Langford blew on his coffee and glanced at the lieutenant. "Glad you and your men were available, Lieutenant," he said. "A little military know-how and firepower is always nice to have out here."

"Well," responded Doane with a twinkle, "I almost didn't make it."

Lieutenant Doane gave the impression that he belonged where he was, as though he'd been leading men through the wilderness all his life. Few would have guessed that his army career covered less than a decade. His Illinois family had taken him to Oregon in 1846. Doane completed his schooling at the University of Santa Clara, joined the army, and spent the Civil War with those who tried to tie down the West.

"I did receive the impression that Major Baker wasn't rushing to support your participation."

"That gentleman helped a great deal," said Doane, nodding in the direction of General Washburn. Henry Dana Washburn was a tall, slender man who carried himself with military bearing. Because of his bright eyes and alert demeanor, he stood out as a natu-

ral leader—the individual everyone instinctively looked up to because he radiated confidence and optimism. At the moment he was
leaning against a cottonwood tree, talking to Cornelius Hedges,
Helena's only Yale-trained lawyer.

Langford knew of Washburn's early involvement in the prepa-
ration of the expedition. He had seen to it that the general's academic interest was converted into action. It was relatively easy:
David Folsom worked for Washburn as a surveyor. Folsom had said
little about the Yellowstone after his scare at the bank until Langford
carefully pried him open. Feeling more at ease now, Folsom pulled
out a map he and Cook had made of their journey and showed it to
another of Washburn's surveyors, Walter DeLacy.

To his surprise, DeLacy had exclaimed, "Aha!" and pulled
out his own map. Like David Folsom, DeLacy had never talked
about his adventure, but he now admitted that he'd been through a
segment of the Yellowstone in the mid-1860s. After some discussion, the two decided to update DeLacy's map with Folsom's data.

Then Folsom shared the seven-page article he and Charles
Cook had written about their trip. After Washburn and Langford
read it, Folsom submitted it for publication. The *New York Tribune*
and *Harper's Weekly* returned the manuscript with polite comments
about overly exaggerated material. *Lippincott's* of Philadelphia
bluntly told Folsom that they did not accept fiction. In June, however, the *Western Monthly Magazine of Chicago* accepted the article for publication. When it appeared, it had been heavily edited.

By then, Langford had enlisted General Washburn, Sam
Hauser, and Warren Gillette for the trip, and had secured a promise of military escort from General Hancock. By mid-August, twenty
men had signed up. Chief Justice Hosmer of the Montana Territory
advised Washburn that Lieutenant Doane at Fort Ellis would be
mighty interested in exploring the Yellowstone. And Fort Ellis was
on the way.

So Washburn sent Doane a telegram to ask whether he could
join the party. His telegram arrived a day or two before the Army
sent notices to the general population of the Montana Territory to
be on the watch for restless Crow Indians. The next day, the number of dedicated adventurers dropped to eight.

Doane filled Langford in the missing details. "I gathered from Washburn's telegram that he assumed I was free to go anywhere, any time. I had to tell him that if he wanted me along he'd have to bypass my C.O. and obtain direct approval from General Hancock. I even suggested that he ask Hancock to send Baker an order authorizing me to go."

Doane raised his eyebrows. "The order arrived seven days ago. I don't need to tell you that it's been a long week."

"What's Baker's problem—other than hitting the bottle too often?"

"Oh, he was all right until that little fracas on the Marias River last winter. But after that, the national press had him for breakfast, lunch, and dinner. Sheridan was the only one who tried to protect him. Sheridan's loyal because Baker served under him in the Shenandoah of Virginia during the Civil War and distinguished himself during the Battle of Winchester."

Doane spoke more softly than before to limit the conversation to himself and Langford. What had become known as the "Piegan Massacre" on the Marias River was a subject that still roused a lot of emotion. While he talked, General Washburn moseyed their way. Doane kept talking. "General Sheridan had enough information about the activities of Mountain Chief's Piegan camp to authorize a preemptive strike. We left Fort Ellis last January sixth, with two companies of cavalry and two companies of infantry we'd acquired from Fort Shaw. Sheridan told Major Baker to hit the Piegans hard."

General Washburn settled himself on a boulder near Doane. "We captured a five-lodge camp on the Marias, then moved downriver," continued Doane. "A few of the captives told us that Big Horn and Red Horn—chiefs we knew were hostile to whites—were camped downstream." Doane shook his head a little and glanced at General Washburn. "One of our scouts, Joe Kipp, said that wasn't the case. He tried to convince Baker that the camp he was about to attack belonged to Heavy Runner, one of the camps Sheridan had agreed to leave alone to ensure the strike was made only against hostiles."

"Well, Baker's blood was up, and he might have been drunk at the time. I didn't have any close contact with him that morning.

Anyway, he ignored Kipp's report—almost had the man arrested when Kipp persisted. Heavy Runner heard that the soldiers were coming in, so he came out of his tent carrying a piece of white paper and was promptly shot by Joe Cobell. Turns out that Cobell, who was our other scout, was married to Mountain Chief's sister. He did not want the Army to find his camp ten miles downstream, so he thought he'd start a little shoot-out."

General Washburn nodded his head. Bad intelligence and hidden motives were often enough to throw entire campaigns into chaos. The Civil War had taught him that.

"As you can imagine," continued Doane, "with everyone's finger on the trigger, one shot was all that was needed. Our boys opened fire and when it was over, one hundred seventy-three Piegans were dead. Many were women and children. I was left to guard captives while Baker went downstream. All he found was empty lodges.

"The rest, I'm sure you know. As a result of the campaign, Congress dropped the idea of transferring the Department of Indian Affairs from the Interior to the Army. They even refused to allow officers to take civilian posts like that of Indian Agent."

"They're chosen from the ranks of religious groups now, aren't they?" asked Washburn.

Doane nodded.

"Any official action taken against Baker?" asked Langford.

Doane shook his head. "Unofficial censure was enough. But he was tarred with the name 'Piegan Baker' and his report about the fight was considered to be self-justifying. He's taken to the bottle and likely ruined any remaining chance of advancement. As I said, Sheridan tried to protect him, but he was no match for the press."

Langford idly poked a stick into the earth. "I was asked to check out the death of Malcolm Clark—you know, that American Fur Company fellow murdered last August. It got around that the Piegan had killed him—wounded his son and took his three daughters. That incident was one of the reasons for the strike on Mountain Chief."

"And?"

Langford snorted. "Clark was killed by a relative. The relative was an Indian, yes, but the killing was an old family feud. The son was wounded in the fracas, but no daughter was kidnapped."

"Good lord!" said Washburn.

Doane enjoyed the rush of a good battle, but some of the Indian issues bothered him. He had re-entered the Army in 1865 after his wife divorced him. He received a commission to Second Lieutenant within a year and was assigned to join Colonel Bracket's company of Second Cavalry. That troop became the first company to be stationed in Montana. At long last Doane was part of what he called the *crest of the wave of civilization*. That part, he loved.

During a lull in the talk, Langford started for the coffeepot. A few yards away, Nute stubbed his toe on a root and fell with an armful of pots and pans. Gillette's gelding spooked, pulled his picket, and headed through camp at a gallop. Langford snared the picket rope as the horse went by, but the animal's momentum pulled him off his feet and dragged him into a log, which he hit with a terrific thud.

Momentarily stunned, he looked up to see Samuel Hauser looking down at him. Langford managed a wry grin and rubbed his head.

"I thought you'd stopped taking unnecessary risks, Tan," said Hauser with a little chuckle. The log against which Langford had snagged was half rotted and full of ants. As he pulled off his shirt and shook it, he replied, "I stopped collecting taxes, didn't I?"

Hauser laughed. He knew some of the hairier incidents Langford had been involved in. The two men had met at Grasshopper Creek in 1863 when Langford arrived with Captain Fisk's caravan. Until Hauser had acquired a case of gold fever then, he had been in Missouri as the chief engineer for the Southern Missouri Railroad. Hauser wasn't the kind who believed in waiting for others to shout "Gold!" Once in Grasshopper Creek, he joined James Stuart's gold-hunting party, a troupe that went by the name of the Yellowstone Expedition. They headed straight into the heart of Sioux country. One dark night while camped in the Yellowstone River Valley, the Sioux took exception to their presence. One of the first shots hit Hauser right in the heart!

While the fight flowed around him, Hauser sat up from where

he had fallen and found that the rifle ball had come to rest in the last pages of a thick notebook he carried in his shirt pocket. After that, he never went anywhere without it. If the brush with death was a sign to start life anew, Hauser took it to heart. He built the territory's first furnace to reduce silver ore, organized a bank in Virginia City, and with Langford's help, built the First National Bank in Helena. He made money from everything he touched, but he never lost his sense of adventure.

6) The Yellowstone Road

The going had been easy. The only members of the group who had had any ailments were Booby and Everts. Booby was the dog that had attached itself to the expedition as it left Fort Ellis. His feet had been cut by sharp pieces of rock, so Lieutenant Doane fixed him up with some rawhide moccasins. He lay in the shade and licked his new shoes, but didn't try to remove them.

As for Truman C. Everts, he had had some intestinal problems from having overindulged in Bozeman. At fifty-four, the transplanted Vermonter was the oldest in the expedition. With his thin, straight hair and wire-rimmed glasses, he resembled a fastidious businessman or accountant. Abraham Lincoln had appointed him assessor of Internal Revenue for the new Montana Territory. He and his assistant, Walter Trumbull, who often rode behind Truman, lost their federal jobs in the patronage scramble after Grant was elected.

As the expedition traveled deeper into the wilderness, the valley walls moved closer together, rock exposures grew more complex, and the country became more varied. As Charles Cook predicted, they came upon a strange formation that ran straight up the mountain. Cook had labeled it "Devil's Slide." The men looked at it, and Private Moore made a rough drawing of it, but no one knew what it was.

The eleventh day out of Helena, they camped at the mouth of Gardiner's River, where the riverbank was composed of sand and great granite boulders. A grove of cedars provided a natural windbreak between the beach at the river's edge and the sage-covered hills to the west. The evening air was a cool forty degrees, the stars and the campfires were bright, and the men were in a good mood. They surmised that they were at the threshold of the Yellowstone, so everyone anticipated strange and exotic sights.

Walter Trumbull remained close to the fire, writing in his diary about the day's events. Like most members of the expedition, Trumbull brought with him an interesting set of skills. The twenty-four-year-old lad was the eldest son of Illinois senator Lyman Trumbull. He'd attended the Naval Academy and had done his part in the Civil War, but had resigned in 1865 to pursue a career as a writer. He had been a journalist for the *New York Sun* and had written freelance pieces for the *Rocky Mountain Gazette*. A few days before he joined the expedition, Mr. Fisk of the *Helena Herald* had asked him to be the paper's special correspondent, so Walter spent the last hour before dusk editing his notes on the day's events and his own musings.

"What are you writing now?" barked Benjamin Stickney. "About Langford's tangle with a picket rope?" Several of the men chuckled. Langford smiled but said nothing. "You should be writing about that Devil's Slide place back there and all the satanic stuff we're gonna encounter."

Several of the men groaned. Trumbull looked at the thirty-two-year-old Stickney with a thin smile. Stickney was a jack-of-all-trades. Langford had chosen him to be chief of the expedition's commissary because of his enthusiasm for the journey.

"Ben, I've already written about what we did yesterday and today," Trumbull said with a straight face. "I can't write about something till I see it or do it. It isn't fair. Be patient." He thought Stickney was a bit silly and not too bright.

"There ain't nothing special where we're going, anyhow," said Everts, who felt like needling Stickney.

"Sez you," retorted Stickney. "I heard Mr. Langford say the water spouts and hot springs and stuff like that were real. And what about Charlie and David's article they got published last month? You saying they are liars?"

Every face turned to Everts. "I ain't callin' no one a liar," retorted Everts, "but I ain't saying they saw what they said they saw, neither."

"What about it, Mr. Langford?" asked Stickney. He got up and tossed another log on the fire in a purposely careless manner. Sparks and hot coals jumped from the fire towards Everts, who was sprawled close to the edge. Everts jumped back and glowered at Stickney.

"I'm not one to speculate on secondhand information," said Langford, "but the stories I've heard over the years have been pretty consistent, regardless of who did the talking."

"How about an example, Tan?" asked Cornelius Hedges.

Langford was immediately transported back to his days as agent for the Internal Revenue. It was the fall of 1865 and he was in Virginia City. His friends had asked him to help develop a business to improve travel between "the States" and the Montana Territory. Their goal was to entice more people to the gold fields by making the journey easier. The Montana frontier had been open for business for two years, but the road to Virginia City remained long and arduous. First, the traveler had to go all the way to Salt Lake City on the Oregon Trail, then cut north on the freighting road to Virginia City.

The new venture was called the Missouri River and Rocky Mountain Wagon Road and Telegraph Company. Langford was elected president; Sam Hauser was elected treasurer. They merged their efforts and funds with the Bozeman City and Fort Laramie Wagon Road and Telegraph Company.

About that time, Jim Bridger arrived in Virginia City. He'd just completed a road survey for Colonel Thomas Moonlight, so he and John Bozeman threw in their interests with Langford's company. Bozeman had opened the Montana Road in 1864. It was a cut-off that linked Virginia City directly to the Oregon Trail at Fort Laramie. Unfortunately, the road went through the heart of Sioux hunting lands. The Sioux called it the *hated road*. In spite of three military posts on the trail, irate Indians had harassed wagon trains and killed several hundred settlers.

Bridger's preferred route left the Montana Road at Red Rocks near Fort Caspar, headed west and north across the southern end of the Big Horns, then followed the Big Horn River north from a

point near the east end of the Big Horn canyon. Then it crossed
some low mountains and entered the Montana Territory near Bozeman Pass. Langford's company elected to use Bridger's Big Horn route.
It stayed away from the Sioux. The route also offered better protection from the weather, experienced less snowfall in winter, and offered more grazing than the Montana Road. Bridger had successfully led wagon trains along this road since 1863.

While Langford consulted with Bridger about the new company, Bridger found a way to recount a few of his adventures in the
Rockies, including those in the Yellowstone. When Langford related Bridger's stories to friends, he didn't label them exaggerated
tales. Langford was well read, and one of the documents he'd read
was Captain John Mullan's *Report* of 1863. Mullan was a soldier
who'd been given the task of building a road west from Helena. His
official report to the Department of the Army said that he'd met
Indians who talked about hot springs and geysers at the head of the
Missouri, Columbia, and Yellowstone rivers.

Langford kept busy with taxes and banking, but he'd never
rid himself of his desire to see the Yellowstone. Two of his Helena
friends, David Folsom and Charles Cook, said laughingly one day
that maybe they'd get there first. They had, but the nature of what
they saw caused David Folsom to shun public speaking.

"Examples," said Langford. "The real good ones I know came
from Jim Bridger. He told me that he'd tramped the Yellowstone off
and on for four decades and claims to have been to the source of
the Yellowstone River a number of times."

Someone behind the campfire snickered. "Ain't he the one
who said he's been in the West so long that the Tetons was a hole in
the ground when he was a child?" The whole group laughed heartily.

Langford held up a hand. "I know, Bridger's a colorful gent,
and he likes attention, but remember, the man's a trapper, a guide,
and blood brother to several tribes. He's been all over the Rockies
and survived a lot of hazardous events. I give his stories credence."

"Well, what did he say he saw?" asked Ben Stickney impatiently.

"The first thing he talked about was the Yellowstone lake. Bridger thought it was a good sixty miles long. But he said you had to watch where you walked when you got close to it, 'cause real quick, the ground could get awful hot."

More snickers.

"And one of the big hot springs he saw took up a whole hillside. It had wide steps down its front like a staircase. He claimed you could cook in the pools high up, and take a bath in the pools at lower levels." He looked into campfire faces and saw expressions that ranged from consternation to pure glee.

"Bridger said that he'd handled pieces of petrified trees and petrified birds; that he'd seen a cliff made of pure black glass; and once saw a body of water the thickness of a man thrown as high as the flagpole in Virginia City."

The men filled the air with "Hot damn," "I'll be damned," and "Glory be!"

"Well, that's what we're gonna find out, isn't it?" shouted Stickney. "I hope we see all sorts of weird things."

"What about the rumor that the devil lives there?" asked Charles Moore in a loud voice. He looked at two of his fellow infantrymen for confirmation. One nodded gravely. No one else spoke.

"I must admit I haven't heard that before," said Langford quietly, "but I suspect that since he likes hot places, he's at least visited!" He smiled, and a number of the men guffawed.

Moore started to protest others making light of his concern, but before he could rise, Cornelius Hedges spoke up. "Maybe the Yellowstone hasn't had many visitors recently, but we shouldn't forget, as Mr. Langford mentioned, trappers have crisscrossed that region time and again. One of the old-time trappers I know said that McKenzie of the Northwest Company was in the Yellowstone as early as 1816."

"That's very early," said Lieutenant Doane.

"That's right. But the Northwest Company was all over these mountains even before that, so it's possible. Apparently, the company divided the beaver country into districts. McKenzie had charge of the Snake River area. According to my friend, he entered the Rockies from the west, crossed one of the Teton passes, then split his men into two groups. He took a handful and went north. At the end of the season, he reported hot springs and boiling fountains in a hidden land the Indians thought was spirit-ridden."

"And don't forget Colter," said Hauser. "If this truly be Colter's Hell, then he ran through the Yellowstone ten years earlier than McKenzie."

"Who's Colter and what was he runnin' from or is that just a way of speaking?" asked Sergeant Barker.

"No, Sergeant, it's recorded fact. Colter was a member of the Lewis and Clark Expedition. They headed to the Pacific in 1803. President Jefferson had asked them to find a route to the Pacific. They were gone three years. John Colter was with them, but in the Rockies on the way back, they ran into a Spanish fellow named Manuel Lisa. Lisa was from St. Louis, on his way into the mountains to trade for beaver. He and Colter chatted and Lisa ended up hiring Colter away from Lewis and Clark. Lisa built a post at the Three Forks, where the Madison, Jefferson, and Gallatin come together."

Hauser looked into the fire and paused as though trying to remember. He knew that any good campfire storyteller let some silence into the telling. It was good for the listener. The fire crackled and sent a light trail of red sparks into the blue-black sky. Everyone waited.

"Lisa figured there was no sense in busting his back and freezing his hands in cold water every spring to catch beaver if he could get Indians to do it for him and then trade the pelts. But he would need to powwow with the tribes. So he sent Colter on a mission to find the tribes and bring back representatives.

"No one knows the actual route Colter took, but he headed south to find the Crow nation and they like to winter in the north part of the Wind River Valley, near the de Noir. Some say there are no entrances to the de Noir Valley in winter, but I suspect Colter had help. After talking trade with the Crow, he headed west toward Jackson's Hole and ended up with a Blackfoot bullet hole in his leg."

"How'd that happen?" asked Stickney.

"Well, I guess somebody shot him," said Hauser, slightly

miffed at being interrupted. Most of the men laughed because they thought Stickney deserved the answer.

"Anyway, with that hole in his leg, Colter made his way to Yellowstone Lake, the one we're headed for, then he angled across the hot parts, warming himself and nursing his wound by taking hot baths in the springs. Some say he avoided a dark-looking waterfall on his way. In the end, he cut across some high mountains, found the South Fork of the Shoshone, and made it back to Lisa's fort."

"So how far was all that?" asked Everts.

"Most give him credit for five hundred miles," said Hauser.

"That's impossible," said Moore.

"Can't be done," agreed Everts.

"Tough man," said Sergeant Barker. "A real survivor."

"I thought Colter was killed by the Blackfoot," said Hedges.

"You're thinking of the time he and Potts were caught by the Blackfoot on the Jefferson," said Hauser. "They disemboweled Potts, but only stripped Colter naked, then let him go. They chased after him, but he turned the game around—killed one Indian and eluded the rest. I guess he got tired of living like that, 'cause he left the Rockies in 1810 and never came back."

The fire was a pile of orange coals. A light wind made stray pieces of wood glow as though they were winking. The men of the expedition sat quietly, each with his own thoughts of past adventures, daring, and death.

7) The View from the Top

Two days later, the expeditionary force trudged along an ancient Indian trail. It took the men high above the valley. As they ate lunch in a low saddle between two peaks, Doane and Langford decided to climb the higher of the two peaks. From on top, they could survey the area.

The incline was steep and covered with boulders and snow. Of the eighteen, only Gillette and Stickney volunteered to go along. The four scramblers caught up with the rest of the expedition that night and unanimously said the view had been worth the four-hour climb. "We saw something that no white man has ever seen," said Doane. "The first impression you get is that you are so far above everything, you could be peering over the edge of an eagle's nest. All around you are nothing but mountains."

"The basin must be fifty to seventy-five miles wide," added Stickney.

"Close in," said Gillette, "the mountains look like a pile of jigsaw pieces; nothin' but confusion: steep-sided ravines, volcanic passes, and blue-black lakes." They all wanted to talk at once, to tell their version of what they had seen.

The peak had been a strange place whose surface was composed of broken chunks of volcanic rock. A gale-force wind had cleaned off almost all of the snow. Lieutenant Doane seemed the only one immune to the wind and cold. He sat up and scanned the scene with his binoculars. With twenty miles of visibility, features of the land stood out like an etching.

To the north and west Doane took the measure of a great plateau. Further west, he saw snowy ranges on the headwaters of Gardiner's River join those of the Gallatin to form a continuous southward-bending rim around the Yellowstone basin. To the east, he scanned a lofty, ragged set of volcanic peaks attached to a parade of mountains that stretched south. And beyond the southern rim he saw three isolated white spots—the Tetons.

Almost beneath their feet, a great canyon cut through the base of two mountains. It was so dark, he thought it might be that gorge Bridger spoke of—the one that absorbed all light and sound. Ten to twenty miles away, they also saw a broad, Prussian blue sheet of water—Yellowstone Lake.

Langford was the first to notice the white puffs. "Is the forest on fire?" he asked. "No. Wait! Look!" Streams of white vapor emerged in tall columns from groves of trees. As he watched, they melted into the air. "I'll be damned. That's not smoke, it's more like small clouds, billows of steam."

"Further south!" pointed Doane with his glasses still to his eyes.

Langford saw two more columns of white rising a good five hundred feet high. Now he was positive. The journey would validate everything he had heard from David Folsom, Charles Cook, and Jim Bridger. Langford felt a tightness in his stomach. Yes! The Yellowstone would more than justify the risk he'd taken.

Last June, he'd taken Marshall's advice and went to Philadelphia to talk with Jay Cooke. The dapper banker had welcomed him and invited him to his home. During dinner, Langford boasted a little about his planned expedition. He was hoping that his knowledge of the Yellowstone plus his knowledge of the resources of the Northwest would make him a good candidate to lecture for the Northern Pacific. Cooke appeared quite interested in what he had to say. He didn't offer him a job, but asked if Langford would share his findings when he returned.

Langford now realized that if Jay Cooke's railroad passed through Bozeman, as planned, the Yellowstone could be made accessible to people from all over the world. Would they understand what they were seeing? he wondered. The region needed to be documented. None of the men in his expedition, himself included, were scientists. Another worry: what was to prevent his descriptions and explanations from being discounted the way David Folsom had feared, as flights of fancy?

Langford half-slid down the last section of snow-covered terrain to where the horses were tied. Someone important and well-known needed to make a detailed examination of the Yellowstone, he thought. Not just anyone; someone who knew the West.

Langford knew the names of the prominent explorers of the day. The most renowned explorer was the young, sophisticated Clarence King. Where was he now? Somewhere in the Southwest, unraveling the country on the flanks of the Central Pacific Railroad.

John Wesley Powell was another candidate. Just last year, the one-armed Civil War hero had challenged and beaten the Grand Canyon with three boats. He might be interested.

The only other candidate was geologist Ferdinand Hayden. For the last three to four years, he'd led surveys through portions of the United States Territories. Hayden was becoming known across the country as the West's most energetic promoter.

Three candidates. After a while, Langford had a pretty good idea which one he could interest in the Yellowstone.

PART 3: FERDINAND V. HAYDEN, 1870

1) The Omaha Recruit

In Omaha, Nebraska, a slender, hirsute gentleman in tidy, but drab-looking clothes stepped down from the westbound train. He tugged once at the bow tie beneath his bent-wing collar, brushed a sleeve, and looked around momentarily as though bewildered. But instead of exhibiting the slow, exacting gait one might expect from his retired appearance, he picked up his bags as though they were empty and marched towards the city with energy and resolve. His name was Dr. Ferdinand Vandeveer Hayden. He was a government geologist, author, and champion of Western settlement. Today, the forty-year-old explorer was in hot pursuit of a new idea.

His destination was the most prominent photographic studio in town, Jackson Brothers, Photographers, at Douglas and Fifteenth streets. Hayden did not know much about the owner, but last summer he had stopped by the shop to examine photographs of the Union Pacific route. One look had startled him, for the prints compared very favorably to those of A. J. Russell.

A. J. Russell was the official photographer of the Union Pacific Railroad, and Hayden knew his work well. A year ago, he'd purchased a number of Russell's prints for his forthcoming book, *Sun Pictures of the Rocky Mountains*. Before this year was over, five hundred copies of his book would roll off the New York presses of printer Julius Bien. When Hayden spoke of the work, he said it was an experiment in writing and photography—his attempt to summarize his seventeen years exploring the West.

Arriving in front of the Jackson Brothers studio, Dr. Hayden set down his luggage next to a tall, closed, wooden box on wheels.

The ungainly shape had Jackson Bros. painted on the side. It was a traveling darkroom. Hayden nodded his head in understanding, then pushed open the studio door. A tinkling bell announced his presence.

Jackson's studio was one large room. Half had been given over to a huge inventory of photographic equipment: cameras, glass plate negatives, seemingly hundreds of bags and boxes and jars of chemicals, and several contraptions that looked like saddlebags made of wood, which Hayden knew to be panniers, used to transport food or equipment on mule back or horseback. The other half of the studio was rigged for portraits. A large view camera on a tripod faced a series of props and colored background canvasses whose selection minimized the need to relocate outdoors for the shoot.

A young, pleasant-faced woman in a plain dress and apron appeared from behind a set of curtains. Her hair was done up in a bun and her face was lightly flushed as though she had been engaged in physical labor. She walked to greet him and introduced herself as Mrs. Mollie Jackson. "How may I help you, sir?"

Hayden took off his hat, ran a hand self-consciously through his thin, straight, black hair, and introduced himself as Professor Hayden of Philadelphia. "I wonder if I might speak to Mr. Jackson?"

"Of course. Please wait here." While Mollie sought her husband, Hayden matter-of-factly snooped through a stack of eleven-by-fourteen-inch glass negatives. They looked recently taken. Their subject matter confirmed his thoughts.

"Dr. Hayden! Welcome!" A tall young man with a full head of light brown hair strode across the room with outstretched hand. "I'm William Henry Jackson. I see you've found some of the additional shots I took last summer along the Union Pacific."

Hayden was pleased that Jackson remembered their first meeting, and was flattered to think that the young man was delighted to see him again. Before he could say anything, Jackson walked to a large box and began to pull out prints. "The only other recent work I might recommend you examine are my Indian portraits," he said, and handed several to Hayden.

"I spent a good portion of the summer of 1868 with the

Winnebago, Pawnee, and Otoe to document the more spectacular of the chiefs and their way of life." Jackson was proud of his Indian photographs and felt confident that his collection, which now numbered in the hundreds, was one of the best in the country.

Hayden took his time. First he studied the shots taken of the Union Pacific along Weber Canyon and the Wasatch Mountains. He noted the strong lines. The light and shadows created marvelous detail and relief. Then he examined several of the studies of Indian life. Here was stark realism in an acceptably conventional manner. Yes, said Hayden to himself, this is what I need.

When Ferdinand Hayden first started exploring the West in the early 1850s, he'd worked alone, so he'd been forced to rely on his own talents to add a visual dimension to his work. He sketched geologic formations, distant mountains, and landscapes. A decade later, with two surveys for the government under his belt, he did what the majority of explorers did, he hired an artist. Hayden secured Henry W. Elliott, a young man of administrative competence as well as great artistic talent. Elliott worked for the director of the Smithsonian Institution.

Sketches, line drawings, and watercolors of the West had been rendered by soldiers and artists since the 1830s. The earliest artists were privy to the West under the patronage of royal sportsmen, wealthy explorers, and surveyors. Hayden had seen images created by Samuel Seymour for the Yellowstone Expedition of 1819 under Lieutenant Stephen Long. The works of Alfred Jacob Miller who accompanied William Drummond Stewart into the Wind River country in the 1830s had been displayed at the Smithsonian. More recently, artists including F. W. Von Egloffstein, Heinrich Baldwin Mollhausen, and John Mix Stanley had been hired to document the great railroad surveys of the mid-1850s.

With each passing year, however, Hayden became more anxious to find a stronger, more efficient way to depict the unique and complex aspects of the country's geology and topographic features. Sketches and artistic studies added a humanistic element but they often introduced a romantic dimension and many assumed a life of their own. Explorers were beginning to use photography to document the country and to strengthen the validity of their findings.

Photography was relatively new. The painter Albert Bierstadt, who joined Frederick Lander in South Pass in 1858, was one of the first to use a camera in the West.

Hayden was forced to take note of the notoriety and acclaim recently accorded Timothy O'Sullivan. The works of the young photographer, who started as a protégé of Civil War photographer Mathew B. Brady, were now exhibited in New York, Washington, New Haven, and Boston. Hayden didn't know O'Sullivan personally, but he found O'Sullivan's photographs deliberate, competent, and compelling. The public attention O'Sullivan was receiving also created a problem for Ferdinand Hayden because O'Sullivan had taken photographs for geologist Clarence King, and Hayden considered King his arch-rival.

Hayden worried constantly that if he did not appear highly competitive, he would lose the attention, interest, and eventually funding of his congressional allies. So this year, he was determined to take along a photographer, especially since his instructions from the Secretary of the Interior stated he must include *thorough* visual documentation. The longer he examined Jackson's photographs, the more potential he saw for his survey and his annual report.

Hayden put down the last photograph. "This is exactly what I need," he said with a yearning voice. "I wish I could offer you enough to make it worth your while to spend the summer with me." His expression was one of resignation, almost of pain.

As Jackson replaced the prints in their cases, he asked lightly: "What could you offer me, Dr. Hayden?"

Hayden smiled and shook his head. "Only a summer of hard work in the Wyoming Territory, I'm afraid. Oh, I have enough to pay for your expenses, but all I can offer in exchange for your labor and time is the satisfaction you might find in making a contribution to science." He glanced at the dashing young fellow, fully expecting to see him shake his head.

Jackson smiled politely while his mind whirled. Hayden had no way of knowing, but he had appeared at a moment when money had become a critical issue to William Jackson. Jackson's brother, Edward, had given notice that he would no longer run the studio. He was off to Blair, Nebraska, to manage his father-in-law's farm.

Unfortunately, Edward's decision had occurred a few weeks *after* brother William had purchased a second studio in town. Now Jackson desperately needed new views to sell. An expedition with the government would provide him protected access to spectacular scenery. No salary, but no expense, either. Jackson thought the offer had promise. Besides, he sensed a boyish enthusiasm in Dr. Hayden's demeanor. Yes, he thought, this Professor Hayden was so caught up in his plans that his eyes glittered. He spoke so fast about his plans he almost stuttered. Jackson thought Hayden's attempt to present himself as an authority in search of expertise was a bit comical. Under all the polite restraints, Jackson saw a man in love with exploration and the excitement of discovery. Hayden was a fellow adventurer if he had ever seen one.

"How long would I be gone?" asked Jackson, nonchalantly.

"Three months at the outside," blurted Hayden, surprised that Jackson had not automatically turned him down. He quickly searched his mind for something positive to say without having to lie about circumstances. "My appropriation is too small to provide you a decent salary, but I could guarantee that you can keep all the negatives you make. I simply want to have photographs available for future use. They will aid me greatly in my objective of familiarizing people with the nature and resources of the West, which, of course," he added with a slight stutter, "is the object of my work."

Hayden's summer geological program had been set in motion eight months earlier, when he wrote the Secretary of the Interior to request an appropriation of twenty thousand dollars to continue his survey of the territories. He asked for funds to support a reconnaissance of Wyoming and Montana, including a small topographical corps to make maps. Feeling that he had nothing to lose, he also requested an additional fifteen thousand dollars to present two quarto volumes of engravings to Congress, but he hadn't been sufficiently alert to include funding for a photographer. Congress gave him twenty-five thousand dollars for everything.

Jackson put away the last photograph. He looked at Professor Hayden but didn't say anything. He was thinking that if the survey covered his room and board and photographic materials, and provided him opportunities to make exposures of new areas of the

West, he would be in the unique position of marketing photographs under the imprimatur of the survey! All he would have to do was supply Professor Hayden with copies. As the moment of silence lengthened, the possibilities began to multiply.

At that moment, Mollie Jackson re-entered the room. Seeing the silent, statuesque poses of her husband and Dr. Hayden, she paused. Both men were obviously in deep thought. When Jackson eventually looked her way she raised an eyebrow.

"Oh, uh, Mollie dear, Dr. Hayden was just outlining his plans for the summer . . ." His eyes were bright, and he made gestures with his hands the way he always did when he was excited.

"And telling your husband how much I would like to take him along," added Hayden with a warm and eager smile.

Mollie's eyes darted back and forth between the two men. At first she grinned, then she laughed, a light and easy laughter that made the two men regard one another. They smiled, hesitantly.

Men, thought Mollie; they've reached an agreement but neither one has enough sense to admit it. "Well, I'm glad you two have worked it out," she said and went about her business, leaving the two men to suddenly grin and shake hands.

Five days later, Jackson received a telegram to leave at once for Fort Russell. "See Captain James Stevenson upon arrival," wrote Hayden.

Mollie read the message over his shoulder. "I can handle the studio for the months you are gone," she said. A grateful Jackson dashed off an order for special equipment and supplies, then the two spent a day preparing a routine Mollie could use for the studio.

The last day of July, William and Mollie headed for the railroad station where Jackson watched his photographic equipment loaded into a freight car. Their farewell kiss was a prolonged one. Neither had any idea where Jackson would be going or what dangers he might face. They had good reason for being a little nervous: in 1870, everything between Omaha and San Francisco was either Indian Territory or wilderness.

During the first hours of his trip, Jackson thought of all of the changes he'd gone through since he'd left New England. Life had been so simple there. He had a good job as a photograph retoucher.

He also painted backgrounds on photographs. And at age twenty-three, he was engaged to be married.

The next thing he knew, he was standing on the west bank of the Missouri River, scanning the waving grass of the Great Plains. He had left New England, his job, and his fiancée, with hardly a word and no thought to the future. He was about to walk across the Plains to the Rocky Mountains with no more than a pocket full of misgivings.

At the end of that first day as a bullwhacker, William Henry Jackson knew he should have stayed home. Between sunrise and sunset, the thirty-wagon freighting outfit had covered fifteen miles. It had been one long, tiring process of shouting and prodding Texas cows, a tedious business aggravated by bruises from having to yoke and chain up the six pair of oxen twice a day. God, how his feet had ached.

June turned to July and Jackson became irritated by the constant diet of bacon sandwiches, beans, and coffee. He was worn out trying to adjust to days full of wind-blown dust and storms, and cold nights. Then, the pain lessened, the chores became routine, and the impressionable William Henry Jackson became caught up in the harsh romance of being on his own in the West. He learned to make bread and to harness his oxen quickly, so his wagons would be in lead position in the morning. It was the only place where a bullwhacker didn't have to eat dust. He learned to snap his whip without touching his bulls and to shake his boots for snakes before he put them on. By the end of July, he realized that he would have been miserable had he remained in Vermont.

Jackson stepped from the train in Cheyenne and looked around. He was greeted by silence, dust, the smell of horses, and curious glances from the locals. He waited a few minutes, but saw no one who looked as though they were waiting to meet someone. He made inquiries, rented a wagon, and made his way to the Hayden Survey camp located near Camp Carlin, a dusty depot a few miles west of Fort D. A. Russell.

At what he thought might be about the right spot, Jackson saw a group of flimsy tents, a few scattered wagons, and a number of men who glanced his way with open curiosity.

"I'm Jackson," he said to the first man he met. "Is this the Hayden Survey?"

"You bet," responded the other. "I'm Elliott. Guess you're the photographer."

"Right. Where do I go?"

"See the captain," said Elliott, nodding toward a bearded fellow with a clipboard standing next to a pile of material. "He'll fix you up."

Jackson stopped his buckboard and examined the solidly built man with the full beard. Inquisitive eyes greeted Jackson. "Are you Stevenson?" asked Jackson. The man nodded. "I'm Jackson, the photographer."

For this information he received another nod.

"Do I get what everyone else gets?"

"I don't think so," responded Stevenson, "unless everyone else here is a photographer, in which case we don't need you, do we?"

Jackson scratched the back of his neck. "Well, what do I need?"

"That's my question," said Stevenson cryptically.

Jackson hesitated. "Should I come back at a later time?" he asked.

When Stevenson didn't respond, Jackson began to turn the buckboard around.

"That's a rental, isn't it? So for starters, you're gonna need a wagon for all that camera gear," said Stevenson.

The wagon he received was an army ambulance. Jackson relocated his three hundred pounds of equipment and supplies from one wagon to the other. First in were his six-and-one-half-inch by eight-and-one-half-inch view camera and a double-barreled stereo camera. The latter produced two slightly different images that created a three-dimensional effect when the prints were looked at simultaneously on a stereoscope.

He was loading his personally-designed portable darkroom with pans, trays, and a canopy when Stevenson walked his way.

"You'll receive your food and equipment from the army quartermaster until we get underway, then it will be up to John to feed you." As he talked, he eyed the camera gear. "Do you really need all that?" he asked.

His voice could have been interpreted as angry or condescending, but Jackson hadn't taken the full measure of the man and had no reason to believe that he'd riled Stevenson. Besides, as the survey's operations manager, Stevenson had an excellent reputation among the three men Jackson had talked to so far.

"Afraid so. I have to make negatives and prints while we're in the field," said Jackson. He held up his portable darkroom. "Look at it as an eight-by-ten-foot room shrunk to a container two and a half feet long, half a foot wide, and half a foot tall." He grinned.

Stevenson looked at him as though he were a beggar asking for money in a foreign language, then started to walk away. Jackson took two steps in Stevenson's direction. "By the way," he added, "I'm going to need an extra mule."

Stevenson stopped in his tracks.

"If I'm going to be exploring the country on horseback," explained Jackson, "I need a mule to carry my photographic gear."

The next day, a man handed him the reins to a butterball of a crop-eared mule whom Jackson immediately named Hypo, short for hyposulfite, the chemical he used to stabilize images on his negatives and prints. The mule looked reliable but pretty well worn. Later on, he learned that Hayden routinely purchased horses and mules for his survey from army rejects.

Jackson had had good experience with pack animals. He knew he could fit his darkroom package into one pannier and his cameras, glass plates, and chemicals into the other. Last but not least, he could secure his large wooden tripod and a barrel of water on top. Jackson looked at his final arrangement, took everything off the mule, and went back to Stevenson.

"Now what?" said Stevenson.

"I need a pair of parfleches," said Jackson.

Stevenson looked at him with a blank expression. "You know," said Jackson, making strange shapes with his hands, "large saddlebags of rawhide with flaps that you can secure. They lace up the front and come with loops that hold them on the crossbars of a pack saddle. The kind that trappers . . ."

"I know what they are," said Stevenson testily.

"Oh," said Jackson. "Well, I need them to protect easily broken gear, like the glass plates I use to create my negatives." He smiled. "I figure rawhide is best." This time he was the one to turn and walk away.

"Hey, Jackson," yelled Stevenson.

This time, Jackson stopped.

"You want buckles or snaps?"

Jackson smiled without turning. "Buckles will do nicely," he said.

2) Documenting the West

Ferdinand Hayden had telegraphed his instructions to Jackson from Denver. While there, he'd discovered that his appropriation for the year had been delayed until mid-July. The delay had worked to his advantage, however, for in Denver he encountered three artists, Sanford Gifford, Worthington Whittridge, and John Kensett. They were friends and all members of the Hudson River School of painting. They told Hayden they were planning to take advantage of the rising interest in the West to find new scenes for their canvases.

"I'd take you all with me if I could afford it," said Hayden enthusiastically. "We'll be crossing the Wyoming Territory to the Wind River Mountains, and if all goes well, we'll also examine the Uintas. You can't beat those mountain ranges for beauty."

Ten days later, on the train to Wyoming, artist Sanford Gifford sat across from Hayden. Gifford had taken Hayden to one side and asked if he could tag along for a month. Hayden readily agreed, because he didn't see how he could lose.

Now on his way to his gathering survey team, Hayden put down his reading to gaze at the lofty peaks of the Colorado Frontal Range. He had told the world that he wanted only to explore and help open the West to settlement. He'd never told anyone why; he wasn't always certain himself. But this year he was leading his fourth government survey. And this year, for the first time, he was going into the field under the title of United States Government Geologist. His appointment and upgrade in status included a small office on the third floor of a building on the corner of 11th and Pennsylvania Avenue, in Washington, D.C. His life now had an orderly pattern and purpose.

"I grew up with a pencil in my hand," said Gifford as he sketched the passing mountains. "Did you grow up leading surveys?"

Hayden immediately pictured the heavy, bearded face of Spencer Baird, assistant secretary of the Smithsonian Institution. Poor Baird, he thought as he chuckled politely in response to Gifford's question; I importuned you until you endorsed me to the General Land Office.

"No. The best answer to your question is that after spending nearly fifteen years exploring on my own, I finally knew what I wanted to do, but it took time to convince Congress that I was the man they needed.

"You see, after the Civil War, the Department of the Interior took a keen interest in the West because most of the land still needed to be mapped. Once you got away from the main east-west trails, you were in *terra incognita*. Some of those regions were as large as the state of Virginia. Oh, a map might have suggestions of mountain ranges and the names of major Indian tribes, but even the direction and links between many of the rivers in the Rocky Mountains and beyond were still unknown."

Gifford continued to sketch. From time to time he glanced at Hayden or nodded to indicate that he was listening. "The center of American life was shifting west, so if you wanted to conduct investigations that supported western settlement, Congress looked upon you with favor."

Hayden had made himself as visible as possible. He told everyone who might help that he was exactly what the government needed. In retrospect, it had been only a question of being seen, but he hadn't known that then. He knew only that he was healthy, curious, reliable, and endowed with an intense desire to make a contribution to science. He also knew he had acquired sufficient skills as a geologist, paleontologist, and naturalist to document the general character of the country and note its special characteristics for those who would come later to settle, mine, and build. He had shown that he could cover large areas of land and work rapidly while noting outstanding features and peculiarities of the land, topography, drainage, and geological resources. He could accumulate tons of data and could provide Eastern specialists with boxes and boxes of paleontological specimens. He confessed to anyone who would listen that he would gladly spend his summers surveying large portions of the West.

"I was given my first government survey in 1867," said Hayden conversationally, "an appropriation to survey the newly created state of Nebraska." He had been thrilled. He had almost raced across the land to describe its surface and subsurface characteristics. He wrote about its mineral sources and the fossils which were key to its geologic history, and personally illustrated his field notes.

"My report sold well," he said. "That was important because then I knew the settlers found my information useful. It took me a few years, but I eventually developed a routine that worked well. I have stayed with it since."

His first official government report was fifty-nine pages long. He had highlighted the information most important to settlers, and outlined the specifics of Nebraska's economic resources. He had stopped short of classifying portions of the public domain before it passed into private hands, and he only estimated the magnitude of the mineral resources he'd located. The more detailed tasks, he decided, would be completed by those who followed.

Hayden's experience working for officers in the U.S. Army Corps of Topographic Engineers had helped him understand what a survey was and what it was not. He set a goal for himself to have his own survey team, one that would put before the public full, reliable, and accurate information. He wanted to motivate public and private entities to commit capital, skill, and enterprise to develop the great natural resources of the country. He knew he was not an intellectual who would produce textbooks or academic monographs. He was, nonetheless, a good explorer, an unveiler upon whose descriptions of the lay of the land the settler could rely.

Hayden's second appropriation of five thousand dollars had supported a survey of the eastern portion of the newly created Wyoming Territory. With a party of nine he geologized the Medicine Bow Mountains and the North Platte River to South Pass. His team also examined timber resources along the Wyoming-Colorado border around the Snowies. He vividly recalled having written his preliminary report at Fort Steele during a raging snowstorm.

The following year, Hayden received ten thousand dollars to explore the geology and resources of Colorado and New Mexico. This time, the Land Office asked him to document agricultural profiles, ores, stratigraphic systems, paleontology, and mineralogy. He was to bring back collections to support his notes. To accomplish these goals, Hayden relied on a cadre of experts. He brought along Henry W. Elliot of the Smithsonian to make sketches, hired Reverend Cyrus Thomas to cover agriculture and insects, and recruited mining engineer Persifor Fraser, Jr., and zoologist E. C. Carrington.

Hayden's approach worked for everyone, the men who worked for him in the field, government officials, and the scientists in Eastern research centers who interpreted his fossils. Although the academics back east thought his reports shallow and unscientific, the narration and descriptions remained a winning combination with the public. Hayden needed no more proof than the notice that the entire eight thousand copies of his 1869 annual report had been snapped up within three weeks.

His love of exploration had not diminished a whit. He would always savor the tactile world of the West, draw energy from its silence and its immense vistas, and find excitement in the freshness of the view beyond each new horizon. And this year he would go into the field with his own photographer.

"Who's the lanky dude?" asked Jim Stevenson, as Hayden arrived in camp. "We already have a cook and enough packers."

"Ah," said Hayden, knowing his friend's penchant for dry wit, "but not artists. That's New York artist Sanford Gifford."

No response.

"Even you should have heard of Kensett."

"Hudson River artist."

"Correct," said Hayden.

"So this fellow is also a Hudson River artist."

"Correct."

"I hope he doesn't eat much," said Stevenson.

A few nights later, Stevenson told Hayden: "Looks like we're ready. I've planned breakfast at four."

Over the next few days, the Hayden survey team of twelve, with its eight packers and teamsters, covered considerable distance. The survey moved up the east side of the Laramie Range, explored Lodge Pole Creek to its source, then crossed to the head of La Bonte Creek. They rested a day at Fort Fetterman, then pushed on to the North Platte River. By late August, after covering one hundred seventy miles, the men made camp at Red Buttes, a protected rendezvous on the Sweetwater. The spot had long been used by immigrant trains. Smaller wagon trains would wait there until another train arrived. When the combined outfits had thirty wagons, they headed west. Smaller outfits that didn't wait, ran the risk of being targets for aggressive bands of Sioux, especially between 1864 and 1868.

From Red Buttes, Hayden sent the Secretary of State the first of a series of progress reports. He took care to mention the *most excellent photographer* he had hired to document the more complex aspects of geology. He also expressed the need for a military escort, explaining that part of the area they planned to explore was frequented by Indian bands which the Army said were hostile. In fact, the officers at Fort Fetterman had been quite vocal about the danger of hostiles along the Oregon Trail in the summer months. Their warning of repeated raids around Red Buttes put the men on edge. Not surprisingly, in the middle of setting up camp, someone yelled, "Indians! Indians! Get your guns!"

Everyone dropped what they were doing and ran to their horse for their rifle. Then the men scattered to shelter under wagons and behind boulders. A large black form broke through the bushes across the river and bounded up the hillside.

"Whoa! Whoa! Whoa! False alarm!" yelled Stevenson.

Several hours later, Hayden wandered into camp, after having explored a nearby creek. Noticing the frazzled and drawn expressions on a number of faces, he asked Stevenson whether something was amiss.

"Everything's fine, Doc," said Stevenson with his typical straight-faced expression. "What you see is simply the aftermath of an encounter with a black bear that sprouted a headdress and carried a tomahawk."

In the middle of lunch the next day, Jackson posed everyone for an exposure. The image in his glass-backed camera included the expedition's two black Labrador retrievers who lay near the skeleton of a butchered deer, the back portion of one camp wagon, and several survey horses that grazed in the distance. Nearly everyone wore caps or hats and long-sleeved jackets. Only half the group was bearded.

Back on the trail, Jackson saw views he thought were important, so he asked the group to wait while he made exposures. At his third request, Hayden chatted briefly with Stevenson, then turned and rode on. The others fell in behind him.

Stevenson rode to where Jackson was examining the finished negative. "You're on your own," he said.

"Can you be more specific?" asked Jackson.

"Sure. See you in camp when you get there." Then Stevens rode off. Jackson and his mule, Hypo, never did find the survey camp that night. They slept to the sound of yipping coyotes, and arrived in camp in time for breakfast.

The morning sun was hot and clear, but the air remained cool so outdoor work was pleasant as long as one could find occasional shade. Jackson spent the morning with Gifford, then the two drifted into camp for the main noon meal. Men stood, sat, and sprawled; some smoked, some chewed, some snoozed, some compared notes. At the clang of the kettle, everyone gravitated to John's smoking kitchen where wild game, beans, bread, and coffee waited. That day, they also enjoyed canned peaches.

Hayden put his fork on the tin plate and leaned forward to

look down the wooden table. It was bulky, but served as a token of
civilization. "Weather looks good, John," said Hayden. "What's
your best guess for tomorrow?"

John H. Beaman, the survey's meteorologist, casually spit a
piece of gristle on the ground. "Not much change, Dr. Hayden.
Still got good high pressure. Tomorrow should be another clear, hot
day. Wind has picked up a bit, so I expect something to happen
maybe tomorrow night."

"Best keep your hat on, John," said Cyrus Thomas from across
the table. Thomas had a naturally stern expression and he addressed
Beaman with a straight face. His comment drew a round of laughter. The medium-built Beaman grinned and tipped his hat to expose his bald pate. His gleaming dome with one small tuft of hair
made him look older than his years.

Thomas belched. "If it gets much hotter, Professor Hayden,
we're gonna have bad 'hopper' problems across this country. I'm
going to give it front-page rating in my report, because no one is
going to bring in much of a crop in this region with this kind of
insect problem." Thomas resembled the stereotypic Bible-beating
frontier reverend. He was tall, scraggly-looking, and gaunt in his
thinness. Between the top hat, the effete mat of his beard and his
straight, high ridged nose, he also looked like a tired Abraham
Lincoln.

When Thomas indicated he had no more to say on the subject
for the moment, Hayden turned to Jim Stevenson. "Our supplies
are getting a bit lower than I would like, Stevenson, so I'm going to
suggest that we move our arrival date at South Pass City up by a
day. Is that agreeable?" No one complained.

"While you guys are out and about tomorrow," said Jackson,
"don't forget to keep a sharp eye out for good views. I have plenty
of plates, but I can't see all the country. Help me out."

"Yeah, and if you like eatin'," said John, the cook, scratching
his short-cropped hair, "some of you might give Raphael a hand."
Raphael was their only hunter.

Henry Elliott and Jim Stevenson volunteered to hunt. When
they stood close together, they looked like brothers, except that
Elliott always wore a tie and a white shirt; Stevenson wore a field

shirt and vest. Also, Stevenson was quieter than Elliott, and had a drier sense of humor.

"Anyone find anything unusual this morning?" inquired Professor Hayden.

"Just an incredible amount of granite," said Carrington. "And a good view of the Wind Rivers from the ridge."

"Oh? Good. I didn't think we were that close." Hayden closed his notebook and walked towards the cook stove. John anticipated him and met him halfway with the coffeepot. "Thanks, John. Good meal."

Hayden ambled back towards his tent, the one surrounded with piles of books. No one would think to disturb him when he was writing. If anyone needed directions or advice, they asked during meals or when Hayden was in the field. At night, while Hayden wrote, the men would all sit around the fire, tell anecdotes about the day, listen to the sounds of the night, and look at the stars.

3) Jim Stevenson

The last day of August was a windy day with sagebrush-colored clouds. Rapid changes in air pressure made everyone jumpy. Towards five in the afternoon, Jim Stevenson saddled and mounted his horse. With a nudge of the knee and a touch of the reins, he guided his big gray southeast, across high, desert country.

Stevenson was in no particular hurry; an occasional ride was his way to enjoy the country. He knew he could leave camp because everything was secure: all the gear had been checked and cleaned, supplies were put away, and the horses' pickets had been moved. One cracked wagon wheel had been repaired, as had two bridles and one cinch strap. The food inventory had been taken again, and Professor Hayden was probably right about moving so as not to cut supplies too close.

When the man he called Doc in private had started developing his survey team, there had been no question of who would be in charge of day-to-day operations. Jim Stevenson had solved the supply and refurbish problems right after the Civil War when he reminded Hayden that the West still belonged to the Army. So the next year, when Hayden was ready to move into the field he collected written endorsements from Generals Sheridan, Augur, and Schofield. Each guaranteed cooperation and materiel from every military post he entered. After that, the Army became Hayden's partner in his survey of the territories.

Each year, Stevenson assumed more of the task of planning as well as operations during the trip. Without him, Hayden could not function efficiently. By the summer of 1869, Stevenson knew enough to establish a pattern that covered the planning and operations of all future surveys. Ferdinand Hayden, the survey's administrator, fund-raiser, and promoter, would restrict his role in the field to general geology and stratigraphy. The crew of specialists would attack select aspects of the land. As a team, the survey would assess the suitability of large tracts for future settlement. Each specialist would write his own narrative and receive immediate credit as part of the survey's annual report. While the work was in motion, Stevenson would ensure that everyone was well fed and that everything remained well-oiled and in good repair.

Stevenson's sturdy quarter horse walked without effort while Stevenson's eyes scanned shades of pastel purple lurking below the jagged horizon. The landforms closest to him were studies in dust-colored grays and yellow-browns. Stevenson marveled at the variety on the high plains; the landscape never looked the same to him two days in a row. There was always the unexpected view, the secret canyon with its hidden game trail, the sudden aroma of dense sage, or the song of an unexpected bird. As for the variegated pastel hues, he did not believe any artist could capture them. They were not meant to be captured; they belonged where they were, wild, free, and as rooted to the mountains as were pumas and coyotes, cactus and scrub pine, rocky crags and dry washes.

Stevenson knew he would never tire of his chosen life. Out in the valley flats of the great West he was at home. His friends were the prairie dog and the rattler, and Stevenson was certain he had a little of both in his blood. After riding for about an hour, he stopped to listen. He thought he'd heard the faint crack of metal on rock. The sound came from a mountain draw, a half mile away. Stevenson made an effort to sit upright in the saddle, he hated slumpers, then angled his horse towards the sound, pretty sure he would find Doc flitting around like a mud dauber, pockets and tote bag full of specimens, sticking his nose into places where it shouldn't go, perching on steep, slippery slopes, ignoring the possibility of snakes and the prying eyes of Indians.

There was no one like Professor Hayden. Stevenson loved him. As he approached the canyon, he thought about what he and Hayden had been through since their first days together in the Dakotas thirteen years ago. Back then, Stevenson had just graduated from a private school. He had already decided that the wharves of St. Louis would be more exciting than the hills of Kentucky.

St. Louis offered young Stevenson a swarm of activity. He used letters of introduction, and was befriended by Charles Chouteau, the man who held the reins over the city's fur industry. Less than a month later, Ferdinand V. Hayden showed up to pay his respects. Chouteau and Hayden had a common passion, fossils, and on occasion, Chouteau underwrote scientific expeditions. At age twenty-six, Hayden was full of energy, enthusiasm, ambition, and full of himself. In Stevenson's presence, Hayden explained that he'd signed on as geologist with an exploration team of the U.S. Army Corps of Topographic Engineers under Lieutenant Gouverneur K. Warren. The group was headed into the Dakota Territory where the army wanted to map and assess potential wagon roads. He was to meet Warren at Fort Pierre the last week of June.

Stevenson told Hayden that he wanted to go with him. Chouteau said Stevenson was eager and smart. Hayden agreed. In Jim Stevenson, he saw an empty vessel, a protégé he could fill with his love of science and his belief in the future of the West.

To fill the hours on their journey up the Missouri, Hayden talked almost nonstop about geology, paleontology, and his wanderings. His first trip west, in the summer of 1853, had changed his life. The open spaces had become his sirens, but in place of luring him like a sailor onto the rocks, they lured him into the realm of badlands geology, with its desert songs.

Stevenson rode into the lengthening shadows of the draw and startled an antelope. It dashed across the hills and disappeared, leaving no trace. "Antelope remind me of the spring of 1855," Hayden had told him. "I left Fort Pierre early in May with two carts, one Indian guide, and a voyageur and his son. We headed for the White River Valley to collect mammalian and chelonian fossils. The trees and flowers were in blossom and the antelope were returning to their summer feeding grounds. Colorful birds were passing through the area, and the watercourses were green."

He said he had paused on the edge of a butte to take in the landscape. "Just before sunset, I circled through a denuded area of high relief." He used his hands to help create the scene. "The sun dropped slowly below the western horizon. The light turned the land into an etching that showed every niche in every formation. The scene reminded me of what the amphitheater of Rome must have looked like. Then, for an instant, the world glowed orange, more intensely than anything I have ever seen. The color faded, and the scene became a study in shades of gray. Jim," he said, "it was evident, as I watched the light change the land, that nature worked on a much grander scale than mankind."

Stevenson believed that the badlands offered Doc a silent beauty and a physical challenge. Who else but a geologist would find such a dry, empty place attractive? In the afternoon, the sun's rays poured onto white, barren walls, reflecting back with double intensity. The only water was standing water. It slaked one's thirst, but the suspended minerals also gave the drinker painful bouts of diarrhea.

Stevenson considered that the prairie desert was probably Hayden's equivalent of Moses' wilderness, a testing place in which to wander for more than forty days and nights, withstanding temperatures of up to one hundred twelve degrees.

Now Stevenson saw his employer a half mile away, high on a slope, probing a thick reddish shale. To Stevenson, Hayden's energy and initiative would far outweigh his shortcomings. In that one-and-a-half-year period in the mid-1850s, Hayden had collected six tons of fossils, which included discoveries of dinosaurs, Pliocene mammals, and new species of reptiles in the Judith Basin. He had organized the stratigraphy of what he called the White River Group by arranging its Titantotheres, turtles, and oreodons in hierarchical fashion, in a vertical column, the way they appeared in the land. He identified the presence of Jurassic period beds on the flanks of the Black Hills uplift, and had found evidence of the Cambrian period, the earliest geological period in which fossils were then found.

Wild days, thought Stevenson. He nudged his big gray into an easy lope towards the distant figure. He believed his boss lacked a lot of common sense, but he didn't know of anyone more devoted to his work. Stevenson had never regretted his allegiance to the geologist.

He stopped his horse and whistled. The shrill sound echoed sharply through the canyon. Hayden stood and looked down at him.

"Time to go back to camp, Professor," he yelled. Hayden waved, collected his things, and slid down the slope like a ten-year-old.

4) William Henry Jackson

William Henry Jackson sat on a granite boulder with crossed legs, smoking a cheroot. From his little rocky knoll, the land rolled away in long hilly waves. Roundish exposures of granite occupied most of what he saw: its uneven forms, cut, gullied, and eroded by wind and water, added exquisite texture to the treeless scene. Close by, both grass and granite were brown under the sun. The view to his left consisted of a stack of intersecting convex crests that ended at a horizon silhouetted with antelope. To his right, the land butted abruptly into a granite hillside. Behind him, a featureless desert raced away to the upswept slopes of distant, purple mountains.

Jackson played with a handful of pink crystals mixed with translucent chunks he now knew were quartz. All were rough-edged granules. Centuries of harsh weather had broken the surface of the rock into its component minerals.

Aside from the Hayden party, the only sign that man had crossed the endless plain was a set of grooves in the rock. The wagon wheel ruts were all that remained of the tens of thousands who had crossed to Salt Lake City, Oregon, and California. Jackson had walked a good portion of the length of the Oregon Trail, including this area called Split Rock. A slight motion in the air carried the smell of dry grass and that peculiar dry fragrance of high plains country. He closed his eyes and inhaled.

"Have you ever seen a painting in which a portion of the composition is out of focus?" asked Sanford Gifford as he examined the image on the glass plate of Jackson's view camera. The black cloth over his head allowed him to see the details of the image.

"The answer, of course, is no," said Jackson. "But while you're comparing painting and photography, you need to mention that artists paint in color, photographers are limited to black and white. And, further, you fellows can paint animals and humans in motion. All we can capture is a blur. Face it, Sanford, there isn't much of a parallel between the two."

The artist emerged from his bent-over position and replaced his high-crowned hat. Everything about Gifford was long and straight, from his straight-sided face to his arms and fingers when he pointed.

"I bet there's more than you think, William." Gifford motioned his thumb towards the camera. "Can you fix it so that nothing is out of focus?"

"Sure, but not from here. Everything in the composition needs to be at least fifteen feet from the lens. A hill or high rock usually works."

"How about that ledge?" Gifford pointed to a flat hump of granite.

Jackson lugged the camera to the ledge and set it up as Gifford suggested. "Fuzziness is part of photography," said Jackson as he leveled the camera. "Besides, what's the difference as long as the main feature of the scene is clear?" Jackson had learned that only certain camera positions and angles resulted in good photographs. As in sketches and paintings, composition mattered, and he always tried to make his views somewhat picturesque, but content was more important to him than arrangement. He also made certain that the prominent subjects, especially geological and topographic features, were clear in detail and contrast. Professor Hayden wouldn't accept anything else.

"Think about it, William," said Gifford. "When everything in your views is in focus, your viewers don't have to guess. And totally sharp images allow all parts of the picture to work together. That gives you more leeway in composing."

He stuck his head back under the cloth. "Speaking of leeway, how much thought have you given to including people in your images?"

Jackson was listening, but he was also enjoying his cheroot and the countryside. "You mean group scenes?"

"No, a simple human form will do . . . someone standing, kneeling, sitting, riding a horse, anything." Gifford surfaced again. "People like to look at people. A person in the scene makes the image more interesting to the viewer. A body also serves as a scale of measurement. Without some familiar shape, even a horse, it's difficult to determine how big or small things are out here. Even the trees don't help very much."

"You're right!" said Jackson, leaping to his feet. "I'm always amazed at how far away the mountains are. Some look like hills, and some distances I have estimated at a mile turn out to be five. And, in case you haven't noticed, there are very few trees out here."

"Did you mean that as a joke?"

"No, I'm simply saying that you're right; since size and distance are well related out here, a human in the photograph will help establish distances." He tapped Gifford on the shoulder. "Excuse me," he said. He handed the artist his cheroot and ducked under the cloth.

The scene in the camera *was* different. How had that happened? The camera was elevated, so even the foreground was in focus. And more than half of the image was terrain. Gifford had pushed the nose of the camera below the horizon. The upper third of the scene was dominated by the diagonal lines of mountains rather than a featureless sky. Jackson's eye was drawn to a few survey tents nestled near granite outcrops in the foreground. They were not highly noticeable until the viewer's eye followed the meanders of the Sweetwater River.

Then he saw a lone figure by the riverbank, facing their direction. Jackson wasn't sure why, but the presence of a person changed the meaning of the photograph. "Hmm. Look at that. What do you think?" It was all he could say at the moment.

Gifford was enjoying himself immensely in his self-assumed role as unofficial advisor. It gave him a break from sketching and an opportunity to compare photography to painting. He puffed on Jackson's cheroot, then used it to point to the landscape in front of them.

"View it in the abstract, William. For the first time, we have mankind in the American West. He's on an adventure. He's a tentative visitor. Ah, but he's also an explorer, a survivor, and we sense that in the long run, he's probably here to stay. Hmm? So the person in the image is undergoing an awakening. Simultaneously the print awakens the rest of mankind to the potential of this country. Is it not a promise of things to come?"

Jackson started to emerge from under the cloth. "No, no. Stay there. Keep looking," said Gifford. "Forget those lonely souls for a moment. Look at the entire scene. What do we have? Overwhelming grass, rock, and sky. The one little man is almost swallowed by nature. He may be part of the picture, but mother nature retains the upper hand. She is exquisite, strong but delicate, and temperamental. What a relationship!"

Jackson's head popped out from under the cloth. Confused, he looked at Gifford and took back his now shorter cheroot. "I'm just a photographer," he said, "not a philosopher." But later in the day as he unpacked Hypo, Gifford's words refused to go away. The advice made him think of other lessons he'd learned from other photographers like Hamilton, Hull, and Savage.

Jackson sat down again and lit another cheroot while Hypo, with his head down, looked at him with hooded eyes. As Jackson gazed across the plains towards the Rockies, he considered that he had learned one hell of a lot since his first days in the West. He'd made it all the way to San Francisco, came halfway back, and settled in Omaha.

At the close of the Civil War, Omaha was a great spot for a twenty-four-year-old lad with talent, energy, and enthusiasm. Jackson could smell the potential. He borrowed money from his father and bought his way into Omaha's photographic business. The Union

Pacific Railroad, headquartered in Omaha, became his largest account. In 1866, the construction of the first transcontinental railroad was national news. Tourists from the East came west to see the sights. Many wanted photographic proof of their visit. Within a year, Jackson bought out his partner, Frederick Hamilton. He then persuaded his brother Ed to join him. That summer, the Union Pacific reached a wide spot in the prairie known as Julesburg.

"Jewelsburg?" Ed had asked. "A mine?"

"No. Definitely not a gem of any sort." Jackson showed Ed where Julesburg was on the map. "That's where I left the wild horses I drove back from California last year."

The Jackson Brothers studio became the leading photographic enterprise in town. Their bread-and-butter work was to photograph business and civic groups, new storefronts and business openings. By the summer of 1868, they were doing so well they bought out their last major competitor in town.

Up to this time, Ira Johnson was their photographer, Ed was the office manager, and Jackson was the colorist. Jackson decided it was time for him to become the photographer. Because of his background in art, he thought he understood the elements of composition. He set out to acquire a photographer's mechanical and darkroom skills. Always on the lookout for views that tourists would buy, Jackson devised a traveling darkroom and drove it to the Omaha reservation where he studied and photographed Indian life. That was the year President Grant declared that his Indian "Peace Plan" would be government policy.

Then Jackson met young, pretty Mollie Greer who was visiting Omaha from Ohio. When she left, she was in love with handsome, easygoing William Henry Jackson. They were married within the year and honeymooned on a Missouri River steamboat, while officials at Promontory Peak, Utah, pounded the golden spike to join the Union Pacific and Central Pacific railroads.

The completion of the transcontinental line increased Omaha's rate of growth. Jackson wanted to photograph views along the railroad line to Salt Lake City, but he was still unsure of his skills as a photographer, so he took Arundell Hull with him. Hull was an accomplished portrait photographer who'd spent two years in the

Colorado, Wyoming, and Utah territories.

The trip to Salt Lake City was an "earn as you go" excursion. The two stopped in Cheyenne and immediately looked for money-making opportunities. At that time, Cheyenne was little more than a railroad depot and storage facility. Saloons, gambling parlors, and "lady's emporiums" still outnumbered the churches and general merchandise stores. Cheyenne's make-up still reflected its days as a "Hell on Wheels" town when the whores and gamblers entertained the end-of-track railroad workers.

For six days towards the end of June, Jackson and Hull took photographs of individuals and businesses, wherever money could be made. They stumbled into Madame Clevelands' and spent two days taking pictures of the girls.

Taking and giving photos to the men of the Union Pacific, and taking experimental shots from the cowcatcher of the engine, Hull and Jackson worked their way to Utah. In Corinne, Jackson was getting low on supplies, when he ran into a fellow photographer named John Crissman who understood his plight and loaned him his darkroom.

Jackson received a telegram from Mollie and Ed that said he needed to return. He and Hull had been away from Omaha two months. On the way home, Hull asked, "How much money do we have, William?"

Jackson looked at his partner out of the corner of his eye, raised an eyebrow, and said regretfully, "About what we had when we left."

"Damn! All that work."

"Not good. If Mollie and Ed hadn't sounded so pressed, I would have been tempted to try it another month."

"Let's see what we have in the way of good prints," Hull suggested.

Jackson pulled out a sheaf of prints, and the two began to select the better ones for display.

"Whatcha got?" asked a new voice.

Jackson Henry looked over his shoulder into an inquiring face. Tourist, said Jackson to himself. He smiled at the man. "Photographs," he responded. "Interested? I might be talked into selling a few." He winked at Hull.

"Oh, I don't know. They any good?"

"Hey," said Hull, "these are the best from the leading photo studio in Omaha."

"Let him look through the stereo prints, Arund," said Jackson.

Hull passed a dozen stereoscopic prints and the stereoscope to the fellow who took a seat opposite them. He placed his bowler next to him carefully before he scrutinized the offering.

"I've never seen images like this," said the stranger after looking at two or three. "They give one a pretty good sense of the West, don't they?" He kept looking at the images as he talked.

"So how many would you like?" asked Jackson.

"Oh, I guess I could use about ten thousand."

Jackson chuckled. At least the fellow had a good sense of humor.

"You see, I manage a postcard distributorship back east. You don't know how hard it is to find decent shots of the West." He glanced through the scope once again. "Yes, I think ten thousand will do nicely."

Jackson jumped up to shake the man's hand but he was still looking at stereos, so Jackson shook Arundell's hand. His money problems had just vanished. And they stayed vanished until the summer of 1870, when brother Ed left and Professor Hayden came knocking.

5) Fort Bridger

South Pass City, Wyoming Territory: F. V. Hayden to Secretary of Interior: Followed Fremont and Stansbury's old track up the North Platte via Red Buttes, thence up the Sweetwater to this point. Very successful. Leave for Fort Bridger tomorrow. Should reach there by September twelfth or thirteenth to explore the Uintas. May explore the Green River and return via North Park.

Ferdinand Hayden sat in a folding chair by his tent, his left leg draped over his right knee. He wore the same old field jacket and wool pants he had worn the year before. The outfit was sometimes too warm during the day, but mighty comfortable when the sun disappeared. The brim of his hat cast a shadow on the notebook he held in his right hand. Books, maps, and sample bags cluttered the area near his feet.

Hayden found the South Pass area abounding in metamorphic slates. In nearly every case, they jutted from the earth at a near-vertical angle. The gold-bearing rock that had created the rush to South Pass in the spring of 1868 was confined to a band of gneissic slates ten miles wide and thirty miles long. Inside these slates were veins of quartz, and inside the quartz was gold. The foothill topography was streaked with gulches. The course of the gulches was controlled by the direction and erosional resistance of the slates. Wherever the gulches crossed the slates, running water had eroded the gold-bearing ore and the gold had been deposited in the streambed. Placer miners had turned the streams upside down with dredges, pans, and rockers. The boom also brought shaft mines, like the Cariso and Miner's Delight, which were extracting fifty to seventy-five dollars of gold per ton.

It was clear to Hayden that the amount of gold was limited and would not support the town much longer. In less than three years, the ranks of profitable mining operations had started to thin, and a good number of miners who couldn't make a living from panning had taken farming land further north in the Wind River Valley.

His survey team had made an extensive examination of the lower range of hills that extended to South Pass on the south side of the Sweetwater. Like the Black Hills and the Laramie Range, the Wind River Mountains formed a complete anticline.

As for South Pass City and its sister, Atlantic City, they were typical frontier mining towns: rough, functional, and devoid of anything that smacked of planning or thought to appearance. They were depots of supply and commerce for those who hoped to find material bliss in a glory hole.

The local survey was complete. Jackson and Gifford had secured photographs of South Pass City and Atlantic City, so the survey made camp at the foot of the Wind River Mountains, under Fremont's Peak. Hayden wrote letters to politicians to keep the

East Coast wheels turning in his favor. Then he took time for a personal letter that began, "My dear Emma."

Not far from camp, William Henry Jackson sat with his back to a ponderosa and wrote to Mollie. *The Wind Rivers are deceptive giants,* he wrote; *when you are close by, the foothills, like skirts, hide the breadth and height of the mountain core. Some day we'll either climb them or find a pass through them. I bet Chief Washakie knows several. He's the chief of the Shoshones, a wizardly-looking fellow who must have been handsome when he was in his prime.*

Dr. Hayden has been anxious to get as many photographs of the Indians as possible. I found a fellow who spoke pretty good sign and some Shoshone. We got Chief Washakie to agree to pose after we presented him a few trade items. You can guess what happened then, all the head men wanted to have their picture taken. I had free run of the camp and made as many views as I needed.

As for the Doc, penned Jackson, *I've never met a more nervous or energetic fellow. I can't keep up with him when he walks. A few nights ago, he suddenly jumped up and started walking around the campfire, claiming that geology was like the Bible because it held a seminar in every verse. He must have gone on for an hour. He's tiring to be with because he's so vehement about everything.*

On the other hand it's hard not to like him because he's so full of enthusiasm for the West. Some Shoshones came begging a few nights ago, and although the professor wouldn't give them any handouts, he invited them to stay for dinner. That kind of attitude has won him success and cooperation. Good thing, 'cause according to Jim Stevenson, he forgets most of the time to take a weapon with him when he goes out, and he often works alone.

The men have immense respect for him. Easy to see why: he shares his thoughts, he listens to others and he takes care of the men. In return, everyone watches him. Everyone ignores his faults because he gives his employees, yours truly included, complete freedom to prove themselves. He also lets everyone publish their work, which I am learning is a great drawing card for good scientists.

We head for Fort Bridger tomorrow.

He signed it, as he signed all of his letters to Mollie, *Your devoted William.*

South Pass was an open plain with a gentle slope. The mountains that defined its north and south ends were miles apart. The only way you knew you were on the Pacific side of the pass was when you could see that the streams ran west. The trip across was uneventful for everyone except Jackson, who decided to use Hypo as a mount. Being a standard mule, Hypo kept his feelings to himself, waiting patiently for the right time to express them. Hypo never let on that his pack was too heavy or that Jackson occasionally cinched him too tight. He may have reached the end of his patience when Jackson mounted him and kicked him in the sides. Whatever his irritation, he waited until the expedition was going down a small incline and Jackson was relaxed. Then Hypo simply planted his front feet and lifted his rear ones. Jackson went over the mule's head like a sack of flour and dented his noggin on the unforgiving Wind River granite.

By mid-afternoon, the entourage arrived at Church Buttes. The badland creations had been formed by the forces of a dry climate working on a geological formation virtually unknown in the East. From the summit of one butte, Jackson, Beaman, and Gifford found a scene that epitomized the entire region.

"It's a ruined city of the gods," declared Gifford. He ignored the treeless plain and saw only the buttes, which grouped themselves along the horizon.

"It's Atlantis," countered Beaman. "When I think of all the fossils in those rocks, I can't help but see the wreck of a former world which teemed with life."

"They're buttes," said Jackson, whose head still hurt.

Fort Bridger was a tidy frontier post located in the valley of the Black Fork. Since the strata were level, the streams cut valleys that were shaped like horseshoes. The men took the first few days to relax, replenish, and repair. Jackson overhauled his equipment to such an extent that the post carpenter finally made him a new dark box. Sanford Gifford said his good-byes and departed for Salt Lake City.

On its first foray into the Uinta Mountains, the Hayden survey team was guided by William A. Carter, the post sutler. The tall, thoughtful Virginian had a gray beard that reached his belt buckle. He maintained a reticent Western posture, speaking only when spoken to on the trail; off the trail, he shared his thoughts freely. At one rest stop, he asked Hayden if he knew the other fellow who had come looking for bones.

The question startled Hayden. "What other fellow?"

"Well, his name slips me at the moment, but he was shorter and rounder than you, and he had a cold eye."

"Where was he from?"

"Some college back east. Well, now I think he said it was Yale."

Hayden jumped to his feet and announced in a loud voice, "My God! It's Marsh!"

Carter nodded his head. "That's the name."

"You say he was through here, that he stopped at Fort Bridger?" Professor Othniel C. Marsh of Yale, a scientist with powerful connections, was no man to cross. Hayden had no love for him, and less desire to run into him in Wyoming.

"It was about two weeks ago that he and his associates arrived," said Carter.

"Associates?" asked Hayden as though in pain. "How many? Who were they? Where were they headed?"

Carter looked at Hayden with a slight frown. "Takes longer to tell if you keep talking," he said. Hayden abruptly closed his mouth, made what passed for a nod of understanding, and plopped down on a log.

"Marsh was with a party of seven. They spent two days at the post. They wanted wagons and horses. Wagons we had. They finally took mules for riding 'cause we didn't have horses to spare.

"He said it was his third trip this summer. He might know them other places some, but he didn't know this country," continued Carter.

"No, this would be his first time here," said Hayden.

"He wanted to go south, over the Uintas, in as much of a straight line as possible to where the White and Uinta enter the Green. I kept telling him there were no passes. The way he spoke, you'd have thought I was trying to make sure he never got where he wanted to go."

"Marsh tends to think a person is either for him or against him," said Hayden. "He makes a lot of enemies that way."

"I gave him my last thoughts about following the Henry down to Brown's Hole as the only feasible way, and left it at that. They were headed that way when they left here."

Two weeks. That should be enough time to keep him out of my hair, Hayden decided. He had no desire to have a confrontation with Marsh.

Snow began to fall on their third day out from Fort Bridger. Jackson was alone in camp attending to some last-minute repairs on his box. Starting out in no particular hurry, he enjoyed the vistas which greeted him between the trees. Occasionally he gave in, dismounted, and set up for a view. By noon, he'd ridden through several heavy flurries and the full force of a serious early snowstorm. Thick clouds swept overhead, permitting the sun to peek through from time to time. At one point, Jackson stopped to button his jacket and wrap a scarf around his neck. He watched a grove of quaking aspen shudder in the wind and understood: it might only be September, but winter was coming to the Rockies.

Late that afternoon, Jackson caught up with the rest of his team. Ferdinand Hayden was seated near a steady fire looking thoughtful. The first voice Jackson heard was William Carter's. The trader was talking about weather. "First storm like this always comes in September," he said. "Most of the time it's just a reminder of the season yet to come, but once in a while she can be a real horse killer."

Jackson rode into camp pulling Hypo and waved to everyone. Hayden stood up and snapped, "It's about time you showed up, Jackson. We've been sitting around here waiting."

Unprepared for anything other than cheerful greetings, Jackson dismounted and tried to think of a proper response. Why would Hayden be waiting? He never had yet. Had he missed some instruction about being back at a certain time, he wondered?

Carter and the others looked his way, half out of curiosity. Stevenson walked toward him as though to help unload Hypo. When he caught Jackson's eye, he shook his head minutely as if to say, "Don't say anything."

Carter said a few more things about the weather while snow continued to fall. Jackson handed Stevenson one end of a black rubber blanket. "Might as well catch a little of this white stuff and melt it to make developing and fixing solutions," he said aloud. He and Stevenson moved to a clearing some distance from the fire. Jackson hissed "What's going on?"

"Don't pay any mind to him the rest of this week," said Stevenson, quietly. "The snowstorm has just reminded the Professor that summer's over. Now he has to return to Washington, D.C., to pay for his fun." Stevenson shook his head. "It happens every year when he remembers that fat congressmen are waiting for him."

"I don't understand."

"When the season is over, our boss has to return, bow and scrape, and play the lackey to ensure that Congress won't leave out his name when it comes to appropriations next year. It's politics, Jackson, politics and money."

Jackson looked astonished. "You have to be funning, Jim. Dr. Hayden has an international reputation. His work is in demand by thousands, isn't it? How could Congress not fund him?" He leaned towards Stevenson, outraged. "Anyone can see that he does more for the development of the West than . . ."

Stevenson held up his hands. "You and I may appreciate that, but congressmen change their minds daily, depending on who's slipping them the right change."

"Well, damn them all!"

"Every year is a race for him, but there's no way out. Our good Dr. Hayden has become quite adept at the game, but only because he works at it and because the money enables him to do what he wants in the summer. It's his one big compromise." Stevenson raised his eyebrows. "He forgets all about it during the summer. Then weather like this reminds him" Stevenson shrugged. "It takes him a few days to accept it. He gets better once his annual report is done and he starts planning for the coming year."

Stevenson knew that his friend and employer had been happiest when he was wandering the badlands back in the fifties, long before he'd ever met a congressman. His success had made him responsible for a survey, complete with a growing staff, budget, deadlines, correspondence, annual reports, and congressional politicking.

Jim Stevenson also knew that Hayden's dream of heading his own survey had been nothing than that for years, a dream. In retrospect, he decided that his employer had no legitimate complaints. How many other men were able to live their dreams? Everything came with a price; in his case, the survey, like a delicate annual flower, had to be reseeded every year.

At the campfire that evening, Hayden talked faster than usual. He carried on about his concept of dissecting the Uinta Mountains into geological zones, long strips that ran parallel to the axis of the range. Everyone listened politely except John, the cook. His plan for elk steak and potatoes had failed. He'd boiled the potatoes, but they'd remained hard as rocks, so he set them aside. The next morning he put the potatoes back on the fire, added snow meltwater, and watched them boil.

With his characteristic early-morning enthusiasm, Hayden poked his head into John's kitchen and asked what was cooking. John responded with confidence, "Scrambled eggs and boiled potatoes this morning, sir."

Twenty minutes later, when Hayden received his breakfast, the plate contained only scrambled eggs and bread. "What happened to the potatoes, John?"

Everyone looked at John who turned beet red. "Honest to God, Dr. Hayden, I sure had planned on having those spuds ready for you this morning. I must have gotten a bad batch. I cooked them for a half hour last night and another twenty minutes this morning. They're still hard. I just don't understand."

William Carter cleared his throat, stroked his beard, and suppressed a smile. "John, you must give a thought to altitude. You're at 12,000 feet. At this elevation you'll do best by cutting everything into small pieces and doubling your normal cooking time.

You can almost put your hand in boiling water at this altitude."

"Yes, of course!" said Hayden. "The air pressure at higher altitudes is lower than it is at sea level. Notice how much more yawning we all do and how we have to breathe more strenuously? Well, as the air pressure drops, so does the temperature of boiling water."

"All right, *Potato John*," said Jackson with a grin from the back of the growing breakfast line, "Let's have some scrambled eggs." The camp laughed, and John was henceforth tagged with the ragging sobriquet.

Several days later, Hayden, Jackson, and Stevenson dined with William A. Carter, his wife, and their four daughters. The sutler was an independent Virginia gentleman whose style of life at Fort Bridger epitomized that of the successful frontier entrepreneur. Fort Bridger was strategically situated on the Oregon Trail. As western migration increased, the post became one of the most important way stations in western America.

Carter's situation as sutler was perfect. Under U.S. Army regulations, only one sutler was allowed on any given military reservation. Carter grew with his opportunities. He owned three sawmills, a limestone quarry, and a kiln. His payroll, which included a freighting business, supported more than one hundred men. He supplied the soldiers at the post with hay, firewood, and vegetables. By the Civil War, Carter had become a major wholesaler, retailer, farmer, merchant, banker, freighter, contractor, cattleman, and speculator. His markets included the Army, travelers, tourists, wagon masters and their men, freighters, miners and speculators, agents of the government, natural scientists, local settlers, and several Indian tribes.

As Shoshone Indian servants cleared the long oak table of linen and china, the men moved to another room for cigars. The conversation turned to the settlement of the West. "The Union Pacific Railroad has surprised a lot of people," said Carter. "I believe it will literally be the vehicle by which the West will sustain rapid growth. What are your thoughts, Dr. Hayden?"

Hayden was a bit surprised by his own answer. "There is no doubt that the West will continue to grow and some day be fully settled; as to when, however, I believe that will depend on the mood of Congress. The government is the only agency with sufficient funds to provide people the information and resources they need to flourish in an untested and unsettled area. And I'm sure the railroad would never have been built without congressional support and grants. In my business, exploring new territory for the government, I work under the assumption that Congress has a vested interest in seeing the West completely settled. But Congress is like a woman, it's hard to judge her mood or what she might do next."

"I understand. You're not alone in your distrust of Congress," said Carter in a matter-of-fact tone. "Too many congressmen have never been West. Few know of our needs. I discovered that two years ago when Congress decided the Army could do without the sutlers. Without us, the soldiers might come up a bit short of what they want, but the immigrants rely heavily on traders like myself to replenish their supplies, their oxen and sometimes their wagons."

"I thought resupply had always been a military function," said Jim Stevenson.

"Not the kind of goods I sell," responded Carter, stroking his beard. "The Army cares well for its own, but it was never designed to deal with civilians or to function with a profit in mind. I convinced a few congressmen to reinstate the sutler at posts between here and the California border. They now call us military post traders."

Hayden remained silent.

"I get the impression you are not certain whether Congress will continue to finance your explorations," continued Carter. "Surely the majority in Congress consider your work to be of major importance."

"I won't tell you how much time I have spent to ensure that I always receive a positive response to that question," said Hayden. "Every year I return to Washington, D.C., I must renew my contract. To date, Congress has said yes, but I'm afraid we are all expendable in the long run. My work could be halted tomorrow."

Congress had approved Hayden's annual request three years in a row. Nonetheless, he remained acutely aware that to return to the field was subject to approval of an annual appropriation. And every time he returned to Washington to face that issue, he feared deep inside that the Appropriations Committee was going to turn him down. To minimize the possibility, he stretched his resources to cover large tracts of territory. He went the extra mile to maintain a smooth relationship with influential congressmen. And he always published quickly. Discovery was not as important as publishing. He who published first received recognition, prestige, and government appropriations.

The apprehensive Hayden was ready to face some new threat every year. This year he feared the lengthening shadows of three other surveys, two of which were sponsored by the Department of the Interior. While Hayden was surveying Nebraska, a twenty-five-year-old geologist named Clarence King had been on his way west with a tidy appropriation. His task was to survey the geology and mineral resources of a one-hundred-mile-wide band between Denver and the east slope of the Sierra Nevada, the route of the Central Pacific Railroad. King's plan had been approved by General Andrew A. Humphreys, Chief of the Army's Corps of Engineers, and signed by Secretary of War Edwin Stanton. King's plan was well conceived. He came with impressive credentials: endorsements from scientists James D. Dana, author of *Manual of Geology;* Spencer Baird of the Smithsonian; and William Brewer of the California Geological Survey. To these, King had added an array of social and political endorsements.

Hayden knew King's name. The scientist had the respect both of California's chief geologist, Josiah Whitney, and of Spencer Baird. What Hayden learned about the man made his stomach cramp and his palms sweat. King was one of the elite, a man of impeccable background who exuded social grace. He was an intimate friend of influential, aristocratic snobs like Henry Adams. King had graduated with the first class of Yale's Sheffield Scientific School. O. C. Marsh had been one of his classmates!

King had all the qualities that Hayden did not have and would never have: natural poise, conversational wit, and unshakable self-confidence. King also enjoyed what Hayden longed to have, the admiration and respect of influential politicians and people of high social standing.

Furthermore, King was charismatic; he had climbed Mount Shasta and discovered America's first active glaciers. He'd published articles in the *Atlantic*. He was renowned for dressing for dinner in the field! As for his work, Hayden had examined King's first volume of *Mining Industry*, which examined methods of digging and treating ores. It was exacting; his presentation was well organized and his writing style lucid. Hayden hoped that King would remain in the Southwest; he had no desire to have to compete directly.

To Hayden, it was enough that he shared the spotlight with John Wesley Powell. The former teacher had taken a trip to the Green River with a group of students in 1867 and had become fascinated with the Grand Canyon. Last year he'd returned to the Wyoming Territory with nine men, embarked from Green River, and bested the raging torrents of the Colorado in three oared boats. His daring won him instant acclaim, and the acclaim won him his own survey, the Topographical and Geological Survey of the Colorado River of the West. His feat was all the more heroic because Powell had lost an arm during the Civil War.

The third survey that Hayden kept an eye on was underwritten by the Department of the Army and led by West Point graduate Lieutenant George Montague Wheeler. Last year, the officer had provided the Army with detailed geographical maps of the deep Southwest, an enormous area not covered by other surveys. Wheeler had the full support of General Humphreys, so Hayden fully expected to hear more of Wheeler.

The competitive situation would not have caused Hayden as much anxiety had there not been so much jealousy and animosity between the governmental departments. The Department of the Interior and the Department of the Army were constantly at each other's throat over who should control the Department of Indian Affairs. The Army considered the Interior Department corrupt, out of touch, and counterproductive to those objectives the Army considered essential to western settlement.

The Interior Department believed that giving Indian Affairs to the Department of the Army was equivalent to genocide. Congressional opinion had shifted in favor of the Army until members read about Major Baker's battle on the Marias River. And since politics knew no rational boundaries, western surveys automatically became an extension of departmental quarrels. Hayden repressed his anxieties, thanked his host for dinner, and returned to camp. The coming year 1871 was full of promise, but like the weather, the picture kept changing. There might always be a string of clouds on the horizon but it was anyone's guess as to how stormy it might get, or how quickly.

6) An Unpleasant Encounter

On the morning of the survey team's second excursion from Fort Bridger, Hayden gave William Carter two letters to mail. Among his other functions, Carter was also the county postmaster. Hayden's letters were addressed to Miss Emma Woodruff of Philadelphia and to Senator Logan of Illinois. Hayden and Logan had become good friends during the Civil War. For three years, Hayden had served under contract as a surgeon and hospital administrator. Since then, Logan had proven a staunch supporter of Hayden's surveys. To increase their bond, Hayden had accepted Logan's recommendations for several specialists in his survey, including Logan's brother-in-law, Cyrus Thomas, whom Hayden considered a great addition. This letter informed Logan that Hayden had named a mountain and a survey campsite after him. He wrote that he planned to send photos of both in the coming month. He didn't need to say that he would need Logan's help during the forthcoming congressional session.

Hayden led his team south to where Henry's Fork emerged from the Uinta Mountains, then followed the stream to its junction with the Green River. From the Green River they rode to Flaming Gorge, then took a three-day side trip to Brown's Hole. On his arrival back at camp, the first thing Hayden heard from Potato John was that an unpleasant, officious man had stomped into camp, loudly demanding to know where Professor Hayden was.

"Who was it?" inquired Hayden. He descended from his horse and stretched.

"Some fuzzy buzzard named Professor Marsh."

Hayden jerked his head around and looked at Potato John with wide eyes. "Marsh? Damn. That's all I need. What was he doing here?"

"He didn't say why he was here, but he wanted to see you."

"Was he alone?"

"No. He had a couple of other fellows with him. I met one, a fellow named Bill Cody." John squinted as though what he had to say was painful. "This fellow Marsh cussed a bit when I told him where you were. Then he muttered something about your not having followed instructions, and went away without as much as a howdy or good-bye."

Oh, bother and disaster! Hayden pulled off his boots, rubbed a sore foot, and tried to measure the pitch of Marsh's emotional state. He was probably fuming because I've entered into an area where he's collecting, thought Hayden. He knew all too well about Marsh's volcanic temper, especially when he was hot on the trail of new species.

Othniel C. Marsh was one of a handful of American scientists devoted to filling large gaps in the paleontological record. The process of discovery had become a race of critical importance to Marsh. It was useless to remind him that Darwin's theory was only a decade old or that Louis Agassiz, Europe's most forward-thinking paleontologist, had not accepted the theory, at least in public. The theory of evolution was rising as a significant force in science and society, and he who published first received first credit! Marsh was hell-bent to ensure that he would be the foremost leader in the field.

Hayden, Meek, and Hall had made superlative discoveries in western Cretaceous and Tertiary strata. Since they worked only with invertebrates, the vertebrates, the bones, as Baird called them, were usually sent to Professor Joseph Leidy in Philadelphia. Some had been sent to Edward Drinker Cope, another Philadelphia paleontologist who was fast becoming O. C. March's archrival in terms of discovery as well as emotional zeal.

But Marsh was the first paleontologist to conduct his own western field trip. No tested field procedures existed for collecting vertebrate fossils, so Marsh was pioneering. He had exhumed

Pliocene deposits in Nebraska, and now he was tackling the Miocene. And who did he encounter fossilizing in his backyard but Ferdinand Hayden, friend of his competition, E. D. Cope!

Hayden wanted no part of the growing rift between the two men. As far as he was concerned, Joseph Leidy was the master of paleontology. Long before anyone had ever heard of Marsh or Cope, Leidy had single-handedly performed the bulk of paleontological work in America. The bones which Leidy received during the 1850s and 1860s from deposits in the West were new not only to American scientists but to European paleontologists. Every specimen seemed to represent a new genus, family, or even a new order.

Leidy had spent decades feeling his way through a dark landscape, but he was a scientist's scientist, inestimably patient and accurate in observation, and conservative in conclusions. He was also a friend of all, a man of peace, and a supporter of Hayden's efforts. Using Hayden's collections from the White River formation of the Dakotas as his primary source of data, Leidy had published a great monograph on vertebrate fossils called *Extinct Mammalian Fauna of Nebraska and Dakota.*

If Hayden didn't do something about the Marsh incident, he would fear the worst and in doing so, become a mass of nerves. So he wrote to Leidy about Marsh's tempestuous appearance. He didn't tell Leidy that he had known for more than a month that Marsh was in the area, or that he knew there was a good chance their paths might cross. He wrote only a description of Marsh's visit, saying that while he had been camped on Henry's Fork, Marsh had been on the Green River, close by, and had stumbled over his camp. *He was in a terrible rage to think that I should follow him,* penned Hayden, after he questioned Potato John more thoroughly. *He says the expedition has cost him twenty thousand dollars and now I have taken the cream of it. He accuses me of not following instructions. He has gone on to San Francisco; if he calls upon you when he returns you must make things smooth with him and not commit me. I do not know what he has got at all, but I suspect not much. I leave the whole matter to you. When Marsh cools off, he will find that I have done just as he would in the same circumstances.*

It was the middle of October when the survey turned due east to follow the line of the Overland Stage. The trail ran south of, but parallel to, the Oregon Trail all the way to Laramie. It had been created in 1862, after Bannock and Shoshone Indians had burned most of the Pony Express stations on the Oregon line. Also known as the Cherokee Trail, the Overland had fallen into disuse since the end of the Indian Wars, but the wagon wheel ruts still showed and the trail was still quite usable. Hayden's entourage poked, chipped, sketched, and photographed its way across Bitter Creek to the Medicine Bows.

When they ended up where they had started, near Cheyenne, Jackson had a portfolio of quality prints and negatives that included images of Flaming Gorge, the Green River at Brown's Hole, the coal-bearing bluffs near Point of Rocks, the North Fork of the Platte, and the Medicine Bow River on the old stage road.

As always, the survey party's last evening was named Camp Farewell. Hayden sent Jackson and Stevenson to Denver, then mailed the last of sixty boxes of fossils and specimens to Leidy, Meek, and the Smithsonian. Another field season was over.

7) In from the Cold

Stevenson and Hayden had breakfast together in Cheyenne after everyone else had departed. It was time to batten down the hatches, close the books, sharpen one's wit and claws, and head for the East Coast to battle Congress for the buck.

"What's that you're eating?" asked Hayden with a frown, pointing to a brown lump Stevenson was about to put into his mouth.

"Bear meat," said Stevenson with a straight face.

"In the morning?" Hayden swallowed a mouthful of coffee and opened the paper. "Oh, God, what next?" he asked with dismay. He pushed the paper across the table. Stevenson read the article Hayden pointed to, the resignation of the Secretary of the Interior Jacob D. Cox. Stevenson grunted. He knew they had just lost a key survey supporter. Cox had been more than Secretary of the Interior; he'd been a fellow student with Hayden at Oberlin. Now there was no one in the Interior office who knew Hayden, his history, his plans, or his needs. He stood to lose an important edge.

He might even be shuttlecocked back to the Land Office.

Ouch, thought Stevenson. He pictured his boss being tossed back into the Land Office, den of the ignominious Mr. Wilson. Wilson would oust Hayden without ceremony. Hayden's surveys would become history, and everything he had worked for would disappear forever, all because Cox and Grant disagreed about reform.

The two men looked at one another across the table. Stevenson chewed his bear meat and matched Hayden's frown, not because of the situation but because he was beginning to think like his boss.

"Delano will follow Cox, yes?" said Hayden. "Isn't that just great. I don't know Columbus Delano from an albino buffalo, and here I sit, in the Wyoming Territory, thousands of miles from where I need to be to protect myself. There's only one thing to do, "

"Write Baird!" they said at the same time, laughing because they thought alike.

You see how I am situated, scribbled Hayden hastily. *If Mr. Delano becomes Secretary of the Interior, will you ask Mr. Henry to place me in the right position before him? Do not let Mr. Wilson get a hold of me. My old teacher, James Monroe, wrote that Cox was elected to Congress. I cannot finalize my plans and will not be in Washington, D.C., before December 1. Maybe you will see Mr. Cox and speak about me.*

Worried that he hadn't made his point, Hayden added: *My success in the future depends much on the character of this officer. Success attends me this year: no accidents, no loss of animals, or any government property lost. Amount of work done in length of time most credible. Much of the annual report is done already.*

The letter was in the mail before Hayden saw the issue of the paper which confirmed that Delano had, indeed, taken Cox's place. Without waiting, he sent Baird a follow-up note: *I see Mr. Delano has moved up and that Cox is gone. Haven't heard a word from Cox in months so I know nothing. Do me a very great and lasting favor by seeing Delano at once.*

While Hayden stewed about being placed in chains and dragged back to the Land Office, he found the discipline to work on his report and act as though he would lead a survey again in the spring. To that end, he wrote his closest collaborator, Meek.

Hayden's missive didn't come without prodding. Meek had queried Hayden about the status of their joint efforts to publish articles on newly classified fossils from the Cretaceous and Tertiary beds in the badlands. *Your letter came*, replied Hayden. *I wish you to become the paleontologist of my surveys. I will settle with you as you say either now or when I return. I wish you could write a kind of essay and prefix it to your report on the fossils. I shall want my fossils from this trip studied and reported by January. My report will be ready for publication by that time. Will not be back until December 1.*

He promised Meek that he would soon publish Meek's portion of the Nebraska Survey. Hayden knew he was often brusque, but he and Meek went back a long way and Hayden badly needed his alliance. *Don't make any other arrangements*, Hayden pleaded. *As soon as I come in I will get you all my fossils.*

Before boarding the train to Philadelphia, he received one more letter from Baird that said Hayden should calm himself, and that he, Baird, would do everything in his power to assist Hayden to resolve his problem of the changing guard at the Department of the Interior. Baird did not think it would bode well to rush since Delano was not taking office until November 4. *No danger of Mr. Wilson's accomplishing anything for some time to come as there will be little occasion for his making the effort. As your appropriation extends over the whole fiscal year, and is for the use by yourself under the direction of the Secretary of the Interior, it is not very likely that the new Secretary will accept any incidental suggestions of the commissioner before you return.*

Return. Return home, such as it was at 1302 Filbert in Philadelphia. Even under the cold, gray skies of December, it looked comforting. Hayden found a stack of mail that included congratulatory notes from distant friends, requests for copies of earlier reports and articles, requests for lectures, bills, and flyers, and one further word from Baird. *Professor Henry has done nothing re Delano, and Delano is too busy with regard to his new office to attend to any matters of that kind,* said Baird without preamble. *However, Mr. Wilson is expected to receive his walking papers. If so, it will obviate any special action on our part.*

With a small grunt of satisfaction, Hayden rifled through the rest. A lightly perfumed letter caught his attention. He sniffed and smiled. Emma. She had been terribly diligent and most thoughtful to write to him while he had been in Wyoming. Having her words to read in the wilderness had been a luxury. A letter from her, waiting for him here at home where he knew she was nearby, was exciting. It raised the promise of seeing her soon.

Hayden pushed aside notes, journals, and correspondence, and turned up the gaslight. With a buffalo bone knife he carefully sliced open the pastel-colored envelope. The scent immediately brought to mind Emma's throaty laughter and the deep sparkle of her eyes. She had a coquettish way of glancing at him then away again while she laughed, as though her ebullience was unladylike. All the while she would hold his hand or touch his shoulder or arm. He could feel her hand in his now.

Dearest Ferdie,

Welcome home, sweet man. Where did you find time to think of me in all the heat, dust, and your constant wandering? Your enthusiastic missives from strange places were touching but I've remained lonely for your company.

I do hope you are whole and well and anxious to share your adventures. May I count on at least one evening for the two of us before you hasten to Washington? You must know that if I do not see you at least at Christmas, I shall be crushed. Wait till you see what I have been making for you. I'm quite excited by it.

Father and Mother are fine and forward their respects. And I must tell you how proud I am of Thomas! He's found himself a partner and plans to open his own hattery on the west side of town. I'll tell you all about it.

After you dust yourself off maybe you'll find yourself thinking of me. If you do, please send a message to let me know you have arrived safely. Can't wait to see you.

With warmest thoughts,

Emma

Hayden sat back and allowed her image to fill his mind. Emma Woodruff. For six months of the year, she smiled at him like a shimmering mirage in the midst of the heat waves that rose from the Plains. For the other six months he knew that when he reached out to speak to her or touch her she was real. Was it possible that Emma had missed him and eagerly awaited his return? What fair hand of fortune had permitted him this glimpse of happiness? Did he even dare to imagine a future that included her? She was so young, so alive, so exciting! What did she see in him? Did it matter? My God, he must not risk losing her due to survey affairs.

It took Hayden several minutes to find notepaper that would not embarrass him. He washed his hands, forced himself to slow down, and wrote with attention to detail. Scribbled notes on dusty journal paper were fine for field communications; not even Emma expected more. Here at home, however, he had little choice but to abandon his field habits and adjust his words and manners to match his new environment.

Could he promise Emma any of his time? How could he *not?* He could never get his fill of her and still accomplish what he needed to keep his survey alive. Nonetheless, he knew he would try. He ended up writing that his report would have to wait the extra day they would spend together.

"Gentlemen! Comrades! Fellow explorers! We have triumphed!"

"Hear hear!" "Three cheers!" "You tell 'em, General."

General Washburn had warned Nathaniel Langford in the last week of November that the men were planning a banquet to celebrate their success. Langford sat at one end of the banquet hall, opposite Stickney. Everyone was there except Lieutenant Doane.

Everyone was also a little drunk, even the current speaker, General Washburn, which surprised Langford. He didn't think the general ever got that loose. Nonetheless, the banquet was a welcome break. Langford had put six weeks into his Yellowstone report. He'd used General Washburn's office to update DeLacy's map and to complete an organized transcription of the expedition. Rather than produce a lengthy technical article or report, he had shaped a narrative he could read aloud.

"I just want to say that I considered it one of the greatest privileges to . . ."

Several men belched, causing general laughter from around the table.

"Hey, I wanna toast the trout," yelled Benjamin Stickney.

"Aw, shut up, Stickney," shouted Walter Trumbull. "I wanna hear the general."

"Gentlemen!" said Cornelius Hedges. Hedges always looked like the lawyer he was when he stood to speak. His heavy mustache flowed over his upper lip and his dark eyes glistened. "There is time for everyone to be heard. I suggest we start at one end of the table and permit each to have his say."

"Everyone will be too drunk by the time I get my turn," retorted Stickney.

The expedition celebration was a blowout. Platters overflowed with elk, deer, bear and beef, oysters and puddings, and glasses were filled with an endless flow of champagne. With each new speaker, the dangers and the geysers grew larger, the hot springs grew hotter, and the narrow escapes became narrower.

Langford saw that everyone except Truman Everts was having a great time. Poor Everts, thought Langford. He still looked terrible after his ordeal. How he had managed to survive for more than a month in the wilderness without a rifle, horse, or tools for a fire, Langford would never understand. The men of the expedition had spent two weeks looking for him. Someone else had found him a week after the expedition gave up. No one except Everts was responsible for his getting lost, but he continued to view his experience with bitterness. Another member of the expedition rose to say his piece. Langford smiled. It was going to be a long evening. What the hell, he thought. He could sit through one more evening of geysers and hot springs. He'd better get used to it.

A week later, he gave his first talk about the expedition to a surprisingly large crowd of two hundred at the Helena library. He titled his lecture, "Recent Explorations of the Yellowstone." The size of the audience indicated there was still considerable interest in the Yellowstone, even if he attributed a portion of the audience to the editorial in the *Helena Herald.* Its editors had suggested that the wonderful scenes Langford would describe would delight any audience. Langford made sure to leave his thirty-pound chunk of petrified wood on the table near the entrance for people to see as they entered. He gave the same talk to a crowd in Virginia City.

By the first week of December, Langford was satisfied that his speaking voice and his notes were well honed. He packed up and headed for the East Coast. Local newspapers suggested that he was taking over where former Montana Territory Governor Ashley had stopped. Ashley had arranged with Jay Cooke of Philadelphia to give a series of lectures on the resources of Montana, all to benefit the Northern Pacific Railroad project.

But Langford had no such arrangement to date. He thought of addressing that issue when he arrived in New York City. Between now and then, however, he planned to visit the offices of *Scribner's* magazine to discuss publication of his Yellowstone material. Then he would begin the new year with a lecture in Washington, D.C.

Yes, indeed, Nathaniel Langford might still be unemployed, but he had new irons in the fire, and the fire was getting hot.

PART 4: JAY COOKE, 1870

1) Jay Cooke and Co.

On the last day of 1869, Jay Cooke's black, covered carriage moved smoothly along the Germantown Road toward Philadelphia. The temperature was a few degrees below freezing. Pockets of ground fog filled the dips and hid the wooded slopes that dropped into picturesque Wissahickon Creek, a tributary of the Schuylkill.

Mr. Cooke wore one of his heavier wool coats over a dark-colored business suit, vest, and bow tie. His long gray beard protected his chin from the cold. From time to time he removed his gloves and placed his hands against his cheeks to ease the bite of winter.

Jay Cooke hated to sit idly, but during the winter months there was not enough light to read on the way to and from work. Between November and March, Mr. Cooke rode alone with his thoughts. This was not always wasted time, however, because Mr. Cooke's thoughts were diverse and creative, and often led him to engage in profitable activities. This morning, Jay Cooke would very much have enjoyed more light (and less cold), for the day marked the end of another year plus the end of a decade, and 1870 hovered like an eagle, a bit fearsome to behold, yet exciting to contemplate.

Possibilities about the future filled Jay Cooke's mind because tomorrow he would sign a document that would set into motion what he believed was the greatest project of the decade. The soft clopping of Sandusky the horse and the swaying of the carriage, a combination that often pushed Mr. Cooke towards the edge of sleep on brighter days, had no effect on Jay Cooke this dark midwinter morn.

The Germantown Road judiciously followed the ridges and hilltops of the Appalachian foothills, leading travelers from the quaint stone mansions and quiet gardens of Germantown and its environs to the noisy, cobblestoned streets of Philadelphia. Commuters like Cooke who lived Northwest of Philadelphia were surrounded on their daily journey by richly wooded, rolling hills. As spring unfolded, the traveler witnessed the rebirth of the world. Flocks of migrating warblers played hide and seek in the overhead foliage, their presence revealed only by brief melodic calls and flashes of yellow. Beyond the treetops, breaking the soft pattern of cumulus clouds, long V's of ducks and geese pointed north. Underfoot, tufts of new grass created patterns on the edges of the road, and tiny purple and white flowers, ensconced in shoots of green, waited for warmer days to announce their true colors.

As spring evolved into summer, a traveler's senses were assaulted by oppressive heat and humidity. In the swales of the endless green canopy, the air was deathly still, so pedestrians and riders alike looked forward to the light breezes that clipped the hilltops. In autumn travelers were caressed by the redolence of the air, the sound of carriage wheels and horses' hooves over dry leaves, and the dazzling pattern of hardwood colors. Even winter, as long as the road was passable, had its picturesque moments of crystal stillness and views of lacy white on white.

Cooke's commute began at his mansion in Chelton Hills and ended at his place of business on Philadelphia's Bankers Row. Most of the time Mr. Cooke traveled in his two-person, one-horse carriage driven by his coachman, Asa Peterson. On the way home, to avoid the often-congested Broadway, Peterson occasionally opted to take the Germantown Road from its point of origin due north of the downtown business district. And once in a while, particularly when Peterson had the day off, Mr. Cooke took the train.

Philadelphia bristled with train tracks, including one set that reached the environs of Chelton Hills. The only significant problem Cooke associated with taking the train was the harried business of finding transportation to traverse the remaining seventeen blocks between the passenger depot at Ninth and Green and his office at Chestnut and Third. His solution had been to hail a hansom cab or take one of the horse-drawn passenger railway cars. whose tracks formed a network throughout the city. Unfortunately, they were public conveyances, subject to delays and crowding. And one had to remember the color codes to catch the correct car. Once in a while it was enjoyable to mingle with the townspeople, but for the most part Mr. Cooke preferred the privacy and comfort of his own carriage.

At the end of the first hour of this morning's commute, Mr. Cooke's coach descended to the river plain on the outskirts of Philadelphia. Small, neat villas and thatched-roof cottages appeared frequently. Side roads and meadows dotted with cattle and horses replaced expanses of forest. Wagons, horses, and buggies vied for the road, and soon, shoulder-to-shoulder homes of lesser quality lined the highway. Soot drifted from coal-fed fires in working-class neighborhoods. All too soon, residential tracts gave way to food and repair shops and huts for the selling of small wares. Now and again the chimney of a small factory replaced a jumble of storefronts.

The country road name became Broadway and in doing so announced Philadelphia's city limits. Under a dark pall of coal smoke, Jay Cooke's carriage rumbled down the cobblestones. Laborers and clerks darted across the road, instinctively dodging horses and wagons. The shops of shoemakers, blacksmiths, and liquor dealers were already open. A mix of odors that reeked of human and animal waste replaced the cool country fragrance of grass and mud. The character of the mix changed rapidly as Cooke's carriage passed from grocer to butcher to cigar maker to iron founders with their heated furnaces.

A full third of Philadelphia's tradesmen and tradeswomen had emigrated from Ireland; half as many had come from Germany. They filled the ranks of the city's coopers, leather makers, weavers, tailors, and wheelwrights. The city ranked as the largest textile manufacturer in America, so any immigrant with skills as a basket or carpet weaver, spinner, gilder, glass cutter, chair-maker, or upholsterer could find a living wage and a decent place to live.

Not that Philadelphia was problem-free. Businesses at the extremes of quality existed side-by-side, and child labor laws were serious issues. Typhus, scarlet fever, and smallpox took their toll every year. A chronic problem was the filthy, poorly-lit, and wretchedly paved streets. Taxes remained high, elections tended to be unruly, and many people carried pistols for protection. Like any city with a population of six hundred fifty thousand, its newspapers reported at least one murder per year. The most notorious act of late was the robbery of one million dollars in bonds from the Beneficial Savings Fund at Twelfth and Chestnut in April of '68.

Nonetheless, Philadelphia's inhabitants were more genteel than those, say, in New York City. There was no jostling, crowding, or cursing conductors, and everyone felt secure enough to take advantage of the city's outdoor parks. For those whose pleasures were more rudimentary, the city offered a thousand drinking establishments and more than five hundred bawdy houses, roughly one for each church.

Peterson guided Mr. Cooke's buggy onto Market Street, staying to the right of center to avoid straddling the passenger car railroad tracks. After successfully edging past one such conveyance, he pulled Sandusky to a halt to permit six pair of mules pulling a string of baggage cars to cross his path.

Market Street was *the* pivotal byway into the heart of Philadelphia, the route followed by festivals and parades. The most recent spectacle had taken place during General Grant's 1868 presidential campaign. Republicans staged a parade for the boys in blue led by General Grant and Schuyler Colfax all the way to Independence Square. The parade was exciting but older residents said it didn't match the fervor of the homecoming parade on June 10, 1865. That was when Philadelphia's own General George G. Meade, hero of Gettysburg, had led Civil War veterans from Camp Cadwalader past the reviewing stands.

Peterson continued down Market until he reached Third Street, then turned right. Here, on Bankers Row, the blocks were crowded with three- to four-story structures, all tightly aligned against wide sidewalks. Square, rectangular, or arched windows looked like eyes in the massive facades of granite and sandstone. Thick columns of the most recent construction squatted next to Byzantine post and lintel structures. The mix created a hodgepodge landscape broken here and there only by a colorful sign of an oyster luncheon or a clock shop.

Bankers Row was dominated by financial institutions like the Guarantee Trust and Safe Deposit Company, the National Bank of the Republic and the Philadelphia Bank. But it was also home to fashionable auction houses like Christie's, downtown theaters and restaurants, and a few higher-class retail stores. And the district boasted several newspapers, including George W. Child's impressive multistory building at the corner of Sixth and Chestnut, which housed his newspaper, the *Public Ledger*,

Jay Cooke was at home here among the businessmen, all of whom dressed and looked alike. In addition to the conservative suit of the day, half of the men wore flat-top straw hats with a dark band; the other half wore bowlers. Most gentlemen sported a full beard and mustache. Mr. Cooke remained in the minority in this regard: over the years, he had chosen to narrow the width of his full beard to mid-jaw. Now, in its elongated state, the grayish mat resembled a Vandyke left to grow as it pleased for a decade.

At 14 South Third Street, Peterson pulled Sandusky to a halt. With a sprightly motion, Cooke stepped from the carriage, removed his hat, and entered his bank. The exterior and interior of Jay Cooke and Co.'s brownstone building radiated confidence and success. Customers entered between six fluted marble pillars that stood for strength, permanence, and refined taste. Above the lintel, the large sign said simply, Jay Cooke and Co. Once in the lobby, the first object to catch a client's eye was a large bronze eagle perched above an enormous fireproof and burglarproof safe. The eagle clutched a red, white and blue ribbon wide enough to carry the name of the firm.

The lobby floor was made of large squares of marble, as were the tellers' counters. The ceiling was frescoed, the chandeliers were fine-cut crystal. The rug was a rich Brussels and all the fixtures were of walnut and polished brass. When Mr. Cooke completed the refurbishment of his office three years ago at the outrageous cost of sixty thousand dollars, the newspapers said he had created the most magnificent and costly establishment of its kind in the state. In addition to opulence, the firm offered its customers the latest in modern conveniences, including attendants in the bathrooms and a gas furnace. The state-of-the-art building was typical of Jay Cooke's "do it right" approach to business.

Cooke crossed the floor with a radiant smile and "good morning" nods to his employees. He stopped briefly at a small corner desk and leaned towards a young clerk. "You did a fine job on that stock evaluation yesterday, Josh," he said. His voice was soft, and his blue eyes bright. The young man stood quickly and stammered his thanks. Then, flushed with pride, the clerk glanced around to see who might have noticed.

Inside his office, Cooke closed the door, hung up his hat, coat, and scarf, and inhaled the room's warmth and comfort. Cooke liked simplicity, but he also liked things his way, so against tradition, he had installed a four-foot by six-foot window into the wall next to the lobby. He wanted to see what was going on and at the same time permit his customers to see that he was available. Cooke prided himself that he put in a full day at the office and had nothing to hide.

On the contrary, Cooke had plenty to show. The wall opposite the window held an oil portrait of himself, a recent photograph of his family in front of his estate outside Philadelphia, a detailed sketch of his retreat at Lake Erie, and a large stuffed pike. The center of the wall was reserved for a lavish display of notices, newspaper clippings, ads, and a large replica of a government bond. The assemblage of memorabilia represented the story of the Five-Twenties, government bonds he had sold to help finance the Civil War.

Jay Cooke's desk was immaculate. In addition to trays marked for telegrams and correspondence, he kept a large hand-carved walnut box for Cuban cigars he acquired through one of his partners, Edward Dodge. Each cigar came in a glass tube etched with Cooke's initials. The front-center spot on his desk was saved for a glass-framed, counterfeit, fifty dollar note, the first one he had spotted when he had worked as a clerk for Enoch Clarke.

The dynamic financial world was like caffeine to Jay Cooke. He still found it exciting to pick up decisive information others had overlooked, to be the first to enter into or complete a challenging financial deal, or to be wise enough to turn down an apparently lucrative investment which he knew was flawed.

And Jay Cooke, the man, was good-looking and articulate. Frequently, not too well-concealed glances of attractive ladies in the company of other men lingered on his figure. Those who met him for the first time were struck by his attentiveness, his bright blue eyes, and his eager business posture. The prematurely gray mustache and goatee that hid his bow tie provided added dignity. He was a consummate gentleman, who wore both expensive clothes and a warm smile. At age forty-eight, he looked every inch of what he was, the head of the largest private banking firm in Philadelphia.

Cooke was engrossed in a report written by engineer J. Milnor Roberts when a clerk announced the arrival of a Mr. John Wiley. Mr. Cooke frowned until he remembered that he had agreed to listen to the gentleman's proposition because he carried a letter of introduction from another Philadelphia private bank. Mr. Wiley was a tall, frail-looking gentleman with wispy hair, who smiled and whispered "Ah, yes," and shook hands diffidently. He perched on the nearest chair, opened his portfolio, and handed Cooke a brief.

"Ah, yes. What I have here, Mr. Cooke, is an opportunity to be first in line in a fundamental but growing service of industry: shipping." Mr. Wiley crossed his legs and rested his forearms on his chair. "I, ah, intend to start a line of steamers between California, Japan, and China to compete with the Pacific Mail Company. This may be a new field of investment for you, but I assure you . . ."

Cooke smiled at his visitor and held up a hand as a way of asking him to pause. He shook his head slightly and extended the brief back across the desk. "Thank you, Mr. Wiley," he said with a firm and steady voice, "but I need to save you your time and me, mine. Jay Cooke and Company is a conservative banking establishment. Speculation in new enterprises is not an acceptable line of investment for . . ."

"Ah, yes. But Mr. Brewer said you had millions to invest, Mr. Cooke, and with your name at the head of my list of investors, we would have no problem in raising . . ."

"I am sorry, Mr. Wiley, but our firm has had to make investment policy decisions and we have ruled out entire categories. In this day and age I am sure you will have no trouble locating eager investors, and I wish you the best of luck in your enterprise."

"Ah, yes. My calculations show that returns, over a period of . . . Ah, yes. Well. I see. Ah, yes; thank you for your time."

Cooke watched Mr. Wiley exit the office and pondered the lack of understanding by entrepreneurs about the boundaries of private banking. Jay Cooke and Co. bought and sold securities, kept deposits, transferred credits, floated securities, handled currency exchanges, and acted as a financial agent for corporations. His bank did not invest in mining or new industry, nor did it become involved in manufacturing or speculative patents or processes. Shipping, indeed. Why, an investment like that wouldn't see a return for five, six, or seven years. For a moment his mind drifted toward the report he'd been examining, as though his thought about return on investment should have some bearing, but the connection faded.

Besides, he thought, if Mr. Wiley's speculative venture was sound, he would draw the interest of active financial capitalists. The active capitalist was a new breed of investor. He participated in the management of the enterprises supported by the loan. He stood between the owner of the capital and the financial user, providing funds and working capital for long-term investment, and took responsibility for the manner in which loans were used.

Because of the tremendous surge in industrial growth and the need to tie Western goods and services to Eastern markets, active investment banking was rapidly overtaking passive investors. Bankers had learned that they could maintain control of profits while they invested their resources in long-range enterprises. The successful involvement of large banks in real estate and railroad development speculations had proven the wisdom of the concept.

A clerk unobtrusively deposited a batch of telegrams from New York and Washington, D.C., into Mr. Cooke's tray. Before he could leave, Cooke asked, "What's it like in the lobby today, Arnold?"

"Very quiet, sir. Since it's the last day of the year, I suspect many people have already left town."

"Oh, of course," replied Cooke absently. Then he smiled, adding, "Tomorrow is the first of the year."

He returned to Roberts's report, an appraisal of the Northwest in terms of where to run the tracks of the Northern Pacific Railroad. The report covered last summer's survey when Roberts and his party traveled nine thousand miles by foot, horseback, canoe, wagon, steamer and train. The party made it from Puget Sound to Bozeman, only to be stopped by rumors of hostile Indian parties in the Yellowstone River Valley.

Roberts estimated that laying track for a railroad through the Northwest would cost eighty-five million, an average of forty-two thousand dollars per mile. His estimates were far below Cooke's best expectations and they contradicted an earlier survey estimate, but Cooke trusted Roberts. Now all he needed was William Marshall's report on the survey of the eastern portion of the line. In a letter a few weeks ago, Marshall admitted that the group did not get as far west as he had intended. No matter; in his heart, Cooke knew he had already selected his path to the future.

He was certain that he had done his homework and properly weighed the odds. If anything, he had been overcautious, but a gambit of the magnitude he contemplated required as many double checks as he was willing to consider. He stopped reading, made a few marginal notes, then pulled down two documents on railroad construction from the growing library behind his chair.

Cooke's preoccupation was obvious to everyone at the firm. No one wanted to disturb him, so they were all pleased that the day was uneventful: no new accounts, no minor market crises to analyze or follow up, no new stock or bond issues interesting enough to pursue, no counterfeit notes, and no attempted robberies like the one in January 1863 when a beggar turned out to be a crook and made off with five thousand dollars.

At noon, most businesses in Philadelphia, including the city government, closed their books. The year had been uneventful. Every year was uneventful compared to 1866, when mother nature pulled the temperature to eighteen below zero and caused the Delaware River to freeze. A month later, flames reduced the value of the James, Kent, Santee and Co. warehouse from a million dollars to ashes. In the fall, Asiatic cholera claimed the lives of nine hundred citizens. The only other well-remembered Philadelphia disaster was the hailstorm that shattered more than a million panes of glass in September of 1867.

America, on the other hand, was winding down from a hectic year of growth and speculation. To Jay Cooke, the highlight of the year occurred on April 10, when the Union Pacific and Central Pacific railroads were linked by the golden spike. The Civil War was becoming a memory. The bond between private capital and government patronage was unleashing a whirlwind of speculation. Cooke anticipated that the future would bring unprecedented growth and prosperity.

2) A Natural Businessman

On his way home, Cooke once again chewed over his choice for the future. The investment market had been shifting. He wanted Jay Cooke and Co. to shift with it. Government securities no longer provided profits worth pursuing. Treasury Secretary Boutwell had opened the sale of government bonds to competitive bidding, a move that effectively removed the edge Jay Cooke and Co. had enjoyed for nearly a decade. The decline in government-related work, in turn, had made his Washington, D.C., house superfluous. Jay Cooke and Co. had to retrench or find other ways to make money. To retrench was to ignore business opportunities. Cooke wanted to shift his firm to an investment area in which he felt comfortable. The path he had selected was one of the toughest, even if it was the most promising. But challenge was part of the stakes, and Jay Cooke never forgot the key moments in his life that had steered him to a life in finance.

When Jay Cooke was twelve years old, he wanted to become a lawyer and politician like his father. That was the year that Ogontz, a full-blooded Wyandot, told him that his father, Elutheros Cooke, had a wolf's eye. Ogontz did not tell him why he mentioned this, but added that having a wolf's eye was a good sign. "The wolf," said Ogontz, "is cautious and an excellent listener, but he can be as bold as he is cautious, and he is a stable leader."

Ogontz made this statement as he and Jay Cooke squatted quietly side by side on the bank of an unnamed stream, two lines in the water. Ogontz wore his traditional loincloth, a dirty white man's shirt, and a wide-brim hat. One white eagle feather protruded from the band. Jay Cooke wore frayed shorts and a cotton shirt. Every thirty seconds or so, Ogontz would tug slightly on his line. Every other try would yield a trout. Jay was dying to ask why he wasn't catching fish while Ogontz was, but Ogontz never taught Jay by telling him anything directly. Over time, Jay Cooke understood that learning was a game. He loved games, especially when he won, so he became a good student. And his friend, this aging Wyandot who had lost both his grandfathers at the Battle of Fallen Timbers, was a good teacher.

That evening, Jay Cooke heard his father say that Lake Erie was large enough to send a representative to the Ohio legislature. Elutheros Cooke planned to fill the need. Mr. Cooke was not a large man, but he made up for his lack of physical size with personal intensity, what Ogontz called a wolf's eye. When he practiced his speech behind the house, he addressed stumps and bramble bushes, but his rousing voice startled squirrels and hawks, and occasionally spooked a deer.

Jay Cooke decided that Ogontz must have known what his father had planned, and in his own way was suggesting that he accompany his father on the stump. So the day Elutheros Cooke saddled his horse, Jay Cooke asked if he could come along. Elutheros Cooke couldn't find a decent reason why his twelve-year-old son shouldn't be exposed to the economic and political issues of the day, and Mrs. Cooke smiled, thinking it would be a good thing for a father to have his son with him.

The wooded Ohio frontier was replete with speculators and energetic, restless, pushy people who had little time for Eastern niceties or regulations. They wanted roads for commerce, tax relief, and fair prices for their goods. In each town, Elutheros Cooke stuck to economic issues and sent the same message: the country was opening up and he could help Lake Erie keep pace economically.

"I know the law. I know the frontier. I know you. Your concerns and problems are the same as mine, because I am a neighbor. Ask those among you who know me. Have I not always been honest, gone the extra mile to help those in need, tended to my family but also lent a hand to my neighbor? I will represent you and your concerns fairly and squarely and you may hold me to account if I fail to live up to my promises."

Jay Cooke sat on benches, fences, barrels, stumps, and steps, and listened to his father and to what the crowd had to say. When Elutheros Cooke was elected, Jay decided it would be wise to adopt his father's values.

Three years later, Jay went to St. Louis with Ted Bascomb. Bascomb was engaged to Jay Cooke's sister, Elizabeth, so Cooke's parents were willing to support his adventure. Bascomb hoped to become established in merchandising in St. Louis, with the assistance of family connections. Jay was going because the trip sounded like a great adventure.

Two days before they left, Jay Cooke met Mr. Willham, a man with a wagonload of factory-made twill shirts from Philadelphia. Mr. Willham's wagon had broken down on the road to Lake Erie and Willham was drinking whiskey to console himself. When Jay saw that the man did not want help and was in no danger, he left, but only after he'd heard Mr. Willham's story. This was the third time the wagon or horse had failed Mr. Willham on his journey, and although he had successfully repaired the situation the first two times, he had missed connections with the partner who was to pay him for his goods. Now Mr. Willham was eager, if not anxious, to sell his wagonload of shirts at cost.

As Jay Cooke walked home, he figured the value of the merchandise and the cost of moving it to St. Louis on the flat boat. Then he figured what profit he might make if he sold only half the items at a reasonable price. Elutheros listened to his son's account, then took the cash box from the hidey-hole in the floor and counted out enough coins to buy the shirts. He had Jay sign a note of indebtedness as one would do when borrowing money, and he taught his son one additional fact about money, that it cost the lender to borrow it. Jay Cooke had to pay his father one percent per month interest.

Bascomb and Cooke arranged for working passage on a flatboat to St. Louis. Conditions on the river remained favorable, so they landed at St. Louis in one piece with all of Jay Cooke's bundles in good condition. After the two were established, Cooke found an empty place among the hawkers near the wharves. He discovered that he was a natural salesman. He sold all the shirts, save five, in seven days. The five he gave to the less fortunate he saw along the riverbank because the effort to sell them was not worth the profit and he believed that a little charity was becoming to a man of business.

With a pocket full of money, Jay Cooke then had to decide between his love of games and his desire to save money. One of the older teens who hustled the docks held a late dice game among the "wharf rats." Bart invited Cooke to join in. Cooke didn't know that several of the locals had kept tabs on his profits.

Bascomb saved him from unpleasant consequences, appearing just then to ask if he wanted to work in the family shop. Jay Cooke said he thought that would be fine. He counted out a small allowance for himself, then gave Bascomb the rest of his money and asked him to keep it until he returned. Jay Cooke joined the game and lost his small stake. When he stood to leave, three of the group blocked his way. Jay said that they should enjoy what they got from him, but that was all there was. Bart spun him around, frisked him, and then looked at him with a malevolent grin. "Well played, Mr. Cooke," he said, "but you should make up your mind who you are and what you want. Some day your desire to play high stakes games may catch up with your desire to be a wealthy man. You can't gamble and be rich, too." He laughed. The others laughed, too. Then he punched Jay once, hard, in the stomach and let him go.

Jay Cooke became very successful at the family store: the customers loved his smile, his quickness, and his guile, which made them spend a little more than they had planned. Cooke knew his inventory and prices, and he flattered his customers. He loved the excitement of making money and the way he could make it grow. After two months, a man named Havercatch, a distant cousin of the Chouteau family, came to see Jay Cooke about a position with his company. He brought his attractive daughter with him. Jane was physically mature for her age and not shy about using her charms to her advantage. Jay Cooke was overwhelmed. When Mr. Havercatch offered him twice what he was making and pressed him for a decision, he stammered "Yes." Three months later, however, when Ted was ready to return to Ohio to marry his fiancée, Cooke went with him.

Jane Havercatch had mixed feelings about Jay Cooke's departure. He wasn't the first boy she had kissed, but he refused to gawk and tremble like others his age when she flirted. And when he did occasionally lean towards her in a suggestive manner, it was not, as she had hoped, to make advances, but to tell her of another way he had just figured out to make his fortune when he returned East.

The most decisive event in Jay Cooke's life took place when he was seventeen, a year after he arrived in Philadelphia. The first year he worked as a promoter for a packet company which offered rail and canal transportation to pioneers trying to get to Pittsburgh. He discovered the best way to promote the line was to be direct. He researched problems associated with crossing Pennsylvania by road, then wrote advertising copy to highlight the advantages of canal and rail travel. By designing posters, and by handing out flyers to newly arrived immigrants on the docks, Jay Cooke managed to attract a considerable amount of business.

However, at the end of the year the packet company failed and he was out of work. Rather than feel depressed, Cooke viewed his situation as an opportunity. He'd acquired confidence and knew what aspect of work he most enjoyed, making money. Cooke bought a new suit, reviewed the business columns in the paper, talked to a few men he trusted, and sought employment where money was handled every day, at the house of private banker Enoch Clarke.

Enoch W. Clarke's bank had the best reputation among Philadelphia's eleven private banks. The short, round man with the soft eyes and unaggressive manner had a keen mind for facts, figures, and financial dealings. Like most bankers, he was cautious and conservative; he had to be to survive. Banking regulations were unstable, and the currency was disorganized. Clarke recently had expanded his investment services to handle securities and long term investment. Now he was evaluating the advisability of expanding his financial services.

Clarke was not looking for additional staff the morning Jay Cooke entered his bank and asked for a private moment, but he happened to be thinking about the future. In Mr. Clarke's office, Cooke made it clear that he was looking for employment. He was alert but relaxed, pleasantly deferential but not subservient. He presented letters of introduction and summarized his background in terms that let Mr. Clarke know he would be an asset to his establishment. When Mr. Clarke spoke, Cooke listened carefully, and when Cooke asked questions he did not apologize for his lack of knowledge nor challenge Clarke's answers. He also looked Clarke in the eye with a personal smile while he talked.

After a few minutes, Enoch Clarke decided that this young, energetic fellow was bright, direct, tactful, and obviously ambitious. Clarke simply couldn't understand why he sought employment in finance. "Perhaps the most important question, Mr. Cooke," said Clarke with a puzzled expression, "is why someone your age, an obviously aggressive young man with a flair for marketing and sales, would want to take on the unexciting responsibilities, not to mention the low pay of an entry-level clerk, of a banking establishment?"

"Quite simply, Mr. Clarke," said Jay Cooke with a quick smile, "I intend to learn the banking business, become a partner of your firm, and make a good deal of money by being more observant and aggressive than our competition."

Clarke sat back in his chair, stunned. *Our competition?* Amazing, thought Clarke. He's already assumed that he's been hired and has started to think like a banker. While Cooke waited, Enoch Clarke thought more intensely about the future. He then leaned

toward Cooke to ask the only other question he could think of.
"When will you be available to start work, Mr. Cooke?"

3) Ogontz

To approach Jay Cooke's million-dollar Victorian estate in
Chelton Hills by carriage at dusk was to discover an Italian castle
in the woods. Near the top of a small rise, a knee-high stone wall
paralleled the road. The wall was not the typical construction of
field stones, but a stone lintel supported by a series of closely
spaced, fluted dowels. The fancy fabrication announced the beginning of Jay Cooke's two-hundred-acre estate.

The wall stopped at a carriage entrance flanked by ten-foot
stone pillars which anchored a set of iron gates. Everything one
might expect could be found somewhere on the grounds of Jay
Cooke's estate. Vistas had been cut through the forest, fountains
punctuated walkways, and sinuous paths wound their way beneath
manicured hardwood covers. The outbuildings were tucked away,
including the house for estate servants.

The house commanded a wooded knoll that rose several hundred feet above Wissahickon Creek, and the main drive led all
carriages to a porte cochere at the front. Here, an unaltered stretch
of wooded ground dipped away to provide a peaceful setting, one
that provoked visitors to consider that the primary purpose of the
home might be to experience nature and the joys of solitude.

Friends often referred to Ogontz as a fortress because it was a
four-story rectangle that occupied an area equal to six Victorian
houses. Because the exterior walls were granite and the perimeter
composed of straight lines, the house appeared to be a composite
of irregular rectangular sections snugged together like a government building. The first two floors were punctuated by regularly
spaced, eight-foot-high windows arched at the top. Flat-roof porticoes accompanied verandahs along the north and west sides of the
house. The fifty-two-room building accommodated five hundred
people with ease.

Cooke had designed his own home. He had borrowed the En-
glish-style arrangement of rooms by which guests were received in

a formal drawing room and individual rooms were designated for special activities. The house included a morning room, breakfast room, library, hunting room, amusement room, music room, and business room. The living room and dining room, kitchen, music room, library, and a theater for plays that could seat one hundred were located on the first floor. The kitchen complex included a scullery, larder, pantry, bake house, and servants' hall.

The second floor, designed for play and sleep, held the master bedroom suite and a dozen guest bedrooms, many of which had attached servants' quarters. Open coal fires kept the rooms warm, yet ample ventilation was provided for the gas-fired lights which illuminated rooms and hallways. Three dozen servants were available to carry basins and hip baths to each guest room and fill the containers on location with hot water.

The impression of spaciousness, luxury, and expert workmanship was not illusory. Cooke had spent more than one million dollars on construction, which began April 3, 1865, the day that Richmond fell. Cooke hired local artisans. He used local stone and lumber. As the structure took shape, he engaged a local frescoer and thirty assistants to decorate the walls and ceilings. Ornately carved walnut trim added the last touch of elegance.

Extravagant mansions of the times, like Ogontz, often implied that the owner thought he was superior, but Cooke was simply delighted to have money, so he did what he wanted to, without airs. Cooke once said that money was the means whereby one could display "a social and generous spirit." He never shied from the physical comforts it brought, but never thought himself a better man because of his wealth.

Ogontz was ready for occupancy by Christmas of 1866. The following February, Cooke held a house-warming party. He hired a band and paid to have a special train run to the closest station. Five hundred guests were shuttled to and from Ogontz by carriage.

Before a full year passed, Cooke had completed the interior decorating with his purchase of three hundred paintings and engravings. A landscape by Thomas Cole and numerous portraits by R. B. Cogswell and William Cogswell ended up with sixty other paintings and etchings in the downstairs hall. Seventy paintings hung in the second floor hall. A third, equally large group found its way to the music room. The largest piece was Worthington Whittridge's fifteen-square-foot *Tributary on the Rhine*. A special place was reserved for Edward Moran's *Shipwreck and Rescue*.

December 31, 1869, was a snowy evening. Under the lights generated by Jay Cooke's private gas works, Ogontz glowed like a fairy castle. Parties at Ogontz were not uncommon; on the contrary, they were routine. This evening, the affable Jay Cooke and his cherubic wife were the center of attraction. At home, Cooke always had his wife close by; next to banking, Dorothea Elizabeth Allen Cooke was the love of his life.

Lizzy, which is what Cooke called her, was a short, full-figured woman with an oval face and deep-set eyes. This evening she wore a full-length, green velvet dress with long sleeves and a high neck fastened by a cameo. Her dark auburn hair, parted in the middle in tight ringlets, provided a perfect frame for her high-polished cheeks and dimpled chin. For more than an hour, she stood outside in the cold next to her husband to welcome the arriving guests. Sometimes she forgot where she was and would talk to one of her friends at length while others waited. When Cooke touched her shoulder or whispered in her ear she would beam, quickly end her conversation, and resume her role of hostess. Her warm smile, dancing eyes, and soft-spoken graciousness endeared her to one and all. From time to time a servant brought her a hot mug of cider or her favorite, hot chocolate.

Carriages drawn by handsomely matched horses with braided tails arrived at regular intervals beneath the stone arches of the porte cochere. As Lizzy welcomed old friends and said hello to new acquaintants, she occasionally reached out with her left hand to touch her husband, an unconscious gesture of her love and occasional need of reassurance. Lizzy had been fifteen when Jay Cooke entered her life. She had been visiting her brother, the president of Allegheny College. Cooke was nineteen and on his way to Sandusky, Ohio, to visit his parents. He'd stopped by to see his brother, Henry, who was a student at Allegheny. When Jay Cooke was introduced to Mr. Allen, he also met Elizabeth.

The two lost their hearts at that first encounter, and for two years, Cooke made time to visit Lizzy in Baltimore. When her family moved to Lexington, Kentucky, Cooke took stock of his financial position. He had been a full partner of Enoch W. Clarke for more than a year. He proposed, and they were married the following August. Had all of their children lived, Jay and Lizzy Cooke would have been surrounded by their five girls and three boys, yet only three children celebrated this New Year's with their parents: Pitt, Sara, and Henry, the youngest. Four of the girls had been carried away by diseases of the day, and the oldest of the clan, Jay, Jr., was away on business.

Congressman William Kelly and his wife stepped down from a black-fringed carriage with shouts of "Greetings!" and "Happy New Year!" Lizzy and Mrs. Kelly fled from the cold while Cooke and the congressman exchanged greetings in a cloud of cigar smoke. Representative Kelly was a tall man with thick curly hair, a short-cropped mustache, and a beard. A congressman since 1860, he was known as the best orator in the House.

The Kellys were to be overnight guests, so servants appeared without command to take charge of their luggage. Cooke and Kelly followed the ladies who were busily chatting. On the way upstairs, Congressman Kelly patted the bust of Ogontz that adorned the post of the stairway railing.

Jay Cooke had known Kelly by reputation since his earliest days in Congress, and on a personal basis since 1865 after Kelly became a member of the congressional Ways and Means Committee. They had a mutual interest in railroad development, so it was no coincidence that he and his wife had been asked to stay overnight.

Downstairs, Kelly joined William Moorhead, Jay Cooke's brother-in-law and partner, who was commenting on Cooke's lifestyle. "Too many people," he was saying. "Too much of everything. I couldn't live like this."

"You of all people should know your brother-in-law. It's his style," said General Ab Nettleton. Cooke had recently hired him to help manage his projects. "I doubt if Jay knows what he has. If it strikes his fancy at the time or if he feels that an organization or local artist needs help, he buys something."

"A very kindhearted soul," said Kelly, "which makes him one of the softest touches in the city. In the past few years he's given more than fifty thousand dollars to Kenyon College. I don't know how much he's given to the church, but I know he's one of the few parishioners who regularly receives personal notes from the bishop."

"Oh hell, he argues with the bishop over church policy, the phraseology of messages presented to the congregation, and church practices," said Moorhead, shaking his head. He told about a luncheon the year before when Cooke had just written a long document to the Reverend Dr. Dyer of New York. He said that he wanted the bishop to revise the prayer book and to remove all signs of religious dogma, ritual and anything else that got in the way between Jesus and his people. What was needed, wrote Cooke, was a plain book for the American people, full of the simplicity of the blessed gospel in which Jesus is recognized as supreme on every page. The book would be a source of edification and dignity to the entire congregation, as long as it wasn't slavishly binding and did not intrude like a "stalking, robed priest" into social and prayer meetings.

"I saw a list of the sums of money our Mr. Cooke gave away to various causes in one month," said Nettleton. "It was enough to support his banking staff. I sometimes think half of his mail is one large request for money. The people of Philadelphia treat him as though he were a charitable institution."

"Money has never been an obsession with Jay," said Moorhead. "He works hard enough for it, but that's just who he is. And when he has it, he spends it." Those who knew Cooke knew that he was genuine. He was no fraud, fool, or snob. He worked at being a banker because he enjoyed business and making money, and he acted confident because he was one of the most successful men in the country.

"And," said Kelly with a short laugh, "he certainly has it. Why, if I had a third of what Cooke has accumulated, I would retire from politics."

"No you wouldn't, Judge," said Nettleton. Kelly had been a

judge prior to his becoming a congressman. "You'd go crazy without issues or adversaries, and you wouldn't have anyone to lecture."

The three men laughed heartily.

"Well, I wish I knew what Mr. Cooke's latest speculation is," said the judge. "I know he's up to something, but he's been pretty quiet about it."

"I believe I know what that something is," said Moorhead. "It's not my place to say, but I think he's gone off the deep end this time."

Kelly and Nettleton exchanged glances and sipped their drinks. "Then it will be up to his friends and relatives to keep him on track," said Kelly with a smile. Nettleton said nothing. He, too, was pretty sure what Cooke had in mind for the future, but he didn't feel comfortable saying anything adverse about his friend, host, and employer; it was too close to biting the hand that fed him.

At eleven o'clock, Cooke set about to locate his compatriots. He looked first for his brother, Henry, a man with an exceptionally powerful way with the written and spoken word. Henry exuded that selective sensitivity that gives one man power over another. In addition to serving as president of the District of Columbia branch of the house of Jay Cooke and Co., Henry used his personal alliances with high-powered politicians to keep his finger on the political pulse of the nation. Without Henry, the firm would have no edge with the government, and without that inside voice, Jay Cooke and Co. could lose more than half its revenue. This influence was one of the reasons Cooke had not made an issue of Henry's six-figure personal debt. Henry's position in Washington was as critical to Jay Cooke and Co. as Jay Cooke's financial wisdom and entrepreneurial bent were to Henry D.

Cooke now motioned to Henry with the twitch of a forefinger. Would he locate brother Pitt and bring him upstairs to the hunting room? Henry nodded and disappeared into the crowd. Family was one of the most fundamental building blocks in Jay Cooke's life, yet the differences between his older brother, Henry, and his younger brother, Pitt, made little sense to him.

Henry had trained as a lawyer, then permitted newspaper journalism to sidetrack him. He purchased the *Sandusky Register*, then the *Ohio State Journal*, and put his influence behind Salmon P. Chase, who was campaigning for governor of Ohio. Chase was elected, but was appointed Secretary of the Treasury just as quickly. Cooke suggested that brother Henry relocate to Washington, D.C., and use his influence to make the family rich.

Pitt's attempts to find a niche in life had been less successful. He had tried West Point, but failed the physical. He then studied real estate. Pitt had enthusiasm, but he was frail and lacked energy. Cooke also thought he showed poor business judgment, but Pitt was family, so Cooke brought Pitt into the firm and asked his New York partner, Harris C. Fahnestock, to watch out for him. "See that Pitt feels constructive and doesn't do much harm." Cooke frowned when he found himself thinking about his brother that way. He made a note to himself to try to think positively about Pitt's more redeeming traits.

Weaving through the crowd, Cooke found Fahnestock talking to William Moorhead. If I know Harris, thought Cooke, he's bending William's ear about the problems the Union Pacific has been having. On the other hand, William might be whining about profits. Fahnestock caught Cooke's eye, and nodded when Cooke pointed to the room directly above them.

Earlier in the evening, Cooke had poked his head into the amusement room and found it full of children engaged in everything from cards to the ball-rolling game of bagatelle. A few of the older children were playing at billiards. Cooke watched four youngsters playing his favorite game, Muggins. Each had five dominoes in front of them. They were making numerical combinations that added up to five on the end pieces. Cooke whispered to a hesitant young girl about a playing opportunity and received a bright smile in return. Two servants were keeping an eye on the creative disorder, so Cooke had to search for another room for his conference.

Cooke then located Congressman Kelly. He was holding court with several well-dressed and attractive ladies and enjoying himself immensely. Rather than interrupt him, Cooke cornered Ab Nettleton. "Ab," said Cooke, "in a minute or two, find an opening in Kelly's soliloquy, disengage him, and lead him to the hunting room for me, will you?"

"Of course, Jay."

The last person on his list was William Marshall, who, like Kelly, had been invited to remain at Ogontz for a few days.

Cooke and Marshall walked upstairs together. "You're acting pretty quiet for a man who has so many irons in the fire, Jay," said Marshall as they walked down the second-floor corridor.

"Patience," said Cooke with a smile. "Your invitation was not entirely social. You have to earn that retainer once in a while."

Marshall laughed and passed a hand over his bald head. What remaining hair he had was confined to arch-shaped strips over his ears. He balanced the loss with a modest beard and mustache. Marshall had just reached the end of his second and final term as governor of Minnesota, but he was reliable and had good connections there and in Washington, D.C. A few days ago, Cooke had retained him at a liberal salary. Marshall told everyone that he'd bought into Cooke's program of railroad development because he thought it would be good for the state. What he did not say, but everyone knew full well, was that he enjoyed the by-product of personal gain that accompanied being an insider.

"I should have guessed," he said. "There is always more than meets the eye with you, Jay. That's probably how you got where you are." He knew where they were headed, so he moved forward and opened the heavy walnut-paneled door of the hunting and fishing room for his host and patron.

4) The Decision

Judge Kelly strolled into the hunting room in front of Henry Cooke, his escort. "Aha," he said, spotting Cooke and the others. "I knew you were up to something, Jay. You had that little gleam in your eye, the one I have come to know over the years."

"Well, Judge, I'm afraid this has nothing to do with pig iron."

The judge laughed along with Marshall, Henry, and Pitt, because they all knew that Congressman Kelly was also called "Pig Iron Kelly" for his stance to protect Pennsylvania's iron producers.

Two servants passed a tray of champagne. "I know this can't

be in celebration of record profits, brother," said Henry with a wry smile.

"Oh, come, it wasn't *that* bad of a year," said Fahnestock with a banker's reserved expression. "Admittedly the gold speculation was costly, but the Philadelphia house had a hundred fifty thousand dollars in profits to share." Fahnestock did not have to elaborate about the gold issue. Jim Fisk and Jay Gould had tried to corner the gold bullion market that fall. The two, who were simple thieves according to Cooke, used their controlling interests in the Erie Canal to buy large quantities of gold and push up the price. When the commodity moved above one hundred fifty dollars per ounce, Cooke recommended to President Grant that he could relieve the unhealthy situation by increasing the availability of gold.

By the end of October, gold was quoted at one hundred sixty-two, a premium of sixty-two cents over every greenback dollar. Secretary of the Treasury Boutwell dumped four million dollars of gold onto the market in exchange for bonds, and in fifteen minutes, the price of gold had plummeted to one hundred thirty-two. Speculators, including the New York office of Jay Cooke and Co., were caught with substantial losses.

"Can I invite you to switch places for a year?" asked Henry, looking at Fahnestock. Henry had thin, light blonde hair, a longish face, and a thin nose that balanced high arched eyebrows. A light-colored mustache and rounded beard softened the expression of his face.

"You must be joking," snorted Fahnestock. "Any attempt to mix Wall Street and Washington, D.C., is like trying to blend lamp oil and salt water. Not only do they not mix well, they ruin each other's better qualities."

"Gentlemen," interrupted Cooke. "Let's drink a toast: to 1870." He raised his glass and waited until everyone did the same. "Tomorrow, as some of you may have already guessed, I will sign a contract on behalf of Jay Cooke and Company to serve as the financial agent for the Northern Pacific Railroad."

Henry and Congressman Kelly beamed.

"I have been waltzing around this issue for several years," continued Cooke, "but I'm convinced that our destiny is to bring into being a new transcontinental line to link Lake Superior with the Pacific Coast. The opening of more than two thousand miles of Northwest country for settlement will be our biggest challenge and our greatest achievement!"

"Fantastic!" shouted Henry. He downed his champagne with a swift tip of his glass, then stepped forward and shook Cooke's hand. Nettleton grinned over his glass, for indeed, he had known what was coming. Congressman Kelly and William Marshall exchanged looks and raised their glasses to each other.

"To your visionary posture, Jay, and your bold decision," boomed Kelly in his best speaker's voice. "I don't need to tell you that this has been a long-held dream of mine. Call on me at any time."

Sensing less than total enthusiasm from his other associates, Cooke felt it necessary to expand on his decision. "Our house will be responsible for raising one hundred million dollars to finance the development of the line. By the time the project is complete, Jay Cooke and Company will own more than half the railroad stock and will have earned millions from the sale of bonds and lands."

"This will be the biggest financial project of the decade," said Nettleton.

"And it will put Minnesota on the map," said Marshall.

"Each of you knows that over the past several years I have spent countless hours weighing the pros and cons of tackling this project," continued Cooke. "The overriding factor was the significance that a completed Northern Pacific railroad will have for America. I know the dangers. We must keep a tight rein on the process, resolve challenges as each one arises, and work as a team to sell the bonds and railroad land to which success is tied."

"Here, here!" Everyone, two more slowly than the rest, toasted to the success of the enterprise, and to the anticipated profits. Marshall immediately moved toward Jay Cooke and began to talk about what he thought had to be done in Minnesota. Henry and Congressman Kelly headed back to the party. Their smiling faces and animated voices told Cooke they were pleased by the decision.

Cooke interrupted Marshall to say that, yes, they had a lot to talk over in the coming week, but he didn't want to begin this evening. "Keep your thoughts, Governor. We'll tackle them tomorrow." Then he invited the ex-governor to return to the festivities. When Marshall was gone, Cooke turned his attention to the two remaining men in the room. The closest to him, William Moorhead, was walking between the table and the rifle rack, making strange faces and rubbing his hands. When Cooke stepped in his path, Moorhead looked up at his brother-in-law with an anxious expression. He had been nibbling the inside of his lip.

"You don't see the possibilities here, do you, William?" said Cooke calmly.

"Jay," said William in return, "I'm leaving the firm."

Cooke did not speak. There was nothing to say. Because of William's demeanor, Cooke had expected some negative reaction, but nothing like that.

"The Northern Pacific project," said William, "is a very unwise move. It . . . it's unmanageable and will be most unprofitable. Remember last summer? You wanted me to go to Europe for you. 'Take the family,' you said. So I went, and out of respect for your wishes, I visited the Rothschilds from whom you sought support."

When William then held up both hands in front of him, Jay Cooke wasn't sure whether it was in protest or to push him away. It was William's "don't get mad but I told you so" gesture. "From the moment that I mentioned American railroads it was clear that the Rothschilds were not interested. Jay, they are the most powerful family in Europe and their attitude towards us and our projects is known all over Europe. To go ahead with this scheme will be catastrophic!" He turned his back on his brother-in-law. "I know that once you've made up your mind, no one can turn you, so I have no choice. I can't pledge my support to a project I believe is doomed." He placed his champagne glass on the table and started to leave.

Cooke moved to intercept him. He touched his shoulder and whispered with an intensity that matched William's. "William, we are family. If you do not want to participate, I will find other activities for you, but I ask that you postpone your decision." Cooke patted him on the shoulder. "In time, you will see that this is simply good business."

William whirled, exposing the angst written across his face.

"For God's sake, Jay," he hissed, "find another project!"
Cooke motioned for silence. "Spend a few minutes talking to
Judge Kelly this evening about your concerns, will you? Listen to
what he has to say. You and I can chat at length tomorrow morning."
Cooke watched his brother-in-law leave the room. Six years
ago, it had been William who had introduced him to railroad financing; it was with William that he had assumed the financial
management of the Franklin railroad. They had accepted responsibility for the purchase of all railroad construction materials. And
with William's help, the road had been finished ahead of time, under budget, and in superb fashion. Now, for some reason, William
had lost faith. He was behaving like a croaker and a sniveler. Jay
Cooke took a deep breath and turned his attention to his New York
partner, Harris C. Fahnestock.
Fahnestock was a slender, dark-haired man with a manicured
mustache and beard. He was then gazing out of the window. When
the door clicked he knew they were alone, but he prolonged the
neutral moment by asking how much snow fell at Ogontz every
winter. He knew the answer, because he'd heard Cooke tell a number of people that it varied between six inches and six feet. As
Cooke responded, Fahnestock could see a white-tailed deer illuminated by the gas lights outside. The deer's tail waggled back and
forth as she trotted through the powdery snow into the woods.
Fahnestock turned towards his senior partner, his eyes a mixture of sadness and resolve. "Jay, for the life of me I cannot get up
your enthusiasm for the Northern Pacific project. I know your posture and your hopes, but at every step in New York I am confronted
by investors who cannot place their railroad bonds in the market.
The six percent bonds of the Central Pacific, which, by the way,
has been completed and is profitable, sells at ninety-four. Missouri Pacific bonds sell between eighty-eight and ninety. Both earn
money, neither depend on congressional favor for their construction as did the Union Pacific and Central Pacific. Even the Kansas
Pacific at seven percent government interest can be bought in
Frankfort at sixty-three, and at seventy-seven here."
He picked up a newspaper from a table and symbolically of-

fered it to Cooke. "Have you looked at railroad stock offerings, or analyzed the number of new issues? Everyone with a million dollars in capital and access to a construction company is building a railroad. The Chicago, Danville, and Vincennes offers seven percent for forty years; the Burlington, Cedar Rapids and Minnesota pays seven for fifty years, and their bonds are free of government tax. Then there's the Chicago and Southern . . ."

Fahnestock broke eye contact to look back through the window. "Jay, you're a marvel and a wonder, but this project is too large to tackle alone. It may break us. The stock you refer to can't be counted on to be profitable for many years, so the money will flow out like a river and none will come in."

He looked his partner straight in the eye. "You are undoubtedly the most competent man in the world to popularize bonds, but to be a success at completing a gigantic enterprise like the Northern Pacific, you must show a way to at least earn the interest. And of all people, you should know that a railroad enterprise can't generate profit for years, not until the land is sold and it creates its own market. Half a dozen years is a fierce, fierce time to wait for earnings."

Fahnestock noticed that Cooke had not moved since he started to talk. He thought he might as well finish. "It is good to look at the facts in the face now before we're committed. However great you can demonstrate your railroad's potential to be, you must compete with the cheaper bonds. Your old friend, Enoch Clarke, bought Missouri Pacific at ninety-five; it's now at eighty-six. Kansas Pacific does not have as much land behind them but they have more road and a land subsidy. And you know full well that the larger capitalists will take a hands-off stance. That will leave you with backers you must reach by personal influence. That's not good business."

Five years earlier, thought Fahnestock, this man had opened new worlds to him with the simple phrase, "Join me." And during those five years, he had come to appreciate Cooke's judgment, sense of timing, and intuition. But he had never held back his own judgment, especially when the financial health of the firm was concerned. The Northern Pacific was a bad call and he wanted Cooke to know how he felt.

"You probably call this croaking," added Fahnestock with a sigh. "Don't. You know me, or should after our years together. I give you facts and figures as I see them."

Two months ago, Cooke had sent Fahnestock a pamphlet entitled *The Northern Pacific Railroad: Its Route, Resources, Progress, and Business.* In return, Fahnestock sent him a letter of warning, pointing out that the market was flooded with bonds. He suggested that people would take the length and cost of the railroad and figure out that the average cost per mile was fifty-eight thousand dollars. For the Union and Central Pacific, those figures were sixteen thousand and thirty-two thousand per mile. Against facts like that, the Northern Pacific did not look attractive.

"Do you really believe I've made a rash move, taken a position without having studied the pros and cons?" asked Cooke softly in rebuke. "I'm not swallowing the Northern Pacific like a fish swallows bait, you know. Their board of directors has pressed me to assume financial responsibility for this project for five years. I repeatedly turned them down. Why? Because they had neither the popular nor the financial base with which to begin. And, in truth, the situation at Jay Cooke and Co. was very good. But President Grant has given the Treasury to Boutwell, and Boutwell has listened to outside voices, and the sale of government bonds is no longer profitable. So I decided to reexamine the project in detail."

Cooke took a deep breath and joined Fahnestock by the window. Both looked out onto the winter landscape while they argued in quiet but intense tones. Each thought he was answering the other's concern, but all they did was reinforce their philosophic differences: Harris Fahnestock was a commercial banker, Jay Cooke was a bond salesman.

Cooke finally banged his fist against the wall in frustration. "What happened to your faith, Harris?" he said with a tremolo Fahnestock had never heard. "What happened to your love of a challenge?" Cooke gestured towards the door. "Henry's for it. Marshall and Kelly are delighted. But a better argument is Roberts's report. The man is an excellent engineer. He has a firm grasp of what is needed and what it will cost."

Jay Cooke reached out and tightened his hand around Fahnestock' upper arm. "I tell you that I am busy night and day about this great matter and you must second me. Trust me when I say that this will be our greatest achievement."

Fahnestock looked down at Jay's hand. Cooke swallowed and silently removed it. There it was, thought Fahnestock. Cooke had set his mind. There was no dividend in bickering.

"All right, Jay. We'll do it your way. You know I will help as much as possible, but frankly, the proportions and complications of this project stagger me. I am not clear as to its practicability. All I see is an incredible, endless task."

Harris Fahnestock moved towards the door, pulled on the latch, and then paused to look back. He never sought an argument, but neither did he ever hold back. "I would feel one hundred percent better if you would spread the load. You are my partner, and you are my friend, but you need to remember that not everyone is Jay Cooke."

Cooke sat in his library with a cigar and watched the smoke diffuse. He wondered if Fahnestock's antipathy was simply a display of his banking philosophy? The two men differed strongly when it came to taking risks. Cooke visualized Fahnestock as a rabbit in a New York tuxedo, content to munch on greens in a protective briar patch. He saw himself as a fox, always on the lookout for new game. Like the fox, he longed to explore the meadow on the other side of the briar patch, and was willing to make a commitment to that exploration.

Other differences? Perspective. Fahnestock did not operate from his gut. He had no sixth-sense understanding of the role or importance of the Northern Pacific project. He lacked the ability to identify with the majesty of a grand challenge. Rather than taste the potential of the project, Fahnestock had been stupefied by the magnitude of the task. With his sense of propriety, he was not galvanized by the vision of ultimate success; rather, he was paralyzed by a fear of the unknown.

Fear! Yes, fear! Cooke wasn't sure whether he'd ever known

fear. In all honesty, he'd never been placed in a position where fear had been a consideration or a force with which he'd had to contend. Did Fahnestock have a right to be frightened? Cooke thought of what was involved in creating a railroad: pushing two thousand miles of new track through a wilderness. He had to catch his breath. Between Lake Superior and the Mississippi River there was not one settlement, only a military post or two and a few Indian agencies and trading stations. The region between the Mississippi and the Missouri remained mostly unexplored, a flat prairie land occupied here and there by buffalo herds and Indian tribes. In the Montana Territory lay a few scattered mining towns, most within shouting distance of the Missouri River. And west of the Rockies? Who knew, other than a few miners, trappers, and surveyors? Why shouldn't Fahnestock consider the project unthinkable, mind-boggling, or even absurd!

But Cooke never considered the possibility of failure because he had never learned how to conjugate the verb "to fail." Besides, everything that the Northern Pacific stood for, and that Cooke risked, was consistent with America's future: immigration would follow the tracks; the new corridor would carry soldiers and supplies to western military posts and thus accelerate resolution of the Indian problem; and the new line would stimulate development of the region's natural resources. In turn, an increase in settlement and commerce would enhance the value of the public trust in those sections of land that alternated with the Northern Pacific land grant.

Yes, thought Cooke. Harris Fahnestock had a right to be scared, to quiver in his desire to have his senior partner rethink the commitment. For a banker, the bottom line was clear: the Northern Pacific Railroad was a massive speculation, because no one had ever tried anything like it before.

But Jay Cooke didn't believe that Fahnestock could measure the people's energy and their faith in the future of the country. He could. He was the only person qualified to see this project through. He could envision what others could not understand; he had succeeded where others had failed. He knew it was his destiny to become involved in projects of national scope. "Everything I have ever done tells me that this is right and that now is the time," said

Cooke to himself.

The clock chimed three. The new year of 1870 was three hours old. Where would the country have been if the world had been left to the fainthearted? As Jay Cooke took a last draw on his cigar, he remembered the moment he set foot in the door of Enoch Clarke's bank. That had been thirty-two years ago. He had stood in the entryway of Clarke's lobby for a moment, tasting the atmosphere, listening to the banking language, and watching the people. He had smiled because it felt right to be there.

And Enoch Clarke never forgot Jay Cooke's reply to his question of why he wanted to enter the banking business. Every article he wrote for the financial columns, every investment recommendation he made, and every analytical report he submitted reinforced Clarke's belief that someday soon, Jay Cooke would be his firm's leading partner. Thus, it came as no surprise to either Mr. Clarke (who made the offer) nor to Jay Cooke (who accepted) when at age twenty-one, Jay Cooke became a full partner of Enoch W. Clarke and began to enjoy a one-eighth share of the profits.

And then, of course, there had been the tremendous success of the Five-Twenties. Above everything else, Cooke's sense of invincibility came from the sale of these bonds.

5) The Five-Twenties

When East Coast residents talked of riches in 1870, they didn't look to the Midas touch, they simply said they wished to be "as rich as Jay Cooke." Cooke's startling rise as a private banker had been a self-fulfilling prophecy. In less than a decade, his name was so well known and so well connected to financial success, that the public viewed him as a genius and patron of Philadelphia. In the halls of the Treasury Department, Cooke's opinions became fact and his recommendations were looked on as preferred policy.

Jay Cooke left Enoch Clarke and started Jay Cooke and Co. in 1861, the year that the nation was fighting for its existence. In the six months before the war, the public debt rose from sixty-six to ninety million dollars. To keep the government solvent, Secretary of the Treasury Salmon P. Chase offered eight million dollars in bonds for twenty years at six percent. When the Treasury extended direct bidding opportunities to banks, one hundred fifty-six responded. Chase accepted bids with a discount of between four and ten percent. Later that same year, he issued another eight million dollars in bonds. This time he accepted only offers of a discount of four percent or less. As a result, he had trouble selling the loan.

From Philadelphia, Cooke watched the government flounder. "Look at this," he said with disgust, as he totaled the Treasury Department's bond sales for the week. "The government will never fund the war using this outdated method of selling."

His audience was a young banker from Pittsburgh, a man whom Cooke planned to hire: Harris Fahnestock. "The country is in dire trouble, militarily and financially, Harris," continued Cooke with fervor. "No one is involved. Everyone conducts business as usual. Where's the opportunity for the people to stand up and say, 'I'll help! Count me in!' Why has no one asked help from the people of this country?"

Later in the year, the state of Pennsylvania prepared to float a loan to its residents to build the state's defenses. Cooke marched downtown bristling with influence, connections, and plans. To the officers of the state treasury, he declared, "I want you to offer the bonds in small denominations, and I want you to issue them at par. I am positive that all three millions in bonds can be sold if they are offered as a symbol of patriotism. Americans believe in America. They believe in its future. They will help. They *want* to be needed. Ask them!" His voice rose to a shout.

Pennsylvania State Treasurer Henry D. Moore agreed to try Cooke's approach. When Cooke found out, he pulled Moore to one side. "Henry, there is one little item I didn't share with your officers last week. My idea of selling bonds using patriotic appeal won't work unless I do it, because I know what has to be done. You have to give Jay Cooke and Co. the contract to sell these bonds."

Moore turned white. "Damn it, Jay, how can I do that?" he protested. "I could lose my job. I can see the headlines now: 'State Treasurer the Target of Corruption Charges.' There's no way," he said, shaking his head.

Cooke kept pace as the two walked down the hall towards

Moore's office. "Don't be silly. In the first place, I've done it before, that's why I was able to convince the board to try it this way. Secondly, my success will become your success, and you will be praised for being one smart fellow. In the third place, I will personally guarantee you an opportunity to take advantage of some little-known money-making schemes. If you work them the way I suggest, they could be worth five times your current salary."

Moore met Cooke's eyes briefly, then muttered, "I'll see what I can do."

Cooke based his pitch to the public on personal appeal and made frequent references to the fact that the bonds were entirely safe and tax-free at six percent. Then he wrote pamphlets, circulars, and newspaper advertisements. Next, he hired a cadre of sales agents, loaded them with instructions and documents, and sent them across the state.

Cooke knew the power of seeing one's name in print. He also knew that people liked to get credit for noble deeds. As the names of the first subscribers came in, Cooke printed every one of them in major newspapers across the state.

The result exceeded all hopes: the people of Pennsylvania rose up and oversubscribed the loan. The result not only proved Cooke's point, the fee he collected for the sales gave him working capital for the first time. As his bonus, his name became known across the state.

Cooke's faith in his approach increased after a second test on a fifteen-million-dollar government loan proved successful. He used half of his commissions to advertise the offering. He even draped a huge flag across the entrance to his bank. Its legend read "National Loan." He sold everything he had been given.

With two successful experiments under his belt, Jay Cooke reexamined the government's financial plight and played his first ace, Henry Cooke. Henry was then living in Ohio. Cooke asked him to move to Washington, D.C., and exert direct influence on his old friend, Salmon P. Chase. *Come to Washington and make your family rich,* he wrote in his telegram. Henry cautioned that his friendship with Chase might not bear fruit. Chase was honest, and he had to be sure that favors were merited before he guaranteed them. That was perfectly all right with Cooke. He simply wanted an inside track.

As soon as Henry agreed, Jay Cooke played his second ace. He located a new branch of Jay Cooke and Co. on 15th Street in Washington, D.C., and placed Henry in charge. By then, Fahnestock had joined Cooke, to provide the firm with expertise in banking procedures.

Cooke's third ace was a meeting between himself, brother Henry and the Secretary of the Treasury, Salmon P. Chase. Chase was an honest, hardworking man and a pragmatist. That afternoon, Cooke led Chase through the logic he believed would solve the government's financial problems, the same logic that would provide Cooke the position he wanted with the government.

"Mr. Chase," said Jay Cooke, "if we brush aside all other issues, the basic problem the government faces is how to raise money to finance the war. I foresee increasing difficulties with your current strategies. Banks will become more adamant in their refusal to accept bonds at par, and the American public will resist increased taxation."

Cooke was rephrasing what Chase already knew, that his attempts to raise money were vulnerable to political conditions. The recent *Trent* affair had been another blow to the people's faith in the government. Captain Wilkes of the frigate *San Jacinto* had stopped a neutral British ship, the *Trent*, to remove two Confederate commissioners, James Mason and John Slidell. England's sympathy was with the South, so when members of Parliament learned of the unauthorized seizure, the halls rang with demands for war.

The commissioners were released, but the affair triggered a downward spiral in the nation's economy. First, the price of government bonds fell sharply, so Americans began to hoard gold and silver. Hoarding reduced the normal flow of hard cash back to the government and forced the government to suspend payment of its debts with hard specie. It also prevented banks from selling bonds.

Chase knew that if he could not collect the money he needed, he had the authority to create it. He issued forty-five million dollars in greenbacks and declared it legal tender. It wasn't the issue of the greenback's stability which had drawn Jay and Henry Cooke to seek a meeting with Chase, it was Chase's second action of desperation when he issued five hundred million dollars in six percent bonds. Referred to as the Five-Twenties, the bonds were callable in five years, mature in twenty. They sat unsold because Chase was too stubborn to sell them at a discount, but no one would purchase them at par.

"I'll be damned if the government is going to lose fifty million dollars by allowing bankers to purchase them at a ten percent discount," he told Henry.

Cooke used Chase's concern as his opening. "Let us show you how to sell the Five-Twenties, and how to sell them the way you want, Mr. Chase. At par."

Chase shook his head. "It cannot be done. I have tried every form of persuasion known to man and politician."

Jay and Henry smiled politely. "I'm sure no one could have tried harder, but we're talking about a new approach," said Jay Cooke. He nodded to Henry, who took a few sheets of paper from his portfolio. "What we are going to show you are results, not speculation or design or forecast." Henry handed Mr. Chase two pieces of paper that summarized the result of the promotion of bonds by Jay Cooke and Co. "These figures are real in hard currency returns."

Henry Cooke made the appeal to Chase on a personal basis. He used cause and effect situations he and Chase had been through together, and he reaffirmed the power of what brother Jay had proposed. In the end, Chase gambled, and Jay Cooke left the Treasury Building with the title of Special Agent for the sale of government bonds.

No one had ever attempted what Jay Cooke was planning to do, sell *one million dollars* in bonds *per day*. He threw all of his ingenuity into the effort. At great cost, he built an organization of twenty-five hundred agents to sell bonds across the country. He called them "minute men" because the speeches he gave them to read were sixty seconds long.

Cooke also contacted prominent journalists, knowing that to get what he needed was simply a matter of paying their fees. He appealed to their patriotism as well as their pocketbook. "You get a bonus if I can determine that your writing has produced results," he told them. "Remember, you will be helping your country, not just yourselves." Journalists cooperated, pocketed his money, and wrote what he needed.

Cooke was driven by a feeling of invincibility, a burning patriotism, and a love of making large-scale efforts hum with success. He became the man of the hour, the one with God on his side. In his company, he was everyone's source of strength and inspiration, the prime motivator, the driver of the program. He combined his reason, righteousness, empathy, and optimism with endless energy. Tirelessly, he planned, wired agents, developed policies, issued goals, directed advertising, and stayed abreast of correspondence. He educated the public and spoke to investors, large and small. He was a whirlwind, a tornado.

Cooke told the people that the bonds he offered were the last best opportunity to get in on the war effort. *Sales of the United States six percent loan called Five-Twenties have amounted for many weeks past to over two millions of dollars daily,* read one Cooke-sponsored advertisement. *The first of July is rapidly approaching when the public will no longer have the right to subscribe at par for this desirable loan, whose principal and interest are payable in gold. All parties contemplating investing in these bonds should at once forward their money through any of the local agencies or direct to Jay Cooke, subscription agent, 114 S. Third St., Philadelphia.*

The money poured in, some days more than two to three million dollars. Jay Cooke and Company was so far ahead in sales that the government fell thirty to forty-five days behind printing bond certificates. An exuberant Secretary of the Treasury extended the loan. When Chase tried to shut down the loan, the flow of subscriptions was so heavy Congress held a special session to legalize the sale of eleven million dollars in excess sales.

On January 21, 1864, the Five-Twenties were closed out. Jay Cooke and Company was credited for having sold three hundred sixty-two million dollars worth of bonds. After expenses, the firm realized two hundred twenty-five thousand dollars, one sixteenth of one percent of the value of what had been sold. After Cooke looked at income and expenses and reflected on the effort, he offered to sell government bonds for nothing if the Treasury Department would simply cover his expenses.

The following year, the government offered another loan: the Seven-Thirties, seven percent bonds for thirty years. As subscription agent, Jay Cooke and Co. was required to sell two million dollars of bonds per day. This time he earned three-fourths of one percent on the first fifty million and five-eighths on the second fifty million. The rate for the rest would be fixed after all of the bonds were sold.

The last year of the Civil War, 1865, was Cooke's most phenomenal year in the sale of government bonds. From the first of February to the end of March, he averaged three million dollars of sales per day. The high-water mark occurred in the last week of February when Cooke took in twenty-seven million dollars.

"I'm terribly sorry, Madam; the government is several weeks behind in printing the bonds. Will you accept our receipt as proof of your patriotism until we can mail one to you? Thank you." Cooke smiled, turned, and nearly stumbled over one of the crowd that had pushed into the lobby. He looked around, seeking help. All he could see was a crushing mob. His ears picked out the murmurs of the clerks in every room and at every counter as they led customers through the process of buying bonds. It was incredible!

Most of the people were town folk. Each bought fifty-dollar bonds. A few purchased a hundred-dollar bond. They were small sums, but they added up. The common people weren't the only ones. Three patrons of the arts, two well-known bankers, and the president of Baldwin Locomotives personally waited for Cooke to take their money that morning. Two hundred thirty thousand dollars in one swoop!

Tuesday of that week, Cooke could not see any of his assistants: they were surrounded by clusters of Philadelphians waving hands and dollars. By Wednesday noon, the line outside the house of Jay Cooke and Co. had disintegrated into an undifferentiated throng. Cooke was getting concerned. The situation might become unruly. How could he keep pace? He waded his way to the front door. "Your patience is requested," he shouted to the crowd. "I guarantee you will be taken care of. God bless you all." The crowd cheered him appreciatively but stood its ground. Cooke wrung his hands and sought his office manager.

"We need more clerks to keep up with the flow," said Cooke.

"Mr. Cooke," said Robert, who was now freely sweating in the body-heated room, "we hired twelve additional clerks and we're using all of the room on all floors in the building. I do not know where all these people are coming from, but this week they have purchased twelve and one-half million dollars in bonds. This event is unparalleled. I don't see how we can keep up the pace."

"We'll find a way," said Cooke, feeling omniscient. "As long as one person remains to buy bonds, we will find a way." Then he pushed through the crowd and walked up Third Street toward Clark and Co., his former employer. We'll use their offices, too, he thought. Enoch will be agreeable. After all, it's all for the war effort.

Jay Cooke and Co. became the chosen target for citizens who wanted to help their country. Hundreds, then thousands sent letters, money, and pledges through the mails. They boarded trains to reach his Philadelphia office. They saddled horses and walked. These were not the wealthy of the world; they were the common people. Of every one hundred bond buyers, twenty-seven were shopkeepers, nineteen machinists, boiler men, and foundrymen; seventeen were soldiers who had been discharged after a term; nine were engineers; five hatters; four barkeeps. Another four were either saddlers, cab men, stallkeepers, barbers or actors. Jay Cooke and Co. was the focal point of northern patriotism, and a miniature version of national mayhem!

Newspapers and journalists compared Jay Cooke to the Rothschilds of France. *Never in the history of nations,* wrote the *Washington Chronicle, has such an enormous amount of money been raised for public use with such extraordinary rapidity and success as in the instance of the great Seven-Thirty loan.* By the fall of 1865, Jay Cooke was being hailed as one of the greatest financial and political figures in American history.

The *New York Times* carried his image to new heights: *In these financial days no name has a more metallic ring than that of Jay Cooke. Possessed of a peculiar talisman, whatever that powerful monetary hand touches it turns into government bonds. Whosoever takes note of these things cannot but half observe the powerful pressure this great house brings to bear upon the market. Whenever a government loan is to be disposed of, to the best advantage, they always adopt the most liberal, practical and productive terms. Their liberality in dealing opens the money drawers, chests, and stockings of the whole country. Universal publicity is another of the instruments they work with. Every farm house, bank, hotel, counting room hears of the loan. The result is that from the state of languor it springs into intense activity.*

Cooke loved a competitive game. And he was accustomed to winning.

6) The Land Grant

The upbeat signing ceremony took place January 3, 1870, in one of New York's finest hotels. "Gentlemen," said Northern Pacific Railroad President Gregory Smith, "I would like to introduce Mr. Jay Cooke."

Amid a firm round of applause, Cooke was escorted to the front stage. A large desk occupied the middle of the floor. In the middle of the desk was a pen and ink set and some documents. Between the desk and the audience was a model train with Northern Pacific painted in red letters on its side. It rested on model tracks bracketed by two bodies of water, one to represent Lake Superior, the other to represent the Pacific Ocean.

Jay Cooke was the only signatory for his firm, but Pitt Cooke had been anxious to be with his brother and to represent the New York office. He stood next to the longtime railroad promoter and former governor of Vermont, R. D. Rice.

When Cooke reached the table, Smith shook his hand, then faced his board of directors who were standing in a line near the desk. "Gentlemen, it's been a long time coming, but Jay Cooke is about to join us in our endeavor. I don't think anyone here is unaware of his incredible contributions to the growth of America."

Spontaneous applause broke out in the room amid scattered shouts of "Here, here!"

"In the financial world of which each of us is a member,"

continued Smith, "Jay Cooke is foremost known for his support of our government during the War of the Rebellion. Some say that our nation might have been in acute financial jeopardy without his creative and astounding sale of government bonds."

More sincere applause. "I am delighted to have Mr. Cooke as an ally, and I know that each of you will pledge total support to ensure that the Northern Pacific will rank among America's greatest achievements."

As the applause subsided, Cooke sat and signed the agreements. He then ceded his chair to R. D. Rice, who was followed by the six members of the board's executive committee: General George W. Cass, President of the Pittsburgh, Fort Wayne and Chicago Line; A. H. Barney of Philadelphia; W. B. Ogden, President of the Chicago and Northwestern Railroad; J. Edgar Thompson, President of the Pennsylvania Railroad; and William G. Fargo, Vice President of the New York Central.

At the catered lunch that followed, Cooke addressed the first requirement of his contract, the need to advance five million dollars to underwrite the construction of the road from Lake Superior to the Red River Valley. "I'll create an investment pool of five million," said Cooke. As if guessing Smith's next question, he added, "The incentive will be stock in the railroad. The offer will look quite good to anyone who has been a client of mine in the past."

"Be sure to save a portion to allot to the members of the board, Jay," said Smith. "I don't doubt that most will want a part of the initial offering. I'll probably spread mine around." He raised an eyebrow. "We have a lot of work to do in Minnesota."

Brother Pitt took brother Jay to the railroad. "Assuming that the pool can be filled," Jay told his brother, "we need to be able to convince Congress to accept alterations in the conditions of Perham's original land grant."

"What the hell for?"

"Because, Pitt, Congress controls the conditions of the grant." Sometimes Jay Cooke thought that his brother was never destined for business. He measured his words. "That's the way Perham wrote it. He was a fool. By that, I mean that he was an idealist and unwittingly caused me a lot of trouble. The official charter from Congress should have included the ability to issue bonds against the value of land grant lands without congressional authority. That's not the case, so we have to correct it."

Congress wasn't his only worry. Fahnestock was right about bond competition. The American market was flooded with railroad bonds and Europeans were reluctant to buy into American railroad enterprises, even *with* government guarantees. Yet the money from bond sales would have to bear the cost of railroad construction until land sales picked up. The success of the entire enterprise rested on his ability to sell the railroad land grant quickly and develop a paying traffic. Could the road be constructed and maintained until settlement of the land occurred? If so, he could use funds from land sales to create a sinking fund to redeem large amounts of bonds at maturity.

Cooke's confidence rested on more than his own track record. He had studied the history of the Illinois Railroad land grant. Land sales from that grant covered nearly the entire cost of railroad construction, yet Congress had provided Illinois one-sixth the acreage per mile they'd allotted the Northern Pacific.

"You sound optimistic," Nettleton had said when Cooke discussed his findings.

"I never go into a project unless I am," rejoined Cooke. "If I don't believe in what I'm doing, Ab, how can I convince others that we have a sure thing to offer?"

The night after Cooke signed the contract with the Northern Pacific, he went to bed and dreamed of success. *Without getting wet, he stood in the water next to a steamer in the port of Philadelphia. The boat had just arrived from Europe. Cooke greeted a wizardly-looking gentleman and assisted him to a train which, in dreamlike fashion, appeared at his elbow.*

"How was your trip, Anton?" he asked, showing concern. Anton looked like all those in Europe who would eventually immigrate to America: an etched face that showed a slight weariness, long artisan's fingers on callused hands, well-worn pockets on his handmade clothes.

"Your agent saw to everything, Mr. Cooke. Everything! He and many of my countrymen saw me off knowing that I was in good hands. There was not the slightest doubt that I was headed for the promised land."

"Have you eaten?"

"Oh, yes. I have no wants at the moment other than to see this glorious Northwest you have been unveiling."

"We are almost there."

In western Minnesota they stood in the shade of a tall pine and looked westward at the waist-high grasses that beckoned under a gentle breeze. At its farthest edges, the prairie grasses tucked into copses of sturdy hardwood and pine forests. Domestic animals grazed contentedly; fresh, clear streams could be heard in the background.

Anton bent down and tested the compactability of the loam, then lifted his hand high, as though giving a benediction. "You are truly a great man, and the fulfillment of your promise is a great benefit to my countrymen and to your nation. How can we thank you?"

"Bring your family, settle here, and thrive. Civilize this wilderness. We have ships and trains to bring you, hotels to house you in until you are ready, building materials at your disposal, and liberal credit terms to ensure your success." Cooke gestured toward the tracks that appeared beside them. A train rushed past them and quickly blended into the horizon as they stood motionless in the field. The train was carrying passengers to settle the land beyond the Missouri.

"Every few days, a new twenty-five-mile section of completed track is surveyed and prominent features of the land plotted on a map," he said. He pointed across the field to a row of small houses, each slightly different from the other. They represented the different models from which Anton could choose.

"They cost from one thousand to two thousand dollars each, and can be erected in one day," he said.

"This is hard to believe," said Anton. "I must see more."

So they traveled west. The country slipped by them swiftly, field after field, farm after farm, town after town. The predominant colors were green and white: green for grass and crops ripening in the

fields; white for the houses, barns, and fences, and the white cloud
reflections in the ponds and streams.
  A buffalo herd thundered across distant hills. Indians appeared,
saluted the herd, then disappeared. The train pushed ever westward,
over high plains, mountain passes, lava beds, and rocky canyons.
They finally arrived at the Pacific Ocean. Standing on the shore of
the West Coast, Anton acknowledged that no one other than Jay
Cooke could have accomplished this feat.
  "Thank you, Anton," Cooke said with a slight bow. "Those in
positions of influence and power are duty-bound for the good of the
country to translate their visions into realities. After all, we're talk-
ing about the future of a magnificent America which is in the pro-
cess of reclaiming land from the wilderness. We must all do our part.
I am lucky that I can do more than others."

     Jay Cooke wrote brother Henry to get in touch with the family's
closest congressional friends. He asked Judge Kelly to identify
problem congressmen and suggest ways to overcome their objections. He directed William Marshall to return to Minnesota to gather
deeds to 500,000 acres of land and to assist with the eastern terminus, which would be Duluth.
     With responsibilities allocated, Cooke drafted an offer to be-
come a shareholder in his five-million-dollar pool. Subscribers were
asked to take Northern Pacific Railroad bonds at par in return for
a proprietary interest in fifty thousand dollars' worth of stock. The
stock would be issued in proportion to completed miles of the railroad. Every person on his list, including Vice President Schuyler
Colfax, Rutherford Hayes, and Hugh McCullough of the Treasury,
knew him well. He issued special invitations with very favorable
purchase conditions to Henry Ward Beecher and Horace Greeley
of the *New York Tribune* because of their ability to influence the
public. If neither paid a dollar for the next year, the publicity and
support they could generate would make it worth carrying both.
     Cooke allotted one-twelfth segments, $466,666, to Henry, Pitt,
and William Moorhead, who both William Kelly and Jay Cooke
had persuaded to remain in the firm. Ten days or so later, Samuel

Wilkeson, now Secretary for the Northern Pacific, wrote that Henry Ward Beecher would, *if sweetened to the highest point*, sell his ten thousand shares of Pacific Mail and invest in the Northern Pacific. The same day, Cooke also received an article and brief note from Harris Fahnestock. The article, from the *New York Times*, said Congress was calling for an investigation into the Union Pacific Railroad and its financial arm, the Credit Mobilier, on charges of corruption, waste, and greed. After the Union Pacific boasted profits in excess of thirty million dollars, it turned around and issued new bonds to pay ten million dollars it owed on construction. Unfortunately, the October gold crisis destroyed market confidence and the bonds sold poorly. Fahnestock's warning was abundantly clear.

Cooke's agreement with the Northern Pacific Railroad Company hit the papers in the middle of the month. Nettleton told reporters that surveyors would soon be in the field, and that construction contracts would be let in the spring. New York and Philadelphia papers gave Cooke considerable credit. One congratulated the Northern Pacific board of directors for their financial connection with the house of Jay Cooke and Co. *The country is to be congratulated. That wilderness will be turned into a belt of settlement and will be the shortest line to the Pacific.*

By the end of January, the pool was fully subscribed. Now Cooke was free to concentrate on the conditions of the land grant. The resolution the Northern Pacific sent to Congress asked that their company be permitted to issue bonds for construction of its road *by mortgaging the land in the land grant in advance of construction*. This would provide bond holders immediate value, not simply future value. The resolution further asked that the company be permitted to build the main line to the Columbia River, and run a branch line from some point on the trunk line to Puget Sound. Lastly, the resolution sought to enable the railroad to select lands from *an additional ten miles on both sides of the current land grant* to make up any deficiencies in the original land grant due to past and interim sales of land.

Speaker of the House James G. Blaine wrote Cooke that since the bill did not require any expenditure by Congress, it might be passed within the month, if pressed vigorously. He suggested that

Henry speak to influential committee members as soon as possible.

The air of optimism disappeared quickly, however, when Henry informed his brother that two bills had been introduced to consider a land grant of the St. Paul Pacific Road. *If it passes,* wrote Henry, *it could damage our grant. You had better have these bills in Washington looked after.* Not a week passed before Henry sent another telegram. One brief message advised: *There is opposition in the air to changing the conditions of the land grant.*

Cooke had heard rumors. So had Gregory Smith, who suggested they buy alliances. *The Postmaster of the House of Representatives can be very helpful to us,* he advised Cooke. *He has kept his intentions quiet that he might be more efficient. He can be fully relied on but will require aid. He will be judicious in expenditures. I wrote to Henry about him. You have to authorize Henry to expend what may be required. The cost will be kept as low as possible.* ·

Next, the Chairman of Public Lands dashed off a telegram to warn Cooke. *Obstacles will be strewn in your path. Mr. Wilson of Ohio, in particular, would have his own little proviso to add to any changes considered in the Northern Pacific Railroad grant.*

When Cooke asked Henry about the warning, Henry told him that it *had to do with the lands sold to settlers. Wilson wants the price of all land grant sales to be limited to $2.50 per acre. He is a power on the committee. Whatever happens, don't expect smooth sailing. In addition to Wilson, Senator Harlan of Iowa and several others have their interests aligned with the Union and Central Pacific railroads. Harlan will oppose the development of the Northern Pacific because we represent competition. They are afraid for the market for Union Pacific and Central Pacific stock and bonds. The Northern Pacific would divert attention from their cause. It is rumored that Harlan has authorization from the Central and Union Pacific railroads to spend thousands to prevent us from altering the terms of the grant.*

Fifteen years earlier, the only topic of conversation in congressional cloakrooms was the first transcontinental railroad. Now, Congress was extremely careful about any support it provided new railroad construction. Too many railroads had sought too much public land, and too much profit had accrued to too few individuals. A growing number of senators on the railroad committee acted as though they were the last settlers to have discovered the promised land. They wanted to shut the gate behind them. Those whose states had already acquired millions of acres from the government were the most vocal in their attempts to shut down what they called "the great giveaway of public lands."

Cooke wadded up Henry's telegram and threw it into the wastebasket. "Those bastards! Two can play that game!" he exclaimed. Angrily, he wondered why the political arena was always the final test of the power of a financial house. But he knew the answer, because the most profitable enterprises of the day were controlled by greedy congressional hands.

Henry Cooke listened as Senator Thurman of Massachusetts settled into his diatribe against the Northern Pacific. Thurman was an effective speaker, and unfortunately beyond reach, because the Union Pacific already had him in its pocket.

". . . and once again, we are faced with a grand profit-making scheme at the expense of the public trust," intoned Thurman. He grasped both sides of the lectern and raised his head like a pastor preaching to his flock. "In the past, Congress has done more than its share to stimulate the growth of the nation. Today, it would be unconscionable to continue a reckless dispersal of the public trust. Congress has resisted financial involvement in this ill-conceived northern enterprise, not once, not twice, but three times. And for good reason: it cannot be justified! Now, in spite of a land grant, its developers plead poverty, and unequal treatment, and they seek even more gratuitous support for their schemes. Their requests are ludicrous, scandalous, and Congress must once again say no!"

Opposition to the Northern Pacific bill came mainly from Harlan and Hemil of Iowa and from Wilson of Ohio. Henry could count on Senators Morton of Indiana, Edmunds of Vermont, Ramsey of Wisconsin, Nye of New York, and Howard of Michigan. The majority of the senate watched from the fence like buzzards waiting to pick up some tidbits once the death struggle was over. Their numbers indicated a growing distrust of railroad development schemes and significant caution about further depletion of public lands. Restraint and controls were needed, they said; restraint and controls.

The opening week was a sparring contest. Senator Harlan documented what he called the lack of financial or commercial justification for the road, but since he needed to show that he was being fair, he compared the Northern Pacific to the Union Pacific, the railroad to which everyone knew he was personally committed.

"When Congress agreed to loan the Union Pacific Company money, it was sixteen thousand dollars per mile, and the company was to make interest payments on the loans. Its officers induced us to yield the prior government lien on the road. Next, we authorized the company to put a prior mortgage on the road to the amount of sixteen thousand dollars per mile for prairie, thirty-two thousand dollars per mile for plains, and up to forty-eight thousand dollars per mile for about three hundred miles through the mountains. As if that wasn't enough, we said they did not have to pay interest on more than half of the amount from year to year. Well, gentlemen, it didn't cost the Union Pacific half of what we gave them, and now the same principles are being brought to bear on behalf of the Northern Pacific."

Mr. Ramsey of Wisconsin asked Mr. Harlan how many acres of land within his beloved state of Iowa had been granted to the railroads. Harlan responded, "I do not happen to have that figure on my tongue, sir, but I'm sure you will enlighten me."

"I will," said Ramsey. "Seven million."

"That's preposterous!" retorted Harlan. "The entire state of Iowa is only nine million. You're implying that the majority of the state is a land grant."

"I'm glad the senator sees my point," said Ramsey incisively, "and I will be pleased to show the senator the source of my figures. And now that I have the senator's ear, perhaps he will concede that financing a railroad through flat farm land is measurably different from financing a railroad through a wilderness that includes mountains, canyons, raging rivers, and thousands of wild Indians?" Ramsey's counterpoint took the sting from Harlan's words, but another week went by and the opposition still had the upper hand.

Senator Hemil attacked the third clause of the bill because it could easily be interpreted as pure greed. "Extension of this land grant is unthinkable," he whined in a high, thin voice. "It's already terribly out of proportion. The grant is enormous, beyond anything experienced in the history of this country. It will be the death blow to all railroad grants if we pass it."

Henry kept his brother advised about battle tactics on a day-to-day basis. *Senator Nye is going to quote Harlan against Harlan, and we intend to get Morton of Indiana, Edmunds of Vermont, and Sherman to make brief pointed speeches on our side and close the debate. Looks like we will reach a vote on Monday. It should be in our favor.*

Harlan had stumbled, exposing his alliance with the Union Pacific, when he blurted, "When you stimulate the construction of competing lines by unnecessary subsidies, you diminish the value of your own property."

Now, the Chair of the Pacific Railroad Committee, Senator Howard of Michigan, asked rhetorically, "Whence is the inspiration of Senator Harlan's objection to the Northern Pacific Railroad? Who tells us that the United States has such a great interest in the Union Pacific and Central Pacific railroads that such interest is likely to become damaged by the construction of a competing line, regardless of how distant it might be located?"

Howard's eyes glowed as he answered his own question. "If I am allowed to indulge in a Yankee guess, I should say that it arises from a dislike by the camp of the Union Pacific Railroad Company. Is it possible that that great corporation, which holds sixty-four million dollars in its coffers, once the property of the United States, a company whose securities are a very high figure throughout the United States, a company who owe all that they are, all that they will be, to the munificence of the government of the United States, the company possessing a road running from the Missouri River to the Pacific Ocean, the grandest enterprise ever contemplated in modern days, a company to which the world points with admiration for their enterprise, and intelligent liberality, is it possible that that company is motivated by pure envy towards the Northern Pacific to such a degree that it stands in fear that its interests will be affected by what the Honorable Senator of Iowa calls a *competing line?* A line that lies *five hundred miles* from its own route?"

The Gilded Age was a period of self-aggrandizement, and Senator Harlan was a product of his time. In 1865, a million men returned home to find that their country had been orphaned by its violent history. In place of security and stability, they found a society in the throes of change, a society that was now a western version of Renaissance Italy, vehement in politics, restless in speculation, and disdainful of former values. In addition, America was poised on the brink of radical changes in production, efficiency, and comfort.

A painting called "The winning of the West," which showed the power and reach of westward-stretching railroads, captured the romance and idealism of the times. The people's headlong rush to reach out and unite East and West was blind to all considerations save the goal, as though the continent were a gaming table tilted in its favor, to guarantee that every bet would become a fortune. The average citizen speculated on his future, and America became engulfed by greed. Entrepreneurism and government patronage formed a partnership like the plow and the mule. The carrot hung before the entrepreneur was instant wealth, wealth without thought of moral value, civic duty, or scandal.

There was, however, no stick, no discipline, so the nation's capital became a labyrinth of patronage, home to spoilsmen and robber barons. The greedy found riches in war contracts, tariffs, subsidies, and bounties; they took appropriations for speculations, and as claim-agents, they reveled in opportunities to collect and spend Federal revenue. All ethical rules were suspended, and Congress was the center of the action.

It's obvious that the Union and Central Pacific are willing to spend tremendous amounts of money to defeat us, Jay Cooke telegraphed his brother. *I cannot sell the bonds and will not do so until I have been given the authority to issue them. It's vastly more important than any other portion of the bill to me when I know the respon-*

sibility of selling the bonds rests in the double capacity of trustee and financial agent.
    Fix it!

7) Ground-breaking

The Reverend Thomas Slater stamped his feet and rubbed his hands as he approached the front of the makeshift platform in the forest clearing near the outskirts of Duluth. Behind him, just clearing the trees, the morning sun tried to make a difference against the chill of five degrees above zero, and failed.

Slater had spent nearly an hour searching for an appropriate passage to read at this opening ceremony. He knew he wouldn't find a reference to railroads in the Bible, so he concentrated on references to great projects. He finally scribbled something from a passage about Noah's ark. Contrary to the reverend's hopes, the ground-breaking ceremony was not a small event. The presence of out-of-town journalists was his second clue. His first clue had been the article in the morning paper, which gave the impression that the railroad was the second coming, rather than a simple means of increasing the efficiency of transportation.

Slater faced a crowd of two hundred people. Even a few dignitaries from St. Paul had braved the February cold to attend. Standing closest to him were some of the one hundred new employees of the railroad line, the same men who recently had cleared a path for the new tracks to connect with the Superior and Mississippi Railroad.

Reverend Slater cleared his throat, glanced at Gregory Smith, General Spaulding, and Ab Nettleton seated on the dais behind him, and realized that this was the largest crowd he might ever address. Duluth had, at best, three hundred people, of which he was lucky to get thirty in his church. But he had been General Spaulding's chaplain during the Civil War, so he'd accepted the task to solicit God's favor for this new enterprise, and had asked a minimal fee. Now he wished that he'd spent a few more minutes in search of a better passage; his reference to Noah's ark seemed inappropriate. He prayed silently that the papers and members of his congregation wouldn't say anything about his prayer.

Slater need not have worried. The front page of the *Minnesotan* the following day contained a sketch depicting General Nettleton accepting a shovel and wheelbarrow on behalf of the workers. The caption below the drawing said *Symbols of progress to be sent to Jay Cooke of Philadelphia.* The paper covered the speeches by Smith, General Spaulding, Colonel Egan, Mr. Hungerford, Mr. Nettleton, and Mr. Luce in about two paragraphs. The remainder of the column speculated on the effect the new railroad would have on the future of Duluth.

Slater was identified as the pastor who blessed the new track. His name was misspelled.

8) Organized Opposition

The reputation of those who attended the birth of the Northern Pacific Railroad came under attack. The first serious negative commentary appeared in a most unexpected place, the *London Times.* The Northern Pacific's objective to sell one hundred million dollars of bonds in Europe was referred to as a *scheme to suck millions from Europeans to aid robbers of the public trust. These activities,* said the *Times, will be strenuously resisted on all sides.* The paper hoped to *open the eyes of the Prussian government to the danger of allowing parties in America to exploit this country in their private interest without offering any guarantee as to the fulfillment of their liabilities.*

Cooke speculated that his agents in Europe had lost favor with the management of the *Times.* Then Cooke questioned whether his European manager, George Sheppard, had created enemies. Sheppard's last communiqué said that the bankers in Paris were looking at the loan with favor, but Cooke knew it took only one jealous banker to muddy the waters.

Americans were inured to inflammatory and prejudiced journalism, but a negative report in the *London Times* was a dark shadow. European investors were all too ready to listen to bad news about American enterprises. First, they had been left holding an empty sack after the Erie and Atlantic and Great Western bonds had failed.

Then the Southern Pacific fiasco had spread a pall over all American railroad enterprises because the primary figure in that case had been an American hero, John Fremont.

When Fremont lost his estates in California, he placed his remaining funds in the Memphis and El Paso, a Texas railroad venture that had been guaranteed eighteen million acres of land. Fremont wanted to extend the line from Memphis to San Diego under the name of the Southern Pacific Railroad. To underwrite the cost of construction, he offered two bond issues totaling ten million dollars.

Fremont's agent in Paris arranged for Paradis et Cie to float the bonds in Europe. In full-page ads in France's leading newspaper, *La Liberté*, Paradis et Cie portrayed Fremont's line as all but completed with three terminals in the East. It declared that the American government had subsidized the line as it had the Union and Central Pacific, and guaranteed the bonds at six percent. Every statement a blatant lie! By the time the outcries subsided, Fremont was blamed for negligence. European investors had been badly burned. To sell any subsequent American railroad bond in Europe was an uphill struggle.

Before the week was out, Cooke learned that the *Times'* report was only the first salvo of an active anti-Northern Pacific Railroad machine. The *Public Ledger* carried an article that said Philadelphia was the *center for the revival of a great enterprise to rob the public domain.* Four railroads had already been granted as much land as was contained in the states of Ohio, Indiana, Illinois, Wisconsin, and Michigan. The leaders of this latest get-rich enterprise, said the *Ledger*, were plying their trade in Europe. The *Ledger* claimed to have discovered that five million dollars' worth of gold-bearing bonds had *been divided among a ring of operators,* the proceeds of which were being devoted to the construction of a line to the Red River. The sum, said the *Ledger*, was twice as large as necessary. Two and one half million dollars would go to contractors and their confederates.

Cooke had scheduled a trip to Washington, D.C., to speak personally to President Grant and the Secretary of War. While he was there, he spoke to Henry about Child and the *Ledger*. "The attacks are personal," he said after greeting his brother. "Child owns the *Ledger*, and he's out to get me." He paused and held up a finger. "Actually, Child is only the agent; the real culprit is Drexel." Henry remained silent.

"It's a personal vendetta," said Cooke, fidgeting. "Drexel and I worked together on a few things before the war. He was friendly enough, but he wanted me to acknowledge the natural superiority of his house. It rankled him when our house became so popular from the sale of the Five-Twenties bonds. He's been waiting for a chance to get even."

George W. Child and financier Anthony Drexel of Drexel and Company bought the *Philadelphia Ledger* in 1868 and changed the name to the *Public Ledger*. Child had an excellent reputation as a publisher. Drexel's bank rivaled Jay Cooke and Co.

"I should tell President Grant that Child was a Copperhead during the war," said Cooke with an ugly expression. "He refused to allow me the usual privileges of popularizing the war loan in the columns of his paper." Cooke's hands turned into fists. "Well, if he wants to get into a punching game with me, he's picked the wrong fellow!"

Congress returned to the Northern Pacific bill in late April. Before the opposition could make new moves, Senator Pomeroy of Kansas decided it was time to close debate and vote. "The issue," he said from the podium, "is building railroads. You cannot put a finger on a railroad in the United States that did not receive some grant or bond assistance from the government. It is simply a question of having no roads at all or giving reasonable grants of land in aid to the construction.

"It is too late to stop this policy. You might as well try to fill in the Erie Canal and destroy the finest monument New York ever reared. You might as well try to tear up the rails of the Union and Central Pacific and return us to animal power to transport our goods across the country. And the policy has been successful. Look at the country, the way in which it has grown, our ability to grow or manufacture goods and move them across the country."

The Senate agreed and passed the Northern Pacific bill by a vote of forty to eleven. Mr. Wilson's proviso to limit the price of land to two dollars and fifty cents per acre was restricted to additional lands granted by the resolution. But one line in the next day's *New York Daily Tribune* editorial stuck with Henry Cooke. It said simply: *The Northern Pacific Railroad bill will not have as smooth a road in the House as it had in the Senate.*

Outside of Congress, life went on. Early the following week, a hullabaloo in the street outside of Jay Cooke and Co. caused the employees to rush to the windows. The street was jammed with Negroes singing, dancing, and laughing. Indeed, in every city, town, and hamlet across America the black population was celebrating the adoption of the Fifteenth Amendment to the Constitution. Now, if the black man wanted to, he could vote: not his woman, no woman, yet, just the man.

The cheery laughter and merrymaking of these new voters created an unusual parity between the races. Whites who gathered along the edges of the parade-filled streets were caught up in the tumult of rejoicing. A sympathetic *New York Daily Tribune* reporter who watched the procession from a street corner wrote: *At last, the children have a future, the young men with the present in their grasp, the old gray heads who to all their long, sad memories, can add this crowning joy. Banners, smiles, the dark pathos of Abraham Lincoln's face, the tender grace of his words.*

Meanwhile, Jay Cooke read that Child continued to assault his project. A *London Times* editorial said that of all the bonds seeking investors in Europe, only two were being outlawed by the Berlin Bourse, a South American bond and the one to be issued by the Northern Pacific Railroad Company. Past dishonesty in the sale of American bonds, especially those that did not have government guarantees, had caused the Bourse to advise the German people to stay clear. Cooke sat down and penned a telegram to brother Henry. *You must lose no time in getting our bill through. All of our friends must understand the vital importance of no further delay. Once passed, we will no longer be vulnerable to rotters like Child.*

Henry wrote back that the chair of the House of Representatives' Pacific Railroad Committee had run into strong opposition by Union and Central Pacific congressional associates. *Hire more lobbyists*, responded Cooke. *Make pledges in the passage of other bills; offer favorable deals on stock and bonds, bank credit. Play loose with gifts.* Congress was a force that would work against him if he did not pay and play by their rules, so he paid.

Henry's team tried to slip the bill through, but first a representative filibustered against it, then an avalanche of debilitating motions was piled against it. The opposition was well organized. When a vote for a third reading was defeated, Chairman Wheeler accepted a move to defer the bill and all amendments to the Pacific Railroad Committee. The move saved the bill from certain defeat.

Henry pulled in all the favors owed him. He learned that it was not the bill *per se* that had riled so many congressmen; it was the pressure Henry's people had used to try to ram the bill through. *We shouldn't have pushed so hard*, Henry told Jay. *Now that I know, I can take care of it.* And he did. The House passed the bill in late May by a vote of one hundred eleven to eighty-five. Cooke forces rushed the bill to President Grant to sign.

When Jay Cooke read the telegram from Henry he closed his eyes. A small smile played across his lips, then died. In perspective, it was just one more battle won in a campaign that had hardly begun.

9) Near and Far

Two days after Cooke Cooke's victory in Congress, Nathaniel Langford arrived in Philadelphia. He carried a letter of introduction from William Marshall.

Cooke had been expecting Langford. Governor Marshall had finally sent in his report on the survey he'd conducted almost a year earlier. In his accompanying note he mentioned that his brother-in-law was on his way to see President Grant. Marshall had suggested that Langford stop in and see Jay Cooke. *He's privy to some very interesting information about Montana that may help promote the railroad*, Marshall had written.

Not knowing Mr. Langford personally, Cooke asked Ab

Nettleton to send him information on the man. Within a few days, Cooke discovered that Nathaniel Langford was well educated, had shown resilience and leadership on the frontier, and was knowledgeable about the Northwest, particularly about the history and resources of Montana. Cooke was always looking for good men to promote his railroad. Perhaps a liaison could be fashioned. He made plans to take Mr. Langford to Ogontz and invited Judge Kelly, an excellent evaluator of men, to come along.

During dinner, Langford responded to his host's inquiry about the territory the railroad would have to cross to reach the Mississippi and Missouri rivers. He described the regions he had traversed, then summarized the eastern plains of the territory. "Laying track should be pretty easy east of the Rockies, Mr. Cooke. It's fairly level. If you have to cross the Yellowstone River more than once or twice, however, it might slow you down."

"I understand that the Sioux. . . ." Kelly started to say.

But Cooke interrupted because he wanted to move on. "Marshall said you had information of some special note about Montana. Is it anything that might be of value to my railroad project?"

"Very possibly. It has to do with the Upper Yellowstone," he said.

"I was just going to ask about it," said Kelly.

"I believe you were going to ask about the Yellowstone River, Congressman, not the Upper Yellowstone. The difference is significant. The Upper Yellowstone is a remote place in the Rocky Mountains. Somewhere in that complex area, a number of major rivers take their start, including the Yellowstone River. The Upper Yellowstone has been the source of mysterious reports for decades. I intend to explore the region myself this summer with a small expedition and an escort of soldiers."

"What kind of mysterious reports?" asked Cooke.

Langford placed his sterling silver knife and fork on the table and wiped his mouth with Cooke's French linen napkin. "Does the name Jim Bridger mean anything to you gentlemen?"

"Wasn't he associated with an Oregon Trail post before the war?" asked Kelly.

"Yes. Bridger had a trading post on the trail in the 1840s. The Mormons ran him out, but the Army took over the post during the Mormon Rebellion."

"Ah, yes, the little Mormon confrontation in fifty-seven and fifty-eight," said Kelly.

"Bridger and I held common interests for a period of time back in sixty-six," said Langford. "I learned that you can't do business with him without hearing some of his tall tales. He's a great storyteller with a flair for gross exaggeration. When someone once asked him how long he'd been in the Rockies, he pointed over his shoulder to a distant mountain. 'See that mountain?' he asked without looking, 'It was still a hole in the ground when I arrived.'"

Both Cooke and the judge both found that amusing.

Langford smiled indulgently. "For that reason, most people believe that Bridger's stories about the Yellowstone are pure fiction. In his stories he spoke of the Yellowstone as a realm of smoke-filled basins and bubbling hot mud pots. He said he once caught a trout in a stream in front of him, then flipped it over his head and cooked it in a pool of boiling water behind him."

Cooke and Kelly laughed heartily. Langford waited until the laughter subsided. "Last summer, several of my friends entered the Yellowstone for a look-see. Upon their return, they spoke to me in confidence about what they saw. What they claim to have experienced validates many of Bridger's tales."

Cooke appeared startled by Langford's words.

"Do you believe this balderdash?" asked Kelly.

"Put another way, I believe in my friends. They are conservative in their values and possess good reputations. It's time for me to see for myself, so I am organizing an expedition into that country this fall. General Hancock has agreed to support my expedition with soldiers from Fort Ellis. We plan to make a thorough reconnaissance. If I am right, this strange region could eventually become one of the largest attractions in the country for tourists and resort seekers. Of course, it would have to be properly accessed."

"By, perhaps, a railroad spur?" asked Kelly with a glint in his eye.

"You know that I am interested in any feature of promotional value that could tie to our railroad," said Cooke. "We may appear to be consumed with Minnesota at the moment, but it's never too soon to market the unusual, even if in the remote West. What else can you tell us about this place?"

"I can give you a pocketfull of rumors," said Langford with a chuckle. "It's best that I wait until I return. Then we'll be dealing with fact—at least more than twenty men will have seen the same thing."

Cooke clipped a cigar and signaled to a house servant to pass his private cigar box to Mr. Langford. "Gentlemen," said Cooke, "let us retire to the library and discuss the implications of this fascinating hideaway. What did you call it, Mr. Langford? The Upper Yellowstone?"

As they stood, Kelly said to Langford, "When you are prepared to discuss the exact nature of what you discover, I believe you will find an open mind in this house."

"Mr. Langford," said Cooke, wrapped in his own thoughts, "have you ever had the opportunity to speak in public?"

"What did you have in mind?" asked Langford.

Even before the ground had thawed, work began in earnest in Minnesota on the Northern Pacific Railroad. Two firms had contracts for the first two hundred thirty miles to the Red River of the North. Completion of these miles would take the railroad to the eastern boundary of the Dakota Territory.

As the first rails were laid in a line due west of Duluth, the political situation in Europe deteriorated. Suddenly the Franco-Prussian War between Napoleon III and Otto von Bismarck was a week old. In the throes of terrible uncertainty, the European Exchange became paralyzed. Every European concerned with finance distanced himself from speculative American ventures. Until Europe enjoyed more stable days, the door was shut against foreign investments, especially railroads not guaranteed by the United States government. Cooke received a cordial note from the President of Switzerland stating that most governments were reluctant to allow healthy citizens to leave until the war issue was settled.

Cooke's plans to build a European base of investment in the Northern Pacific Railroad and immigration to Minnesota faced serious problems.

BOOK II: MERGING PATHS

PART 1: MERGING PATHS

1) The Smithsonian Institution

December in Washington, D.C., was a world of grays. The cloud cover above had the hue of frozen froth, and the earth below was slush. Two weeks before Christmas of 1870, Ferdinand Hayden kicked the icy mush from his boots and climbed into a cab. He was off to the Smithsonian Institution to confer with Baird and Meek. The grinding of the cab's wheels and the rhythm of horse's hooves in the crystalline mud muffled the sounds of the city. A mile ahead, through the trees, the Smithsonian loomed like a castle. To Hayden, it was a haven in a strange and trying land.

The Smithsonian was an ungainly, russet-colored structure, whose formal brownstone facade bristled with abutments, ledges, and a series of high, narrow windows topped with arches. Its late twelfth-century architecture was variously referred to as Lombard, Romanesque, Norman, or Byzantine. But the Institution's sprawling expanse, four hundred forty-seven linear feet with east and west wings, an apse, and nine towers of differing configuration and adornment, was its own architectural archetype.

The mission of the Smithsonian Institution was to support the growth of science in the United States. Scientists involved in research and exploration beamed when they approached the building, because within its walls, they were free to speak their own tribal language and indulge in things scientific. And invariably, before each noteworthy scientist left to do battle again in an unscientific world, he left with verbal if not financial support.

The Smithsonian had been constructed through the generosity of James Smithson, an Englishman. Smithson was an illegitimate son of the Earl of Northumberland, a genealogical quirk that added color to his status as a British scientist. Although he had never even been to America, he bequeathed half a million dollars to the United States to advance the cause of science, proof that he had a profound understanding of what American scientists needed.

Congress proved less forward-looking. Politicians repeatedly refused to endorse the Englishman's bequest. When they eventually changed their minds a dozen years later, they voted that the money should go, not to a center to promote knowledge, but to construct a museum, library, and gallery of art.

The Institution's secretary, Professor Joseph Henry, referred to his charge as "the Norman Castle." He managed to steer the Institution towards Smithson's original purpose by redirecting half of the income. In time, through the efforts of the Institution and through the activities and documents produced by the men of quality it attracted and employed, Smithson's endowment significantly influenced thought and action in the nation's capital.

The Smithsonian Institution occupied a stretch of the Mall, a flat tract of land on "the island" in the southern portion of Washington, D.C. The island was created by the James Creek Canal, an old waterway that ran to the Potomac. Visitors on their way to the Institution, like Hayden, had to contend first with the fetid odor from its waste-filled waters, then with the stench from the Smithsonian's own stock pens. At least the road had been improved. When city officials saw that the Smithsonian routinely drew a large crowd to its evening lecture series, they agreed to construct a wooden bridge across the canal at Tenth Street. Nothing, however, could be done about the smell from the stock pens until the Smithsonian decided to dispose of what amounted to a small zoo.

Hayden's carriage approached the Smithsonian's north side. The entrance was tucked between two towers of unequal height and protected by a carriage porch. Hayden stepped inside the building, closed the heavy door, and watched his breath condense. Accompanied by the echo of his footsteps, he walked down the corridor in search of Assistant Secretary Spencer Baird.

Baird knew everyone and everything. If Hayden was in for some unpleasant surprise, Baird would know. If money was tight, Baird could warn him. If the political atmosphere was troublesome, Baird would know how to bypass it.

Hayden passed door after door that sealed off cavernous, high-ceilinged rooms. He knew that each contained a black potbellied stove and someone's collection of fossils, bones, or hides. At Baird's office, he knocked and entered. The immediate warmth from the stove made him feel welcome. Baird, a large, heavyset man with piercing eyes and a short, gray beard, looked up from a neat stack of papers. His eyebrows shot up and he smiled. "By God, it's Professor Ferdinand Hayden, favoring us with a visit in wintry Washington to relate, one hopes, colorful stories about his latest Western adventures. Pull up a chair, Professor."

As he gave his welcome, Spencer Baird smoothly pulled his watch from his vest and set it on the desktop. Time was precious, and before the day was done he would have to complete some chores attached to other hats he wore. A column for the *Public Ledger* needed writing, and, as the recently appointed science editor for Harper Brothers of New York, he had several articles to review.

Spencer Fullerton Baird was descended from an amalgam of French Huguenot, Welsh, and German ancestors, one of whom had helped to settle Germantown, Pennsylvania. Baird had held the chair of the Natural History Department at Dickinson College until Professor Henry hired him in 1850. Henry had welcomed Baird's endless energy, dedication, and incisive mind almost as much as he welcomed Baird's collection of natural history specimens that would have filled two railroad boxcars.

Baird received an annual salary of fifteen hundred dollars, his own office, and little else. When he discovered he would be working essentially as a Man Friday without a budget, he quietly joined in the Herculean task to build the Institution's reputation and collections. Since he believed strongly in the Smithsonian and himself, he allowed his reputation to become fused with his job. He was successful, in good part because he was able to convince congressmen to smile on appropriations that supported Smithsonian programs. Baird accomplished his fund-raising routines with an unruffled and congenial posture. His reputation was sterling, and by 1870, the Smithsonian was receiving most of what it needed.

"Well, Professor," said Baird, leaning back in his chair, "tell me, how was it out there?"

"Absolutely marvelous," said Hayden without hesitation and began to recapitulate his summer wanderings. No matter what Hayden's position in science or society, he would always be Baird's disciple. When Hayden was maturing as a geologist during the late 1850s, he had always found Baird to be a pillar of support, a source of advice, emotional encouragement, and occasionally, intervention. This was standard fare that Baird offered all young scientists who sought to make some contribution. In return, the Smithsonian received samples of fauna, flora, and minerals. Hayden had been sending fossils and specimens since 1853. Yes, it was always good to see and talk to Baird.

After Hayden wound down, Baird asked a few questions, filled Hayden in on local events and personalities, and soothed his anxieties about predatory personalities.

"What are your plans for the coming year?" asked Baird.

"Eastern Wyoming," responded Hayden, "if Mr. Wilson and Mr. Delano permit me to fulfill my destiny."

"Trust me when I say that Mr. Wilson will not interfere with you this coming year. Also, I believe you will find that Mr. Delano will continue to support your efforts in the field. After all, you have given him no reason to change course, have you?"

"Of course not," said Hayden with a worried look.

"Then relax. Have you already tended to business for next year?"

"How exactly do you mean?"

"Have you put the right politicians in your pocket?" grunted Baird. "Have you forewarned them what you plan to do next year and how much it will cost?" He raised an eyebrow. "You *have* learned what it takes to be successful in this town, have you not, Professor?"

The last thing Ferdinand Hayden wanted to think about was his need to play politics for the coming year. The frontiersman needed to know if the soil was decent for crops, where sources of

potable water were located, and how long the timber and coal might
last. Hayden held the settlers' practical needs in high esteem, and
envisioned an aggressive agenda of western exploration. Not all
congressmen sympathized with the settler's need for pragmatic information, and the Departments of the Interior and the War Department were no more dependable than the politicians who ran
them. Simply put, the scientists they employed were expendable
pawns.

Most people were delighted to savor life in the nation's capital, where they could watch social interactions, political machina-
tions, and the unfolding of an occasional scandal. Washington was
a melting pot of new blood and new money, a half-built and war-
littered southern town that offered the extremes of wealth and poverty, human comfort and suffering. But to Hayden, Washington,
D.C., was a dangerous, stressful place.

The year of 1870 marked the midpoint of the Gilded Age. It
was a get-rich period, a whirlwind for those who showed ambition,
greed, and idealism. Journalists described both the capital and its
notables as lax and corrupt. Houses of prostitution known as the
Division operated between the White House and the halls of Congress. That spring, the chief of police broke up fifteen gambling
places. After Congress adjourned, thirty closed voluntarily.

Power was the key to the city and the proven route to money.
Money, in turn, was the preferred route to reputation, and reputation was what everyone sought. Congress was the seat of power
even if some referred to it as a pig trough. Others described it as an
auction house where the majority in power and their kin were for
sale to the highest bidder. In the first two years of President Grant's
administration, the public had seen the first signs of scandal in the
Union Pacific Railroad's Credit Mobilier. "Boss" Tweed's ring of
influence and corruption in New York City's Tammany Hall was
receiving serious attention from the press. A few congressmen were
still reaping profits from the Whiskey Ring and the Indian Ring.
Most recently, it was rumored that government officials, including
the Secretary of War and White House staff, were selling military
post trader slots at frontier forts across America.

Hayden understood how the system worked. To stay one step

ahead of the competition, he had to secure important congressional support, produce eyebrow-lifting results every year, and routinely name peaks and camps after friendly senators. Hayden had started taking the sons of congressmen with him for a summer. He routinely delivered personalized copies of his reports to those whose support he needed. To date, thank God, no one had asked him to lie, steal, or cheat.

"I only arrived in town last week. I have to concentrate on finishing my report first, otherwise I will have nothing to show."

"I understand," said Baird with a sympathetic nod. "How far have you gotten?"

"I have a good beginning. My contribution may be a hundred pages. But I need to start writing as soon as I finish my business here. Speaking of which, is Meek in?"

Baird chortled. "Where else would you find him?"

As Hayden rose, Baird added, "Stop in before you leave, Professor. I have several documents I think might interest you."

Soft gray light, further diffused by dust in the air, streamed through tall, arched windows. A long, flat table dominated the room. Both the table and the floor were cluttered with bags, boxes, and stacks of fossils. A man was bent over the table, his back to the doorway. It was Hayden's slender, aging friend, Fielding Bradford Meek, engrossed in a box of specimens. Hayden could hear the rustle of packing material as the paleontologist picked up one fossil after another and grunted to himself.

"Meek?" said Hayden. No response.

Hayden rapped on the door frame. "Meek?"

This time he received a faint "Hmm?" but it was not a response he knew was meant for him.

"Meek, it's Hayden." Hayden walked to the scientist's side and waited. "Meek. Hello. How are you?"

Meek turned to him with arched eyebrows and a deeply etched face. "Oh, Hayden! Look! A most interesting collection from King."

"King? You're doing Clarence King's fossils? What for?" asked Hayden, clearly annoyed.

"Because he sent them, and they are interesting," said Meek, nonplused. "That's what I do here, Hayden. Of course, I do your fossils, but I do others as well. I keep telling you."

"Well, I need to speak to you about mine."

"Yes. I understand," said Meek, who nonetheless kept turning the fossil in his hand.

"I need you to devote this month to them. I need the analysis for my annual report. Did you get my letter?"

"Of course. You wrote yours in response to mine. Remember? I told you we needed to talk." Meek replaced the spiny brachiopod in its box, wiped his hands on his apron, then suddenly looked at Hayden. "Did you say something? My hearing's getting worse. I think I may be totally deaf in a few years."

"That's not the problem," said Hayden. He started to lead Meek toward the door, then changed his mind and sat on the corner of a table. "We don't have to go downstairs. We can talk here."

Meek nodded. He didn't like lots of people milling about anyway. He lived in the north tower of the Institution and conducted all of his work in this and adjacent rooms. Baird referred to him as a collaborator. Meek didn't care about titles; he had his work, people left him alone, and he was making a contribution. He was content. It was certainly better than pouring money down the Ohio River by running a failing retail shop, something he had done in years past.

Meek now looked into Hayden's blue eyes with no agenda other than to see how Hayden looked. He always faired well in that harsh, western climate, thought Meek. Yes, he looked healthy. Meek wished that he could say the same for himself. Now a fragile human being, his deteriorating body had become his worst enemy. His Irish lawyer father had died when Meek was three, but Meek learned that he'd inherited his father's weak eyesight and hearing problems. His condition was more than annoying; it was progressive and debilitating.

Meek listened to Hayden harp about his fossils and his needs. When he looked at Hayden it was easy to recall how they met because Hayden's appearance and demeanor hadn't changed appreciatively. Seventeen years ago, Meek had been thirty-six years old, Hayden, a brash twenty-four. Meek's employer at the time, New

York state geologist James Hall, had sent the two of them to the Upper Missouri to collect fossils from Cretaceous and Tertiary formations.

It had been a heady time of western adventure: "firsts" for both of them. They left St. Louis on May 21, 1853, and sailed up the Missouri River aboard the *Robert Campbell*, a weathered paddlewheeler refitted by the American Fur Company. It carried three hundred tons of freight and one hundred passengers.

During the first two weeks, the two were restricted to making visual surveys from the deck. The scenery consisted of alluvial bottoms and islands clothed in sycamore, cottonwood, and maple. Only at night, when the boat was tied up, could they run down the plank to collect plants and insects. When the boat approached the Great Bend where the Missouri turned west, they took off cross-country for two days. When they rejoined the paddlewheeler further upstream, they brought armfuls of invertebrate Cretaceous fossils, including the planispiral shell of the ammonite.

While Meek read and drew fossils, Hayden chatted with passengers like Alexander Culbertson, a representative of the American Fur Company who was well acquainted with the Upper Missouri basin and had provided the Smithsonian with fossils on more than one occasion. Indian Agent Alfred J. Vaughan was on his way with annuities to the Upper Missouri River tribes. He, too, had a keen interest in the fossil beds of the badlands. The well-dressed, twenty-year-old German prince, Nicholas of Nassau, however, showed little interest in natural history.

Hayden kept his distance from the military contingent under Lieutenant Donelson. In St. Louis, the two geologists with Donelson, Evans and Shumard, had made it clear that they wanted nothing to do with him or Meek. What was it they called them . . . "upstarts"? When the geologists learned that Meek and Hayden were on their way to the same region they were headed, they were affronted. The nasty exchange which ensued was Meek's and Hayden's first encounter with the scientific greed associated with the great West.

At Fort Pierre, the two teams of geologists, each with its own wagons, traveled separately toward the fossil-rich badlands some hundred miles distant. Hayden and Meek's little parade included

three carts, six horses, an assistant, a half-breed, and an inter-
preter who brought his wife. After a busy month, they boarded a
flatboat to Council Bluffs, then stepped aboard the *Robert Campbell*
once again. This time, in addition to three thousand packs of buffalo robes and furs, it carried two thousand four hundred pounds of
Meek's and Hayden's fossils.

On the downstream journey, Hayden had talked nonstop about
how he wanted to return to the West. It was his first exposure to its
wonders and mysteries.

"Meek, I think this is it for me," said Hayden. He stood on
the deck and looked West. Then he pounded the railing for emphasis.

"What is what?" asked Meek, only half listening.

"This," said Hayden with an outward gesture. "The West is
'it' for me."

"Hayden, what are you saying?"

"I'm going to spend my life out here. Meek, help me out."

"What do you want me to do? I'm going back east."

"Yes, I know, but I need a sponsor. Do you think Hall would
extend my stay?"

Meek looked skeptical.

"What about Chouteau? His Rocky Mountain Fur Company?
Maybe the Army."

"And if not, how will you survive?"

"I'll find a way." Hayden paced while he talked. "I can do it,
Meek. I can find fossils, describe the land, cover the territory. I
know I can. The West is my destiny. I can feel it."

All Meek wanted to do at the time was to get back to a stable
environment, free of human chaos and confrontation. But Hayden
had persevered and returned to the badlands. Meek intuitively
sensed that his destiny was linked with the enthusiastic explorer,
so he stayed in touch. A year later, he suggested that the two become a team. He would identify Hayden's growing collections, and
analyze the age and the paleoenvironments of the fossils.

Meek understood how different they were. On the surface,
they had little in common. Hayden's personality, talents, and envi-
ronmental preferences were antithetical to Meek's. Hayden had a

quick mind, an eye for stratigraphy, and the ability and motivation to cover large tracts of land and produce solid data in adverse terrain and climate.

Meek was the more experienced of the two, more exacting, discriminating, and patient. He had started his career in geology with Dr. David D. Owen of the Geological Survey of Iowa, Wisconsin, and Minnesota. Owen had taught him how to represent fossils and landscapes with accuracy. Meek had honed his interpretive skills while he worked with Hall.

So Meek assumed the role of counselor and instructor, and to the extent allowed by his personality and their situation, he gave Hayden unrestrained support. He knew enough to keep the reins loose because Hayden had good intuitive senses, was an excellent observer, and learned fast.

Their collaboration became one of the most productive in American natural history. Hayden's collections were superb. Meek found his own calling in the analysis and interpretation of fossil collections and their environment provided by stratigraphic information. A year into the partnership, after they had identified more than one hundred new species, Meek told Hayden that they possessed the right to classify and name the formations of the great Cretaceous and Tertiary systems. The area was larger than Great Britain.

As the Meek-Hayden collaboration grew, Meek's relationship with Hall became increasingly unstable. Meek was a maturing protégé; Hall was his egocentric and paranoiac mentor. With support from Hayden, Baird, and Professor Henry, Meek broke from Hall and moved his work place to the Smithsonian Institution.

Between 1856 and 1863 Meek and Hayden published close to three dozen field notes and reports in prominent publications like the *Proceedings of the Philadelphia Academy of Science* and the *American Journal of Science and Arts*. The two developed a standard stratigraphic section for the West and laid the foundation for future geologic understanding of the Trans-Mississippi West. And the five Cretaceous layers they named in a paper in 1861 became the standard for all geologists.

Near the end of the Civil War, the Smithsonian published Meek and Hayden's *Paleontology of the Upper Missouri*, a volume that, in one thousand illustrations, included more than three hundred fifty new species. The book was readily accepted as the most comprehensive study of regional Cretaceous fossils in existence.

Since Hayden had started his surveys, he kept urging Meek to become his paleontologist. Meek preferred his freedom to investigate the findings of other explorers, a choice he was occasionally forced to bring to Hayden's attention. Now, Hayden was explaining that his survey had grown so much that he was forced to split his time between administration and general geology. He relied heavily on specialists. He needed Meek.

"Hayden, I hear you, but you are only here once in a while. Your visits are separated by entire seasons, and I am not going to go into the field. I need to make you understand that while you are away, I am not waiting for your fossils. This year I have had to describe and prepare drawings of a full set of Cretaceous fossils sent in by Mudge."

"Mudge?" howled Hayden. "What on earth for?"

"Please don't interrupt, Hayden. I'm trying to tell you what goes on here. Then I was asked to do a preliminary examination and final report on King's fossils for his entire 40th parallel report with full descriptions and full illustrations of all new species . . . of which there are a number, I must say."

Hayden, frustrated, walked to the window and turned his back.

"The Ohio geological survey sent a group of invertebrates that needed identification," continued Meek. "Professor Stevenson from West Virginia sent in a collection of carboniferous fossils, and Baird has accepted and sent to me a slew of smaller collections from any number of unknown collectors with the caveat that I should do what I have time for."

Meek walked to where Hayden stood and leaned towards him. "Oh, yes, and I continue to work on the paleontology of the Upper Missouri monograph, which is one topic I am sure you want to talk about."

Hayden faced his colleague. "Are you mad at me, Meek?"

"Mad? Heavens, no, Hayden. I simply want you to recognize that I need more lead time than you normally give me when you rush in and expect me to drop everything and do your fossils."

"Our fossils."

"Humph. I'm not complaining, you know."

"Meek, you don't know how to complain. I only hope you can complete the study of my fossils in time for my annual report. I told you I would make things right with you. Just don't get sidetracked and leave me without a resource."

"I have examined what you sent. By January, I will have everything you need for your report. Is that what you came to hear? If so, perhaps you will tell me what's happening with the Nebraska report?"

"I'm not sure. I'm hoping that Congress will appropriate enough money to get it printed this year. Your report will be printed with all the fossils."

"That sounds rather uncertain," said Meek. He took the last two steps to the window. "It's a bit like saying it will be a nice day if it doesn't rain." And he smiled at the thought.

The cab driver pulled to a halt at the corner of Pennsylvania and Eleventh Avenue and flicked his whip at the dogs that barked at his horse. He tipped his hat to the gentleman who stepped down, checked the flow of carriage traffic, and reentered the flow of traffic.

Ferdinand Hayden crossed the sidewalk and entered the squat brick building on the corner. The directory on the lobby wall announced that the offices of Ferdinand Hayden, United States Geologist, occupied portions of the upper floors. Hayden shifted his briefcase to his left hand and climbed the stairs. Every step up was a reminder of how far he had come. Once inside his cramped offices, Hayden took a deep breath, cleared a desktop and began to organize his notes.

While he sorted documents, maps, and sketches, he ruminated about his position. Mr. Wilson of the Land Office was finally removed from his list of concerns. Baird had defused his anxiety about meeting Delano. And Emma was tucked safely away for the nonce with a promise that he would spend time with her at Christmas. He was free to write his *Preliminary Report of the United States Geological and Geographical Survey of Wyoming and Portions of Contiguous Territories.*

After several hours, Ferdinand Hayden sat back, filled with a sense of accomplishment. The lateness of the season had confined him to Wyoming, and due to limited funds he had not taken a topographer. Nevertheless, his team had covered its assigned territory well. Hayden had voluminous entries about the flora and fauna, topographic forms, character of the soil, and minerals. He had also noted the special beauties of each region.

As for the geology, Hayden had decided several years ago that his task was to present geologic form and structure not only to the scientist but to the layman. This year he planned to distinguish between ridges of elevations and those of erosion, discuss the general nature of granite mountain cores, and describe sedimentary and metamorphic formations as well as the extent of mineral resources. He would also continue the procedure Meek had established in 1857, of including sketches to show the manner in which stratigraphic formations had been laid down. These sketches made sense geologically and paleontologically; even the layman could understand them.

As for original contributions, Hayden had worked out the final sequence of the Carboniferous and Cretaceous rocks. He subdivided the Cretaceous into its Dakota, Fort Pierre, and Fox Hill groups, and could now demonstrate that near the end of the Cretaceous period the ocean had extended all over the area west of the Mississippi. He had collected several interesting fossils in South Pass and had interpreted the probable origin of the granite and gneiss between South Pass and Pacific Springs as sedimentary.

Hayden decided he would write the overview and general geology in detailed chronological sequence, following the route the survey had taken. For the layman, descriptions of what the survey team had encountered would add color to an otherwise sterile, scientific journey. His East Coast specialists would provide him with quantities of new information. He had promised each man that his report would be published as a section of the annual report. Cyrus Thomas was writing on agriculture; Meek could be counted on to cover invertebrate fossils; and Leidy had completed a report on vertebrate fossils studied from previous surveys. John S. Newberry was providing "Ancient Lakes of Western America," and Leo Lesquereux, a Swiss paleobotanist, was finishing "On the Fossil Plants of the Cretaceous and Tertiary Formations of Kansas and Nebraska." Hayden had also promised paleontologist Edward D. Cope room for three reports on vertebrate fossils. Hayden considered this arrangement both natural and fair, especially since many were working solely for the opportunity to be published.

Now, what was he going to do about illustrations? Hayden rubbed his hands and stroked his beard. Jackson would not be back in time to have woodcuts created from his prints. Blast! If he had an illustrator . . . ah, but he did! He had Henry Elliott. Hayden dashed off a quick note to ask Elliott to bring all his sketches so they could make decisions together on illustrations. Now Jackson would be free to print from the last two seasons. No small task: there were four hundred negatives from this season alone.

In the midst of his letters which queried, cajoled, and pushed, Hayden sent off a note to Anthony and Company in New York to ask assistance in making prints. And since he was planning to publish a bound set of "Camp Scenes with the U.S. Geological Survey" to personalize his western adventures, Hayden wrote to Jackson's former Omaha associate, J. F. Jarvis, who managed the largest production of stereographs in the East. Hayden then penned a note for Jackson: *Please be sure to send copies of select views to friends of the survey including representatives of the Union Pacific, Central Pacific, and the Denver/Rio Grande. And please set aside several loose prints for select members of Congress.*

Finally, Hayden began work on his report. He took a deep breath to slow himself. He forced himself to complete his thoughts before he wrote them out. His prior annual reports had drawn criticism for being carelessly organized and sloppily written. Hayden was aware of his tendency to hurry. It showed up in his speech when he got excited, and in his haste to draw conclusions before all the facts were in. But everything seemed to come at him at once.

Hayden worked steadily for the next two weeks. Two days

before Christmas, he drafted his cover letter, the final accomplishment that would set him free to depart for Philadelphia. Christmas with Emma! With a supreme effort, he pushed her once more from his mind. He began the letter as he had others in the past, by thanking everyone who had assisted him during the survey. He even mentioned the officers at Forts Sanders, Bridger, Steele, and Fetterman, and at Camp Stambaugh. Hayden was well aware that his was a government survey. To complete his tasks within budget, he had drawn heavily on the free services provided by public and private officials. To fail to recognize his supporters in the field might be to jeopardize future support.

He then commented on Jackson's outstanding contributions. His photographs *have done much to secure truthfulness in the representation of the mountain and other scenery,* wrote Hayden. *Twenty years ago, drawings were simply caricatures of leading features of an overland exploration. Mountains might be represented with angles of sixty degrees inclination with great glaciers as though modeled upon any mountain model other than the Rockies. Western sandstone mesas have been represented with all the peculiarities of a volcanic upheaval, or of massive granite or an ancient ruin with perfectly square cut joints. Photography has set the record straight.*

Leaving nothing to chance, Hayden underlined the importance of having his report published as soon as possible. *The object of these annual reports,* Hayden wrote, *is to bring before the people at as early a date as possible immediate practical results.* What good was data if it was kept secret or released only after it was needed? Detailed analysis for scientific purposes could come later, tackled by the specialists.

Having outlined his survey's accomplishments for the year, Hayden addressed the future. *Never has my faith in the grand future that awaits the entire West been so strong,* he wrote. *My earnest desire is to devote the remainder of my working days to the development of its scientific and material interest.*

In a moment of speculation, Dr. Ferdinand Hayden wondered what his chances were of returning to the field next summer. He shrugged, shook his head as though to clear it, blew out the lamp, and headed for the train station.

2) Sun Pictures

Ignoring the cold that penetrated the passenger coach of the Washington and Baltimore, Ferdinand Hayden removed his gloves. He deepened his breathing to slow his heart and pressed his teeth together to suppress a nervous quiver as he unwrapped the book in his lap. The crinkle of wrapping paper caused several passengers to glance his way. *Let them look,* he thought. *They should, anyway.* He pulled back the paper to reveal the fabric cover of the massive volume. Its title, in golden letters, made him catch his breath: *Sun Pictures of the Rocky Mountains.*

Hayden turned to the title page, which acknowledged in bold that the book was written by *Ferdinand V. Hayden, U.S. Geologist and Professor of Geology and Mineralogy in the University of Pennsylvania.* He read his name several times before seeking the familiar phrases on the first page. The text was printed in oversized type, the layout open and inviting and the font easy to read. Julius Bien, the Czechoslovakian immigrant who had become a renowned New York printer, had done his work well. Hayden closed his eyes and breathed deeply. *Yes, yes, yes!* he said silently to himself. *At last!*

"My, what a big book," said a large, smiling woman who occupied the seat next to him.

Without looking up, he replied, "Yes. It's about a very large topic, the West." *The West, indeed,* he thought. *The Missouri River Valley, the Black Hills, the Laramie Range, the Oregon Trail. My West!*

"I've been to Chicago," said the middle-aged woman proudly, displaying her knowledge of geography.

"That's nice," said Hayden abstractedly. The first one hundred fifty pages were his alone. Well, perhaps not *entirely* his alone. He had sought advice and comments from Cope and Scudder, and Leidy and Newberry had written the section on ancient lakes that took the reader to the desert of the Salt Lake. But, in essence, the book was his personal statement about the great West. He took the reader on a westward tour, across much of the country he had seen in the past seventeen years.

"I can't say that Chicago was my kind of city," continued the woman, who had been looking for an opening to talk to the interesting little man with the soft eyes and serious expression.

As Hayden turned the pages he recalled the first time he had conceived of this work. It had been Christmas Day of 1855, fifteen years ago. How slowly the pages of life turn, he mused. Hayden sat back and looked out the window while the woman next to him rambled on about her trip to see her brother and four nieces. She had liked the lake, but that was all. "It was too cold," she said. "And such wind!"

Her words and the snowy landscape that filled the window view took Hayden back to the Upper Missouri in the winter of 1855. That October he had traveled from Fort Pierre to Fort Union and then to Fort Benton on a keelboat. The weather had been so severe the river had frozen long before winter was due. The early freeze had been an omen; intense cold followed. The wind found every crevice between the logs. Hayden nearly froze his fingers when he and others had stuffed the crevices with paper and rags, and then packed snow against the outside. The memory caused him to shiver involuntarily.

"It was this time two years ago," said the woman, now leaning a little towards Hayden and trying to catch his eye. "You know, Christmas. And when it's Christmas, you want to be home, on familiar ground. Are you going home? Sir?"

The Christmas celebration at Fort Pierre meant that there were too many men in much too small a room. The odors of animal fur and wet wool mixed with sweat and the harsh smell of spirits. Everyone was embracing one another and singing in several languages. In the midst of the party, Hayden was gripped by a strong desire to add substance to an embryonic idea. He pushed his way through the throng and plunged, head down, into the frigid wind. Back in his room, he stoked the stove, took off one glove, and began a letter to Spencer Baird.

He wanted to tell Baird of his desire to create some kind of summary, an overview, a portrait, so to speak, of everything he had experienced in the Upper Missouri. Of course he couldn't express it in quite that fashion, so he asked Baird's opinion on a number of points. *I have accumulated an immense body of notes on a good many subjects,* he wrote. *I propose first, if it meets with your approbation, to write out a large octavo volume of say 300 or 400 pages, entitled 'Wanderings in the Far West or Three Years on the Missouri River and Its Tributaries.' The kind of life that I have led has given me a better chance to accumulate facts than anyone could have in merely passing through the country.* That letter had been the beginning.

"If you are headed home," continued the woman, "then perhaps this is a gift. If it is, it's a handsome one."

Hayden glanced at the woman, blinked, then returned his gaze to the book and turned a few more pages. "A gift?" said Hayden. "Yes, as a matter of fact it is."

But how did it stand up to the works of other scientists? Had he done well? Who would tell him? He had tried to anticipate and answer questions he thought his readers might have. *At the very threshold,* he had written, *it is proper that we should make some inquiry into the capacity of this great country. Who could live in this country and what would it take to survive? What value does the land have?* He had discussed rainfall, vegetation, soil, and the natural resources of the land. His portrait included everything from Indian culture to his thoughts on evolution, brought about by his fossil discoveries and Othniel Marsh's recent theory of horse evolution.

Sun Pictures incorporated Hayden's love for and state of mind about the future of the West. He had even deemed it proper to discuss the need for explorers like himself. *It is only to the geologist that this place can have any permanent attractions,* he wrote. *He can wind his way through the wonderful canyons among some of the grandest ruins of the world. Domes, spires, towers, and minarets may be seen on every side which assume a great variety of shapes when viewed in the distance. Not infrequently the rising and setting of the sun will light up these grand old ruins, the wild strange beauty reminding one of a city illuminated in the night when seen from a distant point. Many of these lofty peaks and ranges have not yet been explored, geographically or geologically, and these magnificent fields are ripe and waiting for the harvest of science. The far West is vast but the laborers are few.*

Yes, thought Hayden as he read. *I did well.*

"Oh, photographs!" exclaimed the woman who now placed her hand on one corner of the book. "May I see?"

For depth and visual emphasis, Hayden had included thirty photographs taken by the official photographer for the Union Pacific Railroad, A. J. Russell. The prints he had selected, months before he visited Jackson's studio, took his readers from Omaha to Sacramento. They gave the reader an idea of the landscape, the texture, forms, size, and distances that were unthought-of in the East. They presented the West as it was, a realm of awe and power, of openness and promise, waiting to be captured and put to use by man. As he reviewed the photos, Hayden realized that Jackson's photographs were better than Russell's. He would have to find funds to ensure that Jackson became a permanent part of his survey. His work exceeded all of his hopes. Jackson was now indispensable.

Hayden turned the pages to allow the woman to get an idea of the content, but quickly enough to minimize conversational openings. He then closed the book, stood, and tipped his hat. "Merry Christmas, Madam," he said.

At the far end of the car, Hayden found an empty bench, placed his book by the window, and rested his hand on the cover. Outside, light reflected from a quarter moon moved with the train across the snowy landscape. The scene reminded Hayden of the ravines along the Cheyenne River where he'd spent three days eating nothing but snow. It had been his own fault. At Fort Pierre, he'd come down with a severe case of cabin fever, so he decided to explore in mid-February. A few others volunteered to go with him, but when the first storm struck, they turned back. He had stayed. Now, he grunted at his former impetuosity.

He stroked the surface of *Sun Pictures*, feeling empty, as though he had just given a ground-breaking address to an empty auditorium. Of the five hundred copies of his book he had ordered printed, a third were earmarked for select members of Congress, including the new Chair of the Appropriations Committee, Congressman Henry L. Dawes of Massachusetts; the new Speaker of the House, Congressman James G. Blaine of New York; and Senators Pomeroy of Kansas and Logan and Trumbull of Illinois, all longtime supporters of his survey. Copies naturally also went to Baird, Meek, Leidy, Newberry, and other close associates.

Baird had congratulated him on his achievement. Several others, upon receipt of the book, had written their appreciation, but the majority were businesslike replies from colleagues, not family. He had no family. A wave of sadness coursed through him as he pictured his mother and father in their quarrel-ridden home in Massachusetts. He did not try to repress his memories, nor try to edit them as he had for decades. At this time of year, memories that brought pain were better than none at all.

Each time he thought of his parents, his first image was always the same. He was eleven. He had just come back from an excursion to the woods after school. His arms were full of plants and one small shrub, all of which he would add to his collection in the little garden by the house. He was putting the first plant in the ground when he heard loud, angry, and tearful voices. Two strangers spoke in sharp, authoritative voices. His mother was crying; his father was cursing.

Hayden hid by the side of the house and listened without being seen, a move he had learned to make for his own survival. Never get between quarreling adults, especially between Mother and Father when Father was angry. He had never forgotten his Mother's nagging shouts, punctuated by "Asa," and almost always followed by the sounds of slaps. On occasion, he himself had been bruised from having been in the wrong place at the wrong time. Hayden applied these lessons quickly: stay quiet, don't ask questions, disappear when you can.

The voices, one of which was his father's, receded. Hayden peeked around the corner and saw three uniformed men and his father drive off in a wagon. His father, with his hands in front of him, was shouting at the others.

Hayden ran to his mother. "Where's Father going?"

"Ferdinand! Oh, my God! You shouldn't be seeing this. Your father is going to jail. Again!"

Hayden burst into tears. "Why?"

"For using counterfeit money, damn the rot!"

"What's that? What's counter . . ." His mother looked distorted through his tears. He knew it meant something, something bad, but how bad? Bad enough to take his father away?

"Counterfeit is false money; money that is no good to pay bills. Blast his arrogance. 'Don't worry, honey. No one will ever know.'" Her mimicking voice was shrill and venomous. She bent down and looked at her oldest son. Her reproachful expression told him that he was responsible for what had happened. "He's gone for good; this time he won't come back," she spat. "And if he does, he'll find an empty house."

She turned and entered the house but her voice still reached him like a firebrand, searing and permanent. "Get packed, Ferdinand. I don't have the patience or the money to raise two kids. Your brother is the youngest. He stays. You go to your aunt's in Ohio."

Hayden chased his mother into the house, bawling. He raised his arms to her but she knocked them down. "No. The second time is the last time. Stop crying. You'll like Ohio. You'll be living on a farm. Consider yourself lucky."

Lucky, lucky, lucky, said the wheels of the train. Hayden closed his eyes as he recalled the six years at the farm in Rochester Depot, Ohio . . . six years with a loving, but overly religious aunt and stern uncle. They were not insensitive, but they were old and had no children of their own. They did not know how to let the lad know that he was valuable in his own right simply as a human being. "If you're not careful," his uncle used to say almost daily, "you'll end up like your father."

Every night for the first year, Hayden had cried himself to sleep. Somehow, because of him, his father was now in jail. Why else would his mother have sent him away in a rage? As the years passed, Hayden repressed the pain of abandonment. He earned money by tutoring younger students. It made him feel he had something to offer. He also enjoyed nature, so whenever he felt despondent about his banishment, he would take a walk in the woods. Eventually he recalled his joy in collecting and allowed himself to once again reach out into the world. The solitude of nature offered solace to his bruised soul and a world of fresh knowledge to his inquiring mind.

On his seventeenth birthday he walked the fifty miles to Oberlin College. Those who knew him were not terribly surprised. He might have been a diffident, almost subservient lad, but he could be terribly bullheaded once he set a course. Hayden had severe doubts that he would ever amount to anything, but he knew that if he did not leave the farm and try, his mind would wither, and he with it.

The train had its own rhythm that encouraged Hayden to day-dream. His memory of the farm was always followed by the one about his days at Oberlin, especially the day Curly stuck his head into his room in Tappan Hall. "Hey Ferd," he said "Guess who's got a crush on you?" His expression was Mephistophelian.

Hayden put down his Greek grammar book and looked up. His corner of the shared room resembled a vagabond's lair: one ratty chair and a rude table next to a potbellied stove. No rug. No pictures. His jacket had patches and the legs of his extra pair of pants folded atop his books, were frayed. Necessities only, save for one flower.

Hayden stretched and rubbed his hands together. They were still dirty from the day's physical labors. "Huh? Crush? Who?" He grinned uncertainly.

"That little lady you had your eye on last week. Melinda? Don't deny it. You didn't hang around long enough to get anything started, but I saw her watch you leave, then go into a huddle with two of her friends. I got the word she's waiting for you to speak to her."

"You're kidding. Why would she want me to speak to her?" Always open to possible sources of affection, Hayden's heart beat rapidly. Could it be possible?

"Ferd, my boy, don't underestimate yourself."

The next day Ferdinand saw Melinda seated on a bench not far from the playing fields and remembered his friend's words. He pulled down on his jacket and walked over to her.

She was reading and looked up when she saw him coming. She noticed that he had started to run towards her, then had thought better of it. He had slowed to his usual awkward, stooping gait.

"Hi," he sputtered. "I'm Ferdinand Hayden. I already know your name, Melissa, I mean Melinda." He shifted his books and waited.

She nodded sociably, said "Hello," then went back to her book.

"I thought that, uh, that maybe we could talk."

"About what?"

"Oh . . . I don't know . . . whatever seems . . . How about the book you're reading?"

She stood and smiled graciously, her eyes fixed behind Hayden. A well-groomed upperclassman bounded down the hill towards them.

"Hi. I've been waiting," she said to the other. They moved off. She didn't glance back.

Hayden looked at the grass. He noticed stains on his pants and splits in his boots. He kicked a stick and returned to his room. Curly and several of his friends were sitting at the foot of the steps. Curly nudged a companion as he watched Hayden approach. "Hey, Ferd, did you find Melinda?"

Hayden's expression of betrayal and remorse told his story.

Curly nudged his friend again and grinned. "I thought she was going to fall down at your feet. Must have been something you didn't say." The laughter of his friends made it obvious that Curly's comment was outrageously funny.

In his room, Hayden opened a book of poems written by Nathaniel Parker Willis. He read to himself aloud until his voice felt scratchy. Once in bed, he promised himself that one day he would be someone. He would no longer be poor. No one would make fun of him. People would look up to him, listen to him, and ask his opinion. Maybe some would love him. He had no idea then how this might happen, but it had to. He, Ferdinand Vandeveer Hayden, would make it happen. Someday. Someday.

3) Emma

Emma was the picture of Philadelphia fashion as she stood in the doorway beaming at Hayden. "Ferdinand. At last. Come in, come in."

    Philadelphia, like Washington, D.C., and New York, was a city that valued social gatherings and fashion. Christmas Eve required high-fashion dress from those who planned to attend events in the arts. Ladies of social standing in Philadelphia in 1870 wore a full-sleeved and high-necked dress that touched the ground. The style included a modified bustle, an overskirt that came to the knees, and an outer jacket with lace around the collar and fringed sleeves. The bonnet, a winter casque, remained a simple affair with at least a narrow brim and a tie with feathers and flowers. A jaunty, gypsy shape was optional. Capes, once again in fashion, were usually of black velvet or fur.

    Emma's green silk dress was trimmed with crimson silk and dark brown fur. Her hair, arranged in the latest style, fell in folds to her shoulders. She was breathtaking. For one of the few times in his life, Ferdinand was speechless.

    Emma's eyes danced. She reached out and squeezed his hand before she took his hat. When they stood close together, the two were almost equal in height. Hayden could look directly at Emma's round face and full smile, the kind of smile that lifted her cheeks. She was a well-proportioned woman with a larger-than-average frame. He was about to whisper something to her when Emma's father, Edmund D. Woodruff, welcomed him with a handshake, a smile, and a "*Guten Abend* and Merry Christmas, Dr. Hayden."

    Mr. Woodruff was a punctilious hatter who ran a most successful shop. Emma had worked for her father since her days in high school, and had told Hayden all about the business. Since that time Hayden had visited the shop on more than one occasion, mainly to see Emma, although she once cajoled him into buying a very good bowler, and was forced to admit that her appraisal of her father's touch with customers had not been inflated.

    Emma led Hayden into the drawing room, where the rest of the family was gathered. Emma's mother, Elizabeth Woodruff, offered a hand and blessings for a peaceful Christmas season. Hayden thanked her and shook hands with Emma's cousin, Matilda, a girl with whom Emma shared an apartment in town. He then said hello to Emma's older brothers, Edmund, Jacob, and Thomas. Everyone was home for Christmas. It was a close-knit family.

Early in their relationship, Emma had confided to Hayden that as the only daughter, she was the family pet. "I have been working in my father's shop as a salesclerk since I left high school," she told him, "and have enjoyed a freer life than most women of my age. Perhaps I am more independent. I believe I am as close to my family and equally proud of my German heritage." She had smiled boldly and asked, "Do you disapprove of a spoiled but ambitious woman?"

The eight Woodruff families of Philadelphia were all related. Emma's father, Edmund, had married when he was twenty years old, but his first wife died after the birth of their second son, Jacob. Soon after, he married Elizabeth, so there was only eight years' difference between the oldest and youngest children. Edmund provided well for his family. They had a spacious house in a decent part of town and servants for their needs. An Irish girl named Eliza had cared for Emma until she was ten. Rosanna, who was serving eggnog to everyone, made the kitchen smell heavenly with her cooking.

Both girls were taken by Ferdinand, thought Emma. She knew Rosanna was impressed; she had recognized his name. "And is not Herr Ferdinand Hayden, like myself and all of your family, a German name?" she had said proudly. "And, he is a *Doktor* as well. And so dignified."

Mr. Woodruff waited until Hayden had sipped his drink. "So," he said with a smile, "over dinner we are prepared for you to take us on another journey, Dr. Hayden. Where will you take us this time? Emma said you have been in the Wyoming Territory. I must confess, I do not know where that is. America is such a large country. Are there Indians and bears there?"

"There are Indians and bears in all the territories, are there not, Dr. Hayden?" asked twenty-six-year-old Thomas, the youngest brother.

"I have seen and avoided encounters with a number of two- and four-legged adversaries on the plains and in the mountains, so I suspect you are right," said Hayden, smiling. "However, all Indians are not adversaries. I had an opportunity to study the habits and language of several tribes in the Upper Missouri in the late 1850s. I tried to preserve as much information as possible and was fortunate enough to have my records published."

"Yes, yes, I recall you having said so earlier," said Mr. Woodruff, "but we must hear about this year's . . . survey you call it, no?"

"Father," said Emma, quietly, but with a firmness of tone, "why don't we wait until dinner. Let's give Professor Hayden an opportunity to catch his breath. He doesn't have to entertain us all the time."

"No, no, of course not. Forgive me," said Mr. Woodruff.

"You lead such an exciting life, Professor Hayden," said Mrs. Woodruff. "And you are doing so much to help settle the West. Our curiosity gets the better of our manners on occasion."

The Woodruff home had become a second home for Hayden. Emma's family never failed to make him feel welcome. And his visits provided an unusual and interesting change for them because of Hayden's profession. He understood this. Besides, when he was relaxed, he loved to talk about his work, so Emma's family was often the first to hear the highlights of his latest adventures.

Jacob began to ask Hayden a question. Mrs. Woodruff shushed him. Hayden held up a hand, an unconscious gesture he often used in camp to ask for silence. "It has been a full and successful year. And I have never been known as a reluctant speaker. But first . . ."

He leaned down and lifted the package he had brought with him. He held it out to Mrs. Woodruff with both hands. "By the time Emma and I leave for the theater this evening you will have heard enough of the West. If you have any questions after I leave, this may help; it's a little Christmas offering for the family. Careful," he added. "It's quite heavy." He winked at Emma as he sat back in his chair.

The family gathered around while Mrs. Woodruff unwrapped the copy of *Sun Pictures*. When she saw it had been written by Emma's guest, she involuntarily offered a gentle "Oh, my dear." Mrs. Woodruff most thoroughly approved of this Professor Hayden. He was considerate and consistent. The fidelity of his visits told her of his deep interest in Emma, and Emma appeared to be highly

attracted to him. For an eligible woman of good family who had
reached the age of twenty-four, a man like Dr. Hayden was a prize.

Mr. Woodruff stepped forward and picked the book up from
his wife's lap. "Such a book! This is about what you do? Exploring
the West?" Before Hayden could explain further, Mr. Woodruff
leaned forward and shook his hand vigorously. "You do us great
honor, Professor Hayden. Great honor." He then encouraged his
family to proceed into the dining room. "Come; we can talk more
while we eat. I'm hungry."

Hayden waited for Emma. When everyone had disappeared
around the corner, Emma went to his side. They kissed quickly
and gently. "You are so sweet," said Emma, holding on to his arm.
"My father will now be impossible to work with. He'll take your
book to the shop and everyone in Philadelphia will see it . . . after
they learn that you gave him a copy." She smiled and tugged him
towards the dining room. The Woodruffs were waiting for them,
like family.

Hayden broke the monotony of the return trip to Washington,
D.C., by reading letters from Sanford Gifford and Anton Schonborn.
Gifford thanked him for his New Year's present. He was glad to
hear that Hayden's "Camp Scenes" plans appeared so successful
and related that he had recently seen Jackson, who would arrive in
D.C., early in January. *You two need to come to New York*, wrote
Gifford. *We'll have a bachelor's dinner and night on the town.*

Hayden smiled at the thought, but as soon as his mind was
free, it drifted back to Emma and their evening together. Would he
ever have the courage to tell her how he felt? Did he dare picture
her in his life for more than fleeting moments? What could he offer
her? Unable to answer his question, he opened Anton Schonborn's
note. It had been written from Fort D. A. Russell. Yes, he had received Hayden's recent letter asking him if he could break free in
the spring and accompany him as topographer on his next survey.
*General Perry wants me to survey Camp Brown and Camp
Stambaugh,* he wrote, *but I might be able to get away for the survey
nonetheless.* Hayden needed a topographer and he wanted

Schonborn. The man was capable. He just needed a fair chance. Thoughts about the survey made him think about what he had to do when he got back to Washington.

The first order of business would be to finalize his annual report and its cover letter. When Jackson and Stevenson arrived back from Denver, he would offer Jackson a permanent position with the survey. He could afford one hundred fifty dollars per month. He hoped it would be enough. Then he needed to catch up on his correspondence, a thought that reminded him that there should be new letterhead waiting, letterhead that said *Professor Ferdinand Hayden, United States Geologist.*

Hayden reached into his inner jacket pocket where he normally kept a sheet of blank paper. But the document he pulled out was an envelope Baird handed him just before he left the Smithsonian. In the excitement of his book and seeing Emma, he'd forgotten about it. Baird had written a brief note and attached it to several newspaper clippings. The note didn't make much sense by itself, so Hayden read the articles. The first, dated October 14, was from page four of the *New York Times.* The heading read "The Yellowstone Expedition." Hayden came fully awake. He unfolded the column-length article and began to read the editorial which preceded it.

Perhaps the most graphic and effective description of scenery comes from those who are unconsciously eloquent by force of simplicity. The following record of the Yellowstone Exploration is distinguished by this unpretending eloquence. It is a fragmentary account but it reads like a child's fairy tale. We mean no disparagement to the Surveyor-General of Montana in saying this. No unstudied description we have read of the internal scenery of the continent surpasses his notes. The country described had much to his advantage, but to his credit he performed the task unpretendingly and avoided the temptation of the tourist.

Hayden's eyes raced across the article. A fascinating account! He strained his eyes against poor light to scan it a second time. Still in a hurry, he unfolded the second notice. It was an announcement from the *Washington Star.* Ah, a lecture by the Honorable Nathaniel P. Langford on his journey to the Yellowstone. Thursday evening, January 19, Lincoln Hall. *Describing a trip during the past season to a hitherto unexplored region at the headwaters of the Yellowstone, including discoveries of cataracts many hundred feet high, active volcanoes, fountains of boiling water 200 feet high, and many other features of scenery, interesting and striking in the highest degree.*

Now Baird's scribble made sense: *A number of us from the Smithsonian are going. Think you should plan to attend.* As Hayden stared at the note, his mind raced into the future to trace a hundred options. The Yellowstone! Finally! But all at once, he lost all of his enthusiasm. A wave of disappointment, envy, and deep-set panic replaced the momentary euphoria. He knew that he should be giving the lecture. He was the one who had made the vow so many years ago to reach and explore the Yellowstone. Who was this Langford?

The answer was obvious to him. Langford was the man who hadn't dallied. Wasn't that always the way? He had turned his back for a moment, and someone had cut in front of him. His apparent loss turned to anger and his anger to self-doubt. Had his resolution in the Wind River Mountains ten years ago been a simple boast, something to satisfy young Stevenson's ears and his own ego? No! No! No! He'd simply allowed himself to become overwhelmed by his survey. He'd unwittingly boxed himself in with the urgency of the moment, the need to cope with today and tomorrow.

Someday I will . . . Hayden repeated his vow. By God, he had all but forgotten. Now it was too late. Langford had beaten him. There were no second chances in this world. Were there? Maybe . . . if . . . perhaps . . . Hayden's mind leaped from one scenario to another. Sleep was impossible. He held the articles in one hand and rubbed his stiff neck with the other.

4) Hard Choices

"When I'm forced to think about more than one thing at a time, I get a stiff neck, damn it," said Samuel Wilkeson sharply. The secretary of the Northern Pacific Railroad Company looked down the table, past all the faces that looked back. Pitt and Henry

Cooke, William Moorhead, and Gregory Smith of his board of directors sat on one side; he, Harris Fahnestock, and Milnor Roberts occupied the other. Jay Cooke was seated at one end; Ab Nettleton at the other.

Wilkeson avoided direct eye contact with Nettleton. The man was impossible. If things didn't improve in the New York office, he and the "General" would have to have it out. Either that, or Jay Cooke was going to have to make a decision about who would run the office.

"All right, let's take one topic at a time," said Harris Fahnestock. "We can talk about how one situation influences another without getting tangled up, can't we?"

"What's the difference?" said Pitt Cooke. "It's all about money, anyway."

"Pitt, for heaven's sake," said Henry Cooke, visibly irritated. "The decisions we make here aren't just about money. We're talking about our future."

Pitt shrugged.

Jay Cooke had scheduled the mid-January meeting in the hope that new light could be shed on old problems. Instead, the meeting was going nowhere. He tapped on the table. "My friends, please. Let us try our best not to bicker. This is a business meeting. If you want to contribute, either as a partner or as a member of the family, please do so constructively. Otherwise, we will waste all of our time and nothing will be resolved." He leaned back and took a drink of water.

"We are all under pressure," he resumed, "and the situation is far from ideal. Granted. Just remember, we have been through worse conditions before. We have faced and overcome equally difficult challenges. If we put our effort into what can be done instead of dissecting that which cannot be saved, we will be that much further ahead. We will also continue to enjoy our work, something I cannot say I see much evidence of in this room." Silence supported his observation.

Gregory Smith looked at his watch. "Then why don't we finish talking about the European situation. Frankly, I don't see how we can discuss revising our approach to our financial goals unless we agree on a prognosis for Europe."

"I fully agree," said Fahnestock. "It's time to set a value to what we believe will happen overseas in the next six months. We haven't done very well with our forecasting to date."

"Come on, Fahnestock," said Henry, still exasperated. "Who could have forecast the Franco-Prussian War? Without it, we'd see good results from our European sales efforts."

"I doubt that," said Fahnestock. "I have never believed that Europe would produce a tenth of what we needed in bond sales, and I will tell you why. From the outset we have been on the defensive in Europe. We have been forced to spend energy and money dealing with extenuating circumstances. I'm not only referring to the war, which has consumed Europe's attention since July, but to Child, the bad press, and the rumor and innuendo that have a stranglehold on Europe's bankers and investors."

"Trust me, Harris, even under favorable conditions, you'd never get a tenth of what we needed from Europe," said William Moorhead hotly. "That has been clear to me all along. And my conclusions agree with those of our London director, Mr. Sergeant."

Ab Nettleton had to bite his tongue. If Jay Cooke had asked him his opinion before the meeting, he would have suggested leaving William Moorhead, brother Pitt, and Wilkeson out of the conference. They were antagonistic towards one another and they showed poor judgment in making decisions. All they did was complain and backbite. That made them liabilities. But Nettleton wasn't being paid to give that kind of advice. And he knew that Cooke was too much of an egalitarian to ignore the input of his relatives, especially those who were also business partners.

Nettleton looked at the men around the table who represented the core of the Northern Pacific Railroad effort. The Minnesota and Vermont players had been left out on purpose; they'd quickly demonstrated that they would gut the railroad to line their pockets. Nettleton had sniffed the first whiff of duplicity last February during the ground-breaking ceremonies. The deep pocket grafters were in by dint of money, blood, or political position; they had nothing to lose and everything to gain. A number had given themselves away with unctuous phrases and winks in his direction, showing their belief that everyone was on the take.

"Until October last," continued Fahnestock, "we had good reason to believe that Budge, Schiff and Company would spread our bonds throughout the European investment scene. They were going to divide up the continent. We believed that everyone, like ourselves, was in the project for the long range. However, our financial needs were immediate, so we asked for one million dollars per month up front. Brokers and bankers did not appear to have a problem with that condition until the war broke out. They then postponed their commitments and asked for extensions on the contract.

"In the meantime, the railroad is under way. We need funds to maintain progress. We cut our European goal to fifteen million by the first of last July." He grimaced. "The prospect of reaching that goal is dim. Peace in Europe remains impossible to predict. Even if we granted Budge an extension, there is no certainty he would negotiate the bonds in time. The situation has forced us to seek other arrangements to sell bonds in Europe."

Gregory Smith looked down the table at Jay Cooke. "Jay, George Sergeant told me that the problem in Europe has more to do with commissions and perks than the war. We began negotiations with Bishoffstein and we thought we were making progress. Then Bishoffstein backed away. Why? Because of our requirement for cash in advance. I believe that with an extension, Bishoffstein will come in. It's really a matter of commissions."

"It's difficult to negotiate bonds when there are political problems," Cooke agreed. "Experience has shown us that the most money is made when times are peaceful and prosperous."

Fahnestock spread his hands. "All right. Conclusions. In the European investment climate we find fear from the war, distrust of American enterprises, lack of understanding about why it costs so much to lay track in America, and greed on the part of bond houses. My best guess is that regardless of how well we play it, our chances of placing the bonds in Europe are slim. As Mr. Moorhead said, probably no more than one-tenth of the money we need can be raised anywhere in Europe. In the meantime, our expenses continue to approach one million dollars per month."

In the ensuing silence, everyone turned to Jay Cooke, the bond salesman extraordinaire. "We started selling bonds in America the first of the year," said Cooke, "as most of you know. The bond certificates are legal and airtight. Fahnestock made sure they were properly worded and printed on time. At the moment, we're selling them at par."

"Won't that have to change?" asked Henry. "Union Pacific was quoted this morning at seventy-seven to eighty, and other bonds with seven percent interest can be purchased at eighty-five."

"We're not changing anything at the moment," said Cooke stubbornly. "We can't afford to."

"Unfortunately," added Nettleton, drawing attention to his end of the table, "the American market is resisting railroad bond sales, and for the first time, we're seeing a steady demand by buyers for documents they can scrutinize before they purchase. Our sales agents tell us that when they offer a bond to be sold on consignment, the bank wants the documents in hand to examine. The prospectus used to be good enough, but the new practice started by Fisk and Hatch for the Union Pacific has caught on."

Looking for relief from the tense atmosphere, Jay Cooke turned to J. Milnor Roberts. "Milnor, tell us where we are in our tracklaying."

Roberts stood. "As you know, sir, I'm standing in for chief engineer Johnson. I hope you will make allowances." He smiled, but for the first time in his association with Cooke and Co., he was having doubts about the project. He had never seen Cooke so throttled for energy. The man was emotionally wrung out.

"Mr. Roberts," said Cooke softly, "everyone knows full well your capabilities. Please feel free to speak as the chief engineer."

"Well, thank you. At the moment, we have sixteen hundred men at work on the line in Minnesota. Thirty-five miles of track have been laid and one hundred graded. I expect we will begin to lay track on the West Coast by March first. I was out there with Judge Rice to get things started. Rice is still there to hire two thousand Chinese from San Francisco. You may know that we've chosen Kalama as the western terminus. It's on the Columbia River and can be reached by boat. There's a lot of speculation going on now in land prices and negotiating over the construction of stores and homes. About twenty-five houses and six stores have been built, and it looks as though more than two hundred town lots will be changing hands at an average price of five hundred per lot."

"How much are we spending per mile right now?" asked Cooke.

"About thirty thousand. That includes clearing, grading, bridges, cross ties, and laid track. They are contracted prices."

"What problems do we face in construction?" asked Fahnestock.

"Weather, morale, supplies. Nothing unusual. We'll get to the Red River by July as planned."

On that reassuring note, the group broke for lunch. Downstairs, Roberts unwittingly caught a glimpse of a note Cooke had left on the hall table. It was written across an offer from the National Gallery of American Landscape. The gallery was offering subscribers ten by fourteen artists' proofs by Kensett, Whittridge, Gignoux, Hill, Innes, Beard, and Momberger at one hundred dollars apiece. Jay Cooke's note, meant for his wife, said *Pick five.* Roberts returned to the conference room with a slightly better understanding of what it meant to have money. He also decided that the operation was far from going broke.

"I'm turning the meeting over to Ab Nettleton," said Cooke when the meeting resumed. "He is now in charge of advertising and publicity for the Northern Pacific Railroad project. I have utmost confidence in Mr. Nettleton's abilities as a writer, an editor, and a manager."

Cooke and Nettleton had met at a political function in Sandusky, Ohio, five years ago. Nettleton was patriotic and enthusiastic, to all appearances an observant and unaffected man. He spoke with knowledge of politics and finance, and he stated his opinions without editorializing. The two men liked one another instantly. Two years later, Cooke asked Nettleton to come to Philadelphia as his assistant. "I need someone I don't have to watch all the time," said Cooke. "Henry serves the family best in Washington, and Pitt . . . well, Pitt is better off in New York. I have good people at the office, but they lack imagination. I need someone who can grasp the larger concepts, someone who knows how to convey meaning through conversation and in writing. Someone who knows people and will tell me what they think. Please say you'll come. I'll make it worth your while."

Nettleton proceeded to sketch the marketing plans he wanted to implement in the coming year. Many of the ideas had originated with Jay Cooke, but Nettleton was responsible for their success or failure. "First let me tell you about the organization that will deal with the sale and colonization of the land. We're establishing a national land office in the States and a coordinating headquarters in Europe. We plan a number of land offices in Germany, Holland, and the Scandinavian countries. We will solicit and secure assistance from foreign ministers, the press, bankers, and consuls. Your suggestions for able men to run these offices will be appreciated."

"How can we sell land before we have any to sell?" asked Pitt.

"Fair question. As each twenty-five-mile section of railroad is completed, the land will be surveyed and plotted. We can speed up the necessary approval by government inspectors. The land is there. Our main concern is not in making it available, that will take care of itself; our main concern is to have a program that will generate a high level of interest in emigration. We will offer liberal credit terms and persuade buyers to send a representative here to select the land. Each land office will have model houses that cost from two hundred to one thousand dollars. The railroad will build them in lumber country in Minnesota. Each house can be partly assembled, transported to the site, and put up in one day. We also intend to ensure that the journey of our immigrants is pleasant, safe, and speedy. An agent will accompany each group to ensure that the settlers are properly assisted."

"Sounds complex and expensive," said Henry.

"It is," agreed Nettleton, "but we have a lot of competition for immigrants." Since Henry had mentioned money, Nettleton shifted to the advertising campaign they had initiated at the beginning of the year. "We're spending large amounts on print advertising because we believe that will do the trick. We've had to hire editors in New York, produce pamphlets, and of course, lubricate the journalists." He didn't go into the details of how much had been spent on cases of wine, rented carriages and suites, and travel arrangements as well as the printed matter.

"Keene in New York has been able to draft a number of traveling agents for us. They are expensive because of commissions, travel expenses, and so forth, but they are necessary if we are going to get the word to the public."

"I thought you already had a series of lecturers on board," said Moorhead. "Aren't they selling bonds as well?" He was positive that Nettleton and Cooke had spent a large sum underwriting well-known speakers to push the railroad concept.

"Lecturers prepare the people for sales; salesmen sell the bonds," said Nettleton. Nettleton wished they had more lecturers. "C. C." Coffin had created a standard lecture called the "Seat of Empire." For the next few months he would be giving his talk to a different group in New England every week. They also had vice president Schuyler Colfax from time to time, ex-governor Walsh of Montana, and Washington, D.C.'s Recorder of Deeds, who was good in Chicago because he spoke fluent German.

"The advertising budget will remain large for the next six months. I will only admit that to date the results have been disappointing."

Pitt unleashed his frustration into the smoke-filled room. "I really don't understand our problem. In 1865, we sold bonds by the millions, far beyond everyone's predictions."

"This is not 1865," said Moorhead with irritation. "The war's been over for five years and the railroad is not a patriotic enterprise."

"And back then we had Chase in the Treasury Department, not Boutwell," added Henry.

Pitt looked askance at his brother. "So what?"

"Under Chase, our house had a government contract, a virtual monopoly. We worked for what we earned, but every effort was a paying one. Boutwell has removed all the advantages we had in government bonds. On top of that, he nearly ruined the sale of any kind of railroad bonds last November with his temper tantrum."

When Pitt appeared not to understand Henry's message,

Henry plunged on, more irritated than before. "You don't remember his announcement that the Union Pacific Railroad Company owed the government two and one-half million in interest? That he wanted payment then and there? What happened after that, Pitt?"

"The Union Pacific stock, bonds and land grant immediately lost more than half of their market value," inserted Fahnestock dryly.

"Thank you," said Henry.

"Oh," said Pitt.

"He rescinded his demand," added Henry, "but now we have conflicting stories about the Union Pacific. People are talking about corruption at high levels. No one wants railroad bonds."

Nettleton took back control of the meeting. "In spite of the problems others are causing for us, we believe a strong, steady advertising campaign that highlights the name of Jay Cooke and Co. will pay off. We simply have to persevere until the market becomes more accommodating."

On the train to Minnesota, Roberts wrote in his journal of the lack of progress in the face of complex and tenacious problems. No one at the meeting had asked his opinion or solicited his ideas. He had not felt free to add extemporaneous remarks, regardless of their accuracy, to an enterprise that was essentially a family affair.

That did not stop him from drawing his own conclusions. Clearly, the lines of organizational responsibility were poorly drawn and most assignments handed out much too informally. The main action was in New York and Minnesota, yet the "switchyard" for organizational decisions was in Philadelphia. Why did everything have to go through Cooke's hands?

To Roberts, it was clear that the officers of the Northern Pacific Railroad had set up Jay Cooke as an unending source of funds. They were milking him as fast as they could because Cooke didn't have enough direct authority to stop them. He had far too many issues that he was trying to solve at once. Roberts had seen Cooke trying to order materials, solve personnel problems, run a banking establishment, and sell bonds to fund the new line, all at the same time. He was also establishing another branch of his company in Duluth.

In the meantime, the tide of the whole business was turning against him. Recent editions of the *Minnesotan* had carried articles about corruption in the Northern Pacific Railroad. Roberts knew that congressmen opposed to the new line could easily use such articles to justify inquiring into waste and corruption of government aid.

More disturbing to Roberts was Cooke's lethargy. Roberts had known Jay Cooke as a man of infinite enthusiasm who drew others into his plans, leading the way and rolling over doubts and roadblocks with élan. But for the past three days, Roberts had seen a man who appeared uncertain that he could control what he'd created. Cooke's entire history spoke of success; now, in contrast to years of incredible accomplishment, he seemed stymied by a series of business setbacks.

What was it Roberts had overheard Jay Cooke telling his brother Henry just before everyone left? "I would not undertake again such a job for all the money in the world."

In his office, Jay Cooke stood before the display of the Five-Twenties and wondered what special factor had underwritten his success selling them. His mood brought to mind Henry's comment about "changing times." Cooke believed that Henry had been right: times had changed and so had the mood of the people. Even though agents for the Northern Pacific Railroad bonds flooded the American market with advertising, and special commissioned agents probed the financial institutions of Europe, the initial results were pitiful. Money flowed out, little came in. And in the meantime, Gregory Smith and his associates in Minnesota were spending money as though it issued from an aquifer. Maybe Ab Nettleton would come up with something. He had placed everything he knew into play, but the results he sought weren't even on the horizon. He needed something new, something different.

Jay Cooke reread the telegram he'd been holding. Henry had returned to Washington and sent the telegram the same day. Jay was certain his brother had sent him the message to lift his mood. It read: *Good news. Langford of Montana has returned from his adventures into the Yellowstone. He's scheduled for a lecture here in town on the nineteenth. I plan to attend.*

All momentous events have small beginnings, and they needed a momentous event. Jay Cooke believed that a place like the Yellowstone might easily become a prominent part of their advertising campaign. It would draw the public eye to the Northwest. He wrote on the telegram, "Keep me informed of the public's reaction to the Yellowstone," then marked it to be sent to Ab Nettleton in New York.

5) Langford on the Yellowstone

On Thursday, January 19, 1871 Lincoln Hall was packed. The placard on the tripod in the vestibule announced that the Honorable Nathaniel P. Langford of Montana Territory would speak on a recent exploration to the Yellowstone.

Among the masses who scrambled for the few remaining seats in the lecture hall were members of the White House staff, congressmen, a few prominent businessmen, several well-known adventurers, leading scientists from the Smithsonian Institution, and more than the ordinary number of journalists.

The topic, more than the speaker, had drawn the crowd. The eyes of the country remained firmly fixed upon the great West, that expanse of golden sunset which offered romance, adventure, hope, and wealth. The war was a five-year-old memory and the rails of the Union Pacific had tied the shores of the continent together for the better part of a year. More than one hundred military posts peppered regions of the West that a scant decade before had been blank spots on the map. Westward emigration was at its highest point in decades. The country was expanding at a tremendous rate. The West *was* the future!

The American public had savored tidbits from the unusual menu of the West since Lewis and Clark had returned from their trek to the Pacific. In addition to an occasional artist's rendering, the government had printed the highly illustrated Railroad Survey

Reports and reports by the U.S. Army Corps of Topographic Engineers. Rumors of unusual and magnificent discoveries in remote, almost unknown places continued to surface. Most recently, the letters by Captain Sam Adams to Congress added excitement to the air. Adams claimed that the Colorado River was freely navigable for six hundred miles, that pure metals extended up its canyon walls, and that oil floated in its streams.

Once the public heard of Powell's 1869 trip down the canyon, Adams's hyperbole would be exposed, but until that happened, Americans could point to recent gold strikes in California, Montana, and Nevada, and refer to the photographs of the valley of the Yosemite and the redwoods. Who knew the truth? Too much of the West remained unexplored. Anything was still possible.

Now here was Mr. Langford of Montana to shed firsthand light on the discoveries of the Washburn Expedition. Newspaper accounts of the journey had reached Denver, Cleveland, Chicago, New York, Boston, and Washington, D.C. General Washburn's accounts had created such excitement that the New York papers reported the government and the Smithsonian Institution would undertake a scientific investigation of the region in the near future.

In Lincoln Hall, good-natured jostling and last minute greetings subsided. Ferdinand Hayden, Spencer Baird, and Henry Elliott took their seats as the house gaslights were momentarily dimmed. When they were brought back to full light, the new speaker of the House of Representatives, James G. Blaine, appeared on the podium. The popular politician drew enthusiastic applause from the crowd.

Blaine acknowledged his warm reception with a bow. "This evening," he said, "you are most fortunate, because I am going to listen, not speak." The audience laughed heartily.

"Instead," he said, "we are fortunate to have the Honorable Nathaniel P. Langford, a prominent and respected banker and politician of the Montana Territory, who will speak to us about the amazing phenomena that he and other members of the Washburn Expedition witnessed during their journey to a region known as the headwaters of the Yellowstone."

Blaine had agreed to introduce Langford for two reasons:

Langford had approached him with a letter of introduction from John Blaine, the speaker's brother, who had replaced General Washburn as Surveyor-General of the Montana Territory; Blaine had also received a letter from Ab Nettleton in New York, who asked if he would extend himself on behalf of Mr. Jay Cooke to pave the way for the unknown Mr. Langford. The speaker of the house already owed Cooke several debts, some more intangible than others, so he was pleased to help Mr. Langford get off to a good first showing in the capital.

Nathaniel Langford walked on stage, shook Blaine's hand, and took the speaker's stand. He looked into the audience with clear eyes and a broad smile. "Good evening, ladies and gentlemen. To-night, I am here to say that I have seen the elephant!"

The crowd roared its approval. This popular phrase which Langford had selected to open his lecture augured well for an evening of quality entertainment. Assuming correctly that few people in the audience had ventured beyond the Alleghenies, Langford first provided a brief history of the exploration of the Northern Rockies, including the Montana Territory and the Yellowstone region. He dwelled momentarily on Captain Raynolds's 1859-60 attempt to enter the Yellowstone from the south. His failure led to a nice plug for the Montana Territory, because, to date, the only known access into the Yellowstone was the route taken by the Washburn team.

At a cultured but lively pace, Langford described the rumors surrounding the Yellowstone, then talked briefly about the composition of the Washburn Expedition. "In addition to eighteen hardy frontiersmen," he said, "our numbers included a valiant military escort, two unbleached Americans of African birth who kept the kitchen smelling good, and twelve pack animals who carried the gear."

After describing the Yellowstone River's course as one marked by an unending line of willow, he dramatically described the configuration of "Devil's Slide." Langford then took his audience up Mount Washburn, describing in sensory detail the perpetual snow, often twenty feet deep, that coated the sides of the peak. "The valley, which gave the impression of being the size of New Hampshire, appeared as a singular depression, an unsurpassed glimpse of nature. For the first time we saw before us a wild and primitive haven of beasts and Indians. So virginal was this land that we speculated we might find the undisturbed footprints of early trappers. Nowhere else in our country is one able to witness such variety of landscapes as that presented by the glowing peaks of the Yellowstone."

He moved on to Tower Falls. "We were riding parallel to a lively creek that poured its water into the Yellowstone River," he said casually, "when suddenly it dropped more than one hundred feet into a dark canyon. About the head of the precipitate cliff were curious and fantastic shapes carved from solid rock. The material was shale, capped with slate, beautifully rounded and polished, and the shapes were faultless in symmetry. Some resembled towers, others the spires of churches, and others still shot up as lithe and slender as the minarets of a mosque or steeples, rising thirty to sixty feet above the falls. In the moonlight, they reminded one of the portal of the fabled *genii* standing ready to hurl adventurous mortals into the gorge below, which was enveloped by the shadows of the night in impenetrable darkness."

The audience applauded not only the romance and mystery of the scene, but the bravery of the men who had ventured into such a land. Langford then took his listeners to the very edge of the Lower Falls of the Yellowstone River canyon, which he touted as "one of the most remarkable of the world: fifty miles long and one to five thousand feet deep. The brain reels as one gazes into that profound solitude," intoned Langford. "Man cannot help but feel his littleness in his ability to comprehend the architecture of nature. This location is the essence of solemn grandeur that must be seen to be felt. Ladies and gentlemen, it surpasses description."

After a moment of hushed silence, the crowd broke into a murmur and then rapid-fire applause. Langford bowed slightly. Meanwhile, in the audience, Ferdinand Hayden had been swept up by Langford's campfire dialogue. He was one hundred and ten percent inside the Yellowstone, fully tuned to Langford's choice of words, for Langford's generous use of geological terms heightened his interest and his imagination. Without missing a word, Hayden reached into the inside pocket of his jacket and took out a small notebook and pencil.

"The Lower Falls," continued Langford, "is a continuous spectacle of awesome proportions, a uniform body of water instantly transformed into separate though still related streams. The combined appearance is one of molten silver. In the sunlight, the foot of the falls is enveloped in a mist that, in turn, is crowned by a shimmering rainbow. As for the Upper Falls," he said, "it takes strong nerves to stand on the edge and watch this magnificent body of water, compact, perpendicular, wide as a street, and as deep as any river, pour in everlasting fashion over the edge of a two-hundred-fifty-foot precipice. This one falls must be half the volume of Niagara, yet it falls twice the distance.

"Yes, the journey of the Yellowstone River is a watery adventure broken by immense cataracts, falls, and grand scenery. And at the very source of Yellowstone?" Langford paused to heighten the drama. "A beautiful inland sea at a height of seven thousand feet, surrounded by forests primeval.

"How can I sum up its wonderful attractions?" he asked. "It is dotted with islands. Forests of pine, dark, and almost impenetrable, are scattered at random along the Yellowstone River banks, and its beautiful margin presents every variety of sandy and pebbly beach. Its mood is ever-changing, from mirror to raging sea when the winds and storms descend. It is set amid the greatest wonders of Nature that the world affords, and beautified by the grandeur of the most extensive mountain scenery. Not many years can elapse before the march of civilization will reclaim this delightful solitude, and garnish it with all the attractions of cultivated taste and refinement. Probably within our own lifetime, the region will be adorned with villas and the ornaments of civilized life."

After the lake and falls, said Langford, he was certain the expedition had seen the best the region had to offer. "But, as we followed the radius of our circle through the valley, we found ourselves in a volcanic land that abounded in boiling springs, mud volcanoes, mountains of sulfur, and geysers more numerous than those in Iceland. The colors we saw are indescribable: hues of every color. Pure crystallized sulfur rimmed hot spring pools in which color changed like steel under the process of tempering with every kiss of a passing breeze. Yet these circles of magic were also as diabolical looking as the caldron of MacBeth, and needed but the presence of Hecate and her weird band to realize that horrible creation of poetic fantasy."

The room was so silent it might have been empty. Hayden wrote furiously. "My friends, a highly dramatic moment occurred when one of our troop almost fell through the crust into boiling water. Had our friend not fallen quickly backwards in rapid reaction to the failing surface, his would have been a certain and hideous death."

Langford paused. Hayden's pen flew as he recorded the details of Langford's descriptions: volcanic ashes twenty feet deep, sulfurous fumes, boiling springs, seething geysers, treacherous encrustations, desolation. The expedition had obviously passed through a realm of undocumented, large-scale volcanic activity.

Hayden's senses were overwhelmed. He could see the falls, smell the sulfur, feel the heat of glistening waters so "boiling hot, yet tasting vitriolic." He had no interest in how the group had lost the older, nearsighted Everts for five weeks, nor did he listen closely as Langford ended his hour-long talk with a reference to the Northern Pacific. "When, by means of the Northern Pacific Railroad, the falls of the Yellowstone and the geyser basin are rendered easy of access," said Langford, "probably no portion of America will be more popular as a watering place or summer resort. Thank you."

Amid thunderous applause, Spencer Baird turned and said, "Well, Professor, it would appear that . . ."

But Hayden was already out of his seat. Baird watched Hayden's back disappear as the geologist scurried down the increasingly crowded aisle, not towards the exit, but towards the podium. Following Hayden's probable train of thought, Baird smiled. If the inspired explorer was as determined as he thought . . . who knows, there might yet be something in this for the Smithsonian!

Hayden found Langford discussing the accessibility of the Yellowstone with several members of the audience. "What's the real Indian situation out there?" asked one. "How might I get there if I went west?" asked another eager listener. "When is the Northern Pacific Railroad going to reach the Yellowstone?" asked a third.

In the middle of the barrage of questions, Langford saw Hayden and stuck out his hand. "Dr. Hayden? A pleasure."

"Mr. Langford. My compliments. A superb talk. When you have a moment I would like to verify a few facts and clarify a few hypotheses."

"Certainly." Langford excused himself from the gathering and led Hayden to the rear of the stage. When Hayden opened his notebook, Langford said: "Sir, forgive me, but in response to every one of your questions, my best and most honest answer is 'go and see for yourself.'

"I say this for several reasons. First, I cannot satisfy your curiosity as to geologic detail. As for hypotheses, well, sir, you are far more learned than I regarding the history and manifestations of the earth's natural forces and its products. Mine would be but uneducated guesses. And although my presentation today was as realistic as I could make it, it falls terribly short of any scientific validation of what our group experienced. And, of course, that is what the Yellowstone needs—scientific examination."

Langford's words caught Hayden off guard. They echoed in his head. He stumbled. "I found your presentation most intriguing," was all that he could say. "Have you, by chance, brought specimens with you?"

"I'm sorry, I left everything in Montana for fear that some might be lost or taken during some unguarded point in my journey."

"I understand. It sounds as though you have happened across a vast, volcanically active region."

Langford's eyes blazed hot. "With all due respect, Dr. Hayden, our exploration of the Yellowstone was planned and executed in considerable detail. It was hardly happenstance."

"Oh, of course! I meant no disrespect, Mr. Langford. An unfortunate choice of words. I was merely reflecting on the unique geological aspects of the scene. May I ask your plans? When will you be in Washington again?"

"I leave tomorrow morning for New York, where I have a number of appointments. I intend to give another lecture there. I'm afraid my rather tight schedule will not free me for several months."

"Several months," muttered Hayden, in deep thought. "Is there any chance I might obtain a copy of your notes or your map?"

"If time were not a critical element I would be honored to copy the material for you. But I am in the middle of editing an article for *Scribner's.*"

"The new magazine? I have yet to see it. When is your article to appear?"

"No date has been set. I will meet with the editor, Mr. Gilder, and his illustrator, a Mr. Moran, in New York."

"Illustrations? You have drawings? Photographs?"

"Only simple sketches, I'm afraid." Langford opened a satchel and removed a small folder. "One of our escorts, a Private Moore, was sufficiently alert to make these." He showed Hayden some small, crude pencil drawings. "He loaned them to me," added Langford. "I thought Mr. Moran, with some additional detail from me, might make a few decent woodcuts to accompany the article."

"Fascinating country," agreed Hayden as he scrutinized the drawings. "And, as you say, aside from your journey, totally undocumented."

"Yes, a task that awaits someone with scientific skill and understanding. And a task that should be undertaken soon, for my guess is the region will be completely civilized in the near future. Opportunities for the entrepreneur are too great to ignore. Nature's offerings there are too spectacular to keep hidden."

"Indeed," said Hayden. "Indeed." He stared at Mr. Langford, envious and a bit irritated that he had allowed him to get there first. Well, he thought, at least he hadn't taken Timothy O'Sullivan along and lined the walls of Lincoln Hall with photographs.

6) Lobbying for the Yellowstone

William Henry Jackson emerged from his new Washington, D.C., darkroom with two wet prints and hung them next to a dozen more. He looked at the new prints with satisfaction but spent less time looking than he would have liked. He did not have the time. Literally hundreds of unprinted negatives waited, and some of the more striking prints would have to be reprinted five to ten times.

Taking a break from his seemingly endless task, Jackson stoked the stove and poured himself some coffee. In the adjacent room, he picked up one or two of the specimens Dr. Hayden had brought back from their summer trek. He wondered what the professor did with all the rocks and fossils once they had been described. Returning the specimens to their places, Jackson decided they were probably like old negatives, nice to have in your files.

This room also served as the survey library. Stacks of Hayden's latest annual report just off the press, copies of earlier reports, maps, pamphlets, even some correspondence, lay helter skelter. Documents overflowed their boxes. Jackson was certain some would be lost or inadvertently used as fire starter. It appeared the new offices were devoted more to publishing and distributing an annual report than to serving as a survey headquarters. He prayed that the pace would soon slow. He'd had a hectic month himself, traveling to Omaha to see Mollie, then continuing here to Washington, to confer with Professor Hayden.

The trip had worked out better than he'd expected, because Dr. Hayden had offered him a permanent slot with the survey. Surprised and pleased, Jackson accepted. He wrote Mollie that after they sold the studio, they could relocate to Washington. He looked for a permanent residence and began directing the design and building of his new darkroom inside the office complex.

Being separated from Mollie made Jackson disconsolate. He knew he would feel better about his work, not to mention his annual summer away from home, after she was safe with him. In his first letter, he'd suggested selling the whole kit and caboodle, but Mollie wrote back that it might be best to wait. If they rushed, they would sell only to opportunists and lose in the process. She didn't look forward to being by herself much longer, but she was handling the studio quite well. And between his job and the studio, there was money in the till. Not to worry.

This week, with Hayden gone, Jackson enjoyed some unaccustomed peace and quiet. It wasn't that he didn't enjoy his boss's company; he did, but Hayden tended to speak in long soliloquies, often beginning in the middle of a pleasant silence. It was disruptive.

From time to time one or two of the survey, notably Jim
Stevenson, popped in. Henry Elliott came by once to look at maps
and to refer to earlier documents in the library. But Stevenson and
Elliott were quiet and unobtrusive. It was nice to see them once in
a while. Actually, Jackson used their arrivals as an excuse to break
his routine. He liked a brief period now and then to reminisce or
speculate on where they might go next summer. Like Stevenson,
Jackson was ready to return to the field. That was where the action
was.

Jackson wandered back into the darkroom to prepare another
plate for printing. He had printed a third of the negatives he had
taken through the summer of 1870. That meant he had just three
hundred plates to go.

The door to the office opened and Dr. Hayden walked in. Jackson stuck his head out of the darkroom and waved. "Welcome back,
Dr. Hayden." He thought the professor looked flushed, as though
he'd been running. Jackson thought that if Hayden had been a
little younger, he probably would have run everywhere. He'd never
known anyone so hard to keep up with.

Deep in thought, Hayden went immediately to his desk and
began to search through the stacks of papers. Jackson closed the
door and returned to work. If Professor Hayden wanted to talk,
he'd come and get him. But an hour passed and Hayden hadn't
said "boo." His silence intrigued Jackson. It wasn't like the professor to be so tight-lipped. Jackson came out to hang up another
print. He glanced at his employer several times in the process.
Hayden was still sitting at his desk which was now strewn with
open books and several maps. Jackson was just about to ask what
was so interesting when Jim Stevenson came in.

Hayden saw who it was and beckoned. "Ah, Jim, come here.
Sit down. We have to talk."

"Be right there, Professor. Let me get a cup of coffee."

Hayden drummed on the tabletop with the blunt end of a pencil. Jackson had seen him drum on logs, tables, and his notebook
in the field, a sure sign that he was trying to make a decision or
mulling over some new discovery.

Stevenson placed his top hat on the hat rack and went to the coffee pot. He poured himself a half cup of coffee and, looking at Jackson, jerked his head in Hayden's direction with a raised eyebrow as if to say, "Something's brewing. The boss is nervous."

So, thought Jackson, Stevenson had noticed Hayden's preoccupation, too. "What's going on?" he whispered to Stevenson. Stevenson shrugged.

"Come on, Jim," said Hayden impatiently. "I have something to show you. You will find this most interesting. Besides, I need your help."

"Yes, boss," said Stevenson, who used the term only when he wanted to get a rise. Hayden frowned, then beckoned again.

Stevenson leaned over the table to look at the large map Hayden had unfolded. Hayden poked the map in several places and was about to say something when Stevenson grunted. "This is the region we were headed for back in sixty. Remember how Captain Raynolds cussed like a horseshoer 'cause the snow kept him from going where he wanted?"

Hayden said something, but from across the room, Jackson couldn't hear him. Stevenson chuckled in response to Hayden's comment. That did it! Jackson wiped his hands, sniffed them to see how bad the hypo stink was, then joined the two men. The map they were looking at was one that Hayden periodically updated with pencil notations. It was a sketchy map covering most of the territory of Wyoming and portions of the Montana Territory. Jackson didn't think anyone could use it as a guide. North of the Oregon Trail, the only marks within a ten-thousand-square-mile area identified Camp Brown and Camp Stambaugh. The positions of the Wind River Mountains, the Tetons, and the Big Horn Mountains were well documented, but the northwest corner of Wyoming Territory, where Stevenson was now pointing, was labeled *terra incognita*.

"What would you say if I said we should take next summer to explore the Yellowstone?" asked Hayden. "No, don't answer that," he added quickly. "Let me just say that we have an opportunity. I'm wondering whether we can do it in one season."

Stevenson traced the railroad tracks from Fort D. A. Russell

to Corinne, Utah, then north along the freighting line that joined
Salt Lake City, Virginia City, and Helena.

"Where would we go in?" he asked.

Hayden stabbed the map with a pencil. Jackson leaned over
to see and bumped Stevenson, who nearly spilled his coffee.

"Easy, Bill," said Stevenson. "We'll get there." He laughed.

"Just curious," said Jackson.

"Why go all the way to the north, Doc?" continued Stevenson.
"What's wrong with coming in from the west, maybe up the Madison? We could send out guides and find a pass. Might have to leave
the wagons earlier than expected, but . . . ."

"Because," interrupted Hayden, "last summer an expedition
entered the Yellowstone from the north. They made a map. They
have notes on weather and trail conditions, and they documented
the lay of the land. We'll have to travel further, but we'll have the
benefit of following a known trail."

"We'll have to start early, be out of Fort Russell by the first of
June and on the trail a week later. That's a good piece of territory."
Stevenson spoke as if he had no doubt that they would go.

"You realize that none of this line has ever been surveyed,"
said Hayden as he moved his pencil back and forth along the freighting line to Virginia City. "This route has been heavily used since
the early sixties, but it remains unmapped territory. No one has
ever examined the geology. We could continue from where we left
off last summer near Fort Bridger. It all fits."

Hayden looked at Stevenson and Jackson and smiled wist-
fully. "I must say that Mr. Langford's lecture was quite revealing. If
I can convince Secretary of the Interior Delano to let me change
my plans, we'll have a productive summer." He stood up. "The
Yellowstone, Jim; it's been a long time coming."

"What's been a long time coming," asked Jackson loudly, still
feeling left out. "Who's Langford and what's so special about this
Yellowstone?"

Hayden and Stevenson smiled simultaneously. "William, that
was the same question that our Mr. Stevenson asked Jim Bridger
fourteen years ago," said Hayden. "Let's just say that the
Yellowstone is represented to be one of the most unusual regions

on the continent. It's probably a volcanic area that still shows signs of activity. But I should let Jim answer your question."

"Dr. Hayden, Jim Bridger, and me were standing on the east bank of the Yellowstone River not far from where it joins into the Missouri. This was back in fifty-six or so. Jim Bridger was our guide. He pointed up-river with a corncob pipe he always carried and said something about having been to the Upper Yellowstone where the river starts. He said it with a good deal more pride than usual." Stevenson chuckled.

"And?" prompted Jackson.

"So I said what you just said. 'What's so special about the Yellowstone?' Dr. Hayden told me later that it was the only time he had ever seen Jim Bridger astonished."

Stevenson chuckled once again. "Every time I think about it, I can picture old Gabe. I believe he was put out by my suspicious nature. When he recovered his tongue, he looked straight at me with a hard eye and said, 'Well, pilgrim, what would you think about an ice cold spring that gushed from a mountain, and got piping hot by the time it reached the bottom?'"

"This is in the Yellowstone?" asked Jackson, looking astonished. "When do we leave?"

"We're still trying to determine whether a trip is feasible and how much it might cost, William," Hayden said. "Congress will have to approve extra funds and approve a change in plans."

Jackson turned on his heel. As he walked back to the darkroom, he said in a loud voice, "I'll start packing."

Hayden scratched his beard. "Mr. Jackson has more faith in the system than I have."

But Stevenson was already absorbed in figuring out distances and expenses. Based on prior years, Stevenson had worked out a rough *per diem* cost per person. All he needed from Hayden was the total number of persons, the number of days they would be out, some understanding of the terrain over which they would be traveling, and any special requirements. From that he could plan their need for pack and saddle animals, vehicles, food stuffs—not only for humans but also grain for the animals—water barrels, sleeping gear and roughed-out sleeping arrangements, crates or crate materials for packing and shipping specimens, extra parts, cash, and the location of resupply points. And from that, he could give Doc a rough estimate of anticipated expenses. Hayden would then decide who he had to have along and what they could contribute for what they would cost. He would also set aside a large amount to cover the cost of publishing the heavily illustrated reports.

7) Plans

True to Utica's reputation, it was snowing. Langford sat in his hotel room, examining the changes *Scribner's* wanted him to make in his manuscript. He looked out the window as he searched for a word. He was thankful that he would be here for only two days. If his lecture went half as well here as the others had, the auditorium would be packed and the applause would be extended.

His experience in New York City had been especially rewarding. He'd considered the approval of his appearance at New York City's Cooper Union Hall as a great privilege. The Cooper Union Free Lecture Series was known up and down the East Coast for providing important, up-to-date information to the public. Langford followed John Wesley Powell, who had spoken at length the week before on his venture down the raging waters of the Grand Canyon of the Colorado. The scientists who followed Langford spoke on the design and function of the microscope, America's last glacial age, Darwin's hypothesis of evolution, the nature of illuminating gas, and the manufacture of iron.

New York City's newspapers had been most kind in their appraisal of his talk and they had quoted him at length. While in New York, he met with Mr. Wilkeson of the Northern Pacific Railroad Company. Wilkeson attended the talk, then invited Langford to his office. Saying he was impressed by the content and style of Langford's writing and complimenting him on his presentation, Wilkeson then suggested an alternative conclusion to give more attention to the Northern Pacific Railroad.

Langford felt compelled to accept most of the changes, because Wilkeson, himself a journalist as well as Secretary for the Northern Pacific Railroad, had sought him out. To Langford, that meant only one thing: the Northern Pacific planned to offer him a lecture contract. Before Wilkeson left, he suggested that Langford get in touch with Jay Cooke.

Cooke urged Langford to allow time in his schedule for a series of talks at Ogontz and in the Philadelphia area. Langford responded immediately: *Please write me on receipt of this what you especially want me to do, the nature of the lectures to be given, the principal points to be presented, where delivered, and so on. I ask to be advised so that I may assure myself that I can serve the railroad company as well as its officers and friends in New York seem to think I can. And I should be very glad to deliver my lecture on the wonders of the Upper Yellowstone in Philadelphia so that you may better judge my fitness for a field that is so new to me.*

He informed Cooke that his current schedule would keep him busy through April. He suggested that he arrive in Philadelphia in early May. Part of his schedule required him to return to New York to meet with the *Scribner's* editor and illustrator a second time. At his first meeting, Langford talked to the publisher, Roswell Smith, the editor, J. G. Holland, and their new assistant editor, Richard Gilder of Philadelphia. Langford was told that the magazine was going to concentrate on documenting the Trans-Mississippi West. His article fit their needs perfectly. The editors had decided that as long as the article could be well illustrated, there was enough material for two issues.

Smith was adamant about having high-quality illustrations. *Scribner's* competition included *The Atlantic Monthly, The Overland Monthly, Scientific American, Galaxy,* and *Harper's Weekly.* The most successful of these, *Harper's Weekly,* was also the most heavily illustrated.

Gilder was a pudgy little fellow, the kind who looked good in a black suit and top hat. He had a rather soft, round face and arching eyebrows. He saw Langford's sketches and listened as Langford described them in more detail. He then asked his employer to let Thomas Moran do the woodcuts. "He's the finest woodcut artist on the East Coast," said Gilder, looking at Langford.

Thomas Moran was a new employee. Gilder had lured him to New York from Bordentown, the Philadelphia suburb where the two men had grown up together. Moran had already done a fine woodcut for *Scribner's* first issue in November 1870, so Roswell Smith accepted Gilder's recommendation.

Three months had passed since that first meeting with the *Scribner's* staff. Langford was anxious to see what Moran had accomplished. He also wanted to hear about the layout of the articles and find out when the issue would be published. Langford looked again into the dark Utica night. Gaslights from the street illuminated a continuous net of snowflakes. By tomorrow the streets would be knee-deep again.

As Emma Woodruff watched the light snowfall, she began to hum an old German folk tune her mother had taught her when she was a child. The uplifting melody fit well with her sense of well-being and the familiar kitchen activities. Snow, she thought, will make the evening much cozier. She hadn't seen Ferdinand since January. Although they had exchanged letters and an occasional romantic note, she realized how much it meant to her that he was coming to dinner. Tonight would be just for the two of them.

Her mother, bless her heart, said nothing. Although she might have been a bit shocked by the absence of a chaperone, she understood the need for privacy. Still, she had no intention of telling her husband that Dr. Hayden was dining at Emma's apartment.

Emma thought of herself and Ferdinand alone. Ferdinand occasionally looked at her with a most revealing glance, and he obviously enjoyed physical contact, but he had always been the perfect gentleman. He had never said anything definitive, yet Emma was quite sure that he loved her. She stopped what she was doing, pushed back her hair, and wondered if she would enjoy hearing Dr. Hayden promise love and devotion. She almost burned her hand, wondering.

After Cousin Matilda had helped tidy up the apartment, she found she had a prior engagement for the evening, and would not be available to join Emma and Dr. Hayden for dinner. The pendulum clock struck the half-hour. Emma bit her lips lightly to redden them as she thought about what she had to do and how much time she had left before Ferdinand arrived. She covered the dumplings to keep them warm, then went to her bedroom to make some last-minute changes to her appearance. She thought again about what Ferdinand's devotion might mean. He had courted her for more than a year now.

She would never forget the day they met. It was a Sunday afternoon. He appeared in her father's shop saying that he had misplaced his regular hat. Emma supposed he meant the one he wore on a daily basis. In any event, he was looking for a replacement. Something about his manner told her that only she would be acceptable to him, so instead of calling one of the assistants, she waited on him herself.

After he paid for a bowler and left, Emma had smiled to herself. When she understood that she had liked that man, she tried to figure out what had attracted her. She decided that he reminded her of her English teacher, the one who had been patient and attentive on the outside, and youthfully enthusiastic on the inside.

Her father had seen Hayden leave and casually remarked to Emma that it was nice to see that their shop continued to attract famous people. Emma was perplexed. She looked around the store, but saw no one. Her father whispered, "I take it you don't know who you just waited on."

"No. Should I?" she asked.

"That, my dear child, was Herr Professor Ferdinand Hayden." He spoke in the casual, too slow voice that was his way of underlining something important. "He's one of Philadelphia's more noted scientists. An explorer of the West. Members of Philadelphia's scientific circle consider him a peer of Professor Leidy."

"Never heard of him," said Emma. But afterward, she realized that this Dr. Hayden had received *quite* the compliment from her father. Professor Leidy was the president of the Academy of Natural Sciences of Philadelphia. As far as her father was concerned, the man walked two heads above ordinary people, and at least one head above most scientists.

Emma had seen Dr. Leidy at the shop on only two occasions; the first time, her father had proudly introduced him to her, adding that Professor Leidy's father, too, was a hatter. So that was how the two had become acquainted, she mused. The second time, Dr. Leidy caught her eye, bowed and smiled. Her father joined him, and the two left the shop together.

Mr. Woodruff frequently reminded the family that he had not missed an evening lecture at the Academy in nearly two years. On several occasions, he had invited Emma to accompany him. She consistently declined. Why, she argued, should someone her age spend an evening in a stuffy room with old men talking about dead things?

While she moved about, tidying up before the shop closed, she again thought about this man, this Professor Hayden. Now she decided that his attentiveness might have had as much to do with her as with her success in finding him a replacement hat. Indeed, if she reexamined his behavior and his words, she might find that he had dropped rather obvious hints that he was interested in her. She remembered how his eyes had gone from hooded to warm and smiling, and his eyes looked more at her than at the hat she'd picked for him. Now that she thought of it, he had not appeared very interested in the purchase at all, not after she had offered to assist him.

Emma stood by the door to the shop with the key in her hand. Suddenly her father was standing next to her. "Emma, my dear, are you waiting for a last customer or simply keeping the key warm?" he asked. He dearly loved his daughter, and her behavior told him that her mind was anywhere but on her task.

"How old is he, Father?"

"Who?"

"Who indeed? Professor Hayden."

With a little smile in his eye, her father said, "Why should you care? You don't know him anyway."

"Oh, Father." Emma sighed, locked the door, and pulled the blind. Her father's voice echoed clearly from the back of the now-empty store. "Please apologize to your mother, and tell her that I will be a little late for dinner this evening. It's getting close to the end of the month and I have a few accounts to balance. And if you will, Emma dear, please remind her that tomorrow night I need to eat early. The Academy lecture begins at seven, and I don't want to be late."

A few minutes later, as Emma buttoned her coat, she bent down and kissed her father's cheek to say goodnight. "What's the topic at the Academy tomorrow night?" she asked casually as she pulled up her collar.

Her father looked at her with an open grin. "Does it make any difference?"

Emma pulled back her shoulders and pursed her lips the way her mother did when she was offended. "Mr. Edmund Woodruff, you're a terribly presumptuous man, even if you are my father. You should treat your daughter with more respect." Then she laughed in her throaty way. "Just make sure you reserve seats for two."

To her delight, the main speaker of the evening was Professor Hayden himself. She hadn't the slightest idea what he was talking about, other than that the general topic was the geology of some dreary place called the badlands, but he was obviously engrossed in his topic, considered what he had to say important, and handled himself in front of the audience with dignity and poise. In fact, he was vibrant and quite attractive. By the end of the evening, Emma had reappraised Professor Hayden. Her father had warned her that he was an intense, often nervous fellow, a little on the droll side, who talked too fast.

On their way home that evening, Emma felt an inner warmth she was inclined to assign to her brief time with Dr. Hayden. He had seen her in the audience and made a point to seek her out. He might appear droll to others, thought Emma, but his eyes had sparkled when he talked to her, and when they spoke together for a few minutes, he made her laugh often, and blush once. When she thought about his status as a distinguished scientist, her feminine mind made her inquire, "Father, is Professor Hayden married?"

"Herr Hayden? I don't think so. At least, I have never heard mention of a Mrs. Hayden. He is, however, not afraid of women. Just the opposite, if gossip and rumor have it right."

Lost in thought again, Emma did not notice the sly smile that crept across her father's face when he suggested the family might enjoy having Herr Ferdinand Hayden for dinner some evening. Emma merely nodded.

When Emma heard the knock on her apartment door, her own heart pounded in response. With a radiant smile, she opened the door. Hayden's arms were full of flowers but he still managed to kiss her hand. Emma recognized the flowers. Lord! He had purchased the bouquet in the window of the flower shop across the street. She had asked about them, but they were too expensive for her.

"Oh, Ferdie, aren't you dashing this evening." She smelled the flowers and invited him to make himself at home. "Is this a special occasion?"

"Of course it is. It's already special on two counts. First, I am spending the evening with you. Second, I have news."

"Oh, good for you." Instead of waiting, she turned her back on him and entered the kitchen. "I hope you are hungry," she said. "We must eat in a few minutes; otherwise the dumplings will lose their freshness."

Hayden closed his eyes and sniffed appreciatively. When he opened them Emma was smiling at him. "As you know, Emma, home cooking is still an extra treat for me."

"I know." As the first months of their relationship slipped by and they began to see and write to one another more often, Hayden had allowed Emma to learn about some of the more painful aspects of his past. He hadn't dwelled on his early home life, but neither had he shied from answering Emma's perceptive questions. She now knew what attention and affection meant to him.

"I'm glad you like what I fix for you."

"I like everything you do for me and everything about you."

"My, compliments so early in the evening."

Hayden looked at the elegant place settings and flowers on the table. He shook his head in wonder, then laughed lightly. "You can't imagine the contrast, Emma. In the field, everything is so primitive. It's appropriate for the harshness of the land and the climate. We carry our own table and benches so we can sit together, but . . ." He gestured towards the table. "This is so . . .

delicate. Sometimes I have a hard time making the change."

Emma went to him and kissed his cheek. "Just for you, dear."

She admired Ferdinand Hayden terribly. In her mind, what he did, his dedication and perseverance, was nothing less than heroic. She was not shy about complimenting a man, but some things were better left unsaid, at least until both parties knew where they were headed as a couple.

Halfway through the meal, Emma told Hayden she had been thinking about how they met. "I often wondered why I had never seen you before. What made you come to the shop that day?"

Hayden looked at her and said matter-of-factly, "That was not the first time I'd seen you."

Emma looked very surprised. "What? I don't recall . . . Ferdinand, when . . .?"

He wiped his mouth and said, "You didn't see me. You were with your father at the time. I recognized him because he comes to the Academy so faithfully. What intrigued me was his obvious pleasure in sharing his company with a most attractive woman who looked to be half his age. I was just hoping that you weren't his wife."

Emma laughed freely. "Ferdinand Hayden! You never told me."

Hayden smiled. "You never asked. I simply inquired of Professor Leidy when the opportunity presented itself and discovered your identity."

"You mean that . . .?"

"Of course, Emma, dearest. You don't realize what seeing you did to me. My appearance at your shop was no accident. I wanted to see you again, up close. You did not disappoint me."

Emma laughed and her eyes sparkled. "You are *full* of surprises, Ferdie."

"Speaking of surprises, I must tell you what has happened." Hayden took her through Langford's lecture, a bit of what he already knew about the Yellowstone, and then about his plans to obtain approval to explore the Yellowstone the following summer.

"Mr. Dawes has been most supportive of my explorations," he said. "And as head of the Congressional Appropriations Committee, his word is nearly law. After Jim Stevenson and I finalized our estimates, I made an appointment to see him. He not only approved, he wants me to take one of his sons with me." Hayden shrugged and showed the palms of his hands. "What could I say?"

"So, your plans are approved? Is this a dangerous place? It sounds fearsome."

"No, no. That is . . . yes and no. My plans are as good as approved, but Congress has yet to vote the funds to support the project. As for any volcanic activities in the area, I am sure they are quite mild." He examined his silverware. "I suppose, however, that earthquakes and eruptions are not altogether out of the question."

"Oh, Ferdinand, you say that just to frighten me. You will be careful."

"Emma, dear," said Hayden, sounding amused, "you will not lose me to a volcano. Trust me."

"I do." She sighed. "How much longer do I have you?" Emma was delighted at Hayden's success, but that success meant he would be gone for another five months. She thought that in the last year, she had come to accept the demands of his work. She realized how much she missed this professor of hers, with his sparkling eyes, his dedication, and sometimes childish ways. She wondered if she would ever share some time with him in the field.

Hayden leaned forward, looking serious. "Do I detect remorse in your tone?"

"Ferdie, I would never try to dissuade you from doing anything you must do, but it doesn't mean I have to like the idea of your running off again for another four months. You just got back." She heard a slight catch in her voice, so she concentrated on serving the coffee and strudel.

When she returned from the kitchen, Hayden was standing beside the table. "You're not leaving are you?" she asked, startled.

To answer, he walked to her and took both her hands in his. "Emma, you know that you have become an important part of my life. We have a warm, honest, and caring relationship. Once I thought only of geology and my fieldwork. That is no longer true. I am not complete when I am away from you. I think of you constantly. You are a fresh breeze of life to me, and knowing you are here when I return from the field makes all my efforts worthwhile."

Emma had never heard him speak that way.

Hayden took a deep breath. "Emma, I love you. I love you very much. I believe I am in a good position to provide for you and I ask that you consider spending your life with me." He cleared his throat. "Will you marry me, Emma?"

Emma bit her lower lip, sighed, and moved into his arms. "Yes, Ferdinand, my dear, dear man. I will marry you. But only on one condition."

Emma had both arms wrapped around him. He leaned back to see her face better. "Condition? And what is that?"

"That you promise to take me at least once to your wonderful land of adventures so I won't be too jealous in years to come." She looked up at him and he kissed her fully.

On March third, Congress passed the annual Civil Sundry Bill. One of its provisions was an appropriation of forty thousand dollars to the Secretary of the Interior to fund an expedition of the United States Geological Survey of the Territories under Professor Ferdinand V. Hayden, to explore the sources of the Missouri and Yellowstone rivers. Professor Hayden would have a free hand to select his assistants, and, effective July first, his salary was to be raised from three thousand to four thousand dollars per year.

Hayden was determined to make the year's survey one of the most comprehensive in American history. He knew how much he could spend, how long his journey would take, and the rough size of the region he needed to document. He enlisted specialists in zoology, paleontology, mineralogy, botany, and geology. He had Jackson to photograph the regions he examined. If he was lucky, the artist Sanford Gifford would join them again. He had the better part of the next two months to prepare.

Commitment from one of his first new team members came from Anton Schonborn. Initially, Schonborn had doubted his ability to break free of the assignments the Army kept giving him, but that was resolved. He rejoiced at being part of the survey team.

Can leave April first. Hope you need no special assurance that I will work in the best interests of the party. Please let me know what duties you require and when you think you may start. Ice breaking early here.

And because Hayden was in a sufficiently comfortable position to repay past favors to mentors and friends, he was able to write his former natural history teacher, Professor George Allen, at Oberlin. *There is a slot open and I have left it for you. I would like you to do mineralogy (bring a blowpipe) and metallurgical work too and as much geological work as possible. You are the best judge of your physical condition. Don't need much, although a good shotgun might come in handy.*

But when Professor Allen asked to bring an assistant, Hayden said no. *I cannot take anyone else. I have refused more than fifty persons so far and am refusing more every day. My party now numbers eighteen. Politicians have six appointments. General Logan has two; General Negley's son goes; and possibly a son of Mr. Dawes of Massachusetts. All fieldwork must of necessity be of the crudest kind. It is designed to throw some light on matters that are not obvious at once to the eye. There will not be anyone along save you and myself who can make any pretensions to be knowledgeable on these subjects.*

Immediately following the passage of the Civil Sundry Bill, Hayden wrote the new Secretary of War, Mr. Belknap, for permission to draw on equipment, stores, and transportation at frontier army posts. The secretary was quite accommodating. He even authorized a small escort "when deemed necessary and the public service will permit." Hayden had also written officers of the Union Pacific and Central Pacific railroads. They gave free passage for his men. The survey team would congregate at Fort D. A. Russell in the Wyoming Territory. By the end of the first week of June they would head north from the environs of Salt Lake City.

Jim Stevenson completed his preparations and left April first for Fort D. A. Russell. Just before he left, he grabbed the last issue of *Scribner's* to read during the trip.

8) At Scribner's

Two weeks earlier, Nathaniel Langford had arrived at the offices of *Scribner's*. Gilder cleared a table and spread out the proofs of the first part of Langford's two-part article on the Upper Yellowstone. "I believe you will find the final article much to your liking, Mr. Langford. I certainly hope so. It would be very costly to try to alter anything this far into the process."

Gilder laid the proofs of Moran's woodcuts on the table. Langford immediately saw that they were excellent, all the more so because they had been drawn from crude sketches and his own vague, verbal descriptions.

The leading woodcut would set the mood of the article. It portrayed a long line of men on horses making their way along a rock-walled canyon of unusual structure and dimension. The lead riders of the pack were just emerging into an open area. It looked as though they had arrived at their destination and were waiting for the others to catch up. The woodcut captured the sense of a long journey and a surprise destination. In this one image, Moran had distilled the essence of the trip. "Superb," said Langford with an appreciative nod to Thomas Moran.

When he discussed the sketches with Mr. Moran in December, he sensed that the artist was not really hearing what he was saying. Worried that the images might not be as good as he hoped, he suggested to Gilder that he expand his written descriptions. It was now obvious to Langford that the artist worked from some inner visualization. Only the lack of the finest details indicated that Moran had not actually been there.

Langford was equally enthused by the magnificence of the Upper Falls of the Yellowstone. Moran had translated Private Moore's rough drawing into a work of art imbued with texture, contrast, and movement. He had captured the height and force of the falls and managed to endow the scene with a disarming sense of cozy secrecy, as though the falls represented that personal place everyone imagined discovering for themselves.

"They're very, very fine," said Langford. "I do not know of anyone who could have come closer to the truth based on what you were given to work with."

"Good. Now we come to the main topic of today's conversation, these illustrations."

"I thought we had finished with them. Is there a problem?" asked Langford.

"None to date," said Gilder with a deep breath, "and with your assistance we hope to avoid one."

A perplexed Langford looked at Gilder, then at Moran.

"What kind of assistance do you need?"

"Your intercession with Jay Cooke," said Gilder.

"Jay Cooke? What on earth does he have to do with my article and Mr. Moran's woodcuts?"

"Have you told him about your articles?"

"Not personally, but Mr. Cooke's associates in New York may have mentioned them to him. Between the last time we met and today, I joined the ranks of lecturers supported by the Northern Pacific Railroad. Mr. Wilkeson in New York made some suggestions about my presentation and created my late spring lecture schedule. In fact, I plan to give my lecture at Ogontz, Mr. Cooke's home," added Langford.

"Well, he seems to know that Mr. Moran has created a number of engravings and that they are particularly well suited to his publicity needs."

"Oh. And that's a problem?"

"Yes. He wants them."

"What do you mean?"

"Just what I said. He wants them, the engravings, physically in his hands. He made his request last week. It places me in a real bind. He's a very wealthy and influential man. My boss would be extremely upset should I offend Mr. Cooke. I cannot, however, risk allowing these engravings to leave this building. They can be damaged very easily, and should anyone see them before we print, they could be quickly copied. The impact of all of our work and your work, Mr. Langford, would be reduced to an unacceptable level."

"I see," said Langford. While Gilder spoke, Mr. Moran was gazing into the distance as though he was dreaming. Langford thought the artist was probably bored.

"Do you know what Cooke is up to?" asked Langford.

"I think I do now," said Gilder. "He needs a series of engravings to help him promote the sale of his railroad bonds. Wilkeson is enamored with the Yellowstone and wants to use it as a publicity stunt. He probably told Cooke that they should use our engravings to enhance the railroad's image with the public."

Mr. Gilder asked rather than stated, "You and Wilkeson discussed your articles on the Yellowstone, didn't you?"

"Now that you mention it, I believe we did," said Langford.

"Well, we have to turn Mr. Cooke's head."

Langford studied Thomas Moran. Everything about the man seemed fragile: his fingers, his facial bones, even his posture. He continued to look distracted, as though part of him was not in the room. It made Langford hesitate before he addressed him.

"Excuse me, Mr. Moran? Is your schedule flexible enough to provide Mr. Cooke some time?"

"Just a minute, please," said Gilder.

"Don't panic, Richard," said Moran quickly. "Mr. Langford is simply asking whether I might be free to do the work Mr. Cooke needs to keep him from our engravings."

"Yes, I thought . . ." Langford interposed.

"Say, that's an idea," said Gilder. "Can we write him to that effect? See what he says. Anything. I just can't abide the notion that . . ."

"Might we send Mr. Moran, with his and your approval of course, to Philadelphia with the engravings *after* they have been used for the article? In that way, Mr. Moran could talk to Cooke about his illustration needs and protect the engravings en route in case a compromise does not work."

Gilder paced for a minute and sucked his teeth. "I'll accept that. Thomas, you'll have to slide everything back, everything except the second series of engravings for the June article, that is. Can't mess with those. The second article is probably more important than the first. The skeptics among our readers will see by the content of our June issue that we fully back Mr. Langford's veracity and descriptions. There must be an equal number of grand illustrations and we must go to press on time. No exceptions."

"I'll write to Cooke," said Langford. In a moment of pure curiosity, he looked at Moran and said: "Pardon my directness, sir, but you have seemed quite distracted this morning. Is there anything about the article or the woodcuts we have not covered?"

Moran rubbed his long, thin nose with a long, thin finger. "No, it is simply that I so want to go," he said in a high-pitched voice.

"I beg your pardon?"

"If it looks the way you have described, I must see it." In the shadows of the room, Thomas Moran looked terribly hollow-eyed. His appearance heightened the urgency in his voice.

Langford was nonplused. "The Yellowstone?" he asked quietly.

"Your descriptions and the little sketches demanded that I give my imagination free rein. When I work on a series of woodcuts, I work from my own private image. I suppose the images have become somewhat of a fixation. I sense a strange, primitive force out there. The Yellowstone must be one of nature's most marvelous, creative playgrounds. I have been arguing with myself about my need to see this place for myself since I started the woodcuts."

When Moran first read Langford's draft and examined the crude sketches, he had gladly accepted the challenge. But he'd had other things on his mind: his children, Christmas, unfinished assignments, and several paintings waiting to be completed for the art journal, *Aldine*. He had not allowed himself the luxury of becoming emotionally involved in the details of the mysterious Yellowstone. In fact, he did not attempt to visualize the scenes he would eventually translate into woodcuts until the deadline approached. Then he worked feverishly to prepare all seven woodcuts, including Column Rock, Devil's Hoof, and the Mud Volcano. By the time he had finished, the Yellowstone had become an obsession.

As a freelance illustrator, Moran was accustomed to sketching objects he had never seen. It was natural for him to complete a picture using only his imagination. But he had also begun to mature as a painter, a medium that demanded much more than woodcutting. For the past year or two, he had been searching for scenes of "grand nature." In the description of the Yellowstone, he was sure he had found them.

"The Yellowstone was fascinating, to be sure," said Langford. "I'm not surprised that you, too, find it so, especially considering your talent."

"Without offending you," said Moran somewhat woodenly, "I must say that you do *not* understand. I have, in the last five or six years, been more and more drawn to focus my energy on nature's grandeur. I do not think the average man has any idea of how complex, how perfectly splendid if not perfect, is nature's multitude of expression." In the stillness of the room, Moran sounded like a monk explaining the ethereal qualities of angels. "I have always wanted to paint from the more grand scenes of nature, but only once have I been able to find the coincidence of time, money and companionship I needed."

"That was when you went to Lake Superior," said Gilder.

"Yes, Richard. I actually slept outside, on the earth. It was quite an experience." He and companion Issac Williams had gone to Lake Superior in search of the "Shores of Gitche Gumee," the shining, big-sea waters of Longfellow's best-selling *Hiawatha*. The poet had obtained his information from the explorer and anthropologist, Henry J. Schoolcraft, and had translated the aboriginal legends of the area as an entertainment for the public. Moran had been drawn by the poem's primitivism and picturesque possibilities. Upon his return, he completed a number of works based on sketches of the grand portal of the voyageurs, the great cave, and other shoreline features. Each was eventually published in *Aldine*.

It was all Langford could do not to laugh at Moran's comments about camping. He had to remind himself that Moran was from the East Coast. "Well," said Langford, "the Yellowstone is not going anywhere. I'm sure you will have an opportunity to see it someday." To Richard Gilder he said, "I had better get my letter written. With your permission I will write it here. Do you have some letterhead I might use?"

Langford pushed aside his thoughts of the sensitive Thomas Moran and began to pen his thoughts to Jay Cooke. *I write you this favor from paper in Scribner's & Co.*, he scribbled. *They are very afraid that the engravings may be copied, that an artist could easily copy them. They will send the engravings of the May issue and soon*

David M. Delo

after, the others. To avoid unlawful copying, they suggest that the artist who drew them, Mr. Moran, on Norwich Street, can do your work as well as anyone else. It would ensure their safety to place them in his hands. Langford ended by saying that he looked forward to his lecture series at Ogontz in May.

Mary Moran cradled her year-old child and watched her husband work. Feelings of love and admiration flowed through her. She considered herself lucky. She had been married to the gentle, creative soul for eight years. The child in her arms was their third. With a silent prayer and a soft smile, she hoped it would be their last. Not that she wasn't utterly delighted with her children. She was, and Thomas, when he found time, was always there to help. But children cost money, and money was not abundant in the Moran household.

She recalled the tiny loft they had found in Paris while Thomas studied the old masters. It was hard to believe that that had only been three years ago. Perhaps that trip was the reason he worked so hard these days. He had convinced her that he had to go to Europe to complete his training. She couldn't say no. They had a marvelous time together, wandering the countryside, sketching, sharing, learning, and loving one another. They even sailed on a funny little freighter from Marseilles to Pisa, Italy. But they spent all of the money they had, and she knew that Thomas had borrowed more. He had more than enough work to keep him busy, but he was not one to ignore his debts. They were poor enough. The debt had been an extra strain.

Mary went to the kitchen to prepare dinner. Newark, New Jersey, lacked the warmth and familiarity of Philadelphia and the house they rented seemed small, but it had the studio space Thomas needed. That made everything acceptable to her.

Mary Moran was a medium height, full-figured woman. Her soft, round physical features and luminescent gray eyes mirrored the salient characteristics of her personality. She was as comfortable with her unassuming self as she was passionate about life and art. Under Thomas's guiding hand, she was becoming an excellent artist in her own right. She loved growing with him, sharing his enthusiasm, and watching how he made canvas come to life. But she had a few rules in her life, rules she applied on a daily basis. Her first irrevocable rule was that nothing would ever stand between Thomas and his need to paint: not money, not children, not her. Mary's rule was selfish, because she knew that if Thomas felt free to work, to express himself without worry or interference, he would remain the man she had first met, a man full of love for life and for her. Perhaps that was why she had decided to help him find a way to fulfill his latest yearning.

She turned to see her husband standing in the doorway. He yawned, then rubbed his beard. Going to Mary, he kissed her lightly, then looked at their sleeping child in her arms. "It's been so quiet in here lately; where is everyone?"

Mary smiled. "Glad you noticed. The children are playing games in their room because their father wasn't working on anything large enough for them to watch."

"Oh ho!" said Thomas. "Well, it will be a while, at least until I complete the last woodcut for Mr. Langford's articles. I admit my ardor to see the Yellowstone has not diminished. If anything, my desire to see the strange manifestations I have been craving has increased." He leaned over the stove and sniffed the contents of the pot. "It's out of the question and I know it. It will pass."

"Will it?" asked Mary. "Thomas, you are ready for your grand scenes of nature. You have been ever since you completed *Solitude* and your earliest scenes from the *Song of Hiawatha*. You can't put off traveling forever."

Thomas smiled and nodded his head. "I know, my dear. Thank you for thinking of me, but I need to help us catch up, not get further behind."

"Didn't you say that Professor Hayden was making a major expedition to the Yellowstone this summer?"

"Did I? I suppose I did. Someone must have mentioned that to me. Perhaps Mr. Langford. Yes, of course; he's planning to accompany the Hayden expedition." Thomas sighed. "Lucky man. To have been there once and now, to be able to return!"

"Why not write this Professor Hayden. Isn't he from Philadelphia, too? Perhaps he can engage you to do illustrations."

"Mary, darling, I haven't even discussed the possibility of going with Richard. Besides, I have commissions and assignments to keep me busy all summer. And even if I could find a way to get there, I should have numerous expenses and be gone for several months. What would you live on while I was gone, pray tell?" He turned and left the room. "I love you and I'll not have it," he said as he walked away.

And I know you, Thomas Moran, said Mary to herself as she stirred the pot. *You will not sleep well at night, nor will you look at me with the same quality of love we have known. A part of you will be away in the wilds, seeking the grand scenes your heart has sought all the years I have known you. You must go. We must find a way for you to go.*

In his studio, Thomas Moran put away his tools and cleaned surfaces. He shook off a slight fatigue and thought that perhaps he needed a change. Then he decided he was indulging himself. He had just made a major change: he had taken his family from Philadelphia and moved to New York and then to Newark.

Financially these moves had been good decisions. He had listened to his friend Richard Gilder because his need to support his family was more important than his own artistic growth. And that, he told himself, was why graphics still took precedence over painting.

Moran had never made a conscious decision to become an artist. He had apprenticed as an engraver for Scattergood and Telfer, on 57 South Third, in Philadelphia, just up the street from Jay Cooke's private bank. An engraving apprenticeship was a common road for artistic youths with no money. It helped that Philadelphia was famous for its publishing, and that wood was the medium for illustrations. Thomas learned to paint a wood block with Chinese white, then draw an image in reverse with india ink and a sharp pencil. With a bruin, he scraped away the white spaces of the wood block.

All too soon he became bored with the process. Yet he couldn't quit and go his own way. His father had paid good money for his apprenticeship. Scattergood was wise enough to allow Moran to draw for other students. Eventually, Thomas produced a series of watercolors and gave them to Scattergood, who sold them.

As he returned now to his engraving, he felt again a desperate need for an outlet like this Yellowstone. Perhaps, if he could find a way, just this once. He understood that timing would always be a problem, but the journey to the Yellowstone region was a rare opportunity. He often worked up to thirteen hours a day as it was. Where would the extra money come from?

The older children emerged from their room and ran to their father. He turned to them and filled his arms and his heart. "Tomorrow," he told them, "we will all take a long walk in the park." The children yelled with delight and ran to tell their mother. And that, thought Thomas with finality, will have to satisfy everyone's desire for "grand nature."

9) Farewells

To Philadelphians, grand nature meant Fairmount Park. It was the largest city park in America, three thousand acres of natural preserve that flanked both sides of the Schuylkill. It was the Philadelphian's getaway: his playground, her garden. The wooded enclave began at the bridge that linked Philadelphia to West Philadelphia and followed the Schuylkill, what the Indians called the noisy stream, north for several miles.

When Philadelphians entered Fairmount Park, they exchanged the exigencies of life for a wonderland of villas and walkways. They traded their building facades for feats of private landscaping and gardening executed in simple geometric styles. Once inside the park, they read books in the arbors, watched shell races on the river, strolled and listened to birds. They flirted with bows and arrows, or enjoyed a corner of solitude.

The day before Ferdinand Hayden was scheduled to leave for the West, he and Emma walked along the east bank of the park. He had hired a hack to take them to Lemon Hill— a private estate that had been donated to the park. That morning was one of the last days of May. The sun splashed through the boughs, squirrels played hide and seek in new leaves, and the fragrance of forsythia and iris ebbed and flowed with tides of gently swirling air.

Emma vacillated between wanting to be glued to Hayden's left arm and seeking the scent of new flowers. She was in love and the day was warm, full of spring and promise. "For you, sir." Emma handed Hayden a tiny, purple flower.

"Ah. If I take it with me, I shall start a new species in Wyoming," said Hayden with his customary penchant to weave his plans into their conversation.

"You promised me we would not talk about anything west of Pennsylvania today," said Emma with mock severity.

"Hmm," said Hayden. "So I did. Not even indirect references, eh?"

"I'd like to talk about us, Ferdie; our future," said Emma. She tugged her husband-to-be towards a walkway lined with japonica, lilac, and forsythia. A mixed pine and hardwood forest rose up behind the well-trimmed hedges. A slight breeze perfected the weather.

"The last I heard, we were getting married," said Hayden. "If you change the date on me and I'm still in the field, best to let me know."

Emma chuckled. "I can see you now, disembarking from the train in your horse-sweated clothes, handing your pick to a guest as you climb into the carriage, leaving a trail of sandstone dust in your wake."

Hayden bent his head to her. "Sandstone isn't usually dusty, but there are some strata in the badlands that . . ."

"Hayden!"

"Sorry, my love."

"Silly man. You'll be back in plenty of time."

"And I leave our wedding plans in your hands, Emma. Please. Getting married while I try to organize my annual report will be enough to make my head rock."

"That traumatic?" When he did not answer, she looked around. No one was looking, so she kissed his cheek. She clung tighter to his arm. "Mother will help me," she said. "Oh, Ferdie, I am going to make you so happy." Emma beamed.

"You already do," he said.

Until Hayden saw a man sitting on a bench and reading, he had forgotten that he had wanted to tell Emma about Lieutenant Doane's report on the Washburn Expedition. The copy he had finished reading was the one Doane had sent to Baird. The twenty-five-thousand-word document would reach Congress after passing through the ranks of the Army. Hayden had been impressed by Doane's elegant descriptions of what he had seen in the Yellowstone. His words had heightened Hayden's enthusiasm for the journey ahead. He was certain that the Senate would recommend printing Doane's report. He was about to comment when he remembered that the topic was out-of-bounds for the day. Instead, he patted Emma's hand.

They sat on a bench near the Robert Morris estate, surrounded by native shrubs and exotics interspersed with statues, busts, ponds, and fountains described as jets d'eau. Emma chatted about people he would meet and places they could go when he returned. Hayden tried to relax and listen. He was so used to being in a hurry; a pleasant stroll through the park was difficult. He leaned against the railing of the small, circular summer house on the breastwork by the dam and watched a few idle gentlemen fish from the parterres. Golden carp mingled with black bass in the waters below the dam.

While Emma talked about her wedding dress, Hayden was taking in the complexity of the park's waterworks. On the surface, the park's gardenlike pathways led to fountains, the prospect houses, the belvedere, the wheel house and races. Breezy porticoes and peristyles, ultra-Athenian in design, gave the visitor graceful shelter. Yet here within the park a complex of nine wheels drove enormous pumps that pushed eighty-two million gallons of water per day into a reservoir above the park. The exteriors of all of the mechanisms had been disguised.

High above them, built like the bell tower of Florence, was the square standpipe. Hayden wondered if there might be volcanic pipes as large as this standpipe in the Yellowstone. He'd received his instructions from the secretary of the interior a month ago. They reflected the areas Hayden said he wanted to explore, but he was also expected to continue his work of preceding years.

As the object of the expedition is to secure as much information as possible, both scientific and practical, wrote the secretary of the interior, *you will give your attention to the geological, mineralogical, zoological, botanical, and agricultural resources of the country. Your collections should be as complete as possible and forwarded to the Smithsonian Institution. You will be expected to prepare a preliminary report of your labors, which will be ready for publication by January 1, 1872.*

"Would you like to look at houses before the year is out? Ferdie?" Emma asked. She was ready to leave; Hayden was just beginning to relax. His eye caught several steamboats that were sliding quietly towards the pier near the dam. They would leave again at dusk for excursions up the river. Too late for that, he thought.

They strolled towards the entrance, where hacks for hire were plentiful. Hayden's mind slipped back to uncompleted chores. He still had to submit a letter to the secretary of the interior to obtain approval to pay new survey personnel. The request was a formal requirement, but Hayden did not anticipate any difficulty; after all, General Carrington was a former U.S. District Attorney for the District of Columbia, L. A. Bartlett was a scientist and resident of Washington, D.C., and Joseph Leidy and Edward D. Cope were two of the nation's leading paleontologists.

Meek's financial requirements had been taken care of, but Hayden had also spent time to ensure that Meek was comfortable with his role in the survey. He was also able to tell Meek that the report on the survey of the Nebraska Territory, which had stood ready for three years, was finally being printed by order of Congress. He had asked Meek for help in proofing, and made a specific point to tell him that his report on fossils with its eleven plates was part of the final publication.

Emma changed her mind. She wasn't ready to go back, so they went down to the riverbank and sat together on stones and looked across the lake. Here, the tranquil water and gentle slopes dominated. The character of the shore across the river was quite different. Its basin was narrow, lined with rocky slopes and stony ravines. Its pathways zigzagged up the steep slope. When Emma looked across the water, she saw reflections in a pastoral scene.

When Hayden examined it, he saw rock outcrops that reminded him of a half-dozen spots in the Rockies.

The warmth of the sun was dissipating rapidly when they left the park. Inside their carriage, Emma snuggled against Hayden. He thought she might be cold, but Emma was as warm as toast.

Scribner's assistant editor Richard Gilder returned from lunch and turned to the day's mail. It was the twenty-fifth of May. He looked for the most important items. Bills went in one pile, submissions in another, miscellaneous in a third. He was about to place the letter from Nathaniel Langford into the third pile, when he decided it might be important. Gilder was not just an editor, he was also a pragmatist and an aggressive businessman.

The letter had been mailed from Philadelphia, where Langford had been lecturing. Gilder opened it. Langford sent the usual greetings. Gilder's eyes scanned the paragraph about Ogontz. Yes, Langford had spoken to a number of congressmen and foreign dignitaries. Cooke had taken the occasion again to announce that the Northern Pacific planned to run a spur line to the Yellowstone for tourists. Gilder, a skeptic, thought that seemed like a large expense simply to please a bunch of travelers.

In the third paragraph, he discovered Langford's reason for writing. Langford was having problems with his throat. A doctor had advised him to give up lecturing and other strenuous activity until his throat healed. His medical difficulties meant that he would not, as previously planned, accompany Dr. Hayden's survey into the Yellowstone.

Gilder stopped reading. "Damn," he said. He and Langford had discussed another article or two on the Yellowstone, a natural by-product of Langford's second visit to the region. Gilder planned to run the article in the late fall or early winter. Momentum and readership lost, thought Gilder. More's the pity; the illustrations alone would sell thousands of copies.

The more Gilder considered the situation, the more he realized that a pictorial of the Yellowstone, even without an article, might sell hundreds of extra copies. And Thomas Moran was dying to go. If he could find a way to place him with Hayden's party . . . In a moment of inspiration, Gilder remembered that when Moran had arrived in Philadelphia, he'd discovered that the engravings he was doing covered all of Cooke's needs. With Gilder's blessing, Moran had loaned Cooke the plates. Cooke owed him one!

Gilder immediately wrote a letter to Jay Cooke to say that the *Scribner's* artist who had recently assisted him, Thomas Moran, desperately wanted to visit the Yellowstone. He hesitated to make the commitment because he didn't have enough money to sustain his family while he was gone. If Mr. Cooke thought Moran's work was beneficial to his publicity campaign, might he not help Moran reach the Yellowstone and thereby help to create more artistic renderings that could generate even more publicity?

A week later, Gilder received a note from A. B. Nettleton that said, *Mr. Cooke desires to assist Mr. Moran to reach the Yellowstone.* A check for five hundred dollars was attached. Nettleton said further that he had been instructed to take care of Moran's travel arrangements. He had written to Professor Hayden and believed that the scientist would most likely welcome Mr. Moran, especially if he paid his own expenses.

"Thomas!" shouted Gilder. "Thomas, I did it!" But he knew Moran was home, working.

The knock at the door was impatient. Mary Moran hurried to open it. "Yes, yes. Coming."

Richard Gilder stood outside. "Richard!" said Mary. "What a surprise. Please come in. What's happening? You look excited."

"Where's Thomas?"

"In his studio," said Mary, with a slightly worried look.

"Good," said Gilder, removing his hat. He took Mary by the hand and pulled her. "Come with me."

The artist was sitting on a stool with a paintbrush in his mouth. His children were quietly sitting at his feet. The door opened and he looked up, astonished to see Gilder holding a bewildered-looking Mary by the hand.

With a stern expression, Gilder pointed a finger at him. "Tho-

mas, get up and pack your bags, I mean bag. You'll probably only
be allowed one." Then he grinned, hugged Mary, and spun her
around. Still in the embrace of his best friend's wife, Gilder said to
Moran, "You, my dear fellow, are going to the Yellowstone!"

PART 2: THE NEW NORTHWEST

1) The New Northwest

On the twelfth of June, 1871, the placard out side of
Philadelphia's Academy of Music announced an address on *The
New Northwest*. The topic and the speaker, Congressman William
D. Kelly, had drawn four thousand curious Philadelphians to the
auditorium which normally served only two thousand eight hun-
dred.

The Academy of Music had been the permanent home of
Philadelphia's grand opera since it opened in 1857. This evening,
the stage was bare save for a small lectern. The acoustics and seat-
ing arrangements were based on the La Scala opera house, so a
speaker could be heard clearly in the rear corner seats.

Pennsylvania Governor John W. Geary appeared from a side
aisle, said a few words of welcome, then introduced the main speaker
of the evening, a man who needed no formal introduction. Everyone in Philadelphia knew William Kelly.

After a lengthy round of applause, Kelly raised his hand. A
hush came over the crowd. His first words were political and gra-
cious. "I thank you, ladies and gentlemen, for this most cordial
reception, and beg leave to express my gratitude to the gentlemen
who, by their invitation, have afforded me an opportunity to contribute to the completion of a work which, for more than a quarter
of a century, I have regarded as of prime importance to the country
and of special value to my native state."

Kelly had been invited by the Philadelphia Commercial Exchange to speak on what the completion of the Northern Pacific
Railroad might mean to citizens of Philadelphia and residents of

the state in general. The well-known Pennsylvania congressman was a Philadelphian by birth. He was also a promoter of transcontinental rail transportation.

He had always been a popular figure in Philadelphia. He was a humanitarian, an abolitionist, and he was pro-suffrage, he thought everyone had the right to vote. He unhesitatingly encouraged the government to pump money into the economically devastated south. He was the first Pennsylvania politician to address a black mass meeting with black leaders. And after Pennsylvania authorized black troops, Kelly encouraged black men to enlist.

Kelly was also known as the best orator in Congress. His personal history spoke to the common man's view of the world, and his success in life exemplified the opportunities afforded the average man willing to stand on his own two feet. Kelly's father had died when he was two. The only son, Kelly become the man of the family at an early age. To earn money, he trained as a jewelry maker, but his inquiring mind pulled him to the law. By his mid-thirties, Kelly was a judge, and at forty-seven, a congressman. He was now a ranking member of Congress and a member of the Ways and Means Committee.

The huge crowd had been drawn in part because the West remained a realm of high color, drama, and fortune. But they also came to listen to a man for whom they reserved a special feeling. Less than three months earlier, Congress had passed Kelly's plan to create a US Centennial Commission to mount an exposition for the 1876 Centennial celebration. It would be held in Philadelphia.

Out of habit, Congressman Kelly passed a hand through his thick, curly hair before he launched into his presentation. "I do not expect the statement of facts I shall make tonight to be accepted without many grains of allowance by those of you who have not been to the Trans-Mississippi region of our country." He paused, looked into the crowd with a serious expression, then added softly, "And I shall not be surprised if many of you leave the hall with the opinion that I have dealt largely in exaggeration."

"The truth is," said Kelly, raising his chin, "regardless of how well informed a man may be, he cannot imagine the contrasts that exist between the characteristics of our Atlantic and Pacific portions of the country. Only personal experience can impart conviction."

Several people in the front row smiled at the speaker. Kelly wasn't belittling his abilities. His goal for the evening was to overcome the skepticism he knew would float behind the eyes of his audience. With this goal in mind, Kelly had carefully fashioned his presentation on the basis of three important documents and highlights of his personal experience.

The documents were closely related: Lieutenant Gustavus Doane's *Report* of April 1871, on his participation in the Washburn Expedition; an article published in the last two issues of the *Overland Monthly* by Walter Trumbull, son of Senator Lyman Trumbull; and *The Northern Pacific Railroad: Its Route, Resources, Progress, and Business*, written in February 1871 by the Northern Pacific Railroad.

Kelly's personal experience was as broad and rich as the documents he planned to review, especially when it came to the history and development of American railroads. When he needed to lighten his presentation, or when skeptics called for a dose of testimonial, he intended to refer to his cross-country journeys and his personal involvement in railroad transportation

To provide a national context for his points, Kelly intended to review the search for a transcontinental route. To convey a sense of economic importance, he would argue the impact of the best line across America in terms of world trade. And to convey the character of the essentially unknown Northwest in a convincing manner, he would revert to personal observations.

First, Kelly took his audience across the country, following the tracks of the Union Pacific Railroad to San Francisco. He brought the crowds across the cliffs of the Pacific coast, through the redwoods, across the high, wooded hills and valleys into Oregon, to the foothills of the Cascades, and to his final western destination, Willamette, at the mouth of the Columbia. As he talked of the country's weather and soil, and of the influx of thousands of Americans to this extensive frontier, he underscored the economic opportunity that waited for those who would settle in the West and the potential power of a fully settled America.

At the end of his travelogue, Kelly paused. His audience waited. "How can settlement and development of this distant and nearly inaccessible region be accomplished?" he asked. He walked a few feet from the podium, returned, and answered his own question: "Simple: by developing transcontinental corridors.

"The railroads that penetrate the wilderness," stated Kelly, signaling that he had segued to a new topic, "will enable Americans to explore and use the vast resources of their nation, to civilize unused wilderness and fulfill our American dream. We remain a country of pioneers. In Europe, the railroad simply replaces an outworn method of transportation with a more efficient one. Their lands are already fully settled and developed. In America," said Kelly, throwing an arm into the air, "the railroad is the primary explorer of our frontier."

Kelly let the emphasis sink in. "In America," he said more quietly, "the railroad precedes the settler. It aids him in his ever-westward migration. By its presence, it opens new territory, brings in new populations, and creates new wealth."

Kelly raised his head. He caught the audience's attention with a second upraised arm. "Let us return a quarter of a century ago to when civilization had not yet penetrated the Minnesota Territory, when portions of the West were still known as the 'Great Desert.' In 1845, railroads were but a murmur in the corridors of Congress. Then I met Asa Whitney and heard his vision for a transcontinental railroad.

"Asa Whitney! He was a dark, stout and determined-looking man, who had received his understanding of railroads from his brother, who presided over the Philadelphia and Reading Railroad. But do not be misled: Asa Whitney was not a railroad engineer, nor a railroad investor, nor a railroad executive. He was a restless, dissatisfied merchant, who was looking for his purpose in life.

"He found his path and his quest when he was in his mid-thirties," said Kelly quickening his pace. "His purpose came to him in a vision after he visited the distant Orient as a representative of several Philadelphia firms. He brought back the concept of a transcontinental railroad that would reduce travel time between the distant Orient and the East Coast of America.

"Asa Whitney liked the northern route because it was the shortest route to Canton," continued Kelly with a gesture that conveyed nearness. "He also believed that any railroad line laid between these points would serve as a catalyst for settlement. He approached Congress and asked that a strip of land sixty miles wide between Lake Michigan and Puget Sound be set aside for the railroad.

"His scheme," said Kelly, drawing out the word, "was to organize a vast system of immigration from our eastern cities and Europe, without asking Congress for a penny! Congress was highly suspicious. He had offered them no business plan, there was no capital required, no stock to be issued, and no dividends to be made.

'Ridiculous!' they said. 'Unheard of!'

"Whitney responded that the sale of land while the railroad was being constructed would pay for its development. Workmen could be paid partly in land. All the parts of the whole would be interconnected, in a self-supporting network. Once the line was completed, it would create settlements, commerce, and wealth and stimulate production."

Kelly had no trouble convincing his audience that Congress was appalled at the notion! The bolder politicians asked Mr. Whitney, 'What do you want for yourself?' Asa said, 'A salary of four thousand dollars per year.' This altruism fell on disbelieving ears. No one worked solely for the benefit of the country. It was anti-American. Congress decided that Whitney had some vast, hidden speculation in mind. A number of influential people denounced his scheme as a fraud.

Kelly learned towards his audience and hissed. "No one understood."

An undaunted Whitney toured the country, speaking in places like Louisville, Cincinnati, Terre Haute, Chicago, Dayton, Wheeling, and Columbus. He explained how this new railroad would enable a person to traverse the continent in five days at an average speed of thirty miles per hour. The project might take fifteen years, but once it was started, land sales would pay for the estimated sixty million dollars required to build the line.

"Whitney spoke here, in our city," said Kelly, slapping the stand by his side. "December 23, 1846." He wiped his glasses, and grimaced. There was a flash of anger on his face when he added, "It took me six months to collect enough names to sponsor the lecture. And where was it held? At the Chinese Museum."

Kelly's voice was now filled with passion and anguish. "After his presentation, many cried 'Madness! How can that man talk of a railroad through two thousand miles of wilderness, when it is impossible to build a railroad over the Alleghenies!' But, my friends, an awed segment of the audience sent a resolution to Congress to ask that it set aside the land Whitney needed for build his railroad."

The crowd applauded Kelly's words. When it was quiet again, Kelly told how the fates held Whitney on the brink of success. The jealous and powerful Senator Benton of Missouri decided that the opening of the Northwest was not to be. He wanted the first transcontinental line to cross his state instead. So Benton blustered and pontificated until the bill was tabled.

"Elated by the nearness of victory, rather than crushed by the bitterness of defeat, Whitney devoted his time and money for the next two years to promote his concept. The government rejected the project in the name of practicality and questionable data. They didn't know how to react to his idea," said Kelly, throwing his arms over his head. "It was too radical. No one was ready for it."

Kelly then enlivened his presentation. "By 1850, everyone was asking 'What's out there?' Remember the 'Great American Desert?'" he asked. "It literally disappeared from all maps after a detailed survey reported it did *not* exist. The president authorized the secretary of war to make surveys to determine the best route for a transcontinental railroad. Asa Whitney's route was one of six courses to be examined. If the character of the land and the advantages of the route could be properly communicated, building of the line was assured."

Isaac Stevens, Governor of the Territory of Washington, led the surveyor of the northern route. Army Engineer George B. McClellan examined the western half; Stevens examined the eastern portion. He brought prominent road builders, like John Mullan and Frederick Lander, with him.

"Stevens and McClellan found five potential passes through the Rocky Mountains. They also discovered that east of the Rockies the grade is easy and great fields waited to be planted. There was stone for building and water for irrigation.

"Not all the land is suitable for cultivation, but there is rich farming land, good grazing, timber, and abundant minerals for mining. The cost of starting a farm is essentially the cost of the first herd of sheep. Game is abundant. The scenery is rich and variable, replete with lakes, streams, and falls. The summers are Asiatic, the winters no more harsh than upper New York or Wisconsin. From the plains west, the climate steadily modifies until in Oregon and Washington Territory, there is almost no winter at all."

When all the surveys were finished, the government had thirteen quarto volumes called *The Railroad Surveys*, complete with sketches and detailed drawings of plants and animals. The surveys documented the feasibility of six separate routes. Infighting dominated all subsequent congressional debate. In desperation, President Buchanan declared that private industry would have to build the road. Congress would limit its role to providing loans and land grants. The House of Representatives dropped the northernmost and southernmost routes and passed a bill offering land grants to the Union Pacific and Central Pacific.

"Hope for a northern route was then at an all-time low," said Kelly, "but to America and the virginal Northwest, the Northern Pacific Railroad offered everything the Union Pacific and Central Pacific offered the central latitudes of America, perhaps more.

"First, it could place America firmly in the center of world trade, because the route to the Orient is nearly seven hundred miles shorter than even the route to San Francisco. Second, you, as Philadelphians and Pennsylvanians proper, would share in the prosperity. Think what effect the development of the Northwest, with its farm produce and mines, and the increase in international commerce and trade would have on Philadelphia, Baltimore, and New York.

"And as always in this great land of ours, entrepreneurs are making new discoveries daily." Kelly leaned across the speaker's box as if anxious to address each person confidentially. "Who in this room has not heard the rumors of the exotic wonders that lie in the upper reaches of the Yellowstone? As we speak, Professor Ferdinand Hayden makes his way into that mysterious country to unveil its secrets.

"The Northern Pacific Railroad will give Americans access to this unique American wonderland. Only a year ago, a hardy band of men from Helena, Montana, entered this hidden wilderness and wrote about their journey. I invite you to sample nature's incredible wares by reading this month's issue of the *Overland Monthly*."

Congressman Kelly stood as straight as possible and looked into the attentive faces of the audience. "For all the reasons I have spoken of this evening, I regard the construction of the Northern Pacific Railroad as chief among the great works of the future. It will be a magnificent monument to its builders and promoters, and it will abundantly reward their enterprise and labor. More important, its construction will add immeasurably to the wealth, power, and influence of the nation. Good night and God bless you."

Kelly had spoken for two hours. His appearance had had considerable local backing. In addition to the governor, prominent bankers, publishers, and state politicians lent their names as "vice presidents" to the affair. Jay Cooke, publisher H. H. Lippincott, retail merchant John Wanamaker, transportation visionary Asa Whitney, and several generals were among Kelly's supporters.

What Kelly did not say, yet what everyone knew was true, was that his inspired soliloquy was only one of a series of talks taking place around the country in a massive public relations campaign to help the Northern Pacific Railroad finance construction. At one time, more than thirteen hundred newspapers carried advertisements for the Northern Pacific bonds. The Northern Pacific had allocated upwards of one hundred thousand dollars to spend on advertising during the year, forty thousand dollars alone on maps and documents.

Whether congressman Kelly's eloquence would pay off in sales for Jay Cooke and Co. was yet to be determined. In the meantime, the Northern Pacific Railroad line was approaching the Red River of the North.

PART 3: DOCUMENTING THE YELLOWSTONE

1) Camp Stevenson, June 1871

Each day on the high plains of Wyoming, from late May to mid-June, recapitulates the seasons of the year. Winter occupies the night and early morning darkness. Ice covers small ponds, thickets wear hoarfrost, and horses stand haunches to the wind, head down, unmoving. Spring appears when the sun unveils a world of color and warmth. By noon, the last traces of ice disappear and the chalky soil rejects the excess heat. Birds are raucous, and dust swirls high into the air causing men to hold the brims of their hats as they do in summer. By four in the afternoon, a chill pervades the land. Temperatures in the shade fall below fifty; coyotes trot across the hills, and deer emerge to graze before the frost returns. When the sun disappears behind a peak or butte, every living thing finds a warm refuge. Winter returns again, for the night.

Not far from the sun-bleached buildings of Fort D. A. Russell, Wyoming Territory, a lone wall tent fluttered under a cool morning breeze. The tent suddenly collapsed, then disappeared altogether.

From his perch on a small, empty barrel in the shade of the only tree in the area, Captain Jim Stevenson watched the tent disappear. He placed another check mark on his list. That was the last one; everything else had been taken apart, shaken out, folded up, and strapped down. His checklist included forty-eight animals, half of which were mules, five four-mule wagons and two two-horse ambulances which looked as though they had been to California and back; five wall tents, three of which needed additional repair; half a dozen dog tents; and thirty-two humans. Beneath this checklist were twelve other checklists. They included everything from grease to grain and water to whiskey.

Checking the accuracy and completeness of what was loaded onto the train for the annual survey was one of a long, routine series of tasks Stevenson performed. This year, he'd worked with the quartermaster at D. A. Russell for three weeks. The Army kept a lot of old gear that it never used. Stevenson was permitted to buy and occasionally take anything that was written off as old or worn.

This phase of Stevenson's organizational work was one of the most pleasant. He disliked paperwork, but he was in the field where the air was fresh, and he could see a horizon without looking through a window. He was essentially alone, so he could work at his own pace, which meant he could take a moment to sip a beer now and then at the sutler's tavern. And since he wasn't repeatedly pestered, he remained calm enough to use friendly persuasion to resolve his occasional acquisition and supply problem.

Jim Stevenson was a western gentleman by nature, a solitary man who spoke little. When he knew his job and had the time and tools to do it well, he enjoyed his work. He liked being efficient. He stayed in good physical condition, and normally enjoyed a sense of self-confidence. Those he talked to had to listen carefully or they might end up getting their leg pulled, because Stevenson possessed a dry sense of humor.

Stevenson shared his Maysville, Kentucky, birthplace with John Colter, famous explorer of the Lewis and Clark Expedition. Like Colter, he opted to explore the West at a young age. In Stevenson's day, as in Colter's forty years earlier, the far West began at St. Louis. So after he finished his private schooling, he hoofed it to the edge of the Missouri River to take its measure.

When he encountered the energetic Professor Hayden in St. Louis and learned that the man intended to spend his life documenting the West, he threw in with him. This year was Stevenson's tenth season with the geologist. After a few seasons together in the late 1850s, the Civil War had interrupted their relationship. Hayden joined the Union Army as a medical doctor in 1861.

Stevenson joined the 13th New York Volunteers. He made sergeant and received a commission as subaltern, but took his discharge at the end of the war. Each year since his return, Hayden

had given him more responsibility and more leeway, and had relied increasingly on his judgment and advice. Stevenson couldn't
imagine working for anyone except the professor. Hayden was closer
to him than any cousin or uncle. He thought they made a great
team.

A round of fretful neighing reached Stevenson from the loading ramps. He looked over his shoulder toward the sidetracks where
two hands were loading the last of the horses. Two were refusing to
climb the ramp that led to the boxcar. They would get halfway up,
then balk, kick, or jump sideways. Stevenson watched for a moment, muttered something about having to do everything himself,
mounted his horse, and cantered unhurriedly toward the scene.

As he reined in his horse to a walk, the two men walked his
way. "You'll have to trade them hosses in, boss," said a man named
Pete. He had a bent leg and was missing half his teeth, but he was
reliable. The other spat and nodded in agreement.

"Probably. Give me the reins of the roan," said Stevenson
matter-of-factly as he dismounted. The ears of the young, sturdy
roan were back and she was jumpy. She kept looking around as
though someone were prodding her in the rear. Christ, he thought,
this horse is a mare and she's in heat. He slid his hand up the reins
and patted the side of the horse's neck. "Whoa, girl. Steady." He
slipped off his neckerchief and handed it to Pete. "Tie one end to
her halter, pull it across her eyes, and tie it on the other side."

Pete climbed a post fence next to the horse and did as he was
told. When Pete was done the horse stood still. "Come on, girl,"
said Stevenson. He talked to her quietly and led her up the ramp.
"Move them geldings to the far side," he yelled as he approached
the boxcar. "Leave this mare by herself."

Remounted, Stevenson tied his kerchief back around his neck.
"Just make sure the horses on both sides of her are mares. You
know what a mare looks like now, don't you, Pete?" he said in soft
rebuke, then rode back towards his shady tree and his paperwork.
He was fussy, and Dr. Hayden had come to expect him to account
for everything at the end of the season. Whenever something significant was missing in the tally, Stevenson would try to run down
the errant item. Doc would pat him on the shoulder: "Don't fuss at

it, Jim," he'd say. "You're doing more than most. I don't know what I would do without you."

Over the years, as operations manager for the survey, Stevenson had acquired the skills of a first-class scrounge. Hayden didn't have to tell him to get things as cheaply as possible; he knew his employer's concern for looking responsible with public funds. Each summer, Stevenson waged a little contest with himself to see how far he could come under budget. This year he wanted to save twenty percent.

Hayden asked for and most often received free passage for the men and equipment from the Union Pacific. Stevenson was responsible for everything else. He had to purchase Army reject horses and mules, but this summer, after three weeks, he'd managed to acquire nearly a mile of braided rope of different sizes, a few chairs, one table, an old cook stove, a galley full of pots and pans, some horseshoe repair tools, and awls for repairing leather, all free of charge.

As he flipped through his papers, Stevenson found a note he'd left himself. He was going to ask the military post trader to set aside some canned goods. He'd wanted to give them to Hayden as a treat. He glanced at his watch, calculated how much time he needed, and decided it was worth a ride to the little store just outside the post. He could see the fort in the distance from where he stood. No railroad engine was in sight: just the two boxcars and three flat cars that carried survey gear, and one passenger car that contained thirty-four men who were talking, playing cards, and waiting. Stevenson took a pack horse instead of a wagon; it was faster.

An hour later, trailing the pack horse with its panniers full of canned goods, Stevenson pushed his mount over the last ridge. The camp scene looked even more peaceful than before. That's the way it should look, he thought; deserted, now that everything has been packed. After a moment of searching the horizon, Stevenson thought it appeared a bit too deserted. Ah, the train had left. Everyone had gone. He was alone.

"Well, I'll be . . ." he said in exasperation. He pulled his watch from his vest and stared at it. The dials did not move. It was either broke or he'd forgotten to wind it. He'd missed the train. His eyes followed the tracks towards the horizon, but he saw no smoke. Without further ado, Stevenson kicked his horse into a trot towards the train depot. As he neared the railroad siding, he grunted with relief to see an engine on the siding. A few railroad men moved nearby.

Stevenson knew it would be weeks before the men would quit reminding him of this little mistake. Hayden wouldn't say anything directly; however, he'd find a way to weave it into the conversation at least once, and then his eyes would glitter.

Ferdinand Hayden was having trouble concentrating. Most of the time, neither the swaying of the railroad car nor the loud talk and laughter of the survey men bothered him. He shut out the noise while he read a report or reviewed plans. This afternoon, however, he wanted a little peace and quiet to find the right words to express his concern to Spencer Baird. By the time he'd written half of what he needed, he'd decided that he'd better write Richard Dana, too. The letters were not the kind he relished, but he wanted to head off trouble. It looked as though the Yale gang was after him once again. Better to be prepared than to be unpleasantly surprised.

Hayden's problem had been brought to his attention by Henry Elliott. While the Hayden crew was camped at Fort D. A. Russell, a large body of men had ridden in on horseback and camped nearby. It was Clarence King and his survey team. Their presence disturbed Hayden, because he felt uncomfortable in King's presence, so he ignored the group.

Elliott knew several of the men in King's party, so he rode over for a chat. The following day, Elliott told Hayden of his brief conversation with King. King told Elliott that while he'd been back in New Haven, some unidentified person had read him a scathing criticism of Hayden's latest annual report and said that he was planning to have it published in *Silliman's Journal*. Dana was the editor of the journal.

Without any visible reaction, Hayden had thanked Elliott for the news, but the hearsay troubled him. What was the New England clique up to this time? Would Dana permit the criticism to be published? Hayden speculated that Marsh might have been the instigator. That made sense to him after the way Marsh had stormed into his camp last fall. Damn! Why didn't they leave him alone?

He knew why: they wanted all the glory, all the credit, and no competition. And each year that the Hayden survey was funded and his reputation grew, he was more of a threat to them. Yes, he thought, King and his colleagues, those infernal meddlers, would welcome anything that would reflect poorly on him or his survey.

It took Hayden an hour to complete his task. He asked Dana to be on the lookout for the alleged letter and to at least let him know its contents if he was going to publish it. To Baird he wrote, *it will show a hard spirit on the part of the New Haven clique if they kill me off. The center of western exploration would be transferred to New Haven and Cambridge, but my friends must stand by me and be strong.*

Having done all he could for the nonce, Hayden turned to the more pleasant task of reading reports about the Yellowstone. He had time. The train would take two days to get to Ogden. Before he left Washington, D.C., Hayden had gathered all the background material he could find on the Yellowstone. He had a government print of Warren's mid-1850s military reports, and one of the post-Civil War printing of Raynolds's 1859-1860 expedition. The one he had found most fascinating was Doane's report on the Washburn Expedition. Baird had loaned his only copy to Hayden. "It's only a loan, Doctor. I expect a timely return," Baird had said with a gruff smile.

Hayden also had a copy of Langford's article from the May issue of *Scribner's*. Langford also sent Hayden an advance copy of his follow-up article for the June issue. Then Langford sent a letter telling why he couldn't accompany him this summer. As though to make up for his delinquency, Langford included a full-size copy of his map.

When Hayden couldn't find Langford's map, he looked for Stevenson. Hayden stopped a young man ambling down the aisle of the car. "Clifford?"

"Yes, sir." The teenage lad stopped and waited.

"See if you can find Jim Stevenson for me, please? I need him. He could be anywhere."

"Sure, Professor Hayden," said the young man. Clifford Negley, the second son of General, and more recently, Congressman James Scott Negley, turned and sauntered back the way he had come. Hayden watched him go, hoping that the youth would make some contribution to the survey. General Negley was an influential Pennsylvania congressman and had been a good friend during the Civil War. He'd been one of the first to ask if it might be possible to get a young relative out west for a season.

Hayden thought of how many youngsters he had with him this year. His need to accommodate his political friends without padding his team with deadwood was becoming a problem. The pressure to take dozens more had been fearful; turning so many down had been difficult. Each person requesting a favor supported Hayden's surveys and Hayden needed to keep their support. He finally permitted five general assistant slots. Clifford Negley occupied one. One had been given to Chester M. Dawes, a son of Congressman Henry L. Dawes of Massachusetts, one of Hayden's most important supporters. A third went to William B. Logan, the son of his old senatorial friend John A. Logan who now headed the Committee of Military Affairs.

Three other relatively young members of the survey team, Albert Charles Peale, Robert Adams, and George B. Dixon, were Hayden's choice. All were former students of his at the University of Pennsylvania. Each was intelligent, enthusiastic, and dexterous, so Hayden had no qualms about the quality of the work they would produce even if the field of responsibility was new.

Albert Peale, who had recently received his medical degree from the University of Pennsylvania, was from the socially prominent Peale family of Philadelphia. His grandfather was the renowned painter Reubens Peale and his great-grandfather was Charles Willson Peale, famous portrait painter of the Revolutionary War period. This was Albert's first year with the survey, but Hayden had assigned him the important job of mineralogy. The task had been assigned to Professor Allen. Unfortunately, Allen's physical condition at age fifty-eight was not up to the task. When Hayden saw that Allen would be unable to tackle the job, he switched assignments around before the survey left Cheyenne. To his credit, Peale spent every free moment developing the skills to carry out his assignment.

Hayden's second choice, Robert Adams, age twenty-five, had been a bright classics student who had taken several of Hayden's classes. He had graduated in 1868 and now studied law in Philadelphia. Hayden had invited him because Adams was an engaging person, one who displayed an eager interest in the West. Adams also promised to send articles to the New York and Philadelphia newspapers for which he was a freelance correspondent. Free publicity was always a significant plus to Hayden.

Hayden's third selection had been George Dixon of Philadelphia, who was still an undergraduate student studying medicine. At the moment, he held the generic title of assistant.

While Hayden waited for Stevenson, the train began to slow. It continued to decelerate until it stopped on a sidetrack at a little station called Tie Siding. The terrain was barren, a windy plain of granite that extended across southeast Wyoming. Overhead, low clouds moved in a leisurely fashion, but tufts of buffalo grass nodded nervously and Hayden could hear the periodic whump of a buffeting wind. Hayden looked out across the frosty plains to the peaks of the Colorado Rockies. Some day, he thought, I will need to survey those ranges, too.

After a few moments of silence, his inner voice pestered him. Why had the train stopped? How long would they be here? Was an eastbound train scheduled through? His survey team had hundreds of miles to cover this summer. He couldn't afford to start late. The delay triggered feelings of helplessness which agitated him. Jim knew the answers. Where the devil was he?

Cyrus Thomas, seated across from Hayden, broke the silence with his thin Kentucky twang. "Hey, Professor Hayden, looks like something's poppin'."

The second engineer climbed aboard the passenger car, spotted Hayden, and walked to him. As Hayden turned, the engineer stuck out his right hand and handed him a telegram. "It's not a problem, Dr. Hayden" he said cryptically, "We'll wait."

"What's not a problem? Wait for what?" asked Hayden. But the engineer left without saying more. Hayden unfolded the telegram. It read, *You left without me. Will catch you at Tie Siding. If you leave without me again, I won't be responsible. Stop. Stevenson.*

Hayden frowned, then looked around as if expecting to see Stevenson's stoic face. "Oh, for pity's sake," he said, chuckling lightly. Jim was still back at camp.

He handed the message to Cyrus Thomas, who was craning his neck to read it. Now, a number of the survey crew were looking at Hayden as though they expected an announcement. Cyrus Thomas clapped his leg with glee. "Stevenson missed the train?" he exclaimed. "Well now, ain't that a hoot? I bet he's fit to be tied. He don't cotton to things that ain't tied right. He sure don't like being the butt of trouble."

An hour later, while Hayden was in the middle of Doane's *Report*, a lone, black shape puffed slowly across the sea of pink granite. Cyrus Thomas and most of the others had disembarked from the train. The word about Stevenson having been left behind had gotten around quickly. All of the boys were waiting.

Hayden walked to the rear of the car and watched as the driver of the Union Pacific blew the whistle and waved to the survey lads. The men waved back. The engine came to a stop behind the survey train. Jim Stevenson stuck his head out of the cab. Most of the survey team were right next to the engine now. A few were shouting and laughing. Well, thought Hayden, it's a good one on Jim. Stevenson ignored the hecklers and climbed down.

But before he touched ground, about fifteen men from the survey swarmed toward Stevenson. Hands lifted him high. Despite his protests and amid shouts and laughter, he was carried toward the waiting survey train. While Stevenson hollered "Put me down!" and uttered dire threats, some of the boys started singing "For he's a jolly good fellow." A few sat in the dirt and howled at the undignified form of their dignified Captain.

The man who was deposited at Hayden's feet was red-faced and confounded. He dusted his pant legs while the laughter and singing subsided. At the top of the steps, Hayden said "Welcome back. We were beginning to miss you." The men laughed again. A few applauded. Stevenson said nothing.

Camp Stevenson, as Hayden had named it, in part because of the unofficial celebration of Stevenson's return, was located about a mile east and a day's ride south of Ogden. Stevenson set the camp near a stream on an old lake terrace. From camp, they could see the shores of the Salt Lake.

Hayden planned to explore parts of the Wasatch Mountains before they left the area. Local forays would give the men a chance to refamiliarize themselves with the routines of fieldwork and give Stevenson an opportunity to correct any last-minute problems with the gear. Stevenson liked to have everything tight and trim before they left for the Yellowstone; once on the road, there would be no turning back.

The following day was clear and hot, and there were no trees on the bench. Under the pulled-down brim of his hat, Stevenson watched a wagon pull into camp. The driver was familiar; the woman who sat next to the driver was not, but she was very pretty. The driver turned out to be William Henry Jackson, so Stevenson was pretty sure that the woman was Jackson's wife, Mollie. His friend had spoken of her often enough.

Stevenson walked over to the wagon where Jackson was already removing boxes and camera apparatus. "She can't go," said Stevenson for openers. "You'll never get any work done, and Professor Hayden will blame me." He then tipped his hat to Mollie and smiled. "Welcome, Mrs. Jackson, ma'am."

Jackson introduced Mollie to Jim Stevenson. As he continued to unload, he added, "If you listen to anything Jim says, my dear, you'll end up lost, hungry, and surrounded by Indians, so just do the opposite of what he tells you. Everyone does and we're all healthy."

Stevenson held up one or two strange-looking items in the wagon, then looked at Jackson. "If you think you're gonna get a mule to haul all this newfangled gear, you're dizzier than you were last year."

The year before, Jackson had used a camera that accommodated a six-and-one-half-inch by eight-and-one-half-inch glass negative. This year he brought one that took an eight-inch by ten-inch plate. But he also brought along last year's camera for emergencies. The third camera he unloaded was stereoscopic. He had decided to bring that one because stereoscopic views were so popular back east.

"You just going to sound bossy and complain or are you going to help?" asked Jackson. The wagon was full of tins and bottles of chemicals for developing and toning. Jackson had also brought crated photographic glass plates and tightly wrapped bundles of albumen paper. Professor Hayden had emphasized that he wanted quick publication, so Jackson knew he had to have all the necessaries for making prints in the field. To make life in the field easier this year, Jackson had exchanged his old panniers for a new set of sole leather cases which were more accessible for loading and unloading. He also had replaced the cumbersome water kegs with large rubber bags.

"With all this junk, you'll cost us more in freight than you're worth," said Stevenson, with his arms full.

"Mr. Stevenson, sir," said Jackson, ignoring everything Stevenson said, "you'll have to watch your tongue for a while, because Mollie's going to accompany us on some of our local excursions." Jackson, of course, had never heard Jim Stevenson utter a single swear word.

"She's probably a better photographer than you are," said Stevenson.

Jackson lit one of his customary cheroots. "Where's Gifford?"

Stevenson shook his head. "He's not here. Dr. Hayden hasn't heard from him."

"The others?"

"You're the last one." He didn't say "as usual," but it was implied in his tone. The two men walked toward Hayden's tent.

"Most of the old-timers are back," Stevenson said, conversationally: "Elliott, Thomas, Potato John. Couple of new faces, Anton Schonborn and Dr. Hayden's old teacher, Professor Allen." Stevenson shook his head. "Then, there's the new mavericks to break in."

"Well," said Jackson with a laugh as he held the tent flap for Mollie, "you always did need something to keep you occupied."

Stevenson looked at his friend in an unfriendly way and walked off.

Mollie looked at her husband. "Do you two always treat one another like that?"

"Sure," said Jackson. "He's a good friend. Keeps things from getting boring around here." He smiled.

Mollie proved to be a calming ingredient for the week she remained in camp. She stayed close to her husband and assisted him in his trial runs with his new cameras. She also delighted in having her picture taken with the boys. Her gentle manners and pleasing disposition had a healthy effect on the men. Hayden noticed that they were more careful about their language, their behavior, and their appearance. In fact, Hayden didn't think he'd ever seen such a clean-looking bunch of field hands. It made him think more favorably about permitting Emma to accompany the survey for a season.

To date, weather had not interfered with their work. On the contrary, the days had been clear, bright, and invigorating. It was too good to last. After four days of sunshine, Hayden woke to a low ceiling of thick clouds and distant thunder. On this gloomy day, Hayden received a message from the Department of the Army. He'd been expecting a response from General Sheridan to his request for an escort plus his request to have Lieutenant Doane accompany him. When he read the telegram, he grunted in a way that said all was not right with the world.

He tossed the telegram on the camp table in front of where Stevenson sat fiddling with a stirrup. "Sometimes," he said, "I wonder whether our survey will ever get the respect it deserves."

Stevenson heard the discouragement in Hayden's voice and looked at the telegram on the table.

"For heaven's sake, we don't need that!" Hayden pointed to the telegram. "Like it or not, we're to have more company."

"Oh?" That did concern Stevenson. "Who, and for what purpose?" He read the telegram himself.

"I don't know. I made a simple request of General Sheridan for an escort, so now he tells some captain of the Corps of Engineers that he should accompany us. Read the part where this officer says he would have explored the Yellowstone himself if we hadn't already been on the move. You can bet this man won't come alone!"

"What did you ask for?"

"A few soldiers. Doane in particular, since he's already been to the Yellowstone."

"Is he coming? The telegram doesn't mention him."

Hayden threw up his arms. "I don't know. Captain Barlow is from Sheridan's headquarters in Chicago, so he probably doesn't know either. There's nothing for it except to make the best of it. He wants to know where to meet us. What do you think? Fort Ellis? Seems a logical point." Hayden didn't wait for Stevenson to respond. He snatched the telegram and waved it angrily. "This reeks of politics."

The following day, Hayden wrote an acknowledging note to Captain Barlow, and sent his first interim report to the secretary of the interior. *Leaving here the morning of June 9 along the mail route to Virginia City and Fort Ellis,* he wrote. *Already made observations in this valley to connect our work topographically and geologically with the Pacific Railroad. Will examine a band of country one hundred to one hundred fifty miles in width to Fort Ellis. Remainder of the season will be about the sources of the Yellowstone, Green, and Columbia. All is well.* He attached a copy of an article by Peale about the survey team, which had been published in the *Deseret News.*

The weather continued overcast and rainy. Hayden wrote to Baird and sent a note to Emma. To Baird, he described his chosen route and general plans, then took a few lines to express his hesitation about the new ornithologist for the season. He chose his words carefully, for Baird had handpicked Frederick Huse, the assistant secretary of the Academy of Natural Sciences in Chicago, for the position. In contrast, Hayden wrote enthusiastically about Schonborn, whom he called a capital topographer. "I question very much whether King has anyone with him that will be his equal," he wrote.

Hayden spoke highly of Schonborn in part because he and Schonborn were both German and had been fellow members of the Megatherium Club. Named after the great mythological beast, Megatheria, the club was a little Smithsonian social group headed by Baird. It provided young, eager scientists an opportunity to play as hard as they worked. Baird nourished the foolhardy antics of Megatherium members as thoroughly as he nourished the aspirations and talents of its members.

The weather cleared on June tenth. In the blue-gray, dust-free dawn, thirty-two men and seven wagons headed north. Each man was expected to care for his horse, do his job, and stand guard as needed. Most of the men carried butcher knives or pistols, and nearly everyone had a rifle. The daily routine was not military crisp because the men were scientists, but everyone rose for breakfast before dawn and returned by noon for the main meal of the day. Supper was usually skimpy, often consisting of what each already had or could find if he was still working.

Time and circumstance would test the mettle and talent of each person. No one knew exactly what lay ahead or what they would be called upon to do. That was part of the adventure. To Professor Hayden, U.S. Geologist, former lone explorer of the badlands, the survey appeared much too much like a small army on the march.

2) An Obvious Dude

Fort Ellis lay four hundred fifty miles to the north and east. Stevenson stood momentarily in the stirrups and leaned on the saddle horn as he watched the last of the wagons slide into line. Off to one side, three of the younger political legacies herded the mules. Stevenson settled back and nudged the big gray with his heels. The horse moved methodically down the slope, placing its feet on the least stony places. On the flat, Stevenson tugged once on the rim of his hat and urged the gray into a slow canter. It was good to be on the road again.

As they moved towards Cache Valley, one thousand feet above the Great Salt Lake, the rocks of the country looked bold and proud. Colorful outcrops punctuated the flanks of distant gray-green mountains. The landscape's sparse vegetative cover enabled the trained eye to trace strata and geological structure. The only color for miles was a blue, cherty limestone, but side trips yielded excellent fossils like corals, ribbed *Spirifers*, and the walnut-shaped *Productus*, brachiopods of the Carboniferous Period.

Once, while Anton Schonborn was setting his instruments on a high promontory, Hayden discovered that he could see the lines of the terraces that had formed the shoreline of the lake in Pleistocene times. Based on the height above the current shores, Hayden determined that the lake had been a hundred times larger than the Salt Lake of today. He remarked to Schonborn that the geological history of the surrounding country might be traced by linking internal evidence of rocky strata from the earliest period to the present time. "By describing topographical features of the country along our route," he said casually, "I should be able to reconstruct the physical geography of past geological times." He looked at Schonborn for friendly confirmation.

The first few days passed without incident, save for a chance encounter with a small band of Shoshone Indians herding ponies. When the braves discovered that no one was interested in trading, a few followed the survey to beg for sacks of flour, what they called hog meat. Professor Hayden walked towards Potato John, who was trying to keep the Indians away from the food cache. "No hog meat. Go on, now. Beat it."

Hayden spoke enough Shoshone to understand the braves' wishes. He refused their request, but by using sign and their own language, he invited them to dine with the crew. They accepted, but sat together, away from the table. When they finished, they left without a word.

Jackson watched them go, then turned to Hayden. "The Indians ever give you any real trouble, Dr. Hayden?" he asked. Hayden shook his head. "They're just hungry," he said, "and we're an opportunity. Not that they won't take advantage; they will, but if you share, they think twice about robbing you."

The survey continued along the Cache Valley, a broad plain some seven miles wide that extended fifty-four miles north and south. Further north, in the Port Neuf Valley, Hayden examined igneous rocks and strange flow structures in the lava. He traced the perimeter of what he called a "recent lake" of the volcanic flow. Once cooled, the igneous material had been subjected to heavy wind and water erosion. Miles of lava beds had disappeared. On the sides of the Port Neuf Canyon remnants of the lava flow indicated that the waters had eroded channels through the mass. Hayden wrote that he was convinced that this comparatively modern eruption of igneous material had covered an immense area of the country, *a lake of igneous material of which the Snake River Basin was the center.*

Jackson documented their June journey with photographs of the camp at Ogden and Cache Valley. He took shots of Bear River Crossing at the head of Cache Valley, and of their camp on Gooseberry Creek and Red Rock Pass to record the one hundred mile mark of the journey. Hayden asked Jackson to photograph the spectacular scene at Port Neuf Canyon, and to especially capture the way in which the volcanic overflow had filled the floor. While he was at it, he might also capture the stratigraphy of the canyon walls, because they showed five to six thousand feet of quartzites.

The survey paused at Old Fort Hall for two days. The stage that connected Salt Lake City, Virginia City, and Helena brought Hayden three letters, including one from General Nettleton from the Northern Pacific Railroad office in New York. Nettleton wrote that a Philadelphia artist named Thomas Moran was anxious to make sketches of the Yellowstone. The sketches would later be made into paintings. If possible, he would like to join Hayden's survey party at Virginia City or Helena, and travel with them to the headwaters of the Yellowstone.

Hayden read the letter with interest. He had hoped that Gifford would be with them for the summer, but the artist had failed even to respond to Hayden's invitation to return. Elliott was a good artist, but he would be fully occupied. Who was this fellow, this Thomas Moran? General Nettleton said he'd encouraged the artist to believe that Hayden would be glad to have him join his party and would likely extend to him every facility.

Please understand that we do not wish to burden you with more people than you can attend to, wrote Mr. Nettleton, *but I think that Mr. Moran will be a very desirable addition to your expedition and that he will be almost no trouble at all, and it will be a great accommodation to both the house of Jay Cooke and the railroad if you will assist him in his efforts. He, of course, expects to pay his own expenses, and simply wishes to take advantage of your cavalry escort for protection. You may also have six square feet in some tent which he can occupy nights. We shall be pleased to receive occasional letters from you telling of your expedition, your discovery, your opinion of things, etc. And if there is any way in which we can serve you be sure to let us know. Please write on receipt of this saying what you can do in the way of accommodating him so that he may know what to take with him and what to leave behind.*

P.S. Mr. Moran will possibly go to Corinne by rail and then cross over by stage to Helena in time to join you there. Mr. Bierstadt may join you in Montana, but this is only a possibility.

Albert Bierstadt? He was a nationally known artist. That would be most advantageous, thought Hayden. As for Mr. Moran, Hayden wondered how serendipitous his arrival might be. He was worried about the still-expanding size of his party. In addition to Captain Barlow and his crew and now this artist, Thomas Moran, how many others might appear before they reached the Yellowstone?

The second letter was from Baird, a note to encourage Hayden to continue to send status reports. *It will give me something to give to* Harper's Weekly wrote Baird. He ended with a quick aside that, although he had heard nothing of it, he would be on the lookout for the critical article of which Hayden had written. *If there is anything I will obtain copies and send to you.*

A third letter from Captain Barlow in Chicago acknowledged Hayden's good graces in allowing him to join his party. *Captain Heap of the Engineers Company will accompany me with two or three others*, wrote Barlow. *We may bring a photographer. About fourteen people and thirty animals in all.* The number confirmed Hayden's growing fear. He calculated the size of the troop entering the Yellowstone, then finished reading the letter. *Expect to reach*

Fort Ellis in time to start with your party to the Yellowstone, wrote
Barlow. *We plan to record latitude and longitude, but our trip will
be more observation than survey.*

On the twenty-fourth of June they camped at Taylor's Bridge
near the banks of the Snake. The land had flattened out into a dry,
hot plain covered with volcanic dust which, once disturbed by the
hooves of the animals, quickly rose into a choking, motionless cloud.
Far ahead, at the southern tip of the Bitterroot Mountains, their
route would take them over the Continental Divide which marked
the beginning of the Montana Territory. In the meantime, the early
mornings were dust-free and they could see the sharply etched
profile of the Grand Tetons seventy miles to the east. "French
voyageurs used to call them 'Les Trois Papes,' the three teats,"
said Hayden with a man-to-man grin to young Robert Adams.

On the last night of June, the party made camp within hailing
distance of the Junction Stage stop at Monida Pass on the Continental Divide. The air was pleasant and cool, and the sun was fading. Stevenson watched a small group of mule deer browse at the
edge of a patch of woods while he repaired a saddle. Suddenly the
deer lifted their heads, turned as one, and disappeared. Stevenson
heard and saw nothing, but moments later, a stagecoach pulled to a
stop on the main road. A tall, thin fellow with a floppy hat got out of
the carriage. The driver tossed him a soft bag, pointed in Stevenson's
direction, and drove off.

Still working on the saddle, Stevenson kept an eye on the fellow as he walked up the grade towards their camp. He was a young
man, bony in his slimness, with a silken imperial mustache whose
ends brushed his cheekbones and a light brown beard that was
longer than Stevenson's, but not as full, or, thought Stevenson, as
well trimmed. Like most beards of the day, this fellow's totally obscured the lower half of his face. It left the observer to stare at a
long, straight nose and two deep-set, quick-moving eyes.

An Easterner, thought Stevenson. He tugged at the rawhide.
Another dude; that's all we need. Stevenson didn't base his conclusion on the man's dress; the boots, rough brown pants, and red
flannel shirt didn't say much one way or another, nor did the Smith
and Wesson pistol tucked in the man's belt. Anyone with any sense

dressed for survival. Stevenson had merely watched the way the
man related to the country. He kept looking around as though it
was the first time he'd ever seen a mountain, and he walked like a
man who didn't know why he should watch where he was going.
Twice, the man had paused for breath, a sign that he wasn't used to
the altitude.

The young man stopped about ten feet away and dropped the
carpetbag on the ground. "Good afternoon," he said.

Stevenson looked at him and nodded.

"My name is Thomas Moran," continued the fellow. "I'm looking for a Professor Hayden. I don't know whether I'm expected, but
I'm here." While he talked, still a bit out of breath, he pulled a
letter from his pocket and extended it to Stevenson. "What glorious country," he remarked.

Stevenson flashed a quick look around to see what in particular the fellow considered to be "glorious." All he found was a series of smooth, green hills peppered with large, round boulders,
yet almost entirely devoid of trees and brush.

The letter was more interesting than the landscape. It was
from the same Nettleton who had written Hayden earlier. This note
said, *That Mr. Moran will surpass Bierstadt's Yosemite, we who know
him best fully believe. He goes out under the patronage of Messieurs
Scribner's and Co. publishers of New York and our Mr. Cooke on
whom you will convey a very great favor by receiving Mr. Moran
into your party.*

Very complimentary, thought Stevenson.

*I have assured Mr. Moran he would be welcomed by you. Please
do the best you can to facilitate his mission. I read of your progress
in the* Philadelphia Bulletin *with interest. Nettleton.*

Stevenson looked at the artist, who was still examining the
views. Now he was seated on a rock. He'd pulled a notebook from
his jacket pocket and was making short quick lines with a stubby
pencil on the pad. Stevenson took a long look at the frail man's
outfit and scraggly-looking carpetbag, and wondered what kind of
a horse he could give this fellow who had probably never been west
of Pittsburgh.

"Be right back," he said to Moran. What he really had wanted to do was say to the skinny artist, "I'll give you a week before you quit." Instead, he said to himself as he went to find Dr. Hayden.

Ferdinand Hayden was in his tent, writing. Stevenson showed Hayden the letter, waited until he'd read most of it, then casually said, "He's waiting out there for you now, with two Saratoga trunks."

"What?" said Hayden, wide-eyed. He muttered something about how he'd "fix him," and moved swiftly to locate and chastise this newcomer. Two Saratoga trunks, indeed. Hayden spotted Moran relaxed on a rock projection, one knee up, talking to one of the young assistants. Before Hayden reached them, he was shouting, "Sir, with all due respect, what's this nonsense about . . ." He stopped and looked about him but saw only Moran's floppy carpetbag.

Startled at Hayden's sudden outburst, Moran stopped talking. Hayden, caught off guard, scratched a cheek, then glanced toward Stevenson, who was once again quietly working on the saddle. Hayden shook his head and looked at the carpetbag a second time. Then, with a smile and outstretched hand, he said, "I'm Professor Hayden. You must be Thomas Moran. Welcome to our survey."

Hayden noticed that beneath Moran's bony eyebrows, the artist's eyes were an intense blue-gray. His nose was straight and slender. A large, flowing mustache and an undisciplined brown beard made the nose all the more noticeable. After a few quick exchanges, they moved towards the rest of the camp where the coffee was still hot. Hayden was satisfied that the man would not be troublesome. As to what he might contribute, it was far too early to tell.

As they passed Jim Stevenson, Moran nodded. Hayden gave Stevenson a look of exasperation.

". . . immense and towering bluffs whose colors are very difficult to describe. They came right down to the river's edge." Moran's gaunt frame was bent forward. His hands and arms shaped imaginary cliffs. Had his hands been more still, the men on the other side of the campfire would have thought he was simply warming them. "If the train hadn't stopped, I never would have had time to sketch them. They were magnificent."

"Yes, the Green River bluffs are an extremely interesting feature," said Hayden. "We visited the area last year. Is this your first time west?" he asked, certain that he already knew the answer.

"Yes," said Moran. "About ten years ago I did spend one night camping on the shores of Lake Superior." He paused, shrugged, and added, "That doesn't seem to count now, not in terms of what I have seen since I passed Green River."

Supper for the artist consisted of bread, cold beans, and coffee. It was one more indication to Moran that everything "out here" would be radically different from all his other experiences. He was sitting on a flat stone, near Jim Stevenson who had taken a moment to watch the colors fade from the underside of the clouds.

"Breathtaking, isn't it?" said Moran.

"Great color, but most eastern folk find this country high, dry, and empty," said Stevenson, summing up the world he loved.

"Nothing I have read in Parkman's *Overland Trail* or Greeley's *Overland Journey* properly prepared me," continued Moran, as though Stevenson had never spoken. "I didn't realize that everything would be so . . . basic."

"You mean primitive," offered Jackson, extending a cheroot to the artist. Moran accepted, then poked a stick into the fire for a brand.

"Yes, I suppose I do," said Moran. "You wouldn't believe the number of guns all of the men on the stage had in their possession. For a moment I thought they were part of an Army wagon. Everyone kept saying to keep an eye open for road agents. For most of the journey I thought they meant to look out for employees of the stage company."

Everyone laughed except Jim Stevenson. He closed his eyes at Moran's naiveté.

"Have you fired your pistol yet?" asked Clifford Negley.

"Heavens, no," said Moran as he pulled out the weapon tucked in his belt and looked at it. "Someone will have to show me first."

In the ensuing silence, Moran worked over several sketches he'd made earlier in the day. Stevenson studied the artist. He was certain that Moran was too frail to last long, but he noted a resolute quality he had missed earlier. He wasn't sure Moran had gotten his earlier point, so he added, "This is rough country, Mr. Moran, especially for someone not used to its ways."

"To me, it's an adventure I have been looking forward to for years," said Moran. "It's a vision I've had, entering a land that represents what I call 'grand nature.'"

"Plenty of that to come, I assure you," said Hayden. "And tomorrow is another day. Good-night, all." Suddenly, Hayden pointed towards the northern sky. "Ah," he said. "A sign of good fortune."

"What's that?" asked George Dixon.

"That red-orange glow in the sky. That's the northern lights."

"I thought maybe it was a forest fire," said Potato John. "Been that way for several hours now. Flickers now and then."

Those who stood to watch the glow drifted away to sleeping rolls and tents. Soon, only Dixon, Peale, Moran, and Jackson were left to tend the fire.

"You're from Philadelphia, aren't you?" Peale asked Moran.

"Was," said Moran. "I moved to New York City not long ago. An artist, especially a married one, has to earn a living like anyone else. A true bother." Moran did not say that he was actually born in Lancashire, England. His father had been a spinner. Their cottage had been a workshop for cotton as well as a house full of love and children. When Moran was very young, his father moved the family to America. For a long time, they lived on the Germantown Road in Kensington, near Bordentown, a suburb of Philadelphia.

"Everyone here is from Philadelphia," Dixon remarked.

"Not everyone," said Jackson. "I'm from New England. I've never even been to Philadelphia, although I must say it seems like I've been everywhere else. I came out here when I was not much older than you, Dixon. Been taking pictures ever since."

"Of course," said Moran, realizing who Jackson was. "You're the survey photographer. I would like to see some of your prints later, if I may."

"Any time. Perhaps you can give me some ideas. The artist who accompanied us last year, you might know him, Mr. Sanford Gifford of New York, was quite instructive when it came to compositions."

"I'll be happy to assist in any way I can. In exchange, perhaps you'll help me stay out of trouble . . . you know, the kind green-horns tend to get into." Dixon and Peale laughed.

"If you need an assistant, Mr. Jackson," said Dixon, "I'd take it as a favor if you would ask for me. I'm strong and quick and I don't drop things very often."

Jackson pulled on his cheroot and said studiously, "Well, Dixon, I am going to need help, that's for sure, but I think we'll let the mules carry most of the gear."

Moran grinned, knowing that Jackson was having a little fun with Dixon. But Dixon wasn't quite sure what that meant. Was Mr. Jackson saying yes or no?

A moment later, Jackson said, "Tomorrow, tell Professor Hayden that you're with me from now on, at least until you drop something." He burst into laughter which made Dixon blush, and that made all of them laugh.

Late that day, while Hayden was out, Jackson asked Stevenson to show him once again where they were planning to go. Stevenson pointed out Union Pass in the Wind River Mountains. "From here, ten years ago, we saw the Yellowstone rim for the first time," he said. "Dr. Hayden sort of promised that some day we'd get there." He circled the region he knew represented the source of the Yellowstone River.

"I thought he'd completely forgotten. I should have known better." Stevenson rolled up the map and put it away. "As the man said, it's been a long time coming. It'll be nice to put away the manuscripts and get back into the field."

He glanced out the window as he said it. All he could see was falling snow.

3) Virginia City

Saturday, July first, wrote Albert Peale in his leather-bound journal. *Cool and pleasant. The way lay through the mountains, along streams, over hills. Camped on Wild Cat Creek at 8,200 ft.*

Found a variety of metamorphic rocks; hornblende and gneisses. Spent part of the time trimming specimens and trimming rocks. Dawes helped.

To both William Henry Jackson and Thomas Moran, the land just north of the Continental Divide in the Montana Territory was a fantastic realm of long, swooping ascents and descents, a landscape devoid of trees except for patches that marked underground watercourses. The forms, contrasts, and textures created a visual feast.

To Hayden and Peale, the region was a classroom, full of sedimentary, metamorphic, and igneous rocks that jutted from the surface, overlapping and twisted together, presenting a half-hidden jigsaw puzzle created through time. What had come first? Second? How much time had passed between events? How far had materials been carried before they were deposited? Where had they come from? What had the land looked like then?

To Stevenson, the land was a slow but easy haul because the slopes were relatively gentle, there was water for the animals, and the surface was easy on his wagons and metal-rimmed wheels. It had rained the day before, so the soil was still damp and the morning air had a chill to it. But by noon, it was hot and all signs of rain had disappeared.

Monday, July third, wrote Peale. *Left about three o'clock for Virginia City. Suddenly a grand site burst into view. We're on top of an amphitheater, at the bottom of which a line of green shows the course of a stream. Hills, covered with grasses, show modern formations. White rocks exposed here and there. On top is a flat capping line of basalt. Peaks and hills behind and in the distance, a snowy range.*

The survey expedition straggled into Virginia City at eleven o'clock on the morning of the Fourth of July. The valley was about fifteen miles long. Everywhere the men looked, they saw the huge orange and black piles of earth and rock along the hillsides where miners had burrowed. The land had been torn apart in man's quest for gold. Twenty-foot-high piles of gravel, like giant anthills, lined old creekbeds where placer miners and pressure hoses had dug through coarse gravel pockets to get to finer deposits.

Near to the edge of town, the lead survey riders heard music. Around a bend in the road they found themselves in the midst of a parade about ready to enter town. The American flag was flying high and a brass band headed the parade, so the men of the survey doubled their ranks and joined the cavalcade. They shouted and laughed together over the blare of the band as they rode down Wallace Street into the aging boom town of Virginia City with its sun-bleached boards and slanted shanties. Women and children and town folk, including a large number of Chinese, lined the streets, full of smiles, cheering. The survey men waved, smiled, and rode through town to a spot a mile beyond, where they made camp.

In the spring of 1863, Alder Gulch was one of hundreds of valleys to host a swarm of miners who carried shallow pans and a deep hunger for wealth. The explorers were part of the overflow of miners who had discovered gold near Bannack the year before. Had it not been for the gold, the little dale of Alder Gulch would have remained another stream-cut valley of scattered trees and steep slopes in the northern Rockies. But its unpretentious waters held one of the richest gold deposits ever discovered in Montana.

Most of the placer gold in the creeks of the Rockies came from exposed quartz stringers associated with metamorphic and volcanic beds. When the quartz was exposed to the erosional forces of wind and water, particularly water, the quartz deteriorated and the gold came free. Particles of gold joined the stream-load during the spring melt. They tumbled and rolled as the water coursed down the creek. In places where the flow of water slowed, the heavy gold settled out in pockets.

Every stream that coursed through Alder Gulch contained gold. In one season the first established mining camp became Virginia City, a raw frontier town of close to ten thousand people. In the process of creating a town of this size in a matter of months, mankind showed its best and its worst instincts. The miners organized and worked by claim law while the city became a haven for gamblers and whores. Because of the isolation, the town was also a get-rich-quick opportunity for store merchants, casino owners, and bankers, and a wild card chance for wealth for desperate men from Germany, Russia, France, England, Denmark, and Sweden, all the far corners of the world.

While citizens became familiar with the *Montana Post* masthead, the town's former sheriff, Henry Plummer, and his gang killed more than a hundred people and relieved them of their gold. The local vigilante association, which included Nathaniel Langford and Samuel Hauser, claimed the right to establish law and order. They hung more than a dozen men, including Plummer, from the hanging tree on the outskirts of town.

The second year of its existence, Virginia City became the capital of the newly-created Montana Territory. But as gold extraction dried up, so did the town. After digging and washing fifty million dollars from the earth, all but a few hundred souls moved on. Most of the hangers-on were Chinese, who patiently resifted what the hurried Caucasians had overlooked or discarded.

"Mail call!" shouted Clifford Negley. He slid off his horse as late afternoon thunderstorms dropped lightning bolts, and blue-black clouds loosed rain over nearby peaks. He grabbed the saddlebags and headed for Hayden's sidewall tent. Hayden had a table, and besides, most of the mail was for him. Negley grouped letters for Adams, Stevenson, Moran and Jackson into one small pile. People came in, picked up their mail, and disappeared. Done with this last chore, Negley searched for Smith and Adams; the trio was determined to pan for gold.

Hayden opened a letter from Sanford Gifford. From his home on the Hudson River, he thanked Hayden for the invitation to come to the Yellowstone, but was begging off because of work. He extended an invitation to Hayden to visit him. *Hope you will be able to look through these windows with me one day. Kind remembrances to Jim, Elliott, Jackson, Turnbull, and others.* In two other letters, the secretary of the interior sent Hayden an official note to define his duties for the season, and Emma wrote of her work at her father's shop, the delightful spring weather in Philadelphia, and the fun she was having shopping for their approaching wedding.

While afternoon thunder closed in on Virginia City, William Henry Jackson captured the town from the foot of Alder Gulch with his eight by ten view camera. The weathered and disrepaired storefronts and the rutted road told the story not only of Virginia City but of almost every mining town in the Rockies. Jackson exposed the plate, developed it, and protected it until it dried.

As he put away his gear, he considered what he might have missed back in sixty-six by not staying with the freight outfit with which he'd walked across the plains. But he and six other drivers quit and headed for Salt Lake City. He arrived looking exactly like who he was, a young Easterner who'd walked a thousand miles in his last good suit.

Jackson strapped the last pannier to Hypo's side and led the mule back to camp. Later that evening, he watched Moran add clean lines to a sketch he had made earlier in the day. Moran went about his work in a relaxed but focused manner, without the aid of easels or special apparatus. He had only a number of sketch books, some loose sheets of several kinds of paper, a batch of watercolors, brushes, and containers of black ink. The largest item he carried was a stiff-backed portfolio. It held his larger sheets and served as a drawing board. The smaller sketch book fit comfortably in his jacket and the remainder of his materials were packed in his carpetbag and saddle bags.

"My brother, John, is a photographer like you," said Moran, breaking the silence. "He and I used to argue whether photography was an art form. He said that a photograph could be a work of art when made by a person who had the instincts, feeling, and education of an artist. I can see that your photographs are fine works of art, Bill."

Moran approached everything in life, including most of his conversations, as an artist. It was the way he thought and the way he breathed. He never had to make a conscious decision to become an artist the way Jackson had made his decision to become a photographer. Art was not a vocation nor a set of objectives to Thomas Moran. Neither was it simply a way of looking. It was the umbilical cord to his life, the single channel through which everything acquired meaning.

His older brother, Edward, had become an artist first. Moran followed him, more like the way a small boat follows the wake of a larger one, than like a younger brother trying to fill the footsteps of an older brother. Wherever Edward went, Moran went, including excursions into the heart of Philadelphia to view the works of Thomas Scully, John Neagle, Alexander Wilson, and Rembrandt Peale. And, when he could afford it, Moran purchased a ticket to see the paintings at the Philadelphia Academy of Fine Arts on Chestnut Street.

"Perhaps," ventured Jackson. "But I find the business of photography much more mechanical than drawing." He had been drawing much longer than he had been taking photographs, so he spoke from experience. "I have to work when I draw. As a photographer, I get whatever I point at, as long as I don't wait too long to develop the image."

The sun slowly dropped behind the hills, trailing its colorful skirts. It was the time of day when the men gathered by the campfires to drink coffee and smoke. "Consider this," said Moran. "You are the image maker, be it mechanic or artist. You are the individual who, through whatever medium you choose, interprets what nature has to offer. I stress interpretation because I do not believe in imitation. The palette holds more for me than the camera, true, but even the most realistic image can express emotion and that, in one sense, is the very heart of a work of art. Your pictures and those of my brother, John, hold more than the totality of the scene itself. They are statements, personal comments on the land."

"Is your brother still doing photography?"

"Oh yes. For a while all he wanted to do was test the limits of the camera as a tool to create works of art, so he confined his views to portraits and rather sentimental landscapes."

"Why do you say sentimental?"

"Because he chose views specifically for the purpose of generating an emotional reaction. That was his definition of a work of art, the ability to evoke a response."

"Evoking a response" was a phrase that Thomas Moran used quite differently than his brother. First he fell under the influence of James Hamilton, both a neighbor and serious painter after the fashion of J. M. W. Turner. Moran learned Turner's coloring effects, bought Turner's engravings when he could afford them, even created engravings from Turner's works. Then, when British art critic John Ruskin proffered his philosophy of nature, saying that it was the emotional response provoked in the artist that counted, Moran became a devotee. From that point forward, he refused to paint from any posture except the one defined by how he reacted to the scene he was to paint. He never chose a subject or viewpoint hoping to generate an emotional response from the viewer.

"And now?"

"Ah, this year, John is having an adventure of his own." As Thomas Moran talked, Hayden joined them. "He's in a strange, wild place called the Isthmus of Darien."

"Where is that?" asked Jackson.

"Central America," said Hayden, blowing across the top of his coffee to cool it. "I believe that an expedition was sent there to locate the best place to cut a canal to link the Caribbean to the Pacific Ocean."

"What for?" asked Negley.

"To save travel time when you want to go from a city like New York to San Francisco," said Moran. "It's similar to the Suez Canal project in Egypt. Currently, your ship goes all the way around South America, risking the storms of Tierra del Fuego. If you could cut across the isthmus, you cut three to four thousand miles from your journey."

"Sounds like another of Grant's schemes," said Jackson, looking at Hayden.

"Yes, I believe it is, but the concept is sound," said Hayden. "Isn't this the second expedition?" he asked Moran. "I ask, because I thought Clarence King's photographer, Timothy O'Sullivan, was the photographer for the first Darien expedition."

"Absolutely right," said Moran. "John told me it had been a fascinating but most difficult trip. He read Selfridge's report: Thomas O. Selfridge. John said he was first in his class at Annapolis and given command of the expedition at age thirty-four."

"Impressive, but what happened?" asked Jackson.

"The ship left a year ago last January with one hundred men. They landed at the Bay of Caledonia, where Balboa had landed in 1513 to explore the interior. Selfridge's information said that the land was forty miles wide at that point. That was incorrect. Then, the mountains were higher than expected, and the jungle almost impenetrable. O'Sullivan was their only photographer. He personally told John that he had a terrible time developing anything because of the heat and the rain."

"Is Darien further north?" asked Hayden.

"I'm not sure. In any case, there is a dispute about the ease with which one can cross the land at Darien. I'm sure that's what the expedition is trying to determine."

"How long has your brother been gone?" asked Jackson.

"Since last December. I don't know when he'll be back, but I'm sure he's literally sweating it out as we speak." Moran paused, then added, "He's much sturdier than I am, so he'll be fine. He was quite enthused about the voyage."

"Interesting and highly talented fellow," said Jackson to Hayden as they walked into the darkness towards their tent. "Exhibited in the Philadelphia Academy of Fine Arts at age twenty-four and accepted as a member at age twenty-seven. Quite an honor."

"I believe you could say 'amazing.' A rather encyclopedic mind, don't you agree?"

"If you mean he knows a lot," said Jackson, "you're right. I couldn't find a damn thing he didn't know something about . . . including photography!"

The survey party continued to the Madison River, then turned north, up the Gallatin Valley towards Bozeman. As they passed through the little village of five hundred people, town folk were leaving church. A number of citizens stopped and watched with friendly curiosity. A handful of children, dressed in Sunday-go-to-meeting clothes, ran beside the wagons and horses for a ways, shouting questions, caring more about the excitement of new faces than answers.

Thomas Moran, with his wide-brim gypsy hat, bright, friendly eyes, and wild-looking beard, was one of the most colorful of the explorers. He looked a bit amusing with a pillow tucked beneath his rump to protect himself against the unyielding McClellan saddle.

Stevenson had guessed correctly: Moran had never been on a horse before. The pillow was a giveaway. But if Stevenson had doubted Moran's ability to remain in the saddle or endure the hardships of the trip, he had been quickly corrected, for Moran maintained the group's pace without difficulty. He never complained or asked for help.

Stevenson watched Moran stop to talk to the children, and wondered about the strange, likable man who seemed at home wherever he was. There was something simple and sincere about the fellow. A bit of a dreamer. Maybe that's what an artist was, he thought: a dreamer in search of new visions of life.

Nearly six weeks had passed and the survey team had covered more than four hundred miles. The men were closing on their objective.

About three miles to Fort Ellis, wrote Peale.

4) Fort Ellis

On a hot July afternoon, about four innings into a fierce game of baseball between the officers of Fort Ellis and the men of the Hayden Survey, five disheveled men piled out of the daily stage. The first man out beat his hat against his blues and caused a small cloud of dust. The others looked just as dirty, bone-weary, and generally travel-worn. The five had left Chicago July second, nine days ago.

Their leader was Captain John W. Barlow, chief engineer of the Missouri Division, a heavyset man with a naturally gruff expression. With a last swat at his uniform, he strode to the main building to check in with the acting commanding officer, Captain J. C. Ball. He presented the captain with a letter from General Sheridan regarding his need for supplies, horses, and a small detachment of men.

Then Barlow sought out Professor Hayden. He was thinking that if *he* were Professor Hayden on his way to investigate a potential gem of the West, he would not have welcomed the kind of interference that Barlow represented. But orders were orders, especially when they came from General Sheridan. Besides, Captain Barlow was secretly delighted to have the opportunity to explore the Yellowstone. He was a West Point graduate, class of 1860, and although he'd been three times brevetted during the Civil War, this was his first exploration into the wilderness. He looked forward to meeting Hayden, a scientist who had an unmatched reputation as an explorer.

"Professor Hayden? Captain Barlow." Hayden, caught in the process of opening mail, looked up from his travel desk, stood politely, and shook Barlow's hand.

"In four days, you covered what took us a month," said Hayden, regarding the weary officer. "I think I'd rather do it our way."

"It's a damn quick introduction to the land, that's for certain. Didn't mean to interrupt your work, Professor; I simply wanted to say hello, and to let you know that we'll probably be a few days behind you on the journey into the Yellowstone. Please don't wait for us; we'll catch up. I have Captain David P. Heap of the Department of the Dakota with me, and three draftsmen—W. H. Wood, assistant topographer H. G. Prout, and photographer Thomas J. Hine of the U.S. Army Corps of Engineers. I want to reaffirm that we'll be primarily working on a topographic map, not a comprehensive survey. However, if you are planning to capture any topographic data that might help us, we'd appreciate your sharing it."

"My men, like yours, are professionals, Captain, so I do not anticipate anything but the fullest cooperation all around. Let me know when and how we can be of assistance."

Barlow relaxed for the first time. "Thank you, Professor Hayden. That's very good of you. I haven't been able to find much about the region we're entering. What kind of terrain do you think we'll be crossing?"

Hayden scratched a cheek thoughtfully. "You know, I've read a number of reports about the area, but no one has said much about the terrain. This is fundamentally a mountainous region, so you can expect the land to be broken, changeable, and rough."

"It's a wonderful opportunity. I'm pleased to be here. I'm just sorry that Lieutenant Doane couldn't make it. He was roped into serving as a witness at a court martial at Fort Snelling. General Sheridan wouldn't let him out of it."

Hayden nodded that he understood.

"He may join us before we've completed our work," Barlow added. "A lot depends on how the trial goes."

At midday, Stevenson entered Hayden's tent with one of his "You're going to love this one" glints in his eye. Hayden knew Stevenson's mannerisms, so he stopped reading. "What now?"

"Your new friend, Captain Barlow, is picking out horses and mules."

"Yes. So?"

"He's decided he needs two laborers, three packers, and a cook. That brings his team to eleven."

Hayden closed his eyes. This invasion into the Yellowstone was getting out of hand. "My God, I'm leading an assault! When you add the forty soldiers from Fort Ellis, we number eighty-three men. I pity any Indian tribe that happens to cross our path."

Then, as though he had never uttered a worried word about numbers, Hayden began to talk about hiring a guide. "We have enough kitchen support, three cooks, two waiters, and three hunters, but a guide might be worth the money," said Stevenson. "We can afford one replacement because of Professor Allen's departure."

"Yes. I hate to see him leave," said Hayden, "but it was obvious even before we left that he couldn't take the pace. But he's had an opportunity to see some country firsthand, and that's what counts." With Hayden's approval, Stevenson went out and hired a local man named José to be their guide.

In front of the main post building, Jackson set up his camera. He'd decided he might as well document the survey's camp, and the camp was on the post. As he leveled the tripod, he was hailed by someone carrying a large camera. "Hey, is that you, Jackson?" said a voice. "Haven't seen you since Corinne in sixty-nine. How are you?"

Jackson looked into the face of John Crissman. Was that only two years ago? He and Arundell Hull had been photographing scenes along the Union Pacific Railroad. By the time the train got to Corinne, they'd run out of everything from money to chemicals. Crissman had come to their rescue by letting them use his darkroom.

They shook hands. Crissman had lots of stories about the vagaries of life and photography in the West. Jackson listened with interest, but continued to set up. "I latched on to the ear of that Captain Barlow fella, this morning" said Crissman. "Looks like I'm going to the Yellowstone as part of his group."

"That's great," said Jackson. "We'll have a chance to do some work together." As the two talked, the porch of the post main building was becoming crowded. Word had spread that Jackson was going to take some photographs. By the time he was ready, the photo session had become a social event. "All right, gentlemen," said Jackson. "Hold your poses, please." About twenty officers on the steps provided Jackson with a marvelous array of postures and expressions.

The following day, Lieutenants Norton and Jerome arranged a day trip to nearby Mystic Lake. The party eventually included Hayden, Jackson, Dixon, Moran, Schonborn, Elliott, Campbell, and Peale. They took a trail that cut steeply through the densely forested hillside. On more than one occasion, Moran looked down a precipitous slope. Every time the trail zigzagged, it touched the edge of a mountain stream. Water bounced over boulders and dashed against fallen logs on its way down the mountainside. The sound and glitter gave life to the forest of tall, solemn pines.

Mystic Lake was a triangular depression fed by the stream Moran had seen racing down the mountain. It was surrounded by a garden of wildflowers. The mountains in the vicinity reached eleven thousand feet, and pockets of snow covered the hills just a few hundred feet above the lake. Hayden and Peale took off to examine the local geology and collect specimens. Elliott and Norton assembled long fishing poles.

Several hours later, in the middle of lazy conversation, Lieutenant Jerome saw Hayden and Peale returning. "What'cha got, Professor?"

"An odd mixture: fossils and basalt," said Hayden. He dumped an assortment of specimens on the ground. "The fossils come from the limestone beds; the basalt is the most likely reason this whole area is so mixed up."

"Oh, sure. I could have told you that," said Jerome with a light laugh. "What's basalt?"

"A volcanic rock," said Hayden. "The underlying strata in the area in this area are unusually flat for a mountainous area. It seems as though the basalt intrusions have tossed the strata around."

The officers smiled at each other and shrugged. Mountains were mountains.

When it was time to start back, Moran, Jackson and Jackson's new helper, Dixon, decided they would rough it for the night for the sake of photography, sketching, and maybe a little fishing. Lieutenant Norton left his stringer of fat fish with Jackson. "Not that you won't catch more," said Norton with a smile, "but, just in case . . ."

The morning sun appeared through an immense gorge that was fringed with limestone cliffs. Isolated rock projections provided splendid foreground objects for compositions. Jackson took a dozen photographic shots that included a dramatic view down the creek to demonstrate the steepness of the terrain.

When Jackson returned to camp, he found Moran was fixing a fish fry for a late breakfast. "Excellent," said Jackson. "Norton's trout will be a nice change of pace from bacon, bread, and coffee." He watched Moran scrape aside the coals and the ashes from the campfire and dig a hole. "Thomas, what the devil are you doing?"

"Watch and learn," said Moran. He took the cleaned fish, wrapped them in brown paper, and laid the package in the hot earth. When he pushed all the hot coals back over them, that was too much for Jackson. "That's a lousy way to treat good trout," he said.

"Patience," said Moran. He turned his back on the buried meal and proceeded to add several strong colors to a partially completed sketch.

"I have to hand it to you, Thomas," Jackson said as the three headed back to Fort Ellis that afternoon. "The fish were excellent.

Where did you learn that trick?"

The trail had taken the riders to the edge of a steep cliff. As they emerged from the canopy of pines Moran had an unobstructed view to the west. He pulled back on the reins and shouted, "Look. Look!" He was looking through a window of light-blue air. The far-off landscape was a collage of many mountain ranges. Each seemed to vie with one another for space. Streaks of white ice and snow on the highest mountains shimmered in startling contrast to the gray linings of clouds and blue-gray shadows of the landscape.

"Glorious!" shouted Moran. The composition stirred him more than anything he had seen in years. There lies my wilderness, my land of grand nature, he thought. His eyes shone with excitement and his fingers itched for a pencil. The view was a presage of the terrain he would soon enter, the glorious, dizzying realm of the Rocky Mountains. Moran knew, with an unimpeachable certainty, that his destiny as an artist lay inside that scene.

Soon, he thought. Soon.

5) Threshold to Wonderland

The Hayden survey snaked out of Fort Ellis early on the morning of July fifteenth and headed toward the Madison Range and the Yellowstone River beyond. The survey's cavalry escort would follow several hours later. Captain Barlow's crew with its own military escort would depart some time that afternoon.

Hayden's string of horses, mules, and wagons moved in single file, but the narrow trail was never meant for wagons. The lead riders knew what to do. When they had to, they dismounted, took pick and shovel in hand, and altered the terrain to make a passable road. When the hill became too steep for one team, they doubled the teams. It was a slow but proven method. That day, they also battled a hissing wind, wet with snow, and rain. Hayden's men took the delays, the hills, the detours, and the weather in stride. The occasional discomfort was part of the package that offered adventure and the exhilaration of discovery. Now, they were approaching the gateway to the Yellowstone.

A high point on the trail gave them a view of the Yellowstone

Valley. There, the party took a break. To the north, hills rose sixteen hundred feet. The principal range of mountains to the south,
showing the steep straight sides that meant they were volcanic,
looked closer to twelve hundred feet.

When Robert Adams looked into the flat valley, the first thing
he noticed was the Yellowstone River. Dark and green, the river
occupied the middle of the valley floor like a sleeping snake. Adams
took note of the valley's oval shape only after he heard Doc suggest
that the valley appeared to have been part of an old lake system.
All Adams could see was a thin veneer of soil and grass: everything else looked like river gravel.

"Robert," said Hayden to the young man, "this is incredible.
The character of this region is simpler than it looks, but it would
still take months to work out the details. The strata probably belong to a half dozen groups, yet they've been multiplied into a di-
versity of forms. Lifting and crushing forces have left a mass of
confusion."

"What can we do in the time we have, Dr. Hayden?" asked
Peale. "I mean, it's all unexplored, and we only have a few months."

"We can't do everything," Hayden acknowledged. "Our job
will be to lay a base for geologists to come." The idea that major
discoveries might slip through his fingers didn't bother him. He
was the first in, the door-opener, the scout whose safe return was
informative in its own right. Hayden would report on the lay of the
land. That was his job.

They spent a cold, wet afternoon descending the western slope
of the Yellowstone Valley. Camp was soggy. Everyone turned in
early. At three-thirty in the morning, while it was still dark and
cold, the men rose and made breakfast, then broke camp. By the
time the sun poked through they were well along the road. The trail
cut across low, irregular hills, gentle slopes strewn with granite
boulders and dotted with sage. The top third of Emigrant Peak
dominated the view to the south.

While the team rested, Hayden regarded the structure of the
land, examined nearby strata, and took notes. Although ridges of
Jurassic, Cretaceous, and Tertiary sediments were seldom seen more
than a few hundred feet above the surface, the upturned edge of

lower Carboniferous and Jurassic strata extended in long lines across the Yellowstone Valley as far as one could see. Hayden was most fascinated by what was hidden by the volcanic flows. He wrote in his notebook that *beneath the range of volcanic mountains on the west side of the Yellowstone River is part or maybe all the unchanged rocks known in this portion of the West.*

With his camera firmly planted on the valley floor, Jackson documented the scene. He captured the willow-lined river, the snowy range and massive triangular form of Emigrant Peak, the faces of the twelve-thousand-foot volcanic mountains, and the hardworking survey men sitting in the shade.

Late that afternoon the expedition approached Bottler's Ranch, which sat on a high bench well back from the Yellowstone River. Aside from the main ranch house, the Bottlers had constructed three storage sheds and several barns. Pelts of every known animal, from beaver to wolf, were draped over the corral poles, shop roofs and all of the rafters projecting out from the main house. Hayden also noticed a small herd of dairy cattle. Cows meant butter, a true luxury!

The front door swung open and a burly, black-bearded man stepped out. "Yah, hello, all. Come, come," he shouted with a smile. He introduced himself as Philip; his brothers, Hank and Frederick, were out trapping. "Camp where you like; don't shoot the cows, all right?" Philip was always glad to have company. "I get milk for everyone. Drink of milk all around."

While the survey crew set up camp, José left to hunt for elk. Hayden went inside the ranch house with Philip to learn what he could about the trail ahead. The ranch house smelled of wood smoke, roast meats, animal hides, and earth. Once business was conducted, the men shared their ancestries with one another. The Bottlers were from Bavaria. Philip told of his kinfolk in America, and about the trek west. "Philadelphia? We, too, are from Pennsylvania, but long time ago. We try Ohio but much Indian trouble. And Virginia City, but no gold for us. Only hard work. Everyone else gets rich." He laughed. "So we buy cattle, yah? And now we have the furs. Much better."

Later in the day, Frederick and Hank arrived pulling a string of pack horses weighed down with bundles of pelts. After they hung their freshly taken skins of bobcat, bear, beaver, and badger, they joined Hayden and Philip at the rough-hewn wooden table in the main room. Philip deferred to Frederick, in part because he was the oldest, and partly because he spoke better English.

"Too bad you didn't bring women with you, Professor," said Frederick with a huge grin. "None of us are married. Life gets lonely. All we have to look at is bear, moose, and each other." The men of the survey laughed freely.

Frederick said he remembered the Washburn Expedition, especially the general and Mr. Langford. Hank recalled David Folsom and Charles Cook from the year before last. Philip had been away both times. "We don't go into the Yellowstone very often," he said, "because the game is not so good there, and the main trails were made by the Indians. We like to avoid trouble." No, they said, when questioned; there had been no trouble of late.

Hayden said he needed a permanent base camp while the majority of their survey team explored the Yellowstone. For an agreed-on price, the Bottler brothers were most happy to let their ranch be used as permanent camp and mail post. As they talked, the shadows grew long, and the light turned yellow. The colorless silhouettes of the mountains looked bold and massive. Outside, the men built smudge fires of buffalo chips. The smoke kept the mosquitoes away.

Breakfast was a delight of milk and butter, coffee, cream, hot bread, dried apples, and fresh meat, including ham. Hayden's crew were feeling spoiled and privileged by the time the men of F Troop from Fort Ellis rode into camp.

Now that he had a base of operations, Hayden sent an interim report to the secretary of the interior. He wrote that the survey team would leave the ranch the morning of the twentieth and be at the Upper Yellowstone in three to four days. After surveying the Yellowstone and a portion of the main branches of the Snake and Missouri, he would return to Fort Ellis and survey another belt of land near Fort Bridger. Hayden wrote that he planned to take soundings of Yellowstone Lake from a small boat. They were carrying the makings for the craft, but if they ran into trouble, they also had a whipsaw to cut timber for another.

Hayden stepped outside in time to watch Barlow and Heap's party arrive. Barlow had proven to be modest, courteous, and sincere, but the man's words and actions told Hayden that he had no feeling for the wilderness. Why, he wondered, would anyone ride with an umbrella strapped to his saddle? As for the smallish Captain Heap, chief engineer of the Department of the Dakota, Hayden thought he looked like a fop in his fringed buckskin suit and all his traps. Still, Hayden dismissed his critical thoughts, knowing that everyone had something to offer.

Meanwhile, Jackson walked to the corrals where Stevenson, Shep Madera, and Tom Cooper were emptying the wagons and making up packs. "Hey, Jackson, where'd you get that?" asked Shep, referring to the buffalo robe Jackson had over his shoulder.

"Major Pease at the Crow mission," replied Jackson. As he draped the robe over corral poles, he took a more deliberate measure of what the three men were doing. It looked like they were sorting supplies into two piles, one on the ground, a second one inside a wagon. Shep and Tom pulled created mule-sized bundles from the pile on the ground.

"Were leaving the wagons. Right?" said Jackson. "But what's going to happen to all that?" He gestured at the pile in the wagon that Stevenson kept adding to.

"Some things go, some don't," wheezed Stevenson, as he tossed his own buffalo robe into the wagon. "Everything in this wagon stays."

The next box he put in the same wagon looked familiar to Jackson. "Whoa! Jim . . . them's my personables. They go."

Stevenson straightened up and smiled. "All right. Which camera do you want to leave behind?"

"That's not fair."

"I didn't say it was fair, Bill. We're overloaded, so we're cutting back. All of us. One wall tent for headquarters operations. Dog tents for everyone else. Commissary supplies are limited to flour, bacon, coffee, and dried fruit. Our hunters are going to be real busy for the next six weeks. They have to keep us in fresh meat. But, sure, Bill, after we pack all the essentials which, I need to mention, include a disproportionate amount of photographic gear…"

"All right, all right."

"You can try to bribe one of the mules to take another thirty-pound package."

Shep and Tom chortled.

"I get the message." Jackson wandered off to reevaluate his rock-bottom needs for the coming trip. He overheard Hayden telling Stevenson, "I plan to leave our flock of congressional offspring here. The lads can make barometric readings and do other weather-related work when they're not off somewhere fishing."

Jackson was glad he had put in a bid to keep Dixon. When Hayden had asked him about the youngster earlier in the day, Jackson was able to honestly say the two of them put out four times as many photos as he had alone. Dixon had become essential to Jackson's plans.

When Hayden and Stevenson finished talking, Jackson asked the professor, "If you agree, sir, Mr. Moran and I would like to move out ahead of the main party."

"Set your own schedule; just don't get lost," said Hayden. "Maybe you should take José with you."

So the artistic-photographic contingent led off the morning of the nineteenth. José and Alex Sibley, pulling two pack mules, led Jackson, Moran, Dixon, and Crissman.

"Hey, Dixon," shouted Negley as the group trailed out of camp, "don't fall into any geysers." As Dixon waved back, Negley turned to Sherman with a frown. "Damn, how come he gets to go, while we have to stay?"

Dawn was a dismal smear above the mountains when Stevenson made his last check. Everyone was in place. He rode to the head of the column and led the column out. Professor Hayden wasn't ready, but Stevenson left anyway. It was a sensible routine because he was responsible for setting up camp. His party always left first, then made camp eight or nine miles down trail. He knew how far to go, because he kept the odometer. The survey's only vehicle was a simple affair that looked like a rickshaw. Two wooden poles connected the two-wheeled device to a gentle mule. The instruments that measured distance were attached to the spokes.

The trail dogged the west edge of the Yellowstone River. Marks of drag poles spoke of the recent passage of Indians, probably Crow. Aspen, shrubs, and pine embroidered the earth-colored hillsides with hues of green. In front of them, the valley looked like it had been pinched out between interlocking promontories. The mountains appeared to sit right on the valley floor.

That night, the guides and packers checked the animals, gathered around the campfire, and talked about their journeys and experiences. Their conversation eventually turned to the rumors they'd heard about the Yellowstone. The only man attached to Hayden's survey who had been there was a soldier who had accompanied Lieutenant Doane on the Washburn Expedition. He said little. His silence implied that each man should see for himself. Hayden, also content to let the land speak for itself, retired early.

Adams had borrowed Doane's report from Professor Hayden. Late that evening he shared it and his own speculations with Logan, Carrington, Peale, and Elliott.

"So what did Doane say about the geysers?" asked Logan. "I still don't know if I believe in them."

"There must be a whole valley of them," said Adams. "Doane said more than once how the ground shook when they went off. They must be pretty good size."

"Are they all in a row or in a circle or something?" asked Peale.

"He didn't say."

They were quiet for a moment. "Suppose these things are all made up?" asked Logan.

"Doane's an officer in the Army," said Carrington, the oldest and most experienced of the five. "Army officers are pretty careful what they write."

"I think we'll all see much more than we ever thought possible before this trip is out," said Elliott. "I have never been disappointed when I have been with Dr. Hayden."

"Dr. Hayden's a funny man," said Logan. "He looks tired, but he moves around like a rabbit. Ever try to follow him? You can't keep up. He wore me out a few days back."

"Dr. Hayden is the best geologist in the country," said Adams.

"He's always finding something new, talking about how something might have happened, and you'll notice that he's real careful to record everything." Then he laughed. "But you're right. He can appear and disappear faster than anyone, and I've never known a man to get so excited so easily."

"It's like he wants to say everything at once and can't get it out," said Logan, laughing with Adams. "He'd never make a politician like my father."

"I hope he never tries," said Carrington. "He's got a temper, and he's skittish. But he's a fine man to work for. This is my third summer with his survey. I'd go anywhere with him."

The easy laughter of the evening had turned to quiet anticipation by morning. Stevenson looked down the trail, knowing that somewhere close by lurked the Yellowstone. He had to admit, if only to himself, that it was a little exciting. The path led him up and out of the valley. The survey followed. From high up on the slope, the men could see how the valley was pinched like an hourglass in the middle. At the "waist," the river dashed over volcanic rocks, covering them in a pale green wash. The bedding planes of strata exposed along the canyon wall stood on end, straight up and down. In many places, it was impossible to tell where one set began and ended. The lines in the rock walls were convoluted, squeezed together, impossible to sort out. One didn't have to be a geologist to see that incredible forces had acted upon this land.

The trail took Stevenson back to the river floor and into a second valley fifteen miles long and two to three miles wide. The floor was flat and empty save for scattered sage and a little vegetation that grew along the river. Reddish-brown and yellow-brown colors, like those in the desert, dominated the scene. A fine dust covered everything.

Around noon, the main party caught up with Moran and Jackson, who were just finishing their documentation of the feature Doane reported as "The Devil's Slide." The structure began at the valley floor and rose straight up the steep incline of the western bank, remaining hidden from the trail until a rider was almost on top of it.

"What do you make of it, Jim?" asked Jackson.

Stevenson looked at the formation, which now swarmed with members of the survey. He tried to dissect the formation in terms of hard and soft strata, but the feature still looked strange because the bedding planes were all vertical. It was obvious that the softer material had succumbed to erosion. As a result, two prominent, parallel walls of rock one hundred feet apart jutted several hundred feet into the air. The feature took up a quarter of a mile of the mountainside.

If Stevenson let his imagination loose, something he rarely did, the formation made him a bit uncomfortable. "It does appear to be well-named," he said. "I bet Dr. Hayden will have a lot to say."

"Well," said Hayden, after taking a few additional notes, "Devil's Slide is a series of alternating beds of sandstone, limestone, quartzite and volcanic dikes. They're all vertically elevated. The softer strata, wearing away rapidly, have, left the more durable formation like isolated flanges."

"See, what did I tell you?" said Stevenson proudly to Jackson.

"You didn't say all that," said Jackson quickly.

". . . and that band of bright vermilion clay is the one everyone mistakes for cinnabar," concluded Hayden.

Moran and Jackson had been at Devil's Slide all morning. Moran had completed two detailed pencil sketches. He found the view from the south more dramatic because the sharp edges and contrast stood out better. In his usual manner, he had outlined the major features, then added watercolor tints to key points. Not content, he added word descriptions about color and vegetation. He jotted down a reminder to himself to raise the peak of the hill for greater compositional strength. For fun, Moran added a cluster of rattlesnakes in the foreground. In his second sketch, he offset the face of the slide and enlarged one of the major slabs. A single tree on top of the hill provided scale and indicated distance.

"Gentlemen," said Hayden, as he occasionally did when caught up in the thrill of anticipation, "these are not simply mountains, but the results of incomplete processes."

"What does that mean?" whispered Jackson to Stevenson.

"That means," said Hayden, who overheard him, "this site has undergone recent geologic violence. As we proceed, we should expect to see more of the unusual. Be alert for additional products of incomplete processes."

"Sounds downright dangerous," muttered Jackson as he returned to his horse.

6) White Mountain Hot Springs

The men mounted their horses the following morning under low, heavy clouds. Soon a quiet rain began to fall. Yellow warblers darted between the bushes along the riverbank. Kingfishers flew up and down the river, scolding. A small hawk circled overhead; Hayden thought it might be an osprey.

"Geysers, here we come!" shouted the irrepressible Mr. Logan. A number of the men smiled and barked approval. The Devil's Slide had been a good portent, for it looked the way it had been described. If the character of one strange feature showed true, it augured well for what they would find in the valley. Geysers and thundering lands, indeed!

The full survey traveled together that morning. Hayden told Stevenson that the trail would leave the valley floor and he wanted everyone together. The hills they now approached on the west side of the valley looked as wrinkled as a blanket. Waterfalls and tiny cascades streamed from crevices.

Six miles upstream, the survey approached a mountain stream. It rushed down the hill and reached the Yellowstone, where a crowd of massive granite boulders jammed the river. Instead of crossing this stream, Hayden's guides began to climb the hill.

"Where are we going?" Dixon asked Jackson.

"I'm not sure," said Jackson, "but last night I heard Professor Hayden say that one of the guides found a strange series of springs up the Gardiner's River. I guess this stream is the Gardiner's."

The hillside was steep and uneven. Horses' hooves slipped in rain-soaked earth. The land, the trees, the men, and the horses were shadowless. Every man was gray: not one ray of sunshine could be seen and the canopy of gray clouds dripped on them like sodden cloths. A number of volcanic vents jutted from the slopes, which were covered with a dark, volcanic breccia and a pale, clay-ish earth. Dixon thought the material looked like residue from an old furnace, lots of mud and ash cemented together.

Dixon pulled off his hat and shook it. Rain had been running from the brim into his face for the last hour. He was struck by the notion that they might come across a vast cemetery. Everything about the weather and the countryside pointed towards something nasty like that.

"This place is spooky," said Dixon with a shiver. "Does it always look this weird?"

For the next two hours, they continued up the gray, sterile landscape. The guides stayed away from the cut where the river flowed. There was no trail near it, and the riverbed consisted mostly of large boulders.

The party had climbed about a thousand feet above the valley floor, when Hayden and Stevenson crested a ridge. There they stopped. Behind them was a steep slope, devoid of life, that led back to the valley of the Yellowstone. In front of them, just beyond a small stream, rose another steep hill. This one was pure white. It resembled a cascade of foam, as though a white froth had been poured down the hillside, covering all forms beneath it. Its crenu-lated surface glistened in spite of the cloud cover. Nothing moved; the white cascade had been arrested, frozen in time.

"What trick of the devil do we have here," Stevenson said, only half in jest. "Is this the froth of hell, or some kind of hot springs grown out of control?"

"Exactly," said Hayden with enthusiasm. "Look! See the steam rising from the water high on the hill? The entire hillside is one huge deposit of travertine. It must be a thousand feet long. See how the deposit has spread from a few points as it moved downhill. It's created a triangle." He quickly deduced that mineral deposits from the hot springs had landscaped a square mile of the mountain into this series of intricate, interconnected terraces. Each terrace, like a basin, was semicircular in shape and held one or more pools of water.

"This must have required thousands of years," said Hayden

in awe. The other members of the party who had gathered at the river's edge now plunged their horses into the stream, hooting and hollering as they galloped towards the terraces. Their disbelieving laughter echoed between the hills.

"What an incredible sight," said Hayden, still unmoving. "It looks like the work of fairies."

Before the light of day faded, Hayden and Peale had climbed the hillside. Near the top, a stream of water six feet wide and two feet deep emerged from the earth. At the surface, the water entered a channel of travertine that was pure white with streaks of orange. The channel disappeared over the edge of the cliff, where a whole network of basins began. Where the landscape had been spared calcification, Hayden found flowering sage, dwarf cedar, species of daisies and penstemons, and a rich growth of grass.

As they made their way across the hillside, Hayden and Peale encountered a terrace of travertine one hundred yards in diameter. It formed a balcony that jutted straight out from the hill. A steplike series of basins filled with water lined its flanks. They resembled concave seashells with their highly scalloped and irregular rims that varied from a few inches to six feet in height. The sculptured edges contained tiny crenulations, wrinkles, and little fissures, a study in miniatures on top of miniatures.

The two men eased their way down the slope, stopping to gaze into pools of water. Wild combinations of colors shimmered and changed as water and minerals dribbled steadily over the terraces. The travertine was a true white-on-white. Hues of iron oxide, from light buff to rich red ochre, provided a fairyland of color.

The transparency of the water exceeded anything Hayden had ever seen. Peale dipped his fingers into the water of one basin, then quickly withdrew them and sniffed. "Very hot bathwater and a lot of sulfur," he said.

"With plenty of dissolved lime and iron, no doubt," said Hayden. He was certain that the shapes had been formed exclusively by the deposition of travertine. The massive formation was the result of one long, continuous process. The newest layers were blinding white; the older deposits, where springs were no longer active, appeared as dull as gray pewter. The dry basins also had a withered look. The skeletons of trees, captured in the deposits, stuck out from the basins in stark, angular postures.

That night, the men compared travertine samples and listened to Hayden explain how the terraces had been created. "A fairly simple process, really. Hot water in which an enormous amount of calcium has been dissolved flows to the surface and down the hill. As it flows, it cools, and as it cools, the minerals in suspension are deposited. These deposits build up and create the forms you see now. I believe the colors come mostly from minute amounts of iron and other oxidized elements."

The next day, at first light, Hayden began a systematic examination of the hot springs. He was most interested in the source and chemistry of the deposits. He kept detailed and highly descriptive notes and made a few sketches. He instructed Jackson to document the formation with a complete series of negatives, for as he kept repeating, "Written description can never do justice to this unique expression of nature."

The largest single basin they discovered was twenty-five feet wide and forty feet long. The colors inside the basin ran from pure white to a brilliant cream yellow. Hayden broke off some of the scalloped deposits, holding the pieces of delicate beadwork with reverence. The lines of deposition, like rings in a tree trunk, were clear and easy to see even within the most translucent material.

The water of the hot springs pools was perfectly transparent. When steam did not obscure his view, Hayden could see strange rounded deposits on the bottom. He might well have been looking into an ultramarine glass with deep streaks of pure blue and purple. He was sure that these colors came from the reflected blue of the sky, but he left the scene feeling that he had gazed at colors never seen before. On his way back to camp, he came across smaller basins with green and yellow stains as brilliant as aniline dyes.

He found Peale near the bottom of the hill on a subterrace, looking at a cone-shaped mound with a twenty-foot diameter that towered fifty feet high. "This made of travertine, too, Doc?" he asked.

"Oh, yes. Look at the layering, Charles. The lime layers make the cone look like layers of straw on a thatched roof. Water under great pressure built its own crater. This cone may have been a geyser at one time. It shut itself off with its own deposits." Hayden walked around the structure. "From this angle, it resembles the caps worn by colonial patriots during the Revolutionary War."

"I'm a little young to remember that one, Doc," said Peale.

"Nonetheless, Liberty Cap's a good name," said Hayden, and he made a note in his journal to that effect.

Peale's job included taking samples and measuring water temperatures. He found the temperatures ranged from one hundred twenty-six degrees to one hundred sixty-two degrees. Every sample of water contained a great amount of calcium carbonate and sodium carbonate, alumina and magnesia in solution.

Hayden discovered large quantities of carbonic gas. On the underside of some travertine, he also found rosy stalactites, exquisitely formed by dripping water. By the end of the day, the men had determined that most of the pools were four to eight feet in diameter and one to four feet deep.

That evening, Stevenson reported to Hayden that he'd talked to three men living near-by. "They've taken out claims on the place. They call it Soda Mountain and claim that the waters reduce the symptoms of their disease."

"What kind of symptoms?" asked Hayden.

"I didn't ask, but some of them have bad skin problems. I'm sure two have advanced cases of syphilis."

"Well, they're in the right spot. If their claims are honored, they'll make a fortune when the Northern Pacific Railroad lays tracks to this place." No one had to ask how Hayden knew this; the Northern Pacific had issued a press release announcing its intention to run a spur into the Yellowstone.

The two artists, Jackson and Moran, spent the day scrambling over the formation like a couple of kids. Jackson's first photo of the hot springs included Moran in the picture. Throughout the day, the two collaborated. On occasion, the composition they selected for the camera so thoroughly appealed to Moran, he sat down and sketched while Jackson and Dixon set up the camera.

Jackson would set up the tripod, attach the camera box, focus the lens, and adjust the composition. Dixon would lay out the chemicals Jackson needed to prepare the negative. After Jackson sensitized a plate, he or Dixon would cover the plate to protect it from the light, then insert it in the camera and expose it while it was still tacky. Sometimes Jackson would remain with the dark box to sensitize a second plate while Dixon took the picture. Then it was Dixon's turn to hurry back with the exposed plate so Jackson could develop it before it dried.

Following a hunch, Jackson immersed one of the still tacky negatives in the hot water of one of the springs and discovered that the heat cut his negative drying time in half. He turned to Dixon with a satisfied expression. "You never know how things will turn out, do you? It normally takes us forty-five minutes from the time we set up until we have a finished negative. Today, because we didn't move the camera around much and were able to cut our negative drying time, we're finishing each shot in less than a half hour. Not bad!"

Jackson tapped Moran on the shoulder to share his discovery. Moran looked up with obvious distress. "Look at that!" said Moran, his voice filled with frustration. He pointed at the pool Jackson had just finished photographing.

"Yeah. Magnificent, isn't it?" He glanced at Moran's sketch. "I don't see any problems. You've captured all the elements. What's wrong?"

To Jackson, each scene was texture and form, for his was a world of black and white. To Moran, texture and form were only two anchors in a composition that moved with the swirl of color. The smallest cloud reflected marine colors from the surface of the pool, colors more vivid than the sea. From the basin's depths came blue-green hues that sparkled with an internal brilliance. As he was about to explain, a light breeze passed over the surface of the basin. Swirls of bright color swept away all existing patterns as though the entire surface had become a kaleidoscope.

Moran pointed to the radical change. "See that? I start with one set of colors and 'whoof,' in an instant they're all different. How can I capture that?" he said.

"Cope," said Jackson with a comforting pat. He picked up his camera and moved off, knowing he couldn't help. He'd faced Moran's quandary. Each artist had to work out his own problems.

Moran went back to work, first with pencil, then with water-color washes. Back East, he had yearned for grand nature; now he was surrounded by it. It didn't take long for him to learn that scenes in the West required a new approach. Until now, he had used his sketches as detailed blueprints for finished works. He could define each surface, record the nuances of surface texture, and model the geometry of rocks and tree trunks. He had always denoted shadow and halftones for rocks and foliage with hatch marks, a time-consuming technique, but one that produced a drawing rich in values, easily brought to completion in his studio.

Western landscape had little in common with its eastern cousin. There were no leafy river valleys or dense forests here, no foggy mornings that suggested intimacy. Nothing was dense or compact. Nature had had no need to be economical in the West. Here, the dominant surfaces were rock formations, some of which covered areas as large as towns Moran had lived in. Trees, rather than birds, boats, or people, now provided scale; to ignore this reality was to make height and depth unmeasurable. And the vistas! Western vistas were classical, truly a plane on which horizontal and vertical lines merged. They had to be captured with strokes that pulled the eye tens of miles along the horizon and thousands of feet along the vertical. The adjustment was intensified because the clarity of the atmosphere brought distant objects into close focus.

So everything he saw and touched told Moran that he had to discard his routines, his habitual techniques. He had already made several adjustments. With the expedition constantly on the move, he couldn't take the time for detailed studies. Besides, contours dominated most of his scenes, so lines drawn with economy were better suited to the land. Every time he tried to fill in the details, they ruined the feeling of openness he wanted to capture. So he turned to shorter, simpler strokes.

As he worked to capture the essence of what he saw in the hot spring, he began to understand how the clarity of the air at seven thousand feet enhanced the brilliance of natural colors. Another major difference between East and West! Moran created a rough outline, then added strong watercolor tints. When he didn't have the right hue or tint, he made notes. After a while, he held the sketch at arm's length. Yes! This he could take home and complete. When time permitted, he would hatch in select features and cover the full surface with watercolors.

Moran finished one watercolor of the hot springs on an illustration board, then dashed off a second using a mixture of pencil, opaque white, and watercolor. At the pool they had named Diana's Bath, he spent hours testing combinations of colors to capture the rainbow effect of reflected light. The translucent water was color-saturated, and delicate traces in the deposits provided an endless variety of detail. Initially, the combination was baffling, so Moran distilled its complexity into its primary forces.

The survey men learned that as the water from the hot springs flowed downhill, it lost a lot of heat. Near the bottom, it was cool enough to use for drinking and cooking. Toward dusk, Stevenson saw Jackson peeling off his clothes next to a large pool at the edge of camp. "And just what do you think you're doing?" he asked.

"If it's too risqué for you, you can go somewhere else, "said Jackson. "I'm joining the herd and taking a bath. I like mine luke-warm. Mr. Dixon likes his hotter, so he's further up the hill." Jackson slipped into the pool and sighed. "Ah! Sheer heaven." The lining of the basin was a spongy gypsum that was soft to the touch. "Better than any hotel."

"Why don't you spend the night there," said Stevenson. "Perhaps you'll calcify and become the first human fossil."

"You'd love that," said Jackson with a laugh. "I'd end up spouting water and you'd put me in your garden."

"Consider," said Hayden to Schonborn the next morning, "the manner in which the springs have been formed." He, Schonborn, Elliott, and Barlow had climbed the hill again. "The hot water seeps through the limestone, dissolves the lime, and redeposits it as the water cools. And since this is an ongoing process, it appears that these deposits are in the very throes of formation. My question is, where is the limestone source?"

In addition to eventually discovering fifteen hundred feet of limestone beneath the surface, Barlow, Hayden, and Peale located some old chimneys and craters along the west side of the formation. One led to a vast cavern. They also found a series of extinct geysers that animals had used as dens. The caves were filled with sticks, bones, and swarms of bats. "Some of the pine trees that have grown over these mounds must be a hundred years old," said Barlow.

"Right," said Hayden. He examined his notes. "We may have one common heat source for all these features. Note that when the heat is checked in one place, it finds its way up through another vent. Heat rises through the fissures. However, I believe the heat here is abating; that suggests that the entire complex is dying. Eventually nothing but the deposits will remain."

As they turned to go back down the hill, Anton Schonborn slipped and went down hard. As he gritted his teeth in pain, Captain Barlow laughed. "I wouldn't try to slide down the hill if I were you, Mr. Schonborn," he said.

Schonborn flashed Barlow a look of hatred and started to respond. Hayden stepped between the men and extended Schonborn a hand. "You all right?" he asked.

"I don't like being laughed at," was all he said in a deep voice.

That evening, hunters from Barlow's party brought in a bear and three cubs. Over a dinner of bear steak, everyone exchanged stories of the day. Barlow added his adventure with the caves. "The first cavern was about thirty feet across and its vaulted ceiling forty feet high. I could see into it so I knew that it was empty. The second one was a bit too dark and gloomy to enter. I threw a few stones into it." He laughed and the men laughed with him, but it was clear that they all remained cautious about this strange land.

A new moon climbed over the eastern escarpment that evening. It cast a ghostly luminance over the steaming pools. The travertine shimmered in an unnatural way. While campfires blazed, Hayden wrote that one startling aspect of the hot springs was their isolation. The visitor was given no opportunity to prepare for the sight: the springs simply "appeared." *At close inspection,* he wrote, *individual creations within the complex show what nature can do given time and freedom. There is no standard size or shape to the pools:*

each terrace of travertine is a separate and unique exhibition of sculpturing. The Chinese who terrace their hillsides would be envious at the artistry.

"Enjoy your baths," he said to the men of the survey. "Tomorrow we move on."

Their new trail followed the south bank of the Gardiner's River. When the river turned to the east, the trail led south. The men heard the fading roar as the river rushed through some distant canyon. The trail cut across several tributaries that flowed into the Gardiner's, then rolled over a series of hills and topped out on a broad plateau. Here, the men were greeted by vistas of towering mountains and sweeping valleys. Sharp, volcanic-looking peaks stood out beautifully, set off by large snowfields. The change in landscape was immediate and pronounced.

"My word," said Captain Barlow, "I didn't know this country would have such spectacular scenery."

But the drama of the scene was no more than Hayden's men had expected. Their real adventure had started with the springs. Now they anticipated that their wonderland would continue to unfold unabated. "I'm ready for geysers," shouted Jackson to no one in particular.

"In due time, I'm sure," replied Hayden, who was directly behind Jackson.

The air was clear and invigorating, and the sun was bright against a uniform blue sky. Streams they crossed continued to run northeast. Their horses waded through thick stands of purple penstemons. Patches of shade and streambanks were covered with clusters of white cow lily, pink and yellow monkey flowers, wild geraniums, and lavender-colored asters. On the lower slopes, stands of aspen broke the somber line of pines. Above them, limestone and sandstone cap rock defined the horizon.

The next morning at breakfast, Dixon found Jackson. "You missed the fun last night," he said.

"What fun was that?"

"Being roused out of bed in the middle of the night to find the horses," said Dixon.

Jackson laughed. "Oh, you had an adventure. What happened?"

"Who knows? Stevenson said he thought a grizzly bear might have spooked them. He was afraid the horses would try to head back to Bottler's."

"And?" said Jackson, waiting.

"We found them."

"Sounds like you had fun," said Jackson.

"Not really," yawned Dixon. "I lost a lot of sleep and didn't even see the bear."

"Count your blessings," said Jackson wryly.

The crew spent most of the day exploring the geology exposed in the ravines and canyons of the Yellowstone River. They came across Baronet's Bridge, built the year before, where the Yellowstone merged with the east fork. Jackson took a photograph of it. "What's next?" he asked of Stevenson, who was looking at the map.

"A place called Tower Creek."

"Don't we expect to find a waterfall at Tower Creek?"

"You're asking the wrong person; I just crack the whip around here," said Stevenson with a straight face. There was no evidence that Stevenson ever carried a whip, but Jackson refused to give his friend the satisfaction of asking. He turned to Hayden.

"A waterfall. Yes," said Hayden. "Allegedly it's a spectacular falls that begins at the end of a tortuous course through some strange formations. The men of the Washburn expedition said the falls began in a gloomy canyon they named Devil's Den." He raised his eyebrows and smiled. "We'll have to see, won't we?"

Once again, without warning, the countryside underwent dramatic change. Slopes in the land around them steepened abruptly, and Tower Creek appeared one hundred feet below them, running through a dark, heavily forested valley. Then it vanished, to reappear two hundred yards before it merged with the Yellowstone River. Strange rock configurations stood like sentinels at the point where the stream disappeared.

The sun was behind Jackson, so it looked like the water disappeared into a black hole. He rode downstream to get in front of the falls. He could hear it now. Knowing that his best bet was to photograph directly into the falls, Jackson looked for a way into the valley. The slope was steep, rocky, and full of brush. He couldn't ride down; in fact, he wasn't sure that he could negotiate the slope on foot, not with a camera. Nonetheless, he tried, using the legs of his tripod to keep himself from slipping. The brush hindered his footing, and more than once he came close to losing his balance. At the bottom, he looked back up. He'd come down a good five hundred feet.

The waterfall was splendid. The water appeared to fall effortlessly, a single pour that dropped through a series of towers. From Jackson's vantage, the towers appeared to rise fifty to one hundred feet above the lip. He found a good site and positioned his camera. Then he walked back to where he had come down. "Dixon," he yelled. "Get everything ready for a negative. I'll be up in a few minutes." Jackson paused at the base of the slope, considered the effort he would have to expend to get back up, and wondered why all good shots were in impossible places.

Twenty minutes later, Jackson wrapped the wet plate in wet paper and wrapped the holder in a wet towel. Dixon set out a second measure of chemicals to develop the negative, then followed Jackson, who half-walked, half-slid down the hill.

By the time the two were back on top with the exposed plate, they were wet with perspiration. Nonetheless, the development and fixing of the negative was a success, so they started the process again. By the end of the day they had completed four round trips. With Dixon's assistance, not one plate dried out.

The negatives showed a rigid wall of water that leaped with military precision into a dark hole with rough, vertical walls. The walls were black and angular. Mist from the splashing water appeared like a light veil over a portion of the image, but much remained in shadow. Jackson knew he had been around Hayden too long when he observed that the force of the water striking the canyon floor was probably responsible for the size of the pocket. He also recognized that the canyon walls were composed of volcanic breccia that had withstood the forces of erosion.

Moran stayed on top to complete one sketch of the falls and two watercolors of Tower Creek. He focused on the bizarre sculptured forms that crowned the lip of the falls. Grayish-brown tints matched the mood of the scene, and nearby rocks and trees formed a natural foreground.

Hayden looked at Moran's work with approval: "Gloomy-looking sentinels are they not?" The sketch reminded him of Lieutenant Doane's description of the falls: *Nothing could be more chastely beautiful than this lovely cascade hidden away in the dim light of overshadowing rocks and woods, its very voice hushed to a low murmur at the distance of a few hundred yards.*

7) The Grandest Canyon

The good weather held. The following day the Hayden party found themselves on a trail that led directly to a high, distant peak. "Mount Washburn, huh? Looks a bit like the axle of a wheel," said Moran.

"I don't see that," said Jackson.

"Look at how the ridges come together. Don't they look like spokes on a wheel?"

"Maybe the roots of a cypress tree," offered Jackson. The two artists enjoyed seeing through each other's eyes.

The trail followed a sinuous ridge that gradually rose above the valley floor. Soon the men were riding higher than the forest. Nothing grew on the slopes of the ridge, so they had a clear view across the valley. The views were pastoral, picture perfect. Jackson saw splotches of dark green woods and light green meadows. Streams issued from small depressions at the base of the mountain. Mount Washburn rose in the middle of the picture. Had the party remained on the valley floor, the riders would have found themselves trapped, facing the high walls of a cirque-like pocket in the side of the mountain.

By noon of the following day, the party had ridden to the southwest flanks of the mountain. "I want to go to the top," said Hayden to Barlow during a rest, "but the flank here is too steep. I suggest we backtrack a few miles and climb the west slope. Coming?"

Stevenson and the main party continued on while Hayden, a few of the survey men, and a number from Barlow's party made the ascent. By the time they reached the tree line, the pitch of the wind had increased to a low howl. They tied their horses to the highest clump of trees. As they looked to the north, they saw how the ridge had taken them to the flank of the mountain. They also saw that most of the north-facing pockets high on the mountain contained deep wells of snow. Almost as one, they turned into the wind and started climbing.

Nothing grew on the summit, and everything but sedimentary slabs and volcanic rocks had been blown away by the wind long ago. The air was cold and clear, and the sun was bright. The wind made normal conversation impossible. Hayden walked around the summit in a tight circle, taking notes with his back turned to the wind. Barlow tried to make some drawings but the wind ripped the paper from his hands. Elliott hunkered down and managed to complete two sketches.

Later, they estimated that they were able to see fifty to a hundred miles in every direction. A wall of distant mountains defined the rim of the Yellowstone basin, as though they were conspiring to keep the valley secret from the rest of the world. Volcanic peaks, three and four deep, presented a continuous sawtoothed horizon. In places, the ragged profile pierced the clouds. In the northeast, the mountaintops appeared to rise several thousand feet higher than Mount Washburn. In nearly every case, the highest mountains showed the smooth, steep-angle slopes that spoke of their volcanic origin.

To the west, mile upon mile of black pine forest led to the bald peaks of the Madison Range. To the south, the land was more complex. Close in, Hayden saw a gigantic rent in the earth through which the Yellowstone River coursed. Perspective made the walls pinch out. Further away, a huge lake interrupted the land. Its deep blue spread out in the sunlight. Although still twenty miles away, the limpid pool seemed to lie at his feet.

"What are those?" shouted Barlow to Hayden, who was rapidly making notes about the lake.

"The isolated spires? South of the lake? Those are the Tetons," replied Hayden. "Magnificent, are they not? I haven't seen them since 1860. They are true monarchs of all they survey. I believe their summits are perpetually covered with snow."

Eventually the party returned to their waiting horses. No one spoke. The view had said everything.

The following day the survey party entered a region of bubbling mud springs. The air was filled with an ugly smell and the sound of the popping bubbles. One mud cone, shaped like a horn and buried in a hillside, belched, hissed, and threw a light-colored clay thirty feet into the air. All of the trees within a mile had been devastated by the mud and gas of the hissing fumaroles and associated springs. The colorless fumaroles contrasted strangely with the delicate red geraniums that grew in profusion along the rims of grass. The unlikely partnership was one more reminder that the survey team had entered a one-of-a-kind world.

Late that afternoon, as they rode in pursuit of Stevenson's latest campsite, the air softened and the wind became a gentle presence. Hayden was thinking of a hot cup of coffee and some rest. His reverie was interrupted by Peale.

"Professor Hayden, can you hear that noise?" he asked.

"What noise?" asked Hayden.

"A faint roaring, like far-off thunder. But it's too steady for thunder; besides, there are no clouds."

Hayden turned in the saddle. "Anyone else hear a distant roaring?"

A few men nodded. When the wind shifted Hayden thought he, too, could hear a deep, continuous rumble. It was impossible to guess what additional wonder or creation the sound might portend, so he didn't speculate on its source.

As they descended the mountain, the roaring grew in volume and definition. The sun touched the horizon. Its rays revealed details of the high mountain landscape to the east. Distant peaks appeared to increase in height, slopes sharpened, and hidden intricacies of the landscape were exposed. The riders descended the last slope of the mountain. They lost their view as they were enveloped by the trees of the forest.

The roar continued to grow louder. The forest came to an abrupt end and the riders entered a large clearing. Here, the roar was deafening. Hayden could feel the earth tremble. The noise and vibrations were coming from a huge gash in the earth, a chasm that stretched north to south without apparent end. The men dismounted and walked to the rim of the huge canyon, mesmerized as it yawned wider and wider with every step. It looked as though some stupendous force had pulled the crust of the earth apart to expose its inner structure. The size and depth of the chasm were as overwhelming as its voice. It was difficult to believe that the noise they had been hearing for miles had come from a canyon, but they could now see the source of the sound. In this enormous canyon, the river was transformed into a majestic waterfall.

Moran was in awe. Here he was, a simple man, a creature of the world, privileged to witness one of the faces of God. It was an obvious truth to him, as a painter, that until such an event as this was witnessed, it could never be painted because it could not be imagined.

The men of the survey stood in the shadow of the pines. On the far side of the canyon, the land was awash with the glow of sunset. Amid a flurry of exclamations, everyone scattered to find his own vantage from which he could examine this river of rivers, this canyon of canyons, this spectacle that was both waterfall and miracle in one place.

Charles Peale walked to a point of rock, sat quietly, and looked into the canyon. The sight made his stomach quiver. From where he sat, there was nothing between him and the silver thread of river at the bottom of the slope thousands of feet below. That river looked no more than five feet wide, but as he watched its antics, he could feel its power.

The far wall of the canyon looked as vertical as the one he sat on. Pine trees crowded the rim. They looked no larger than small bushes. A half-mile upstream, he could see the water hurtle over the ledge of the falls in perpetual motion, continuously replaying a fall that measured hundreds of feet. A cavalcade of rainbows hovered where the falls became river again, where falling water was converted into mist.

Jackson and Moran moved along the rim in tandem, delighting in new angles and new views with variations in the foreground. Moran was shocked by the color in the canyon, especially in the diminishing evening light. The walls were bright yellow, brown, and a range of yellow-orange hues. Great pinnacles of reddish stone jutted from the walls, here and there. As he surveyed the slopes, he kept finding hues he knew he had never seen before. For a brief moment he wondered whether he could capture this vision at all.

Here indeed, everything was grand nature. Above the falls, the river flowed through a grassy meadow, calm and steady. As with all phenomena in the Yellowstone, the river gave no warning that it was about to rush over a precipice one hundred and forty feet high, nor that, a quarter of a mile later, it would leap another three hundred fifty feet. Moran kept taking out his sketch pad to make rapid sketches, but the available light was fading fast.

The next morning, before the sun appeared, members of the crew disappeared in pairs to tackle the tasks for which they had been hired. Hayden walked alone. He suggested that Peale examine the rocks and minerals on the canyon walls; he himself wanted to spend the morning examining the geological processes that had created these features.

The ledge of the upper falls proved to be massive basalt. Below that resistant layer of rock, Hayden discovered soft conglomerates of clay and sand. The action of the hot springs in the area accelerated the rate of erosion. On the sides of the walls Hayden noted a thick growth of vegetation that was nourished by the continual spray. It took an effort to concentrate on the geology when the beauty of the place was so distracting.

Aside from what knowledge he gained by standing on the lip of the falls, Hayden was thrilled by the force of nature. The curve of the falls before him appeared to be directly proportional to the speed the water gained from the rapids further upstream. The one-hundred-foot-wide mass of water detached itself in one incredible pour and hurled into space. It fell, first as one adhesive body, then ablated slowly into snow-white, beadlike drops. As the water struck the rocky basin below, foam and spray rebounded through the air for hundreds of feet. From a distance, the dynamic event resembled a mass of snow-white foam.

Hayden knew what he would find at the lower falls: the same mass of water gathering itself once again to plunge three hundred fifty feet. True to his thoughts, the lower falls did not disappoint him. The mist that rose from the foot of the falls was so dense he could get no closer than several hundred feet. He thought of Langford's comment about the water resembling molten silver. He was right; and indeed, in the sunlight, the foot of the falls *was* crowned by a shimmering rainbow.

As for the canyon, *no language can do justice to its wonder, grandeur and beauty,* wrote Hayden. He estimated its depth as twelve to fifteen hundred feet and its width as more than half a mile. The walls, whose slope had stabilized at a very steep incline, were crowded with towers, spires, and gothic columns. Some sections resembled the fronts of fortresses. In places, landslides of brilliant-colored debris extended the full length of the slope to the water's edge. Gothic columns exhibited great variety and more striking color than ever adorned a work of human art; mixes of gas and water had also left a range of fantastically expanded hues from the palest yellow to the mellowest reds of old brick, and from pearl gray to the deepest jet black. From the canyon rim, the river was a streak of silver foam that traveled through a channel of earthen colors, yellows, reds, browns, and whites, all intermixed and blending into one another.

Hayden picked up his journal and observed that the prevailing color of white came from decomposing feldspar. At the bottom of the page he noted that *as one looks into the abyss one cannot but realize the littleness of man when he is compared with the work of nature.* When he was not writing, he scurried back and forth along the rim, humming with pleasure at his tasks. Everything about the Yellowstone, its size, the magnitude of its features, its colors, geology and sheer beauty, far exceeded anything Hayden had hoped.

In the late afternoon, he came across Jackson sitting on a boulder. The light was just beginning to fade. "Well," said Hayden with an energetic note, "Have you run out of plates or out of energy?"

"Neither. Dr. Hayden, this place is nothing short of incredible," said Jackson. He gestured toward the canyon. "I have never encountered anything so remarkable, so strange, or so challenging. What happened here?" he queried. "Is this some kind of freak accident?"

"On the contrary, the canyon is a direct result of nature working steadily over time. In place of unyielding rock like we found in the Wind Rivers and South Pass, we are standing on top of some complex geology. Beneath us we have a huge deposit of soft, volcanic ash, with harder seams of dikelike eruptions, breccia, and basalt. I have hypothesized that this whole region was once the basin of an immense lake. At some later time it also became a center of volcanic activity. Vast quantities of lava cooled in the water. That would account for the basalt which directly underlies the upper falls.

"Volumes of volcanic ash and rock fragments, thrown out from craters, sank through the water to form breccias which mingled with the deposits of siliceous springs. Subsequently, the whole region was slowly lifted. When that happened, the lake drained away. That set the stage for what we see today. The easily eroded breccia along the river channel was cut deeper and deeper as time passed. In the meantime, springs and creeks and falling rain combined to carve the sides of the canyon into the fantastic shapes you now see. The hot springs deposit was originally white as snow, but it's been stained every shade of red and yellow by mineral waters."

"But why the falls? I mean, why here?"

"The key is the basalt," responded Hayden. "Erosion of the soft layers was arrested at the upper end of the canyon by a sudden transition to the hard layer of basalt. While the water cut the canyon, the basalt resisted erosion. The river water kept coming, hence the falls."

As he talked, Hayden wore the slightly pensive expression he donned when he taught classes at the University of Pennsylvania. Inside, however, Hayden's emotions were running amok. He was thrilled beyond words to be where he was. What an incredible opportunity to be the first to unravel the geology of the Yellowstone. And when he returned, his report, supported by Jackson's photographs and Mr. Moran's paintings, would rock the country.

On the steep canyon slopes seven hundred feet below, Peale started to slide past Henry Elliott. Elliott yelled "Here!" and grabbed Peale's hand. Had he missed, Peale might have slid, rolled or tumbled the remaining three hundred feet into the river.

"Good lord, be careful; this stuff is treacherous." Elliott held on while Peale dug his boots into the bank.

"Let's face it," said Peale. "We'll never get to the bottom this way. There's nothing below us except a steeper slope, and there's nothing to get a foot into." He laughed nervously. "If we go into the river, we've had it." He glanced at the river that rushed past them, crashing and foaming out of control as it surged among the rocks. Its speed created a great complex of waves. The river was so swift and so filled with eddies and whirlpools that any fall into the water would be fatal.

"You're right," said Elliott, "and we can't travel sideways in this stuff; we've got to back up."

Peale was sweating heavily. His face, arms, and clothes were covered with yellow-gray dirt and powder and his muscles were trembling. Under a very blue sky and cool river wind, they had climbed more than five hundred feet down a seventy-five degree slope. Their immediate surroundings were composed of loose ochre-colored rubble. On the opposite bank, at their elevation, a few trees grew in a cluster. Peale looked up and took a deep breath. "Getting out of here may be the ultimate challenge."

Nothing grew within a hundred yards. Peale took a step up the slope and immediately slid backwards. Elliott realized that on the way down they had given no thought of how to get out. "I have a pick," said Elliott. "We can use it for climbing." He swung the pick and buried the point in the slope. "This is what they don't tell you about when you decided to spend another summer with Professor Hayden."

"Maybe we should gather specimens on the way back, at least have something for our effort," said Peale.

"You can't fool the boss," said Elliott. "He may act like he doesn't know what's going on, but you'd be surprised how much he knows about what everyone is doing."

"Let's do it," said Peale. "You go first. I'll push, then you can pull me up."

Two hours later, the two lads, somewhat gouged and scraped from unforeseen encounters with sharp rocks, stretched out on the cap rock. Scarcely five minutes later they looked at one another, nodded, and began to search for an easier way down. The initial slope of the one they chose was hardly less than eighty degrees, but in the end, they stood on rounded boulders at the edge of the river. The wind was strong and the wet wind felt refreshing. Elliott looked at the barometer he carried in his rucksack. It showed a descent of one thousand feet.

"We must be the first men on this spot. Think of that!" said Peale as he looked around. He grinned. "Who else would be crazy enough to come down here?"

Light reflected from the waves, then bounced back and forth between the canyon walls. Each set of rocks featured its own prominent color. Some were stained red ochre, others bright yellow from the sulfur. The overall effect was one of a series of light, pastel stains. Peale gathered specimens; Elliott sketched the river and the strange configurations that rose from the walls.

They returned to camp about the time that Stevenson was introducing a local trapper to Professor Hayden. "This is Jefferson," said Stevenson. "He traps in the valley. Says he knows where we can find a geyser near here."

"God's truth," said Jefferson. He spat and wiped his mouth with a leather sleeve that was missing most of its rain strands. "Ain't far from here and as long as we get there before sundown, it'll blow."

Elliott, Peale, and some of Barlow's party ended up going. Hayden looked for, but couldn't find Jackson. "He'll have a fit if he misses anything," he said. But they left nonetheless.

The object around which the men gathered looked innocent enough. It was a small travertine mound with a hole about the size of a cannon bore in its center. The hole was nearly filled to the brim with still water. Everyone waited. Toward dusk, conversations dwindled. Without warning, the water rose in the pool and flowed over the edges. After thirty seconds, it began boil. Suddenly, all of the water in the pool was thrown upwards in a continuous stream. It rose to a height of ten feet, subsided, then shot up again and remained as a high arch of water, like a fountain. A cloud of steam accompanied the spout. Every man in the group backed up and gazed upon this spectacle. No one spoke until the flow finally stopped, twenty minutes later. Then the pool was smooth once again. Nothing remained to give evidence of the geyser's performance.

"Happens about four times every day," said Jefferson with satisfaction.

Back in camp, the blinking eyes of an animal in the woods reflected a yellow campfire. The only sounds were the occasional clink of metal pots, the snap of burning wood, laughter, and a voice trying to replay the rise and fall of the geyser for those who had not seen it. Some distance away, coyotes barked.

Hayden savored the moment. A marvelous land. Would nature's fantastic forms never cease? What would they discover next?

8) The Artist's Reach

"We'll see you at the lake, Jackson," said Stevenson, astride his handsome gray. "If you don't fall into the canyon."

Jackson grinned in spite of himself. "I didn't know you cared," he replied.

Stevenson turned his horse and disappeared. Jackson, Moran, Dixon, and Crissman were staying behind to document the canyon and falls. Everyone else was leaving; too much territory to cover, not enough time. Hayden had said it was better to return to selected spots a second time for more definitive work than to miss an important feature altogether.

On the first three days, the four men were up at dawn. Every new viewpoint offered a composition, but they chose only the best for photos and sketches. The days were busy, tiring, and wonderful. Most exhilarating perhaps was the thought that they were in the presence of one of the greatest natural views that had never yet been captured by artist or photographer. Jackson worked with Moran, backing up his sketches with photographs.

On the last day, Jackson was up before the sun. He banked the campfire into a roaring well of heat to push away the morning chill. With coffee in hand, he reviewed his efforts of the last three days. He'd taken about all the photographs he needed from this side of the river, the upper falls from the rim of the canyon just below the falls, and several good close-ups; a half-dozen good negatives of the lower falls and several views from far down the canyon. The rim shots gave good detail for geological analysis; the more distant shots showed the relationship of the falls to the canyon and country.

Jackson, Crissman, and Moran had also examined the canyon thoroughly from above the falls itself to a point one mile below it. They thought they knew every feature by heart. Jackson's last shot yesterday had been looking downriver. From that vantage he could see the river rapids disappear behind a bend. The banks of the canyon were interrupted by clusters of volcanic spires. They looked like overgrown stalagmites. The full power of the place came to him as he watched cloud shadows race down one slope and up the other. The treacherous slopes, arid and worthless soils, and dangerous rapids all spoke of a forbidden and forbidding place.

It was time to cross the river, explore the far side, then move on to Yellowstone Lake. "Well, George," said Jackson, nudging his assistant awake, "this is our last day here, partner; let's make the best of it."

Dixon sat up and rubbed his eyes. "Right," he yawned. Crissman emerged from his tent about the same time. Jackson lifted a coffee cup in salutation and watched his fellow photographer for a moment as though to assure himself that everything was all right. The man looked tired and resigned. The camera Jackson had brought along as backup stood on a tripod outside Crissman's tent. Jackson repressed a twinge of pity for Crissman, then replaced that feeling with the knowledge that he had helped ease a bad situation. He wondered how he would have reacted had he been in Crissman's boots.

The day before, the four of them had been working the west edge of the canyon. Crissman was set up not more than fifty feet from Jackson. They found it pleasant to work together. They did what any two photographers would do when shooting together: compare thoughts about the light, compositions, and exposures, and share materials. A little past noon, a series of cumulus clouds appeared from the west. A light, variable wind announced their arrival.

Jackson was looking up the canyon, thinking that here, in the Grand Canyon of the Yellowstone, they had the opportunity to present to the American people images never before imagined. Here were formations and erosional processes totally unknown in the East. Suddenly, Dixon tapped him on the shoulder. Crissman was sitting near the rim, his head in his hands.

Something was desperately wrong. They hurried to him. "Hey, John, you all right? What's happened?" asked Jackson.

Dixon realized Crissman's camera was nowhere in sight. "Gosh, Mr. Crissman, where's your camera?"

"It's to hell and gone over the edge, boys. I'm finished," said Crissman. He looked as though he was about to cry.

"What?" Jackson rushed to the edge and looked down. Pieces of camera box and tripod were scattered for hundreds of feet on the slope below. A black cloth was caught on a bush that jutted out from the canyon wall; it fluttered in the wind like a sign of mourning. Jackson immediately looked to where his own camera stood and felt an enormous wave of relief when he saw that everything was still in place.

"I must have planted my tripod too close to the edge," said Crissman. "I wanted a view of the lower falls without a lot of foreground. It looked fine, so I made an exposure and went back to develop the plate." Like Jackson, he kept his developing box in the shadows near the edge of the woods. Crissman moaned. "I can only figure that the wind took it."

"Come on, John, let's go have some coffee." Jackson couldn't think of anything else to say. What could he say? If he'd lost his camera he'd . . . well, of course! He'd have his backup camera.

He grabbed Crissman by the arm. "All is not lost. Hah!" He pulled the distraught photographer with him to his supply pack, where he dug out a large box. With a big smile he handed the box to Crissman. "Now we're even, my friend," he said.

Crissman unwrapped the object. It was Jackson's smaller view camera. "Use it as long as you need," said Jackson. "You saved my bacon two years ago in Salt Lake City. I couldn't have gotten along without the use of your darkroom."

Crissman sighed heavily. "Thanks, William. This means a lot."

Jackson and the others had broken camp and moved above the falls to the river's edge. Jackson's horse drank from the river while Jackson looked across. The body of water looked cold, swift, and deep. There was no way around it: to cross meant everyone was going to get wet and cold. This kind of crossing wasn't new to him; he'd driven a whole herd of wild horses from California to Colorado, back in '67.

Jackson led his horse into the river first. As the water deepened, the gelding balked and tried to back up. Jackson encouraged him forward. He figured the bottom was full of boulders, making it difficult for the horse to find solid footing. After making a small circle, he discovered places that were more than three feet deep. He returned to shore.

"Wrap a line around a nearby tree and feed me line as I go across," said Jackson to Dixon. "When I get to the other side, tie off your end. You two can use it as a safety guide. No sense in losing one of us over the falls, hey?" Grinning, he prodded his horse and re-entered the torrent.

Holding the rope with one hand, Dixon led his horse around a sturdy lodgepole pine, then looped the rope once around his saddle horn. He fed the line as Jackson rode slowly across the river. The horse stumbled once and Jackson got wet to the waist, but he patted the animal, signaled the others that he was all right, and emerged safely on the opposite shore.

Moran and Crissman took the plunge together. Crissman went first. He was the more seasoned rider, so he took the downriver position in case Moran or his horse had trouble. They set a slow pace, and a pale Moran bit his cigarillo in half on the way across, but they had no trouble.

Dixon tied the rope to the tree, waved his hat, and plunged

his horse into the rushing river. In the middle of the torrent, his horse found a hole and fell forward. Instead of pulling back on the reins, Dixon grabbed for the rope. The horse lurched up and ahead to regain its footing, and Dixon fell sideways into the water.

Dixon had hold of the rope, but it stretched until Dixon's head was just one more round bump among the rocks that occasionally broke the surface. Jackson and Moran tried pulling on the rope to bring Dixon to the surface, but the force of the water was too great. Crissman leaped on his horse and went back into the river. The lad's hands still held the rope, but the rest of him was buried in the turbulence. Communication was impossible.

"Can you grab his shirt or his belt?" yelled Jackson.

Cautiously negotiating his horse to where Dixon was clinging to the rope, Crissman reached down and grabbed one of Dixon's arms. Desperate, Dixon clutched Crissman's sleeve and nearly pulled him from his saddle. Crissman wrapped his free arm around the saddle horn and dragged the half-submerged Dixon to shore. Jackson and Moran, leaning into the river as far as they could from waist-deep water, pulled Dixon to safety.

Dixon collapsed, coughing and spitting water. He began to shiver. Moran, who looked equally exhausted, pulled a flask from his saddle, took a drink, and passed it to Jackson. When Jackson gave it to Dixon, the lad took a deep pull and immediately began to cough again.

"That's enough excitement for a while," muttered Moran. He gathered wood and built a fire while Jackson found some dry clothes for Dixon. A few minutes later, a subdued Dixon raised his still-blue face and asked, "Well, did you at least get a photograph?"

The upper falls dominated the center of the image in the camera. Water poured through a deep erosional cut in the basalt. This waterfall was wider but fell less distance than the lower one. Shadows on the west side of the slope added to the composition. Jackson took his eye from the viewfinder with a sense of satisfaction. From Gifford and Moran, he had learned to reduce the amount of sky, emphasize horizontal lines, and make better compositional use of trees and rocks to dramatize the setting.

He owed Hayden a vote of thanks, too. Not that Hayden knew anything about photography, but nearly every evening, Jackson had learned something new about the processes and products of geological forces. The need for scientific content had so taken root in his mind that he found himself considering geology before other factors in the selection of his views.

With Dixon's help he adjusted the tripod legs one last time. They had about an hour left before the sun slid behind the mountain, making a good negative all but impossible. Jackson remembered having seen Moran sketching directly into the sun. "How can you do that?" he had asked. "Doesn't that hurt your eyes and erase all the detail? It does for me."

Moran paused. "It's something you learn," he said, then returned to his sketch. "The landscape painter, Turner, used to paint while looking into the sun. It's a useful technique."

Jackson decided it must be something that only artists did.

"It has to do with essence," added Moran.

Jackson wanted to ask more about Turner, but Moran was involved. His questions could wait.

Thomas Moran was in three places at once. His physical self was seated on a rock, sketch pad and palette at the ready to capture the bizarre shapes and hard-to-believe tones that streaked the slopes of the canyon. The horizons of the image were defined by vivid tapestries of earth tones and columns of wondrous form. At the moment, he was at a loss for how to mix the right color. The natural tints were beyond anything he had ever tried to record. It wasn't that he doubted his ability, but that he realized he'd have to complete the process in his studio. His tints and notes next to his sketches would have to be right.

Moran's emotional self, the artist within, was detached from the scene but not from the creative process. Every artist experienced one spiritual revelation. The Yellowstone was Moran's epiphany. Every element of the Yellowstone landscape, from aspen leaf to lichen-covered boulder, was pure western nature. Nothing here dealt with man: all was form, color, and light. Moran swirled the brush through a yellow ochre-white, blended it with white to an earthy cream. He touched the brush into the paper and pulled it down. Here, undisturbed, in this land of giants and mythology, Thomas Moran was able to express the ecstasy of his soul.

The third Moran, his pragmatic self, was on the periphery, selecting elements of both the canyon and the falls for his first large painting. He had studied the scene from as many vantage points as had Jackson. Indeed, the two had been almost inseparable. Moran had sketched the lower falls and the great sweep of the gorge, but was moved almost as much by the eloquence of the upper falls, whose violence, snow-white arch, and ethereal spray inspired one of his best watercolors.

Now he studied the spectacle of that falls, memorizing the minutest details, seeking the keys of how to reproduce the dazzling highlights of the sun as it reflected from the cliffs. As a lithographer, printmaker, and wood-carver, Moran had trained his mind to hold a thousand details. He had often astonished his wife, Mary, with his ability to recreate, in vivid detail and color, scenes he had not visited in years.

His first major painting of the Yellowstone would be woven from a myriad of sketches such as the one he now worked on. As a printmaker he'd learned the need to create a series of sketches from which his final composition would be shaped. The strategy left him free to create tension between detail and atmosphere, and to link the apparent gulf between intimacy and the vastness of space. He also knew how to adjust the point of view and insert people to add the human element as needed.

He could already envision the final coalescence of images. Turner's "grand idea" had become a reality. As he added streaks of paint and notes to his sketch, he thought of the unique character of each object, and imagined how he might place each color and tree in the painting of his mind's eye.

An early teacher of his had emphasized painting directly from nature, but creating one's own impression rather than trying to imitate her. Moran wanted accurate representation, but he had no desire to recreate scenes. What mattered was to convey his personal vision and interpretation. Nature's scenes were motifs, not the final work. When all of the elements of his masterpiece were absorbed in a single glance, his interpretation would be conveyed.

Thomas Moran stretched and stared at different parts of the upper falls. He found it difficult to connect the beauty of the steady-state waterfall with his knowledge that the river had created the canyon. But Moran was a romantic, not an analyst, so he felt no urgency to explain why this moment and this setting were so right for him. All he knew was that at this point in his life, he was at the peak of artistic readiness.

While Jackson and Dixon packed for the journey to Yellowstone Lake, Moran sensed that the Yellowstone marked the beginning of a new level of awareness, a new phase of his work. He was anxious to nurture this new beginning and to see what would become of it, for he knew he was not yet finished with the Yellowstone.

9) Anna on the Lake

Captain Barlow hurried his horse along the trail to catch the main group, on its way to the Mud Volcanoes, ten miles ahead. Hayden's party, he surmised, was probably at the lake by now. No matter. Barlow was enjoying the pastoral landscape. Nothing hinted at volcanics, hot springs, falls, or canyons here. The Yellowstone River was a broad, smooth stream flowing silently in a slight cut, lined with gentle, well wooded slopes. Barlow turned to his associate, Captain Heap. "I wouldn't be surprised to come across a farm or hamlet in such a peaceful valley," he said.

Barlow spoke too soon. Within minutes, the landscape changed. After crossing several small creeks, the rolling plain turned into a prairie that was alive with steam jets that rose from numerous cracks and apertures. From horseback the two officers could see acre after acre of volcanic features. Barlow and Heap left their men and approached one of the formations, the kind that the hunters called "soda mountains." One side of the mound had been blown away, creating an amphitheater. When Barlow dismounted, he could feel the heat of the earth through his boots. The crust began to crack under his weight. He bent down and picked up a piece of broken earth. A myriad of tiny, pure crystals of sulfur had grown on the underside. They sparkled in the sunlight.

They stopped again at a huge boiling spring that tossed black mud so fine that it had no perceptible grain. "What do you think, David? Hasty pudding?" joked Barlow.

"Not with that smell, Captain," replied Heap. The air reeked of alum. Barlow remounted and rode clear of the soft crust to where a spring threw water several feet in the air. The water was thrown out in pulses. He could feel deep vibrations from within the cavern.

"I am constantly astounded by the phenomena that suddenly appear from nowhere," said Barlow. "First we have an open prairie with expansive vistas, a few streams thick with marsh grass, and voilà, a mud volcano." The crater he gestured to had formed on a timbered hillside. The surface opening was twenty-five feet across. "Look at the trees," he said. "They're covered with mud. To have thrown material so far, this volcano must have been much more violent than it is now."

As they left the scene, a geyser spurted water to a height of thirty feet. Waves dashed against the sides of the surrounding basin and clouds of steam accompanied the display; all the while it rumbled like an earthquake. Barlow was now keen on getting to the lake. He wanted to talk to Professor Hayden. He figured, correctly, that they would catch the advance party by the following evening.

That next morning, Hayden stood on the edge of Yellowstone Lake. "I would estimate that this lake is twenty by fifteen miles," he said to Anton Schonborn. In the heavy shadows of the early morning, the lake was a sheet of glass streaked with hues of ultramarine blue.

"You think, perhaps, one day, it was bigger?" asked Schonborn.

"Oh, most certainly. What we see today may be only a remnant of the lake that existed in glacial times. What an incredible sight. Well," he sighed, "we only have so much time. Best get everyone in motion."

His concern was unfounded; the men, as anxious to explore the region as Hayden, were already assembling the boat. The sound of hammers, the smell of heated pitch, and the uneven noise of conversations of men at work filled the campsite. By early afternoon, the work was finished. The boat, twelve feet long and three and a half feet wide, was covered with stout ducking, and well tarred. A mast stuck up from its center.

"What are we using for sail?" asked Hayden.

"A blanket," said Stevenson.

"Are you going out?" Hayden asked.

"Eventually," said Stevenson. "Launching honors go to the intrepid Private Daniel Storr."

Hayden chuckled. Storr had been a member of the Washburn Expedition, but Hayden's amusement had more to do with Storr's character. A highly likable fellow, Storr was a massive man with a powerful voice and infinite sense of humor. Both Stevenson and Hayden had found him reliable, yet reckless and wild. He was the perfect choice to test the boat.

"We've rigged a sounding line with a lead weight in the back of the boat," said Stevenson. They walked to the beach where Storr was getting ready to make sail. The wind was light and steady.

"So," said Hayden to the assembled members of the survey. "We need a name for our new creation."

"Call it *The Hayden*," shouted Elliott. "*The Explorer*," said Dixon. "*The Intrepid*," suggested another. "*The Jackson!*" said a loud voice. That drew laughter.

"What do you think?" Hayden asked Stevenson.

Stevenson rubbed his beard. "I think it's a marvelous opportunity to make points with your political friends back East." His eyes twinkled. Everyone in the party groaned. "Whose favor do we need most this year?"

Hayden laughed. "Congressman Dawes, to be sure. He holds the power of the purse."

"Yes, well, I happen to know that Congressman Dawes has a daughter named Anna."

Most of the men laughed, and a few whistled.

Hayden looked appraisingly at his friend. "You're getting incorrigibly familiar with the system, Jim; perhaps next winter I should remain in the West and send you to Washington to look for money."

Stevenson shook his head. "You don't pay me enough for that, sir," he said. Storr painted the name *Anna* on the side of the boat in tar, then signaled that he was ready. Amid cheers and grunts of effort, the men pushed the boat into the water.

After Storr proved to one and all that the boat was lakeworthy, Stevenson and Elliott took over. "Let's try the island first," said Stevenson. The lake was almost too calm for the sail. Elliott rowed and Stevenson steered. When the boat touched the shore of the island, Elliott shouted, "I name this Stevenson's Island."

They proceeded to explore the oval-shaped hummock, which covered ten acres but did not prove inviting. It was thickly overgrown and had nothing more interesting than the tracks of lots of animals. "The next time you want to name something after me, let's wait until we've explored it," said Stevenson dryly as he got back into the boat. "Then I'll tell you whether I want my name on it."

Back on the water, they took some depth measurements and made a crude map of part of the nearby shoreline. By noon, the water was becoming roily. The wind only increased as the day wore on. After doing battle with whitecaps several feet high, they rowed the boat closer to shore.

That evening, they reported back to Hayden. "The boat handles well," Stevenson told him, "but waves appear as quickly as prairie dust devils. Our best bet is to complete the depth soundings in the morning and stay close to shore in the afternoon."

"How deep is it?" asked Hayden.

"We found one spot a bit over three hundred feet," said Elliott. "Not surprisingly, the bays are shallow and the deep spots are toward the middle."

"Is the lake as large as I thought?"

"Hard to tell until we get more data," said Stevenson. "It's shaped a bit like a human hand with south-pointing fingers. We didn't do any fishing, but I hear that the fish have worms so I guess we didn't miss anything."

"We're finding that all the fish above the falls have been affected. They carry intestinal worms up to six inches long. The worms get into the flesh, so it tends to put one off eating anything that comes from the lake. Too bad; they are quite pretty fish, light gray above, light yellow below, with brilliant orange fins and heavy spots all over the body."

The next day they moved camp ten miles further down the shoreline. The site gave them a grand view of the lake. Stevenson and the survey's meteorologist, J. W. Beaman, took the *Anna* out again to complete the depth soundings. Upon their return, Carrington and Elliott used the data to make a complete map of the shoreline.

Captains Barlow and Heap arrived that afternoon. Barlow immediately engaged Hayden in discussion about their travels and discoveries. After listening patiently to stories about the geysers, Hayden nodded and said that they had named the noisy one Locomotive Jet. "The steam from that geyser was exceedingly hot. Elliott measured 197 degrees."

"Did you examine the hot pots that threw out all that mud?" asked Captain Heap.

"Do you mean that alum-saturated slough where the surface was so thin?"

Yes," said Barlow. "Quite so." He was becoming accustomed to Hayden's way with words.

Hayden raised an eyebrow. "I examined it a bit too closely, I'm afraid. I was walking between the vents when the crust broke. I burned both legs rather badly to the knees."

"Good God, Hayden! It's amazing that you're still walking."

"I agree. I have used a lot of ointment. The pain is all but gone, but I mention my mishap to advise you to be quite careful."

"Duly noted," said Barlow.

"All of these marvelous natural features," said Captain Heap. "How long do you think this region has been this way?"

"I don't believe that any of these hot springs have broken out in modern times. My best guess is that the springs formed during the last one to two thousand years."

"My word!"

"Most of the forces that created what you currently see started well before the last ice age. For example, we're in a very large basin. I believe it encompasses most of the area that feeds the lake. Chances are quite good that the basin was a crater from an ancient volcano. It's huge, nearly forty miles long."

"Good Lord," blurted Heap. "Is there a chance it might erupt again?"

"No, no, no. The hot springs and geysers represent the closing stages of volcanic activity. However, the area was once the scene of considerable volcanic activity." He leaped to his feet and pointed to the surrounding mountains. "Look! Hundreds of cores of volcanic vents remain as high as ten to eleven thousand feet. The hot springs and geysers act as escape pipes, safety valves, if you like."

"Fascinating," said Barlow.

"What is most remarkable to me is that this miniature volcanism you see around you is a feeble manifestation of what occurred in the past. The internal forces that acted here must have been enormous."

10) Geyser Land

The next morning, Beaman watched Peale rush around to gather his things.

"What's up?" asked Beaman.

"We're headed out to find the geyser basin." Peale grinned. "At last!"

"Great. Good luck to you!"

The party included Hayden, Schonborn, Elliott, and several others, and José as their guide. Hayden stopped at Barlow's camp about eight, but he was not ready. "How are you headed?" Barlow asked.

"Straight into the woods," said José, who was in charge of directions. "Ees faster."

"Our man seems to think we're better off returning to the Mud Geyser, then cutting west over the hill behind the wood," said Barlow. "Guess we'll see you there."

Hayden and his men ended up picking their way around and

over piles of thick downed timber. In contrast, Captain Barlow's party rode easily through a gentle valley with side streams of pure mountain water and a panoply of wildflowers. Then Barlow reached the woods and it was his turn to stumble over dead trees while Hayden's men rode over treeless hilltops.

José paused as the band topped a low ridge. Hayden could see Mount Washburn.

"Madison that way," said José, pointing west. "Maybe a few miles. We follow Colonel Barlow's trail."

"They got ahead of us?"

"Si."

José led off and soon they caught up with Barlow's party. The two groups camped together at the eastern extreme of a little unnamed creek. Tomorrow they would find the basin.

Well past ten that night, Thomas Moran and William Henry Jackson were exhausted. They had waded through heavy cover and clambered over downed timber for nearly thirty miles. Now their world was a deep shadow with silvery gray forms lighted by a gibbous moon.

"I don't understand why we can't find a decent trail," said Moran.

"It's obvious. We missed it," said Jackson testily. He had given up riding. He walked, carefully leading his horse and trailing mule around and over the hazards. He wondered how long it might be before he heard the crack of his glass plates. Then he heard braying and whinnying. "Oh. Success at last. Give your horse his head, Thomas. We're almost home."

The moon was above the mountains by the time they made camp. Its eerie golden glow reflected across the placid waters of the lake in a belt of light as brilliant as the moon itself. Everyone was asleep. No one stirred even after Jackson and Moran noisily searched among the pots and pans for something to eat. At last, they unrolled their sleeping gear and fell asleep.

The united Hayden-Barlow party descended a hillside that proved to be the headwaters of a fast-growing creek. Clusters of small hot springs, conical mounds, chimneys, and orifices lined with brilliant crystals of sulfur told Hayden that he was looking at the remnants of dead and dying springs.

They followed the stream for six miles, struck a good trail, passed through a canyon, and came into a valley where the stream merged with a larger one. "This is the junction of the east and west forks of the Madison," pronounced Hayden. "We were camped on the east fork."

The nearly level valley that opened before them was enormous: fully two miles across and three miles long. Most startling was the total absence of trees and vegetation. Raised rocky platforms were scattered about the basin, each with its own steam vent. The whole country was like a vast lime kiln in operation. One geyser basin occupied a circular area one half mile across. No one dismounted; the view from horseback was too captivating. As they watched, blue sky was pierced by a white spout of steaming water. A light breeze caught the descending vapors and created a bridal train of mist that shimmered like a million diamond fragments.

"The geyser basin," said Hayden in a hushed voice.

Mesmerized by the sights and sounds, the party rode slowly through patches of shadow and sunlight. On the periphery of the basin, where the woods started, pink and yellow monkey flowers nodded to passing rivulets of water. Boulders of limestone were bordered with purple lupine, white asters, and mountain bluebell, and grassy slopes sported yellow patches of arrowleaf balsamroot and radiant daisies.

The travelers emerged into the sunlight, where the hooves of their horses echoed on rocky ground. In a world that hissed with the sprays of water, the men examined the sculptures created by the deposition of geyserite. Occasionally their preoccupation was shattered by the eruption of a nearby geyser. None appeared to have much in common with one another, save for the common thermal source. Even those that appeared linked had different cycles of activity.

Mindful of the survey tasks that had brought them here, they measured pools with diameters of several inches up to more than fifty feet. Warm water lay placidly in finger-deep pools and in thirty-foot iridescent ponds. Carbonate, travertine, and siliceous sinter deposits abounded in unimaginable forms. The overall impression was one of infinite variation. The mix of smell, color, height, drainage, and periodicity created a huge range of experience for the human senses.

The variety and beauty of the basin were exhausting. By the end of the first day, Hayden knew he had broached the inner secrets of a once-in-a-lifetime land. The lengthening shadows promised even more discoveries on the morrow. In this strange world, the explorer might encounter something totally new and unforeseen behind the next hill of broken rock. Today he had discovered a basin as large as a small lake, yet when he peered into it, he could see the bottom clearly. The refracted forms created a fairy-like palace adorned with brilliant colors and decorations, more delicate than anything made by human hands.

Hayden's men moved their camp closer to the geyser field and spent the next three days exploring, collecting, describing, and documenting. Each morning, steam from hot springs and geysers ascended to more than one hundred feet, and each evening the men felt the ground beneath them shake.

"I was telling Professor Hayden," said Peale to Barlow, "that I found an interesting group of thirty to forty geysers with sulfur deposits and an impulse spring that rose and fell every second at one hundred ninety-two degrees. One threw a stream of water twelve inches wide and two inches deep at one hundred eighty-two degrees."

"Were those representative temperatures?" asked Barlow

"Yes, sir; many ranged between one hundred eighty-nine and one hundred ninety-nine degrees."

"Any places we should visit that we have not yet seen?" asked Barlow.

"Elliott and I found the Fountain Geyser that Lieutenant Doane described in his report; it's a natural fountain that shoots water thirty to sixty feet high. Rather magnificent, if you haven't seen it. It overflows itself along a ten-foot rim."

Barlow found Anton Schonborn transferring instrument readings into notes. "Ah, Mr. Schonborn. One of my men suggested that your efforts and theirs might go faster without the duplication we apparently have. Perhaps you could divide the remaining work into sections."

Schonborn shook his head and kept writing. "I cannot do that," he said.

"Oh. Why not?" asked Barlow. "It makes sense, doesn't it?"

"Meaning I do not?" asked Schonborn sharply.

"No, I simply meant that . . ."

"I work for Dr. Hayden and his survey. I don't work for you. I do as Dr. Hayden says."

"It was simply a suggestion."

"As simple as your laughter when I fell down?"

Barlow stared into the angry eyes of the German, but said nothing more.

During their stay at the geyser basin, nighttime temperatures were growing colder. The first morning, one of the men had left a cup of water under a tree. The next morning it had ice in it. Another noticed that particles of ice had formed on the underside of their blankets. On the third morning, the thermometer showed twenty-eight degrees. The fourth morning it rained, and a dense fog lay across the valley, bold signs that summer was coming to a close. Winter in the Yellowstone might be only a mountain ridge away.

They doubled their efforts to finish surveying the basin. "Look, Peale," said Hayden, pointing to a series of deposited rims. "The water deposits nothing except by the process of evaporation which takes place rapidly at the edges." Among his notes he wrote about the clear water that bubbled in an eight-foot-diameter pool, six feet deep. He also described a ten- by fifteen-foot pool whose one-hundred-twenty-eight degree water rippled with transparent hues of blue. They assigned names to the geysers to match their forms and actions: Prismatic Springs, Overflow, Steady Geyser, Architectural Fountain, White Dome.

The party found a second geyser basin towards the headwaters of the west fork of the Madison. It was clear that they were in the midst of the greatest geysers in the world. After setting up camp, a tremendous rumble shook the earth. Soon thereafter, a column of steam burst from a crater near the east side of the river. After the steam, a huge column of water six feet in diameter rose by a series of forceful impulses to a height of two hundred feet. The men stared at this new and awesome event. Hayden shouted to make himself heard over the fountain: "This must be Bridger's Geyser." They renamed it The Grand.

"I would support what is called the Bunsen theory of the geyser," said Hayden that evening. "I believe it to be the most simple and the most correct."

"Could you explain a bit more, Professor," asked Captain Heap.

"Of course. The building blocks of the geyser are silica and carbonates. They are held in solution and eventually deposited to form the geyser's shell. Inside the tube, for lack of a better name, the temperature remains below the boiling point. The higher we go in the tube, the lower the temperature at which boiling can take place."

Drawing a geyser cross section in the earth with a stick, Hayden continued. "Water rises in the tube before an eruption, right? The column is pushed up by steam that rises through ducts at the bottom. Water is lifted to that part of the tube where the boiling point is actually lower than the temperature of the water. Therefore, there exists an excess of heat inside the water, which is used to generate steam. The higher the water is pushed, the more steam is generated. Suddenly the water is thrown into the air and we have a geyser." He scratched several parallel lines to indicate geyser action.

"Is the water actually boiling as we know it?" asked Captain Heap.

"It depends on the pressure, but the water has to be very near the boiling point before action can occur. You may have noticed several occasions where eruption failed to occur. The water was clear and there were no deposits nearby."

The following day, Captain Barlow took descriptive notes on

several of the one hundred springs in the area. Peale told him that
the water temperature ran from a low of one hundred forty to a high
of one hundred ninety-seven degrees. The most formidable of the
springs was more than two hundred feet in diameter. The pool walls
were twenty to thirty feet high. An immense flow of water drained
from the springs into the river. The men named these creations the
Bathtub, Punch Bowl, Giantess, Castle, Saw Mill, and Grand.

When Barlow found Hayden alone, he mentioned Schonborn's
attitude. Hayden looked thoughtful, then thanked the Captain. He
didn't plan to speak to Schonborn, but decide to keep an eye on
Him. He knew Schonborn had a violent temper, but the German
had promised that he would do his work and stay out of trouble.

Hayden heard someone shouting. He turned to see a huge
mass of steam issuing from a crater at the base of a hill a hundred
yards away. The steam was accompanied by a volume of water that
rose higher than any geyser he had yet seen.

Barlow was walking in the general direction of the geyser when
it erupted. He hurried over, but the fountain subsided before he
could get close. He was walking to the edge of the basin to inspect
the orifice, when the geyser again roared like a tornado. Barlow
ran backwards, throwing an arm upwards to ward off the heat. Water from the geyser gushed forth in a strong, steady stream, until it
was the height of the nearby Fairy Falls, a full two hundred fifty
feet high.

Their last night in the geyser basin, an ensemble of geysers
began to spout. The men could not see them, but they could hear
and feel them. The earth rumbled and vibrated. Last but certainly
not least, about ten in the evening, the Grotto began to erupt. Barlow
saw it in the moonlight. He decided not to record his impressions:
the scene was too ethereal to be brought down to earth with words.

Thomas Moran rubbed his sides in hunger. He'd only had
four biscuits per day for the last four days. *The hunters*, he wrote in
his journal, *have had a hard time of it and no supplies have come in
from the ranch.* A few hours later, Moran saw a small contingent of
soldiers on horseback coming into camp. Hayden was still away in

geyserland and Stevenson was nowhere in sight. No one moved to meet the soldiers.

"Who's that?" Moran asked Jackson.

"Let's go find out."

Then Stevenson appeared. "That's Lieutenant Doane," he said. After introductions, Doane said he had come to get the escort.

"They're with Hayden and Barlow," Stevenson said.

"All but six will have to return to Fort Ellis," said Doane. "The Northern Pacific Railroad is running a series of surveys to mark their new line, and the Sioux are having fits. However," he said with a light smile, "I thought I would stay for a few days with the remaining six."

"Professor Hayden will be delighted. He thought he'd missed any chance to talk to you."

"You want to come with us, Mr. Moran?" asked Lieutenant Grugan.

"I was going to suggest that," said Moran. "My sketchbooks are full. It's time to begin painting. I hate to miss the geysers. Are they close enough for a brief visit on the way out?"

"Since I have to wait for Dr. Hayden to return with my men, I'll take you and any of the others who haven't yet been. We call it the Firehole Basin."

"Well," said Jackson, "that includes me. I've been waiting to see geysers since we got here. I'll be packed in fifteen minutes."

"Good," said Doane, "but we won't be leaving for several hours."

The Hayden-Barlow expedition returned to a nearly empty camp. "Where are Messrs. Moran and Jackson?" Hayden asked Beaman.

"Gone with Lieutenant Doane to see the geysers, sir."

"Ah," said Hayden. "Lieutenant Doane. Good. And the whereabouts of Mr. Stevenson?"

"Gone to Bottler's."

Hayden took the occasion to catch up on his correspondence. He wrote a brief report to the secretary of the interior to tell of the documentation of the geyser basin, of Jackson's photographs, and of his hope to complete a topographic map. He planned to remain in the Yellowstone until the first of September.

The next morning, Hayden emerged from his tent with a bucket that had a half-inch of ice on it. He noted the date, August 14, the fact that the temperature had hit a low of fourteen degrees, and reflected on the worn condition of the animals. When Stevenson returned from Bottler's, Hayden greeted him with his decision: "We must complete everything and return by the end of the month!"

"I'm surprised you plan to stay that long," said Stevenson, dismounting. "Aren't you pushing it?"

As if to answer his question, they had rain, hail, and snow showers the next few days. They ate poor deer and a boiled goose that tasted like rubber. Two of the boys hung the carcass on a tree and used it for target practice. They had bets on whether the bullets would bounce.

Hayden ignored the weather and made extensive exploratory trips with Schonborn and Doane to the Continental Divide. After a four-day search for the source of the Snake River and Bridger's lake, Hayden concluded that the lake did not exist. Doane took exception: he said that he'd been there.

By the last week of August, the expedition had circumnavigated the Yellowstone Lake. Hayden had climbed Mount Stevenson and Mount Doane, and pronounced both to be remnants of an immense crater. Three days ahead of schedule, the expedition was back at Bottler's.

Hayden considered the trip highly successful. *After thirty-eight days of exploration and documentation, no portion of the West has been more carefully surveyed than the Yellowstone basin. We surveyed the shoreline of the lake and took its depth. The hot springs districts have been charted in detail and more than six hundred temperature readings have been taken. We will ship a complete collection of natural history and botany. I anticipate arriving in Washington, D.C., in October to complete my report. Anticipate hundreds of pictures, sketches, sections, and a careful topographic map.*

Before they left Bottler's, Peale went in for a last drink of milk.

Several weeks later, the survey party approached the Union Pacific line. Hayden rode over to Jackson. "William, I would like you to postpone your return home if you will."

"Oh. I was counting on seeing Mollie pretty soon. What's up?"

"Did you hear me speak of the Pawnee villages in Nebraska on the Loup Fork one hundred miles west of Omaha?"

"Not recently."

"Well, the government is planning to move them pretty soon. I'd like you to make a side trip and document the way they live. They still use aborigine huts. Photographs of their way of life now would be invaluable."

"Whatever you say, sir. I should be able to do that in a week."

Hayden and Peale were off geologizing along the railroad cuts when the train they planned to catch left Ogden. They ended up walking along the tracks a ways. Peale tried to keep up, but few could match Professor Hayden on foot. Peale was content when he found the professor waiting for him at the next siding. They boarded the next train.

It had been a full Yellowstone summer.

BOOK III: GREAT EXPECTATIONS

PART 1: A COALITION OF INTERESTS

1) Intimations of Disaster

Ferdinand Hayden had decided long ago that if he couldn't read, write, or make plans while he was on a train, he would waste a good chunk of his life. So far, the return trip to Washington, D.C., had proven productive. He had a seat on the north side of the train where the sun didn't blind him half the day, and no one had interrupted him. Having reviewed what he had to do in the coming months, he was also reasonably assured that he could accomplish everything on time.

When Hayden focused on his work, he paid little attention to the world around him. Now, an hour outside of St. Louis, he was becoming increasingly aware of the voices of other people on the train. A thin, distant wail came to him slowly, as if he were awakening from a deep sleep. He heard a murmur, then an occasional clear word. Some of the passengers gasped; others spoke in hushed, sibilant voices, as if they were speaking of the death of a neighbor.

Hayden raised his head from his work. He saw only that the train was approaching the station. Two women sitting ahead of him burst into tears. What in the name of heaven was going on? The more he listened, the more he heard agitated voices, saw strained facial expressions. What did they know that he didn't?

Hayden glanced out the window as the train came to a halt. A paperboy was holding up the latest edition, shouting its headlines. Across the October tenth paper bold type screamed: *Fire and Death in Chicago: The Most Disastrous Conflagration That Ever Occurred in America. Over One-Third of the City in Ruins.*

Chicago! He was headed there. Hayden jammed his papers together, stepped into the aisle, and was almost pushed out of the train by the crowd. He stepped down and to one side and bought a paper. The first article said the fire had started around midnight Sunday, on the west side of town, in a barn behind Patrick O'Leary's home on DeKoven. That was less than two days ago, thought Hayden, yet a full third of the city had been consumed in the flames?

Hayden moved away from the crowd to read further. In less than an hour after the blaze started, a high wind and flaming brands had spread its flames across the river. Driven by heat-generated winds, burning planks sailed through the air for hundreds of yards. The debris set fire to buildings in advance of the main fire. Fire devils, another name for superheated air, accounted for the quick spread.

Hayden signaled to a conductor. "Are we still headed for Chicago?" he asked.

"Yes sir. As far as I know. The railroad yard hasn't been touched. I'll announce any change."

Hayden was going to ask another question, but the man said, "I'm sorry, sir, I just don't know anything more."

When Hayden reboarded the train, the only topic of conversation around him was the fire. Hayden didn't see anyone he knew, so he returned to the paper, which said that Sunday night, residents of the city who were preparing coffee for friends discovered their houses on fire. The more alert citizens ran through the streets, shouting to awaken a still-sleeping neighborhood.

In minutes, the streets were full of people in nightgowns and slippers. Nightshirted men dragged children to safety. They raced down streets filled with carts, carriages, and wheelbarrows loaded with precious belongings. Children cowered in fear. Behind those who fled, the night sky glowed a bright orange. The paper's vivid portrait compared the fire wind to a hurricane, but one that covered the safety-seekers with ash, soot, and blinding, hot dust.

Hayden put down the paper. A feeling of despair swept over him. Who did he know in Chicago? A number of people, associates, friends. What had happened to them? It was impossible to know. What could he do? Nothing.

The paper said that by Monday morning, thousands of Chicagoans were huddled by the shore of Lake Michigan. Many were so afraid they stood up to their necks in the water. The fire was so hot, it melted the iron in stone buildings. Mortar, stone, and marble disintegrated, and buildings fell in on themselves.

The fire finally consumed itself Monday evening. The paper reported that this morning, the city resembled a war zone. Eighteen thousand buildings had been consumed; two thousand acres of the city had vanished. It was as though a huge bomb had exploded leveling everything except the most resistant facades. Two hundred people had lost their lives; more than one hundred thousand were homeless. Initial estimates of losses exceeded two hundred million dollars.

Nothing in the paper prepared Hayden for what he saw as the train entered the Chicago station. Chaos! People were still fleeing the city. The train station looked like a refugee camp. Hayden pulled his window down. The air tasted like sour, burned wood. The people he saw, young and old alike, wore robes or overcoats with nothing under them. Some were shoeless. Others had sooty faces. They sat alone or back-to-back, in groups, their faces expressing bewilderment. They were part of the tens of thousands who had lost everything, homes, businesses, and family.

Hayden was unprepared to deal with the emotions evoked by this catastrophe. He was not involved, yet the outcries of the masses importuned him. He felt trapped, so he closed the window and retreated to his work, thinking that he had to make some progress on his report. He hoped to have at least a partial draft before he arrived in Philadelphia. Once back in Washington, his schedule would be hectic. He focused on his last sentence and hoped that his train would soon leave.

If Hayden's agenda in Washington had consisted only of completing his survey report, he might have accepted that the trip home was a total write-off. Unfortunately, upon his arrival, he faced severe deadlines for a number of items of equal importance. Not all were planned. A week ago, at Fort Hall, Hayden had received a letter from *Scribner's* editor Richard Gilder.

Gilder began by saying that Moran had returned and had spoken warmly of Hayden's courtesy. Then he said he originally expected Mr. Langford to accompany Dr. Hayden's expedition. Hayden remembered that Langford had asked about joining. He would have been most welcome, but he had heard nothing further. *Moran thinks that the hot springs on the Gardiner's were the most extraordinary phenomena seen*, wrote Gilder. *He will put them on the block and engrave a general view of the spring, an extinct geyser, and the like. Now we have the sketches, yet we lack literary accomplishments. We need an article in about a month, perhaps later. Can you do it for us? It need be only four or five magazine pages long. If you could not send us such an article, could you do it for us when you get back to Washington?*

The opportunity to author a national piece was too tempting. Hayden had agreed, although he had no idea where he was going to find the time. He had a major report to orchestrate, not to mention that little matter of getting married on November ninth.

Hayden dropped his briefcase on the floor. His desk was overflowing with mail. Where was all the secretarial assistance he had been promised? He wanted to sweep the whole pile to the floor. This kind of situation always made him nervous and irritable. He pushed the publications and letters to one side. It wasn't the mail itself, it was the time and effort he would have to use to get through it. He didn't have that kind of time. Admittedly, he had placed himself in a tight situation. When he thought of his schedule and the chain of events he needed to initiate before the month was gone, and still present himself in one piece to his patient bride . . .

Hayden sighed in an effort to find his composure. He dropped into his chair and began to sort through the mail. His final administrative and budgetary reports needed submitting. He should begin to draft his section of this year's field report. At the same time, he would have to review everyone else's reports and decide what had to be done for illustrations before Jackson returned from Omaha. Somewhere along the way, he had to write the article for *Scribner's*.

Hayden stopped sorting. Heavens! Where were he and Emma going to live after they were married? He couldn't think. He was sure they had taken care of that before he left last spring. Hadn't they? Finally, without an answer but too pressed to think of it further, he shrugged. If not, he thought, it will be an interesting situation.

While reviewing some of Peale's draft documentation on the hot springs, his elbow knocked a stack of unopened mail to the floor. A small pile of newspaper clippings spilled to one side. Hayden was curious to see what the world had been told of his adventures. He would have been surprised had nothing been reported; after all, his report would clear up all of the mystery about the Yellowstone, and during the trip, Elliott, Adams, and Peale had written a number of articles for their newspapers. Hayden had even supplied Baird with material for *Harper's Weekly*.

A September note from the *Helena Daily Herald* said that Hayden's report would *excite a curiosity and interest which the wonders of Vesuvius, Niagara, and the geysers of Iceland have never caused to be felt*. While Hayden had been at Bottler's, writing the secretary of the interior, the *New York Times* had summed up the nation's attitude towards the Yellowstone:

There is something romantic in the thought that vast tracts of the national domain remain unexplored. As little is known of these regions as the topography of the Nile or the interior of Australia. They are enveloped in mystery. Their attractions to the adventurous are constantly enhanced by remarkable discoveries. Sometimes the precious metals are found in such marvelous abundance as to cause an immediate rush for the tempting deposit. Sometimes, as in the case of the Yellowstone Valley, the phenomena are so unusual, so startlingly different from anything known elsewhere that the interest and the curiosity excited are universal.

A party that left for the Yellowstone Valley early in May has lately been heard from. They are in charge of Professor F. V. Hayden, United States Geologist, who planned the exploration of the wonderful Yellowstone Lake region. Some of the marvels of that district have already been discovered and published in these columns, and there is a strong desire on the part of the public to learn of the unique and the extraordinary. It is hoped that Dr. Hayden's report, which will be printed as soon as possible, will do much to satisfy the general curiosity.

Hitherto, most reports we have had on the region have been popular reports rather than scientific observations. We have the right to anticipate that those now to be furnished will be trustworthy, exact, and comprehensive, and will thus supply much needed information on one of the most wonderful tracts on the American continent.

And so they shall, thought Hayden. As he put the pile of mail back together, he noticed an unopened telegram stamped with yesterday's date. He wondered what it could be. It was too late for more administrative handslapping from government officials, and few of his associates knew he had returned.

He tore open the telegram. The first word he saw was *suicide.* His stomach lurched. It was Anton Schonborn, his old friend and topographer. Schonborn's housekeeper had found him in his room at Omaha House, where he had lived for the past three years. He had departed this life with a violent gesture: he'd cut his throat.

Anton. My God, why? But even as he asked himself, he had to admit that the man was a bit strange. When they first met, Schonborn was Captain Raynolds's artist and topographer. They got along well. They were the only two Germans in the party, and Hayden thought that might have made a difference. On that trip, Hayden learned that Schonborn had a university degree and spoke five languages.

When Schonborn came to Washington, D.C., Hayden saw to it that he was initiated into the Megatherium Club. And Hayden had hired him for the Yellowstone expedition because the Army had found him thorough and accurate. Hayden also thought the man needed the opportunity.

Then Hayden wondered if Schonborn had been intoxicated when he took his life. He knew the man drank to excess. He'd never seen Anton drink when he was working or on duty, only when he was alone. How could anyone cut . . . ? He recalled Schonborn's open anger at Captain Raynolds. He showed that same anger with Captain Barlow. Hayden decided that Schonborn must have hated himself deeply, or harbored some unreachable devil.

While Hayden mourned the passing of his friend, his practical half nagged him about Schonborn's role as the survey's chief topographer. Now Schonborn's work remained unfinished. His notebooks were full of symbols, diagrams, and figures that represented months of work. They were seeds for maps critical to Hayden's Yellowstone report. Now what am I supposed to do? Hayden asked himself. He would have to find someone who could translate Schonborn's notes into a finished map. At the moment, he had no idea. Damn!

Hayden did not handle death well. Life was hard enough to understand; death was beyond him. He looked at his desk, the stack of unopened mail and the telegram in his hand, and decided in a moment of depression that he would never have control over his life.

Jay Cooke finished reading the *New York Times* article about Ferdinand Hayden's survey of the Yellowstone and decided that Dr. Hayden knew who he was and what he could do. He certainly appeared to have his world well under control.

The contrast between Hayden's summer and his own was painful to consider. Hayden had launched his summer plans with a government appropriation and a team of dedicated men. By the end of summer he had fulfilled his original purpose. Cooke's summer had started with bad news, then turned tragic. He doubted whether the trend could be reversed.

The first blow had been the summary report on the sell rate of Northern Pacific Railroad bonds. Compared against his plan, it was pitiful: by July first, combined sales in America and Europe totaled less than twenty million dollars. Subscribers in Europe had purchased less than a quarter of the amount. Monthly sales were averaging a half million, and the potential for additional sales in Europe was drying up as rapidly as the fall leaves were changing color.

Moorhead might have been a whiner, thought Cooke, but he knew now that he might have done better had he listened to Moorhead and Fahnestock's judicious advice, especially after the firm's failure to make an alliance with the Rothschilds. It was all

very clear now, his attempt to manipulate Europe had been unwise. Had he been less stubborn, he might have understood that
Europe was out of his league. He admitted now that he never had
understood the European mentality. He had also lacked the connections with the bankers and politicians that he had in America.
Perhaps contributing to the failure, he had not selected the best
people to woo European bankers.

Then the Franco-Prussian War had struck. When it had ended
last spring, every European banker broke his promise and escaped
his obligation to sell Northern Pacific bonds. Now Cooke's bonds
were no longer viewed as privileged opportunities, but as fair game
for those who wanted tremendous commissions. His overseas man-
agers had referred to the bankers as scoundrels, crooks, and black-
mailers. In the end, his vision of fifty million dollars in European
bond sales had vaporized.

Cooke lighted a cigar and scanned the latest Wall Street report. Since the bonds were dead in Europe, he had to sell the remainder in the States. He remembered Fahnestock's warning that
to compete with other offerings they would have to be sold in the
low eighties, a huge discount. He put the paper down. Nothing
encouraging there. Even though heat records had been set on the
East Coast that summer, the press spoke of an early winter. An
early winter, thought Cooke. Last year, it would have been best had
it remained winter the entire year in Minnesota. Then the perma-
frost would not have thawed and the tracks of the Northern Pacific
Railroad would not have disappeared into the marsh.

Gregory Smith had downplayed the disaster, but it was clear
that the contractor had laid track on frozen ground. Newspapers
had asked pointed questions about competence and the possibility
of corruption. Cooke credited the Vermont-Minnesota clique with
the damage. He speculated that he might have to dump the whole
lot. If he was going to survive, their kind had to be shut out from
the project.

Had sinking tracks been the worst of his problems, his summer might have been a break-even proposition. Cooke got up from
his desk and walked to the wall on which a photograph of Gibraltar,
his house on Lake Erie, was displayed. He reached out to touch

the home where the worst of all possible events had occurred: Lizzie had died.

How could God have let this happen? Lizzie had been tired. She needed rest. Her lassitude increased and soon she had a difficult time sitting up. Cooke's doctors had no idea what was wrong. Cooke thought that taking her to Gibraltar might make a difference. Once there, he moved her to the porch. Before the first week was out, in the afternoon sun on the porch, she died without a sound.

They buried Lizzie on a warm, cloudy morning. Cooke stared at her coffin but heard few of the words that were spoken. His senses felt clogged, his nerve endings numb. Only when the members of his family joined hands in prayer around Lizzie's coffin did he sense the cold fingers of reality. The carriages departed. Jay Cooke remained. Fahnestock wanted to stay, but Cooke shook his head. He wanted to be alone with his wife. He and Lizzie had been best friends and lovers as well as husband and wife for twenty-eight years. As Fahnestock walked away, Jay Cooke knelt beside the grave of his most beloved treasure, clenched a handful of soil, and wept.

Cooke heard later that Fahnestock had hardly recognized him. Fahnestock spoke of him as a man in depression. Cooke's eyes had become black holes, his face sagged, and he walked with obvious effort. The emotional vulnerability he showed shocked those who knew him well. Had they not seen him with their own eyes, they would not have believed it.

Now, Cooke wondered: was he going to press on? Where would he find the energy and enthusiasm he needed to fight Anthony Drexel? The second largest banker in Philadelphia had joined forces with J. P. Morgan against him. Drexel and Morgan were members of a new breed. The pair owned the *Public Ledger*. J. P. Morgan's influence extended to London. They were adept at using power and obviously had decided to undermine Cooke's credibility at home and abroad. In normal times, Cooke would have contacted men who owed him favors, sent telegrams to influential people, and devised a scheme to nullify Anthony Drexel and Co.'s organized animosity. He could not envision such moves now; something about Lizzie's death had dulled his combativeness.

362 David M. Delo

Cooke had stumbled through August and September, absorbed in the bitterness of his loss. With whom would he now share his life? To whom would he bring his problems, his successes? His family was dispersed: the last of his children had married earlier in the year. Lizzie was to have been with him for the years to come. Now she was gone. Did she know the vital part of him she had taken with her? She had been his wellspring of enthusiasm, she had given him confidence to tackle the future.

If October had been full of undesirable surprises for Ferdinand Hayden, it was far more unsettling for Cooke and the railroad. Cooke had anticipated that the proceeds from land sales would surpass the income from bonds to sustain the railroad through its construction period. According to projections, when the line reached the Mississippi River, the railroad would show earnings due to passenger trips to Montana. But Gregory Smith, president of the Northern Pacific Railroad Company, still waited for U.S. Commissioners to inspect the Minnesota roadbed and to release the first portion of the land grant for sale. The land office in New York was not effective. Construction was behind schedule. And the Chicago fire had further depressed an already poor bond market.

Cooke ordered Smith to cut expenditures. Smith replied that Cooke did not understand the labor and materials involved. He had to haul one hundred thousand tons over the road, not to mention supplies to contractors to keep work going. He had to take care of all the outside freighting and passenger traffic. He needed merchandise to satisfy settlers who were already on the line, to say nothing of business from the Hudson's Bay Company, which they anticipated next spring. All of this was supposed to take place on a single track with limited facilities.

With his response, Smith submitted a contract for three thousand tons of iron rail for Duluth and four hundred tons for the Pacific. *It is not an easy matter to apply the brakes to a machine like ours*, wrote Smith. *Our track is one hundred ninety-six miles from Duluth and will soon be to the Red River. We are gaining strongly in public confidence by the very energy and boldness with which we are pushing the work and cannot afford to lose our prestige now. I will be as prudent as possible but certain things must be done or we must stop entirely at great sacrifice and loss in both money and reputation.*

Cooke meant to respond quickly and sharply to Smith's irresponsible actions, but since Lizzie's death, he had had a hard time concentrating. Financial figures lost their meaning. He wondered whether the world was rumbling along at a pace that was leaving him behind. His need for a time-out brought him a moment of bright anguish as he recalled the time he and Lizzie had taken a barge down the Ohio. The edges of their world had been the riverbanks. The leisurely pace of their insular world was temporary, but for awhile they luxuriated in doing nothing except watch others. It was narcissistic and intoxicating. Now, Cooke felt like he was back on that barge, this time, alone, and without oar, rudder, or power to do more than watch.

Cooke wrote an apologetic note to Smith. The bond market remained slow, and the Chicago panic had hurt the financial streets. It was unwise to incur additional liabilities. They were running out of money. He had asked the directors to pledge their thirteenths of the initial five-million-dollar bond. *I have more courage than is good for me but my common sense tells me that we are to have a bad, bad time. Money is tight in general because the people don't trust the market. It's time to hold back a little. I have advised you as frankly as I can so if you go ahead it will not be my fault if you have trouble. The money market simply took a turn and there is nothing to do but to realize it and wait.*

He gave Smith as little hard data as possible. The draw on Jay Cooke and Co. by the Northern Pacific Railroad Company had left the Philadelphia house in the red. In July, it owed the New York house more than a half million dollars. Now the debt had grown to one million. Fahnestock reminded Cooke that the New York house was carrying the London office and the Washington office. He urged his partner not to waste more money sending additional emissaries to Europe.

Everything goes out, nothing comes in, telegraphed Fahnestock. *If this keeps up many will break. That one and one half million dollars locked up in Lake Superior, Preston, South Mountain, Pennsylvania Canal and other bonds would be very valuable to us.* He was giving Cooke direct advice: put more cash into the business, the money tied up in other avenues was becoming a liability. Take a loss if necessary. Sell unneeded holdings. Do it now!

Toward the end of the month, Cooke received a long, discouraging letter from the manager of the Lake Superior and Mississippi Railroad, Frank Clark. The railroad was running out of money, he wrote. *Mr. Cooke, let's face facts: the situation rests with you. Unless you take hold and carry us, the Superior and Mississippi road must fail and the failure means direful things. The amount of money needed to save the road and carry it to a self-sustaining point is, in comparison with the amount you have invested in it, small, but I nonetheless urge you to negotiate a sale. I have hopes of a sale or second mortgage bonds abroad, but a sale is the best thing.*

Clark wanted to point out the irony that everything was working as planned. *Our land will produce one hundred fifty thousand dollars net for the following year, we are getting a good number of settlers on our lands, and we have sold six thousand acres in the last three months at an average price of four dollars and fifty cents per acre. The demand for lumber is increasing because the prairie is being developed, so the value of our pine lands has increased greatly and the land grant will much more than pay off the bonds on our road.*

Cooke paused in his reading. Yes, that was the irony: everything he'd set in motion was justifying his faith, but far too late.

We're feeling the effects of the blunders of the road, of the original faulty financial programming. Considerable money is required to carry us to a self-sustaining point. Make up your mind to put up the necessary money and all your investments are safe. I simply needed to put the situation squarely before you as it is. I urge you to do nothing except the sale. Do as you think proper.

Last but not least, Milnor Roberts sent Cooke a report that outlined his frustrations for the summer of 1871. As soon as the tracks crossed into the Dakota Territory, an Indian war party had hit his track layers with a barrage of arrows. Every man had quit. They said that they were getting paid to lay track, not to fight Indians. Roberts asked them if military protection would convince them to remain on the job.

When they said yes, he telegraphed Generals Philip Sheridan and Winfield Hancock to explain his need for troops. Bluntly, he said that track could not be laid without a survey, and a detailed survey had yet to be completed between the Missouri River and Bozeman. In front of them was a three-hundred-fifty-mile stretch through Sioux country. The Indians were constantly challenging the surveyors and track layers. His conclusion? No troops, no railroad.

The first soldiers assigned to accompany Roberts's surveyors came from Fort Rice under General Thomas L. Rosser. The good news, Roberts told Cooke, was that everything went according to plan: a good portion of the survey work was completed without additional harassment. By the middle of October everyone had returned from the field.

Two additional escort parties were pulled from Fort Ellis to protect surveying teams. The party, under Major Baker and Crow Indian Agent F. D. Pease, was composed of men who had escorted Professor Hayden to the Yellowstone. They accompanied Roberts down the Yellowstone River Valley.

A second Fort Ellis party was assigned to protect Colonel Muhlenburg's men, who were surveying a section of the Yellowstone River Valley further east. Roberts believed that Muhlenburg had underestimated his time requirements. His men were in the middle of the plains in mid-October. One day, within a few hours, the balmy Indian summer temperature dropped below zero. Out of a sunny sky, a blizzard blanketed the land.

Muhlenburg was caught totally unprepared, wrote Roberts. A number of men became lost in the whiteout. *By the time every soldier was located and the men found their way back to Fort Ellis, twenty-three had severe cases of frostbite. One man had to have both feet amputated.* All the offices on the East Coast had heard was that work had come to a halt due to bad weather.

In the New York offices of the Northern Pacific Railroad Company, Nettleton's publicity machine continued to show the public a rosy picture. The *Washington Evening Star* carried his reports unedited, so the public read only the company's version of events. Some parts were true: *The Northern Pacific Railroad is fast ap-*

proaching the Red River Valley and a section between the Columbia River and Puget Sound is under way; the plan is to complete nine hundred miles of road in Minnesota and carry the trunk line nearly a third across America by the end of 1872; Hudson's Bay Company has leased warehouse space in Duluth, and settlers are occupying land at a steady rate. Some were half true: *It is anticipated that business income alone will meet the interest on the cost and finished portions of the railroad; the next two million acres in Minnesota will be placed on the market by the first of the year and proceeds of the sale will be used to purchase steel and cancel the company's Seven-Thirty bonds.* Some were blatantly false: *Northern Pacific Railroad bonds continue to sell rapidly and gain favor with the American public.*

2) Invitation to a Park

Congressman and former judge William D. Kelly walked briskly along the sidewalk. He climbed a short flight of steps without showing his age, and nodded to the doorman as he entered the stone and metal edifice that housed the offices of the Northern Pacific Railroad Company. Kelly had not visited New York for more than a month. Although he enjoyed Philadelphia, he found the hustle in New York more to his liking. It was a businessman's city.

Each time politics or personal business required him to go to New York City, he tried to find time to see Ab Nettleton. The two had hit a common note the first time they talked. *When was that?* Kelly asked himself as the lift took him to the fourth floor. *At Ogontz, of course.* That Jay Cooke had hired Nettleton did not surprise him; everything associated with Cooke and his little castle was either elegant or profound. Kelly had found Nettleton to be intelligent, well read, and in his new position as the director of advertising for bond sales, always on top of the latest developments in the market.

Kelly pulled open the metal grill, exited the elevator, and walked down the corridor. October, he knew, had been a month of momentous happenings for the railroad. Change was exciting. Uncertainties led to analysis, speculation, and generally lively conversation. For example, what was the long-run impact of the Chicago fire on the Northern Pacific Railroad Company? The attention given to the conflagration had subsided in the third week of the month, only after newspapers recounted close to five hundred million dollars in damage and two hundred lives lost. To offset these losses, the spirited American people had donated millions of private dollars: New York City alone gave three million. Residents of the City of Brotherly Love gave three hundred fifty thousand.

Closer to home, Boss Tweed had dominated the front pages. His arrest the evening before, October twenty-seventh, was reported in this morning's papers. Bail had been set at two million dollars. The event encouraged the *New York Tribune* to award Mr. Tweed of Tammany Hall the title of the most corrupt official to ever hold public office. Kelly and Nettleton would have a lot to discuss.

Kelly tipped his hat to a middle-aged couple exiting the Northern Pacific offices and caught the door before it closed. He asked the secretary to advise Mr. Nettleton that Mr. William D. Kelly was in the vestibule. A calendar on the wall advertised the benefits of owning Northern Pacific bonds.

"Bill! Good to see you! Come in. What are you doing for lunch?" Nettleton led the way to his well furnished office with its view of downtown Manhattan.

"Letting you bring me up to date," replied Kelly with a light chuckle.

"Done," said Nettleton. "But I need a favor first. Sit and read the morning paper if you haven't done so, for fifteen minutes. I need to review some campaign literature and get it off to the press before noon."

"Take your time," said Kelly. Nettleton always had several copies of the *New York Times* in the office. He routinely cut copy for his files and sent copies to Cooke in Philadelphia when he deemed it advisable. Kelly had not read today's *Times*. On page six he discovered the most recent article about Dr. Ferdinand Hayden's expedition to the Yellowstone, by one Henry Elliott, Hayden's expedition artist.

The *Times* editor prefaced the article by saying that he had received the article with a cover letter from Professor Henry of the Smithsonian Institution. The article gave a vivid account of the

Yellowstone region, but the editors felt it their duty to be cautious. *Even now, and with every respect to the new witness, part of whose evidence we shall quote, the official narrative of the Hayden exploration must be deemed needful before we can altogether accept stories of wonder hardly short of fairy tales and the astounding phenomena they describe.*

Elliott's account focused on the more splendid aspects of the Yellowstone: the Grand Canyon, the upper and lower falls, Yellowstone Lake, and Elliott's favorite spectacle, the geysers of the Firehole Basin. Elliott described how it felt to stand next to the Grand Geyser while it emitted a column of boiling water six feet in diameter. The huge volume of ejecta rose with a single bound to a height of two hundred feet. It paused there for an instant before it fell back to its silicified basin *in a thousand watery streams, in a million prismatic drops.*

"This Yellowstone region must be simply incredible," said Kelly, momentarily forgetting that Nettleton had requested silence. Nettleton grunted.

"After all these years, those sketchy rumors from trappers and explorers, to finally document, in scientific detail, the marvels . . ." Kelly looked towards Nettleton, who was furiously editing. Seeing that Nettleton was not listening, Kelly ceased talking and returned to the article. But when Nettleton got up to leave the room, Kelly couldn't contain himself. "Have you read Doane's report?" asked Kelly.

"Who?" asked Nettleton?

"Lieutenant Doane. He accompanied the Washburn Expedition the summer of 1870."

"No. Be back in a minute." Nettleton disappeared.

It's too bad that Nettleton hasn't seen that report, thought Kelly. He considered how limited Nettleton's knowledge of the Yellowstone might be. He hadn't been present at Ogontz last June when Langford shared his proposed exploration. Nothing firm had come from that evening of talk, but Langford had piqued Jay Cooke's curiosity. Cooke was all the more intrigued by the possibility that the Yellowstone might represent an ace in the hole, might become the ultimate destination for every American tourist who dreamed about the West.

Kelly knew that Hayden's report was due soon. The final word would be out. How different could it be than the articles by members of his survey team, or for that matter, from Doane's report? As the politician's mind churned, Nettleton appeared and whispered: "Let's go before something else comes up." The two of them bounded down the stairs and out the door like kids playing hooky.

The Manhattan Men's Club on Thirty-Fourth and Second Avenue was serving a seafood melange. Kelly scraped oyster shells as Nettleton talked about the problems and personalities of the Northern Pacific. Kelly found himself only half-listening. His mind kept drifting back to the Yellowstone. Finally he held up one hand while he dabbed his chin with a linen napkin with the other. Without prelude, he said, "Ab, we have to do something about the Yellowstone."

Nettleton had been discussing the "arrogant" Mr. Wilkeson. Kelly's introduction of the Yellowstone struck him as a *non sequitur*. However, he had learned never to dismiss Kelly's remarks, no matter how oblique they might seem to the topic at hand. The man was too intelligent and too experienced to babble.

"All right, Bill. Let's talk about the Yellowstone. What did you have in mind? And, if I may ask, what does it have to do with anything else?"

Kelly leaned forward. "I know this is abrupt, but I've been thinking. The Yellowstone is a one-of-a-kind region. Now, this fellow, Langford, the one who made speeches about the Yellowstone region, he impressed me. You know I met him at Ogontz a year ago last spring. I also heard him speak last May. That was his last talk, come to think of it; he'd acquired some kind of throat infection. Anyway, Jay and I agreed that the natural spectacles that Langford described were exactly the kind tourists would pay handsomely to see. And the Northern Pacific is planning to run a line toward the region to take advantage of those opportunities. Right?"

"Right."

"Langford stirred up a lot of speculation. Professor Hayden is bringing back documentation of what actually exists in the Yellowstone. Once he publishes his survey report, there will be no more questions."

Nettleton said nothing. Sometimes it was best to simply listen.

"Now," said Kelly, "put yourself in the shoes of the western entrepreneur. You know now that the Yellowstone has tremendous financial potential, hmm? You would be foolish if you didn't make your move and claim all rights to the access of the Yellowstone wonders as soon as possible. Then what's going to happen?" He waved a hand to indicate that the question was rhetorical. "Think about what has happened to our other great American landmarks."

"You just lost me."

"There are only two sights in this country that compare to the Yellowstone," said Kelly. "One is Niagara Falls; the other is the Yosemite."

"That's out of my league," said Nettleton. "I know where they are and that one is private and the other is public."

"That's sufficient for this purpose. Have you been to Niagara?"

"Yes, as a matter of fact, I have, several years ago. Can't say I was deeply impressed."

"Why not?"

"Well," said Nettleton, "part of the problem was the clutter and the constant rousting. It was hard to isolate yourself from the infernal stalls and gabbing tourists. It was like a circus. Nothing like I imagined."

"Exactly!" said Kelly, his eyes gleaming. "Now what about Yosemite?"

"I have seen only photographs, although I understand Bierstadt plans several paintings there."

"Then I will tell you. Yosemite remains pristine. No stalls. No rousting. No milling crowds. The main difference between the Yosemite and Niagara Falls is that the Falls is controlled by financial interests, while the Yosemite is controlled by the state of California. I supported the bill to protect the Yosemite Valley and Mariposa Grove of redwoods back in 1864. I have also been to Niagara Falls."

"What did the bill do?"

"Well, after the committee made it clear that the area was unique in all the country, Congress agreed to take it out of the hands of private interests and make it into a park for the people."

"Ah. Now I follow you. You think that if the Yellowstone is as great as Niagara and Yosemite . . ."

Kelly lifted his wine glass and interrupted. "I don't believe there are any 'ifs' here, Ab."

"All right. We assume that the Yellowstone region is as great a natural *and* national wonder as Niagara Falls and the Yosemite Valley. You believe that if left to private interests, the region may well go the way of Niagara, that its pristine character will be better protected if it remains out of private hands."

"If I thought that the Northern Pacific had the money to purchase the region, I would suggest that course to Jay, but that isn't possible." Kelly sipped his coffee. "So, yes, we need to find some way to keep it out of greedy hands. Remember, the Yellowstone will be made accessible by a Northern Pacific spur line."

"But, as you say, private hands will most likely dictate the region's future. Who's going to stop them? I don't see any problems here, Bill. The Northern Pacific has dealt with private interests before. We can cut a deal to run a branch line to the region. We just don't have control over which parties we deal with."

In the silence that followed, Kelly sat back and smiled. "Indeed. Maybe *that's* my point. Maybe we *do* have a choice. Tell me, my friend, why should not the Yellowstone, like the Yosemite, be set aside as a public park?"

The thought set off a chain reaction in Nettleton's mind. As director of publicity for the Northern Pacific, he knew that an open park combined with their spur line would provide the most favorable base for promotional developments. The number of people who would travel to see a slice of the West like the Yellowstone might be nothing short of astounding. A scenic attraction in the midst of the Rocky Mountains? It could double their estimated railroad traffic.

"Who owns the land?" asked Nettleton.

"It's part of the public trust. Technically, the government owns it, until someone files."

"So we're in the clear."

"No. Without a specific act of Congress, it remains open to

private interests."

"Then we tell the Montana legislature to claim it and set it aside."

"The Wyoming Territory legislature is apt to take offense at that suggestion," said Kelly. "When we dealt with the Yosemite, we only had California to deal with. Here we have at least two territories. We might have to deed it to the government. Make it a government park, or, in your terms, a nationally owned public park."

Nettleton still looked skeptical. "A national park of public lands. Sounds very strange. You think we could pull it off?"

"No, but Congress could."

"Why don't we chat with Jay about this the next time we get together at Ogontz," suggested Nettleton as he signaled for the bill.

"Forgive me if I sound pushy," said Kelly, intercepting the bill. "But time may not be on our side."

"You're only pushy when it comes to grabbing the bill," said Nettleton. "Do you want me to send Cooke a telegram? He's the promoter. He'll know what to do."

Kelly didn't answer. He appeared occupied with scraping the last crumbs from his plate. Slowly he put his fork down. "Ab, this idea should not come from anyone associated with Jay Cooke and Co., including myself. I'll tell you why. An initiative like this by any associate, however remotely connected to the Northern Pacific, will be seen as a move to create hegemony over the Yellowstone. Quicker than you can say 'envy,' it will be shut down by Union Pacific interests."

"Then how?"

"We need someone whose hands are clean. Someone not aligned with railroad interests. Someone who is viewed as nonpartisan, who has a good reputation."

"How about Blaine?"

Kelly thought for a moment, then snapped his fingers. "Why not a scientist, a man who has been to the Yellowstone and who is writing the definitive report about its wonders?"

"Professor Hayden. Of course! Congress funded his survey."

"I recommend you send Hayden a telegram, Ab. Propose something specific. Ask him to recommend in his report that the

Yellowstone be set aside as a public park. Ask for a response. If he agrees, we can tell Jay, and Jay will know the strings to pull to see it through."

Nettleton shook his head.

"You're skeptical?" asked Kelly.

"No," said Nettleton. "Sometimes I think you are a walking national treasure."

The following day, Hayden opened a telegram from the offices of the Northern Pacific Railroad. He read:

Dear Dr. Hayden:

Judge Kelly has made a suggestion which strikes me as being an excellent one, viz.: Let Congress pass a bill reserving the great Geyser Basin as a public park, forever, just as it reserved those far inferior wonders, the Yosemite Valley and the big trees. If you approve of this, would such a recommendation be appropriate in your official report?

A. B. Nettleton

Hayden grunted. The Yellowstone region . . . a park? For the public? What in heaven's name for? Who would be interested in a geological laboratory? He shivered. The room was cold. He dropped the telegram, got up, and went to the stove to build a fire.

Why would the Northern Pacific be interested in . . . oh, of course, a tourist attraction, Hayden thought. He lit the fire, stepped back, and waited until it was going before he closed the door to the stove.

What was wrong with leaving the place as is? he wondered. He didn't think it would be a place anyone would want to settle: the valley was too high to grow much, and the place was too remote. He had simply assumed that private interests, like the little ranch near the White Mountain Springs, would develop the area for tourists. He remembered seeing the shacks and recalled discussing how rich the men might get when the Northern Pacific Railroad opened the region to the public with a spur line. Then people could come and see it whenever they wanted to.

The fire crackled. Hayden rubbed his hands in the radiant

heat. Was there any merit to Nettleton's suggestion? Would he look foolish by supporting such a notion? He could not imagine a nationally owned picnic ground at eight thousand feet in such a remote area. As he returned to his desk, the request stuck in his mind.

The West and all of its great natural resources were there for man to exploit. Hayden couldn't honestly say that he thought the Yellowstone offered much in mineral resources. Its primary value rested in its beauty and uniqueness. You don't find active volcanism every day. He recalled his wonder and delight at the colors and sculptures of the hot springs, his astonishment at the geology of the canyon, and his awe of the geysers. He had every intention to sing the praises of the region to the public. But a park?

Hayden could not think of any precedent for such an idea. Parks were city affairs. Paris had its Bois de Boulogne, London its Victoria Park. His own Philadelphia had the Fairmount. Quite sufficient. Hayden wasn't sure that cities needed parks. The countryside was there, everywhere, for anyone to enter and enjoy. But he knew that even before the Civil War, William Cullen Bryant had argued that land for recreation and pleasure was disappearing. Bryant had encouraged New York City to reserve land for a central city park and had hired Frederick Olmsted as chief architect.

Hayden reread the telegram. Nettleton had compared the Geyser Basin to Yosemite. Hayden had seen Carlton E. Watkins's photographs of the Yosemite Valley. Toward the end of the war, he'd read about the move to preserve the Mariposa Big Tree Grove and the Yosemite Valley. Hayden searched his library for a reference on the California bill. The one he found said that Congressman John Conness had asked Congress to grant California the right to dedicate the area to public use, resort, and recreation for all time under the management of the governor.

The area of the Yosemite that was reserved was forty square miles. That was smaller than Yellowstone Lake, thought Hayden. And Conness's justification? The valley and big trees were more than spectacular, they made the land unique. The inherent values of the sites were above commercial considerations. The Yosemite was the first tract of land in America to be set aside for the public.

Abraham Lincoln had signed the bill. Reaction had been favorable.

Hayden closed the document. Parks were the affairs of congressmen, socialites, and editors. Why had Nettleton asked him to endorse the idea? He was a geologist. He didn't run in the same circles with statesmen, poets, and philosophers, and he didn't hobnob with members of the Romantic movement or the philanthropic set.

The image of a shimmering Yellowstone Lake with a background of majestic geysers filled Hayden's mind. Perhaps Nettleton was flattering him. Hayden knew that the American people were waiting for him to satisfy their curiosity. Wasn't it his job to simply report his findings? Or should he also make a recommendation on how the land should be classified?

He wondered what Emma would think of a Yellowstone public park.

Several days later, in Helena, Montana, Milnor Roberts stamped the dust from his boots and hung his hat on a peg in his rented office. A telegram from Jay Cooke lay on his desk.

We are delighted to hear such good accounts of the Yellowstone expedition from both ends. Gen. Hancock and Gen. Sheridan have both telegraphed that the report the army will publish will be a splendid one.

Dr. Hayden will propose in his report to Congress that the geyser region around Yellowstone Lake should be set apart by the government as a park, similar to that of the great trees and other reservations in California.

Please give me your views. It is important to do something speedily, or squatters and claimants will go in there. We can probably deal much better with the government than with individuals in any improvements we may desire to make for the benefit of our pleasure travels.

Jay Cooke

3) Popular Geology

Hayden remained in Washington, scrambling, fussing, and occasionally muttering in his effort to get everything done. He checked off tasks and put wheels into motion, keeping one eye on the clock and the other on the calendar so he wouldn't make himself, his bride, or his future in-laws nervous about his appearance at the wedding. When he finally left for Philadelphia, he still felt behind schedule. The last item he'd attended to was a long letter from Richard Gilder of *Scribner's*.

Gilder wrote that Thomas Moran had selected nine views of the Yellowstone to illustrate the article Hayden was to write. The views were comprehensive: two of the great spring near Gardiner's River, the overflow on the east face and the Pools of Diana; Liberty Cap; extinct craters and the formations on top of the great plateau of travertine deposits; Yellowstone Lake, where the Yellowstone River exits; the great geyser basin of the Firehole; the Grand Canyon of the Yellowstone; the miniature mud volcano at Crater Mountain; and a sketch that showed the difficulties of traveling through the Yellowstone by pack train.

Hayden had watched Thomas Moran capture the tints, curves, and tiny crenulations of the hot springs, and watched him sketch the power of the canyon. He knew exactly what Moran was creating for *Scribner's*. "Pictures are engraved," wrote Gilder in his standard telegraphese. "When can we expect the article?"

Gilder told Hayden that by writing the article, he was doing them a great favor, getting them out of a scrape. Hayden had written back in his own blunt hand, "Why can't I have Moran's engravings for my report as well?" To soften his request, he sent Gilder the first portion of the article. He had taken the majority of the narration from his annual report. Both were written for the common man.

Ferdinand V. Hayden and Emma C. Woodruff were married in Philadelphia in a civil ceremony the evening of November ninth. A number of the Woodruff family were present. Jim Stevenson acted as Hayden's witness. The moment Hayden kissed his bride, he wondered how he had been lucky enough to find such a wonderful woman. Then he wondered how many days he would have to stay in Philadelphia before he could return to Washington to finish his report. He wasn't worried about leaving Emma; he was sure she would understand.

He was right. Less than a week later Hayden was back in Washington. A letter from Captain Barlow was waiting for him. *You will sympathize with me, my dear Hayden, when I tell you that our great fire swept away all my photographic plates before prints were taken from them. Only sixteen prints were made on Saturday previous to the fire which Mr. Hine had taken to his house. I lost some of my notes also, though my journal was saved from which I can make a report. The map notes were up at St. Paul and Captain Heap has sent me a sketch of our route. As we only partially surveyed the lake, I depend upon your work in that particular and hope to receive a copy of your map soon.*

I shall have to trust to our old friendship and your generosity, now, respecting an exchange of photographic views. I can offer you only sixteen, not the two hundred I expected to have had. Not one single page was saved from my office. All my instruments, maps, books, and everything brought back from the Yellowstone, including specimens, were consumed. I have to begin anew.

"Jim!" yelled Hayden. "Where's Jackson? He's got the only negatives of the Yellowstone!"

"Jackson's in Nebraska where you sent him, Doc. The negatives of the Yellowstone are in the back room waiting to be printed. But Hine and Crissman both took photographs, so . . . ."

"No, no, no, Jim. You don't understand," said Hayden, waving Barlow's letter. "Hine's photographs were all destroyed in the Chicago fire, and Crissman is nowhere to be found. The only photographic proof of the phenomena we encountered at the Yellowstone is Jackson's negatives. He's going to have to do double duty." Hayden strode to Jackson's desk. "We'll have to send Barlow something, for sure . . . maybe even a whole set. Oh, bother. When's Jackson due back?"

Then he remembered: Jackson had gone to document the customs of the Omaha and Pawnee. He said he'd only be gone a week.

But then he returned to Omaha to put his personal affairs in order before he came back to Washington. He told Hayden that he would try to sell the studio, then, as soon as feasible, bring his most-pregnant wife to Washington. Hayden knew that Jackson's wife had managed the studio all summer. They had tried to sell the business, but no one had made them a decent offer. Naturally, they were reluctant to sell at a sacrifice.

Hayden returned to his desk, grateful that at least he'd been able to secure assistance for his map: Professor Julius E. Hillgard of the U.S. Coast and Geodetic Survey was working up Schonborn's topographical data. He made a note to ask Hillgard when he would be done, then he settled down to work on his 1871 annual report. He called it the *Preliminary Report of the United States Geological Survey of Montana and Portions of Adjacent Territories, Fifth Annual Report of Progress.* As he picked up his pen, he glanced at Emma's picture. Her smile made him recall their conversation the night before he left for Washington.

"Why can't you simply tell them you need more time?" she had asked after dinner.

"Some deadlines are not negotiable, my dear," replied Hayden. "I hope you know that I would much rather stay, but I have a reputation to maintain and I can't leave myself open to criticism. I needn't remind you that the coming summer hinges on the acceptance of this year's report."

"That's so unfair. You've produced so much more than anyone else. What do they want?"

"It's not the men in charge, Emma; it's the system. Every year is a new game, often with a few new rules. Very nerve-wracking if I do say so, but I have my survey and I aim to keep it. I will make my report simple but as comprehensive as possible and structure it much as I did last year's report. My diary approach saves time, and it lets me address the concerns of the public as well as scientists."

"I thought you said a number of your colleagues criticized you for your approach last year."

"True. Should I change everything because of that? One thing I have learned as a report writer: it makes no difference what approach I take, there will be criticism. People are jealous of my survey. But I have vowed to share my discoveries with the public and I consider that task fundamental to the value of my work. What good is it to discover, to document vast new regions of settlement, if the people who will live there can't understand what you write or don't have access to your conclusions for years?"

Emma smiled. She walked to him and placed her hands on either side of his face. "You're a good man, Professor Hayden. I shall be waiting for you when you have finished your work." And she kissed him in a way that reminded him she was still a bride.

The day after Barlow's letter, Hayden received Gilder's reply about Moran's engravings. *We can't afford to go to such large expense for original illustrations without getting back part of it from some quarter,* Gilder wrote. *Even Harper Company with its immense resources is largely dependent on its reproductions and it cheapens illustrations to have them appear in reports. We would hardly allow the woodcuts to go out of our possession even temporarily. However, if you send me five hundred dollars, I will send you copies of Moran's engravings for your report.*

Gilder's request irked Hayden. I have no extra funds, he replied. Let me borrow your blocks. Your magazine would not have gotten the pictures in the first place if I had not allowed Moran to accompany us.

Hayden wrote Part One of his report as a general narrative on geology, topography, and natural resources, a chronological journey that took the reader through the Yellowstone. If it exceeded one hundred pages, at least the description was of primary significance. It was his job to enlighten the public, to describe the wonders of the region, and to analyze the geology behind the Yellowstone phenomena. While so doing, he laid the groundwork for geological problems to be pursued by future investigators.

He intended to see that the reports of his specialists were included in his annual report. To ensure he could afford it, he set aside a good portion of his annual appropriation to cover printing costs. Part Two of the report belonged to Cyrus Thomas's lengthy examination of agriculture, timber, and water resources. Thomas was planning to recommend that Congress create a national timber reserve and set aside alternate sections to western states to be used for canals and irrigation ditches.

Part Three would be devoted to a host of reports from earlier survey work: fossil flora by Leo Lesquereux, the Cretaceous paleontology of Kansas, vertebrates of the Wasatch by Edward D. Cope, plus vertebrate fossils of the Lower Tertiary formations of Wyoming by Joseph Leidy, to whom Hayden had provided vertebrates for so many years.

Hayden had also promised space to Fielding Bradford Meek, who invariably worked up his survey's fossils; Campbell Carrington, assisted by a variety of the young political tagalongs, had completed a study of butterflies. Elliott Porter was writing a study of plants. J. W. Beaman would cover meteorology, and A. C. Peale was writing on the mineralogy of the region.

As the sun set that day, Hayden said goodnight to Jim Stevenson, and walked out into the city. He was always surprised at the noise people could make simply moving from one place to another. He shut out the sounds of horses' hooves and carriage wheels to fill his mind with images of the Yellowstone's sawtooth horizons with their pockets of snow and swaying treetops. He inhaled deeply, and realized that he felt more satisfied than perhaps at any other time in the past decade. He and his team had done well. In less than one hundred days, they had covered eleven hundred miles, gathered enough data to map the Yellowstone, created hundreds of pictorial sketches and sections, sketched and sounded the lake, taken three hundred photographs, charted the hot springs district, taken the temperatures of more than six hundred hot springs, and returned with complete natural history collections, all without accident or loss of government property.

It wasn't very cold, so Hayden decided to walk. He'd been sitting too long, and the exercise felt good. As he walked, he thought about what he had written. He had especially wanted to share his conclusions about the origins of the Yellowstone basin. He wrote that the Yellowstone Valley might be called one vast crater, *made up of a thousand smaller volcanic vents and fissures, out of which the fluid interior of the earth poured in unlimited quantities. Hundreds of the nuclei or cones of these volcanic vents now remain, some of them rising to ten or eleven thousand feet above the sea. All that is left of the terrific forces which threw up these lofty mountains and elevated the entire region to its present altitude now finds issue in occasional earthquakes, hot springs, and geysers.*

Hayden passed a clothing store with a large sign advertising the attributes of beauty and elegance. Hayden snorted. To him, beauty and elegance were the attributes of Old Faithful. To help his audience picture the geyser, he wrote, *Those who have seen representations of Aladdin's Cave and the Home of the Dragon Fly as produced in a first-class theater can form an idea of the wonderful coloring of the intricate frost work of this fairy-like yet solid mound of rock growing up amid clouds of steam and showers of boiling water. The beauty of the scene takes one's breath, overpowering, transcending the visions of mausoleum's paradise. The earth affords not its equal. It is the most lovely inanimate object in existence.*

Gilder's return mail letter ignored Hayden's second request for the blocks. He reminded Hayden that they were expecting the remainder of his promised article. He then had the nerve to say that the Department of the Interior should view the article as part of its good work of exploring the far West. After all, wrote Gilder, *the object of these explorations is knowledge and the people will more highly appreciate the work the department is doing if the results are presented in popular form.* Hayden didn't think it would have mattered if he'd sent his completed article to Gilder months earlier. The man was intolerable. Miffed at the editor's unyielding posture, Hayden tossed the message into the stove. He wanted Moran's woodcuts.

The next day, Hayden received a second letter from Gilder, saying that he had changed his mind. Hayden could make electrotypes of the blocks without charge. *We thought that Uncle Sam would be rich enough to pay about half costs, but if it is a matter that affects your own pocket, let me pack up the blocks and send them to you that you may have electrotypes taken as you desire.*

Hayden immediately telegraphed Gilder his assurances that the blocks would be returned undamaged. Gilder managed to get in the last shot with his reply: *We will express the blocks tomorrow.*

Now I look for you to stand by me, my dear doctor, in the future, if we can get back some of this western money legitimately from our government I hope you will help that end and do all in your power to make the fourth of my coming articles fully graphic and successful.

By the end of November, Hayden had completed a solid draft of his annual report and had nearly completed his article for *Scribner's*. At the last minute, he decided to close the article with his recommendation that the Yellowstone be set aside as a public park. The message was consistent with his report, and he wasn't sure when the report would be made public. Making the same recommendation in both places could not hurt.

4) Toward a National Park

The same day Emma kissed her husband good-bye and watched him leave for Washington, D.C., Nathaniel P. Langford arrived in Philadelphia. He'd recovered from his throat infection, but he still looked tired and pressed. He'd been back in Helena only a few days when he received a telegram from his brother-in-law Marshall in Minnesota. The contents caused him to take the first stage out of Helena. Since the Northern Pacific tracks were still some distance from the Rocky Mountains, Langford took the stage to Corinne, the Union Pacific Railroad to Omaha, then several other linking railroads to St. Louis, Chicago, and Philadelphia.

His last form of transportation had been a hack hired at the Philadelphia train station. He started to give directions. "To the offices of Jay Cooke and Co.," he said, "at the . . ."

"I know where, sir," said the cabby, interrupting. "Everyone knows where Mr. Cooke hangs his top hat. Can't call yerself a cabby in Philadelphia without knowing Mr. Cooke and his banking district. No sir."

Once at Cooke's offices, Langford made it clear that he had no intention of beginning another lecture series on the Yellowstone.

"Of course not, Mr. Langford," said Jay Cooke affably. "I have a much more important job for you. It does not involve speaking, but it does concern the Yellowstone."

Langford listened, asked several questions, then accepted the assignment even though it meant remaining in Washington for some time. He wondered if that rascal Marshall had known what was in the wind. Of course he had; Marshall probably recommended him. Marshall's telegram, however, had suggested only that if Langford was interested in doing something lucrative on the East Coast, he should board the first conveyance to Philadelphia to see Jay Cooke.

Cooke told Langford that he was not to mention his employment with Jay Cooke and Co. Langford understood; otherwise he would be viewed by others as a member of Cooke's team. "However," said Cooke, "I'd appreciate it if you would inform me by telegraph every few days until the situation is well in hand. Your first task should be to see Congressman Dawes. But we'll let him know who you're working for."

A carriage took Langford up Capitol Hill towards the House of Representatives. On his way, he reviewed what he knew about Congressman Henry L. Dawes of Massachusetts. Although only in his mid-fifties, the Yale-educated congressman had been in the House of Representatives for fourteen years. That meant he had considerable seniority. Some considered Dawes the most influential congressman on the hill. He had administered the oath of office to Speaker of the House James A. Garfield and now chaired the Appropriations Committee.

According to Cooke, Langford could expect an agreeable session with Dawes. The congressman was an ardent supporter of Ferdinand Hayden's surveys; in fact, his son, Chester, had accompanied Hayden to the Yellowstone. Cooke knew that Dawes preferred to conduct his more serious business in the cloakroom and committee room rather than on the floor of the House, although his presentations to that body were always dignified and lucid.

To make the situation easier for Langford, Cooke invoked his emissary approach, a proven tactic he used to solicit assistance from Washingtonians. Cooke wrote out exactly what he wanted. Langford, acting as emissary, would read Cooke's message aloud. If the message went to a person already in Cooke's debt, the letter might read more like an instruction; if the politician was friendly, but independent, the message might sound more like a request.

His approach avoided the problem of having his interests inadvertently misrepresented, and by having the message read aloud, Cooke placed himself in the room.

Langford read Cooke's letter one more time. It sounded very much like a request. Once in Dawes's office, Langford unfolded Cooke's letter and asked permission to read it. Mr. Dawes nodded; he was familiar with Jay Cooke and his ways.

When Langford had finished, Dawes smiled. "Interesting. Mr. Cooke is an astute and highly motivated individual," he said. "Those who stand for the man say he's principled. He has always been forthright with me, so I will accept his intentions as communicated. But I need to ask you man-to-man, Mr. Langford, what's behind this park business?"

"First, I must say that the region is unique beyond description," said Langford. In case the congressman had not read his article or attended his lecture, Langford mentioned his trip to the Yellowstone. "From the standpoint of protecting the Yellowstone, the proposition has considerable merit. Mr. Cooke is, of course, interested in anything that will assist him to increase the sale of Northern Pacific bonds and increase passenger traffic once the line is completed."

"Granted and valid. Any hidden agendas in this proposition?"

"None that I know of."

"And your opinion about a 'Yellowstone public park?'"

"Given the manner in which other landmarks in America have been exploited . . ."

"What do you . . . oh, you're referring to Niagara Falls."

"Yes, I am. And given the delicacy of so many of the features in the Yellowstone, I don't give the region much of a chance unless some protection is afforded it."

Dawes moved to his cigar box. He offered one to Langford, who declined, then lit one for himself. "I can tell you that Congress is not in the mood to spend money on anything frivolous. A request to preserve a piece of public land in the middle of the Rocky Mountains damn well falls into the frivolous category. Therefore, unless this project is almost totally free of appropriations, it won't stand a chance."

Dawes looked thoughtful as he puffed on his cigar. "I suggest we leave Jay Cooke's name out of it entirely, as he suggests, and meet again when Senator Pomeroy arrives in town. He chairs the Committee on Public Lands." Dawes pointed his cigar at Langford. "Who else is working on this?"

"I'm the entire delegation to date. Professor Hayden has agreed to recommend that the region be made into a park, but beyond that, I do not believe anything has been done."

"What's Mr. Clagett's position?"

"I haven't contacted Montana's territorial representative. I believe he's still in the West. Mr. Cooke strongly suggested that I see you first."

"Well, we have some time. Congress does not officially open until the seventh of December. Let's meet a few days before Thanksgiving to outline strategy. I suspect we'll need at least two weeks to get everything done. See Clagett when he arrives and tell him I approve. He may not have to do anything, but I'll invite him to meet with us. No sense in causing problems through oversight."

Langford didn't know William H. Clagett personally, only that he was an attorney in Helena and the first Republican to represent the Montana Territory. But he left Dawes's office confident that Cooke's project was off to a good start.

The second time Nathaniel Langford entered Congressman Dawes's office, the smoke was equally aromatic. The congressman spent a few minutes chatting with Senator Pomeroy and Representative Clagett about current events and items of personal interest. Clagett had been campaigning for Edward F. Noyes for Governor of Iowa.

Langford, Pomeroy, and Clagett sat in overstuffed chairs facing Dawes, who presided from behind his desk. He addressed Pomeroy first. "Sam, Mr. Langford and his associates, who, I might add, include Professor Ferdinand Hayden, believe that the recently documented Yellowstone region should be set aside for the public. It's obviously as unique as the big trees and Yosemite, and it's a finite piece of land rather high in altitude. If some form of protection is not afforded it soon, local claimants will take it over." He turned to Langford. "Am I representing the issue correctly, Mr. Langford?"

"Yes sir. I can't stress enough the uniqueness of the region. It's quite unimaginable until you witness it."

"This is where all those geysers and hot springs supposedly exist," said Pomeroy. Then he seemed to remember who Langford was. "Oh, that's right, you were there last year, weren't you. I'm sorry I missed your lecture."

"Excuse me, but is not the Yellowstone a territorial affair?" asked Clagett. "Or have I missed something?" He fingered his trim mustache and goatee. "I'm sure that I can get our government to restrict activities in the Yellowstone. I had no idea that anyone was interested in preserving it as a public place."

"Montana is only one of several interested parties, Mr. Clagett," said Dawes. "A portion of the Yellowstone belongs to the Wyoming Territory, and a small piece belongs to the Idaho Territory. If it was simply a Montana piece of business, we would not be meeting."

"Then we can't handle it like we did the Yosemite back in sixty-four," said Pomeroy.

"No, Sam, but we can apply a good deal of that approach to creating a national set-aside," replied Dawes.

After an hour, the task of preserving the Yellowstone became clearer. To push through a bill this session, they would need a tight case. After too many railroad land grant battles, Congress was openly hostile to disposing of any more of the public trust. The delegates who pushed legislation for this park would need to document the uniqueness of the features and justify the need for precipitate action. Congressman Dawes told the other three that one key to passage of any bill was money. "No money. Not a penny can be attached to this bill." Dawes looked at Langford. "Be sure that Hayden knows this."

Dawes asked Mr. Clagett if he had any thoughts on the issue. Clagett said that he was not in the best position to offer strategy. He had been elected only a few months earlier and was still new to the legislative process. "I am, however, quite familiar with the Yellowstone, and not only from what has been printed." He turned to Langford and said: "I have talked rather extensively with Walter Trumbull, the journalist who accompanied your expedition into the Yellowstone. He reported on my Montana campaign."

Clagett brushed back his light-colored hair. "Unless the area is a rich mineral resource, I can't think of any reason why we shouldn't proceed along the lines you have suggested, Mr. Dawes."

As a master of congressional legislation, Dawes suggested they divide the work. Langford should leave passage of the bill to Senator Pomeroy, Representative Clagett, and himself. They would see to the drafting of legislation before Congress met. Pomeroy and Dawes would use the same principles and legislative framework they had used to preserve the Yosemite Valley of California in 1864. Since the majority of the area was inside the Montana Territory, Clagett could polish the bill, then copy and introduce it in the House of Representatives.

When the meeting broke up, Langford heard Pomeroy tell Clagett that he would like the opportunity to introduce the bill to the Senate first. Then he felt a hand on his shoulder. "Mr. Langford," said Dawes, with the avuncular expression that was second nature to all seasoned politicians, "I will leave it to you to ensure that every member of Congress knows about the Yellowstone. You will have to put together a promotional program. Find out what Hayden has that you can use. Better yet, get him involved. He has the ear of a good number of congressmen. He doesn't bluster or parade, so men of influence will listen to him. And for everyone's sake, keep Cooke and the Northern Pacific Railroad out of it."

The following day, Langford visited Hayden at his office. After he told the professor about the problem that had kept him from accompanying the survey, he asked Hayden about the trip. Hayden showed him some of the prints Jackson had made in the field. The photographs provided Langford a natural opening. "A small group of people are planning to introduce a bill to Congress to make the Yellowstone a national park."

Hayden nodded. "Yes, that's what I recommended in my report."

"Well, sir, as you know, introducing legislation is one thing; getting Congress to pass it is another. Would you be willing to help promote the public park concept? Far too many congressmen are yet unfamiliar with the region. Dawes is fearful that some may consider the bill one more incursion into the public trust. Your support would add significant weight."

"Yes, of course. But you'd better tell me what you need and how much time it may take. I have a number of serious deadlines."

"The bill won't be introduced to Congress until mid-December, Professor Hayden. As to time, I must leave that to you. It was suggested that we ensure that every congressman has a firm understanding of the uniqueness, beauty, and fragility of the region. First, we need to know how much land we're talking about. Would you define the boundaries for us?"

Before Langford left, he added: "Congressman Dawes suspects that Congress might accept the idea without a struggle as long as there is no money attached to the bill. That means you can't ask for money in an enabling bill or later ask for money for roads or other improvements."

"I understand," said Hayden. He was already examining a map of the Yellowstone to find the natural boundaries that would enclose its important features.

Langford did not intend to keep his organizational activities secret, but since nothing had yet happened, he was surprised to receive a clipping from the *Helena Daily Herald* that said he and several scientific and literary gentlemen were engaged in an effort to have the Yellowstone dedicated as a national park. The article described the region as unusable for agriculture or manufacturing, but rich in scenery, hot springs, and geysers. *They propose to have the area forever dedicated to public use as a grand national reservation.* Langford suspected that the *Herald's* Washington, D.C.-based correspondent, Walter Trumbull, had gotten wind of his activities from Clagett or his father, Senator Lyman Trumbull. The promotional campaign was off and running, even if he hadn't fired the starting gun.

5) The Yellowstone Bill

As citizens of a young and optimistic nation, Americans normally looked at the bright side of issues. Yet the mood of the nation that December was unsettled, as though the populace waited for some inevitable disaster. The mood had been created in part by the Franco-Prussian War. Closer to home, the Great Chicago Fire had further depressed the outlook of many. Americans also had been unsettled by a hard, early winter, and by rumors of corruption in the ranks of Washington's politicians and in the boards of directors of major transportation companies.

Perhaps because of an unconscious need to lift the nation's spirits, newspapers played up three stories towards the end of the year. The first identified those who had given to the poor and homeless of Chicago. The outpouring from cities big and small, and from both the wealthy and the working classes, was a reminder that in time of need, Americans always helped Americans.

The second story focused on William Marcy "Boss" Tweed, a bittersweet event because the stories that came out after his arrest exposed the lengths to which some men would go to satisfy their greed. Between 1853 and 1870, as a New York state congressman, Tweed built a ring of close supporters in the offices of the district attorney, New York Supreme Court, and governor. As Chair of the Board of Supervisors for New York, he created a new city charter that gave him control of the city treasury. He and his associates falsified up to eighty-five percent of all leases, vouchers, jobs, and services. When the *New York Times* received and verified this information from turncoats, Tweed offered the editor an outrageous sum of money not to publish. As Christmas approached, the nation read of Tweed's imprisonment at age forty-nine.

To cap off the year, the papers reserved their best fonts and fine phrases for Alexis Alexandrovich Romanoff, the Russian Grand Duke. The duke's visit to the United States was the first by a Romanoff, and America had not forgotten that Russia was the only country to have supported the Union during the Civil War.

Perhaps as important to his welcome was the fact that the duke was a romantic figure, at age twenty-one, he was six foot two inches tall, with broad shoulders, military side whiskers, and a yellowish mustache over a firm, well-cut mouth. The youthful Romanoff was also an admiral of the Russian Navy. After two weeks of baronial balls and lavish receptions in New York and dinner at the White House, the duke arrived in Philadelphia. General George Meade, the chairman of the welcoming committee, took the duke's entourage on a tour of the city in an open barouche drawn by four black horses.

Against this backdrop, Congress went into session on December seventh. In Bozeman, Montana, that same day, the editor of the *Avante Garde* made a last-minute pitch to have Montana oversee the Yellowstone. Exploration had repeatedly taken place *from* Montana, he argued. The region had been opened *by* Montanans. Further, the headwaters of *all* of Montana's important rivers were located in the Yellowstone, and the Yellowstone River ran the full length of the territory. It was *only right* that its hot springs and geysers be granted to the state for the convenience of local legislation.

As Dawes had foreseen, and the boundaries that Hayden had drawn, confirmed, the Yellowstone region overlapped portions of the territories of Montana, Wyoming, and Idaho. The potential snarl of territorial interests could be bypassed only by placing the Yellowstone under federal protection. Accordingly, on December eighteenth, Senator Pomeroy introduced Senate Bill 392, designed to set apart a certain tract of land lying near the headwaters of the Yellowstone River as a public park.

"It has been ascertained within the last year or two," he said, "that there are very valuable hot springs and geysers at the headwaters of the Yellowstone. It is further thought that they ought to be set apart for public purposes rather than have private preemption or homestead claims attached to them. Professor Hayden has made a very elaborate report on the subject."

Without waiting either for comment or objections, Pomeroy added: "This bill is to set apart the whole tract, about forty miles by fifty, as a public park. The bill places the land under the direction of the secretary of the interior to keep it from preemptions and homestead entries and from sale and to reserve it from any grants that may be made to be disposed of hereafter as Congress may direct."

In the House of Representatives, William H. Clagett stood to introduce a bill that sought the removal of the Flatheads and other Indians from the Bitterroot Valley. He then introduced the Yellowstone public park bill, H.R. 764. After reading the bill, he suggested it be referred to the Committee on Territories. It ended up with the Committee on Public Lands. As Clagett left the room, he heard Representative John Monroe, a former classmate of Hayden's, introduce a joint resolution to provide for the printing of the preliminary report of Professor F. V. Hayden's geological survey.

William Henry Jackson dropped his suitcase on the floor, spread his arms open wide, and said dramatically, "Where is everyone and what's so important that I should have been here yesterday?"

Jim Stevenson looked up from his desk. He gave a half-smile. "Isn't it nice to be needed?"

"I came here directly from the station."

"They're trying to turn the Yellowstone into a public park," said Stevenson. "They need you to turn out a whole pile of photographs for the politicians."

"You're joking."

"I am not," said Stevenson. "Mr. Langford and the professor have decided to make an all-out assault on indifferent and ignorant congressmen and to set the Yellowstone area aside for future generations."

"So how many copies of what does he need?"

"Dr. Hayden laid out everything for you on your desk," said Stevenson. "I suggest you take a deep breath."

"You know," said Jackson as he glanced at several notes on his desk, "Mollie and I had all of three days together at my parents' house in Nyack. I hope this pace is temporary."

"Don't count on it. We may be at this until late spring."

Then Jackson was yelling. "Fifteen complete sets of the Yellowstone before the end of the year! What does he think I am, a printing machine? I can't do that." He looked at Stevenson with a pained expression. "He's more reasonable than that. Isn't he?"

"What did he say in his telegram?"

"Drop what you're doing, get here as soon as possible, and start making special prints. I finished that Indian business. Then I returned to Omaha to help Mollie sell the place." Jackson poured himself a cup of coffee. "I found a buyer. I didn't get what I paid for it, but the buyer didn't get my cameras or any of my negatives."

"Bring them with you?"

"I left everything at my parents' house. Mollie was exhausted from the effort to keep our studio going. We were planning to spend a few weeks together. I left her in my folks' care. You knew that we're expecting, didn't you?" He shrugged. "So much for plans."

As if on cue, Hayden walked through the door. "Ah, Jackson. Get my note?"

"Fifteen sets?" asked Jackson. He shook his head. "I don't know, Dr. Hayden. I can bring in my brother Edward for a while, and I can hire a couple of assistants, but our productivity is still going to fall short of what you need."

"Then let's talk about what has to be done."

They spent two hours reviewing the photographs Jackson had taken during the summer. Jackson had blanketed the scene: wide-angle views of the lake and mountains; shots of the survey crew; peculiarities along the shore of Yellowstone Lake; a variety of waterfalls; geysers of every kind, Lone Star, Beehive, Castle, Mud, and Old Faithful, plus long-distance views of the Upper Firehole River; hot springs of every size; geyserite formations; and campsites. He had even taken a photograph of the odometer.

They decided that Hayden would ask for assistance from Edward Bierstadt, the brother of Albert Bierstadt and a photographer who owned a large New York photographic studio. As it was, Hayden negotiated with Jackson to make ten sets of prints of the Yellowstone: five for General Humphreys, Chief of the Army Corps of Engineers, and the other five for Captain Barlow in Chicago.

"I hope you guys don't mind the smell of hypo; that's all you're going to get for the next three weeks," said Jackson as he disappeared into the darkroom.

"As long as it doesn't resemble that mule of yours," said Stevenson with a straight face. "I think that mule broke wind with every step he took."

Ten days before Christmas, Cooke received a telegram from the New York offices of the Northern Pacific Railroad.

Jay: Nearly three years ago, I told you with energy and feeling that the Yellowstone valley was paradise. Milnor Roberts's report is in and I am putting it into type. It will confirm and justify my wildness of appreciation, for Roberts goes wild over the Yellowstone and he is an older and colder man than I. Jay Cooke, feel to the end of your toes that we have the biggest and finest thing here on earth!

Samuel Wilkeson

PART 2: THE FIRST NATIONAL PARK

1) Promoting the Concept

For Ferdinand V. Hayden, the year 1871 ended with a snow flurry and a quiet week in Philadelphia with Emma. She had decorated their home and involved Hayden in Christmas in a way he had not known since he was a child. When he arrived home a week before Christmas, Emma had placed a wreath on the door and decorated a tree in the living room. In a rush of emotion, he realized that he'd neglected to consider Christmas. Starting today, he would make the effort to treat the season like something he had routinely celebrated.

He saw how Emma had artistically wrapped a variety of packages and placed them neatly by the tree. Little cards told him what the gifts were: new gloves and a wool scarf for the field, a bright sweater for the Christmas season, and a pair of house slippers. The gifts represented Emma's sense of practicality as well as romance.

In the face of these detailed preparations, Hayden acknowledged that he had been detached from the more ordinary events of the year. Either that or he had been a bachelor and field geologist far too long. Before the day was over, Hayden ducked out of the house to attend to a simple and obvious task he had overlooked, Christmas presents for his bride.

Returning to Washington, D.C., after the first of the year, Hayden completed the draft of his annual report and mailed his finished article to *Scribner's*. It was obvious from the stacks of prints and negatives around Jackson's desk that photographic printing was still under way. One pile of prints was labeled "Barlow," another "Congressmen, etc.," and a third "Survey Report." In his pile of mail Hayden found a note from the lithographer Julius Bien in New York, informing him that two hundred copies of his map of the Yellowstone were ready.

Things were coming together. Not only was his report under control, he had completed his article on the great geysers of the Yellowstone for the *American Journal of Science and Arts*. In fact, one morning when Langford appeared, Hayden was writing Dana to request support to survey remaining portions of the Yellowstone. *I believe it would be best if you wrote to the Honorable James A. Garfield, Chair of the House Appropriations Committee*, scribbled Hayden. *With his support, my year will be firmed up.*

Langford was carrying two large bundles which he dropped on the floor. "Four hundred copies of my article, 'Wonders of the Yellowstone,'" he said. "Since we'll be promoting the park together, I thought we might keep everything in one place." He looked around the cluttered office. "Do you have room for them?"

Hayden followed Langford's glance. "I'm sure we have space even though the piles will grow significantly before we're through. This office generates a lot of reports."

They didn't call their subsequent talk a strategy session, yet by the time they shook hands and Langford left, they had defined all the elements of a military campaign. To create the nation's first national public park, Congress would have to pass some version of the bill which had been introduced to both chambers. Little had happened in December due to the holidays, but Langford and Hayden knew they would have to press their case with haste. Because of the publicity about the bill, and their certainty that individuals would file on land within the Yellowstone during the coming spring, Congress would have to act before the session closed. The first question was where should they spend their time and energy?

"Not knowing what you might have available, I brought these copies of my article with the thought that we could hand them out to individual congressmen and bend their ears at the same time."

"A good start," agreed Hayden. "I, too, have an article, two in fact, but they are scheduled to be published in *Scribner's* and the *Journal*, and are not yet available. I'll get extra copies as soon as I can. In the meantime, I'll contact as many congressmen as is possible. We can take advantage of our normal activities to pass on information about the Yellowstone, but I suggest we contact select congressmen to explain the nature of the Yellowstone, our reasons for wanting it set aside, and the need to pass the bill this session."

Hayden wrote hasty notes to himself as he talked. "I will give you a list of the politicians I know best. Perhaps you will do the same for me. We can divide the rest according to time and need."

Langford had tried to locate other proponents of the park idea. He looked for well-connected individuals who had time to give, who knew something about the Yellowstone, and who had a good reputation. He knew Cooke could call in favors, but working in the name of Jay Cooke was out of the question. Congressman Kelly was a natural choice, but there wasn't much he could do for Langford, and he was identified with the Cooke camp. Besides, he would do what he could for the cause on his own. Nearly everyone else had too many other priorities. Smiles and vague promises were all Langford had obtained to date.

So as Hayden talked, intermittently rushing about to find written support for his thoughts, Langford realized that most of the brunt of the Yellowstone campaign might fall on this nervous and energetic man. Hayden seemed to be the right man in the right place and at the right time. He was the nationally known and respected geologist-explorer who had documented the Yellowstone. His veracity as a scientist was heightened by his association with the Department of the Interior. He was thus a respected source of information on the unexplored West, not only for Congress but also for journalists. And as a member of the Academy of Natural Sciences of Philadelphia, he could call upon other members of the scientific community and academic centers throughout America.

Equally important, Dr. Hayden's offices were located in the nation's capital and he had proven himself to be an experienced lobbyist. He knew the arguments that swayed congressmen. As one who had wrested funds from a penny-pinching government, he'd taken the time to become personally acquainted with senior senators and representatives. When he spoke about the Yellowstone, he displayed intensity and enthusiasm, and in spite of a tight schedule, he was willing to spend time to promote the park concept.

Langford looked around the room. "Your articles may be tied up at the press, Professor, but you have an effective array of other documentation. I'm thinking of your collections, Mr. Jackson's photographs, and Mr. Moran's sketches. Surely we can make use of them?"

"Oh, indeed. I first thought of asking Jackson to prepare an exhibit, but he simply does not have the time. As it is, I have had to arrange for outside printing to help him complete the photographs. Nonetheless, we intend to see that key congressmen have an opportunity to view a portfolio of photographs of the Yellowstone."

"A portfolio?"

"Yes. I plan to prepare a limited number of copies of a comprehensive pictorial of the region."

Everything Hayden had brought back from the Yellowstone was housed at the Smithsonian. Hayden and Langford agreed it would be proper to ask congressmen to visit the Institution. A copy of the portfolio would be available when they viewed the collection. The uniqueness and delicacy of the materials would speak for themselves.

In addition to interviewing congressmen, Hayden listed a number of scientists he believed would support the concept. He also made a note to ask Thomas Moran to loan him a group of his watercolor sketches.

Langford left Hayden's offices with the belief that if anyone could motivate Congress, it would be Professor Hayden; once he committed himself, the man was a bull.

". . . and this, Mr. Garfield, is a piece of travertine. An intriguing product of mother nature because it deposited one drop at a time. One entire hillside was covered with this material. It had grown over thousands of years into a complex of delicate sculptures, the like of which will never again be seen on this continent."

With Baird's blessing, Hayden had cleaned out a small room in the Smithsonian for his Yellowstone collection. He laid out a complement of fossils, some colorful sedimentary and metamorphic rocks, eye-catching samples of travertine, pieces of siliceous sinter, chunks of black volcanic glass, and a number of the strange, walnut-sized rocky nodules they had found in the Yellowstone River near the lake. The last pieces in the sequence were chunks of petrified wood and tree branches coated with travertine.

James A. Garfield had responded immediately to Hayden's invitation to meet at ten o'clock that morning. Garfield had been voted in to replace Henry Dawes as Chairman of the House Committee on Appropriations. He knew Hayden's history of survey work but did not know the man well. He thought he owed Hayden the courtesy. Besides, he was curious about the Yellowstone, and he needed some firsthand information to judge the value of the bill to set aside the Yellowstone Valley. Its passage would set a significant precedent. Garfield found Hayden's exhibit fascinating.

After Hayden had steered Garfield from one specimen to another, he opened Jackson's portfolio of the Yellowstone and guided the congressman through the photographs. Hayden and Jackson had chosen photos that allowed the viewer not only to see where the samples were collected, but also to see the spectacular formations from which they were taken.

It was the first time Garfield had looked closely at large contact prints of the West. He was particularly impressed with their clarity and detail. "Good heavens, these photographs make me feel as though I was standing in the valley itself," he said. "They certainly do make an unrefutable case for authenticity."

For once, Hayden said nothing. He let Mr. Garfield peruse the prints at his leisure. "The uniqueness of the Yellowstone is undeniable, it is not? My, my, my. Most impressive." Garfield kept turning the pages and making sounds of surprise and delight.

Hayden never passed up an opportunity to impress a key congressman with the importance of his work. When he noted Garfield's reaction to the photographs, he underlined the importance of Jackson's work as a member of the survey. "You know, Mr. Garfield, twenty years ago most images of the West came to us through artists. In their enthusiasm, they often represented mountains with unrealistic slopes and great glaciers, images modeled mostly from European mountain ranges. I have seen the lines of a sandstone mesa contain all the peculiarities of a volcanic upheaval with square-cut joints and masonry that would do credit to a master mason."

Hayden stabbed a finger dramatically at one of Jackson's photographs. "This is truth. The large-format camera that Jackson uses has done much to secure accurate representation of the western scene."

"Yes, yes, I see. Fascinating."

"And I must stress at this point that what you are looking at is not only beautiful and unique, but in dire peril."

Garfield squinted at Hayden. "Yes, so the bill mentioned, but I confess that this concern mystifies me."

"It has taken tens of thousands of years to create the Yellowstone as it looks today. Many of its features are delicate and vulnerable to the thoughtless action of others. Lack of protection will open the Yellowstone to wanton destruction. Collectors and wholesalers may quickly destroy the beauty and value of what you see in these photographs."

"But Professor Hayden, this region is miles removed from habitation, is it not?"

"It is. And our West is quickly being settled. We arrived in time to see people waiting to enter the region this very spring to take possession of these curiosities, to make merchandise of these specimens, and to fence in the wonders so that they might charge others a fee."

Hayden tried to find words that might be significant to the politician. "Mr. Garfield, one may travel the entire continent and not see such a sight at any other place. Politicians like yourself found it fitting to preserve the big trees and the Valley of the Yosemite in California. The Yellowstone is no less majestic or worthy, but it lies inside three territories. It will be up to Congress to protect it. It will be much easier to do so now, while the Yellowstone is still on public land."

"Very persuasive." Garfield nodded, still absorbed in the portfolio. He still had a few more photographs to look at and although he had other appointments, he didn't want to miss a single image.

Garfield was not the only one impressed with the details and graphic impact of Jackson's photographs. While the bill was waiting to reappear from the House Public Lands Committee, one newspaper editor, who had been privy to Hayden's documentation from the region, said, *Jackson's photographs of the Yellowstone prove that the truth about the area is more remarkable than the exaggerations we have heard.*

To those who said they could not find time to meet, Hayden sent copies of Langford's articles and key photographs. A handful of the more influential congressmen received a copy of the complete portfolio. And when Hayden found a spare minute, he wrote notes to accompany his offerings.

He saw Langford only once or twice during the subsequent weeks to discuss who had been interviewed or who had received materials, and who still had not been reached. At the end of the month, Hayden handed out copies of his forthcoming *Scribner's* article, which contained his recommendation for a public park. He continued to divide his time between congressmen and his bride, much more time to the former than the latter. His need to ensure passage of the bill was becoming a minor obsession. Quickly, and unintentionally, he assumed ownership of the concept.

Outside Washington, a series of articles about individuals' experiences in the Yellowstone began to appear in papers and magazines. The November 1871 issue of *Scribner's* ran an article called "Thirty-Seven Days in Hell." It was Truman Everts's hair-raising story of how he had survived after having been lost during the Washburn Expedition. Henry W. Elliott published a brief article on the geysers in *Leslie's Illustrated.* Captain Barlow provided a detailed account of the trip to the *Chicago Evening Journal*, and an abbreviated one to *Harper's Monthly.*

2) Congressional Moves

"I've been instructed by the Committee on Public Lands to report and to recommend passage of Senate Bill 392," said Senator Pomeroy, addressing the Senate. "This is a bill to set aside a tract of land known as the Yellowstone and to consecrate the use of that country for a public park for public use."

402   David M. Delo

The seasoned senator took his time. January was coming to a close, and Pomeroy knew how to pace the introduction of new legislation. He also knew which key facts would garner the most attention and support. "An appropriation of about ten thousand dollars was made last year to explore the country in question. Professor Hayden and his survey party have been there and this bill is drawn on the recommendation of that gentleman. The land area contains about forty miles square. It embraces the geysers, those great natural curiosities that have attracted so much attention."

In a rather offhand manner, Pomeroy told the Senate he would like to have the bill acted upon at this time. "The Committee felt that if we were going to set it apart at all, it should be done before individual preemption or homestead claims are filed on the land."

"I'm sorry, Senator," said a voice behind a sheaf of papers, "but there are other bills and matters of business pending this morning."

"I withdraw my motion," said Pomeroy quickly, "and shall wait for a more propitious moment."

A week later, Senator Pomeroy reintroduced the Yellowstone bill, with the comment that the Public Lands Committee would appreciate the general consideration of the Senate.

"I recommend the Senate support this bill with a unanimous vote," said the vice president. "It will be reported in full, subject to objection."

"Well, are there any objections to this bill?" asked one senator.

"Not an objection, but a question, yes," said Cornelius Cole from California. "For example, how many acres, how much land is being considered under this bill, and is it necessary for the park to belong to the United States?"

Pomeroy explained that Professor Hayden had platted the area. "North and south, about forty-four miles; east and west, about forty."

"Several times larger than the District of Columbia," offered Simon Cameron of Pennsylvania.

"True," said Pomeroy, "but there are no arable lands and no agricultural lands within the proposed boundaries. It is the highest elevation from which our springs descend and cannot interfere with settlement for legitimate agricultural purposes. When we set apart the Yosemite there were a few who had claims there, and it went to the Supreme Court to decide whether those who settled on surveyed land before the government took possession had rights against the government. The courts held that settlers on unsurveyed land have no rights against the government. The government can make an appropriation on any unsurveyed lands."

His statement caused a few murmurs among a number of senators. "As this region would be attractive only on account of preempting a hot spring or some valuable mineral, it was thought that such claims would be better excluded from the bill. There are several senators whose attention has been called to the matter, and there are photographs of the valley and its natural curiosities which the senators can see. The only object of the bill is to take early possession to avoid occupancy by settlers."

"Is this bill under consideration at the moment or is the discussion simply for clarification?" asked a senator.

"Clarification," said Senator Cole. "I have no objections."

"Well, I do," said Senator Thurman, standing. "Mr. Cole says he has no objections, but I'm just not willing to take it up at this moment. When I have time to consider it, fine; but not now."

The following day began with the chaplain's morning prayer. The prior day's proceedings were read and approved, and the Senate then moved to general business. The first topic was appropriations for the American delegation in Japan. The Committee on Appropriations wanted fifty thousand dollars to defray expenses of the embassy. The Senate acceded.

A number of claims against the government were read into the record. The Senate also voted on improvements to the falls of the Ohio River; asked for a modification of the bill about President Grant's conduct; and dealt with several matters related to mail contractors and financial deficiencies in the post office.

Pomeroy waited patiently. When he found an opening, he told his fellow senators that he wanted to take up the Yellowstone bill. The motion was agreed to, with the understanding that the bill would be laid aside informally if Senator Cole had something important to discuss.

"Well, I believe the Senate first needs to address Senate Bill 625," said Cole. "It is to enable one of the departments to close its accounts." The Senate concurred. The business was settled, and Pomeroy made his fourth attempt. The Yellowstone bill was read as amended by the Committee on Public Lands, boundaries of the proposed park were described, and the Senate was informed that *the land would be withdrawn from settlement, occupancy, or sale under the laws of the United States, and dedicated and set aside as a public park or pleasuring ground for the benefit and enjoyment of the people. Anyone who settled after the act was passed would be treated as a trespasser.*

The second section of the bill placed the park under the control of the secretary of the interior. He was to *establish and publish rules and regulations for the care and management of the park.* He was also to *provide for preservation from injury and spoliation of timber, mineral deposits, and curiosities and wonders and retention in their natural condition.* The secretary was authorized to *grant leases for buildings not to exceed ten years, small parcels, and the erection of buildings to accommodate visitors.* All proceeds and revenues related to road and bridle paths would be expended under his direction and he *would prevent wanton destruction of fish and game and cause all people trespassing to be removed and take other measures as necessary to carry out the bill.*

The vice president recognized Mr. Anthony of Rhode Island. "The destruction of game and fish for profit is forbidden by this bill, is that correct? I want to ensure that this feature is very clear. This is to be a public park; we don't want sportsmen going in there shooting as they please at anything that runs or flies."

"Senator," said Pomeroy, "I believe that 'wanton destruction' is the key phrase. I have no objection if people wanted to go in and camp and fish and shoot game for their own sustenance."

"Fair enough, but the park should not be used for sporting."

"I agree," said Pomeroy. He made a note that Anthony was satisfied.

"If the place is a public park, a place of national resort," said Mr. Tipton of Nebraska, "there should be a prohibition against the destruction of game for any purpose, for once the door is open I fear that there will be destruction of all game in the park."

"Since the bill clearly defends against the destruction of game, it would be up to the secretary of the interior to make rules and be vigilant." Tipton agreed.

"I have taken great pains to acquaint myself with the history of this region," voiced Mr. Edmunds of Vermont. "It is so far elevated above the sea that it cannot be used for private occupation. It is probably one of the most wonderful regions in that space of territory which the globe exhibits, and therefore we are going to do no harm to the material interests of the people to preserve it. I hope the bill will pass."

"With all due respect to Senator Pomeroy and his desire to hold treasures of our great land for the public, I must express my concerns with the propriety of passing this bill," said Senator Cole loudly. "First, the curiosities of which you spoke cannot be interfered with. The geysers will remain no matter who owns them. Therefore I do not know why settlers should be excluded from this tract. There is an abundance of parklike land in the Rocky Mountains that will never be occupied. It is all one great park. It cannot ever be anything else . . . large portions of it at any event. If people want to come and attempt to cultivate it, they should be allowed."

Senator Edmunds thought he knew Senator Cole. Cole had recommended that a portion of the Presidio in San Francisco be given to the city for park purposes. He was also in favor of preserving buffalo, elk and antelope in the territories from indiscriminate slaughter. His objection, then, might have a financial basis.

"The land is north of latitude 40 and is over seven thousand feet in elevation, Senator," said Edmunds. "You can't cultivate that."

"You are probably mistaken, sir, but even if it can't be cultivated, why bother to make a public park of it? If it can't be occupied, why protect it against occupation? I see no reason in that. If nature has excluded man, why set it apart and exclude man from it?"

He looked around as though appealing to his fellow senators. "If there is any sound reason for passage of the bill, I won't oppose it, but I don't see any."

"The experience with the wonderful natural curiosity in the

senator's own state should admonish us of the propriety of passing such a bill as this," said Senator Lyman Trumbull of Illinois. "There's the wonderful Yosemite Valley and you have a couple of people there now with claims by preemption. Here's a region of the country away in the Rocky Mountains, the most wonderful geysers on the face of the earth, country not likely to ever be inhabited for purposes of agriculture. But it's possible that someone will go there and plant himself across the only path that leads to these wonders and charge every man who passes along the gorge a dollar to five dollars. He may also place an obstruction, a toll booth."

Trumbull knew that Hayden and Barlow had found people with claims on Gardiner's River and at an encampment called Chestnutville. They had also found two Bozeman men who had built a cabin on the hot springs terraces and who said they had laid claim to the springs. In addition, there was Bart Henderson, a man with a vision of cutting a permanent road from Bozeman to Yellowstone Lake, by way of the hot springs, for those interested in viewing the wonders of the region. His road would be a toll road.

"This place is uninhabited," continued Trumbull. "No one lives there now. Never trod on by civilized man until a short while ago. Perhaps a year or two ago was the first time anyone saw this country. It's now proposed in this condition to preserve it, put it away. It's a very proper bill to pass and now is a good time to do it. We set apart the region of mammoth trees in California, and we have undertaken to preserve the Yosemite Valley, but there is a dispute about it. Before we get into a dispute about this area we want to set it aside for the general disposition of the public and reserve it to the government. If at some future time we want to do so, we can repeal the law, if it's in anybody's way, but I think it's appropriate."

Trumbull's argument struck home. Around the Senate chamber, heads nodded. With a request from Senator Pomeroy, the bill was read a third time and subjected to a voice vote. A resounding majority said "Aye." The bill was then sent to the House of Representatives.

About this time, Hayden received advance copies of his article for *Scribner's:* "Wonders of the West—II: More About the Yellowstone." In this article, as well as in his article about the geysers, he had asked: *Will not Congress at once pass a law setting the Yellowstone apart as a great public park for all time?*

The Yellowstone *will be a park worthy of the great republic,* reported the *Helena Herald* a few days later. *It will embrace about two thousand five hundred square miles and include the great canyon, falls, and lake of the Yellowstone, with a score of other magnificent lakes, the great geyser basin of the Madison, and thousands of mineral and boiling springs. Should the whole surface of the earth be gleaned, not another spot of equal dimensions could be found that contains on such a magnificent scale one half the attractions here grouped together.*

3) An Idea Whose Time Has Come

Since the introduction of the Yellowstone bill to the House, neither its initiator, Territorial Representative William Clagett, nor influential House members had thought to inquire about its status. The action in the Senate seemed more important. When Langford inquired about the House bill, he discovered that it remained on the speaker's table.

Not having any immediate inroads to the House of Representatives, Langford sent a telegram to his brother-in-law, William Marshall, to ask that he place a little pressure on Minnesota Congressman Mark H. Dunnell. Dunnell was the chair of the subcommittee of the Committee on Public Lands, the committee responsible for action on the Yellowstone bill. Almost immediately, the secretary of the interior received a note from Representative Dunnell requesting a report on the Yellowstone, preferably one by Professor Ferdinand Hayden.

The first months of the year were constant turmoil for

Ferdinand Hayden, but they did not appear to throw him off track. He had become somewhat inured to the strain of juggling a number of balls in the air while he also tied up loose ends. That was the norm every year when he organized support for his annual survey. In any case, calm was not Hayden's forte. His purpose now was to return to the Yellowstone for another season. First, he wanted to ensure that the Yellowstone bill passed. It seemed to him that every day he received either a missive from his wife asking about his schedule ("When are you coming home, Ferdie dear?"), one more detail to attend to from the editor at *Scribner's*, or an inquiry from Fielding Bradford Meek.

At his desk, Hayden sighed from combined exasperation and fatigue. He didn't begrudge the time and energy consumed in promoting the park, but he wondered when it would end. He rubbed the bridge of his nose, then reread the latest note from Secretary of the Interior Delano. Now the secretary wanted him to prepare a special report for Congressman Mark Dunnell.

Hayden shrugged fatalistically, pulled out a pen, and decided that a five-page summary should suffice. He included three main points. The land was not susceptible for cultivation and thus not desirable for settlement. *Winters are too severe for stock raising,* he wrote. *Mountains that surround it are ten to twelve thousand feet high with snow on their peaks all year. They are all volcanic and probably do not have any precious or minable minerals. And frost occurs most of the year.*

Second, the region's value lay in its unique natural features. *The whole region is filled with wonderful volcanic activity. Hot springs and geysers represent the last stages of volcanic manifestations of internal forces. Springs are adorned, the decorations more beautiful than the human eye or hand can conceive which have required thousands of years by the cunning hand of nature to form.*

His final point related to the need for immediate action. If Congress did not act now, the region might well be destroyed. *People are now waiting to enter and take possession of these curiosities. In a few years, this place will be a resort for all the classes of people from all portions of the world. If the bill fails to become law this session, the vandals who are waiting to enter will in a single season despoil beyond recovery these curiosities which have remained for thousands of years. The withdrawal of this tract from sale or settlement takes nothing from the public domain and there is no pecuniary loss to the government but will be regarded by the civilized world as a step of progress and an honor to Congress and the nation.*

Hayden sent off the report, then returned to the pressing matters of the day. A telegram from Bierstadt's photographic studio in New York read: *I send you by mail today proofs of the three negatives received from Mr. Jackson which I trust may be satisfactory. We can take right hold at once and can furnish the pictures as fast as required. We can print at about the rate of five hundred per day.*

Good, thought Hayden. Jackson will welcome some relief. Thinking of Jackson made him smile for a split second. The day before, the man had been euphoric about becoming a father. He had talked incessantly about all the things he planned to teach his son, until someone reminded him that he didn't know whether he would have a girl or a boy. After the laughter, Jackson said it didn't matter; his daughter, if that was how it turned out, would be the first female William Brady Jackson. At that point, Jim Stevenson made some dry comment that set the entire shop to laughing.

The next letter was from Meek, who wanted to know the status of the Upper Missouri paleontology treatise. He said the plates had been complete for some time and the text was almost complete, but his need for money kept pulling him away from the work. *If I understand you correctly,* he wrote, *you intend to publish the whole of the Upper Missouri paleontology in connection with the report of your survey of the territories. I am to be appointed paleontologist of the surveys at a satisfactory salary during a time when I become so connected to it. To avoid further delay, I am not to undertake any more work from other states while so connected. Is that correct?*

Hayden, don't you understand that this arrangement places our partnership on a whole different footing? It needs a new and full understanding. If we publish 'Paleontology' as a volume of your survey, your name will be on the title page. What I propose is that this shall appear as my work with my name alone on the cover as author of the report.

This, Professors Baird and Henry say is fair. You get all the

410   David M. Delo

credit for the general geology; if I do the paleontology work, it should stand in my name. I have to cite the species of genera that have already been published. I shall take on no more outside work, but must complete those in process. Some items can be postponed and the Upper Missouri paleo given priority.

Hayden wrote a response, put Meek's letter back in the envelope, and said, "Amen, Fielding. So be it."

Later in the month Hayden received distribution copies of his article on the hot springs and geysers for the *American Journal of Science and Arts.* The article included Hayden's wish to see the Yellowstone bill passed this session. He mailed an autographed copy to James A. Garfield with his compliments.

Then Hayden received one more long note from Gilder with an enclosed check for one hundred dollars for the article on the Yellowstone. Gilder noted receipt of Hayden's requests for extra copies of various articles. *We've run short of February notes, so I sent only copies to Secretary of War Belknap; Secretary of the Interior Delano; General Cowan; Congressmen Dawes, Ketchum, and Garfield; Speaker Blaine; Mr. Clagett; and Mr. Glastnell of the British delegation.*

On February 20, Ferdinand Hayden completed his cover letter for his annual report. In addition to thanking everyone for assistance, he made a point to thank *Scribner's,* who *has done a lot to spread the word of the remarkable scenery and resources of the far West, and for the use of the woodcuts to illustrate this report.*

"No one can claim I didn't earn my salary this year," muttered Jackson to himself as he rifled through a stack of just-dried photographic prints. "Ed," he shouted towards the darkroom door, "where's the second set of Old Faithful prints?"

William's brother stuck his head out of the darkroom. "Five minutes," he said.

"I sure hope all this work pays off," said Jackson. He stuck out his hand as Stevenson handed him a stack of mail. He looked for a letter from Mollie. Finding none, he scanned the rest of the stack. He pulled out a letter from General Sheridan's headquarters in Chicago and a telegram, and tossed the rest on his desk.

The envelope from Chicago contained a check for three hundred and six dollars to cover the prints Jackson had made for Barlow. In an accompanying note, Captain Barlow wrote that he thought the views were exceedingly beautiful and that General Sheridan was very pleased.

"Hey, fellas," said Jackson with a grin as he tore open the telegram, "we must be doing something right; ole Sheridan himself likes our work."

As his eyes scanned the message, time stopped and so, it seemed, did his heart. *Mollie and your son died in childbirth. Have no words to comfort you. Come to us when you can. Mother and Father.*

Stevenson wandered his way, chewing on the end of a loaf of bread. "Better watch out, William, General Sheridan is known for getting what he wants." He bit off another mouthful of bread. "If you get . . . Bill? Bill? Hey? You all right?"

Jackson slumped forward, his head on the desk, his hands covering his head. The telegram protruded through his fingers. He moaned as if he were in severe pain.

Stevenson pulled the telegram from his fingers. The words stung like wasps. "Oh, my God. This can't be true." Stevenson was motionless for a few moments. He had no idea what to say or do. "I'm more sorry than I can say," he muttered, then walked quickly into the darkroom to tell Jackson's brother what had happened.

"Bill! Bill!" shouted Ed. He rushed out of the darkroom. "Not Mollie and your first child. How is that possible? Was she sickly? You said she looked well. This is horrible. Bill, talk to me!"

Jackson's face was ashen. The deaths of his wife and child were incomprehensible. He felt as though God had kicked him in the face. He and Mollie had worked so hard to get where they were. Everything had been falling into place. He had a permanent job with the survey, they had sold the business, he'd found a place to live in the city, and their first child was on its way. Now he had nothing! Mollie was gone. And so was their child.

Jackson's brother Ed went with him while he packed. They said little to one another. "I loved her a lot, Ed. What am I going to do now?" said Jackson.

Stevenson appeared at the train station. The three men walked down the platform to find the train to Nyack. In a cracking voice, Jackson said, "She sure put up with a lot from me." He walked with a shuffle, as if placing one foot in front of the other was too much of an effort.

"Stay as long as you need, Bill," said Stevenson. "Professor Hayden would want you to."

"I'll take care of the shop," said Ed. "The bulk of the work has been done. You've worked hard and it shows."

Jackson dropped his eyes and disappeared into the train. Jackson and Stevenson watched, wondering why tragedy would strike such a fine fellow. He was just beginning to enjoy the reputation he deserved for the fine work he created, thought Stevenson.

As the train pulled away, Stevenson asked Ed, "Do you think Bill will return to the survey? We'd sure be a lot less without him."

"I don't know," muttered Ed. "Chances might be about fifty-fifty."

The gavel in the House of Representatives resounded throughout the rotunda. General business for the last day of February included the mutilation of currency, the stamping of counterfeit notes, and the regulation of commerce on the Schuylkill River. The House also settled the issue of the Texas Pacific Railroad, voted to build a bridge across the Arkansas River, and approved the survey of Washington harbor.

When House Bill 392 was brought up, there was a momentary silence. Representative Glenn W. Scofield of Pennsylvania stood. "I request that this bill be sent to the Committee on Public Lands." Immediately, Representative John Taffe of Nebraska attempted to redirect the bill to the Committee on Territories.

Congressman Henry L. Dawes rose to speak. "Gentlemen, I would hope that everyone here is already familiar with this bill. I have the greatest hope that it will be put upon its passage at once, as it seems to be meritorious."

While Dawes spoke, Representative John B. Hawley of Illinois was looking around for William H. Clagett. He leaned over and asked Dunnell, "Where's Clagett?"

Dunnell whispered back, "The last I saw of him he was trying to get support to remove the Flathead Indians from the Bitterroots. I believe he's still in conference at the other end of the Capitol."

Hawley grimaced and, with a nod from Dawes, took the floor. "My fellow representatives, the question of this bill was originally referred to the Committee on Public Lands. The house bill is similar in all aspects to Senate Bill 392, which was passed by unanimous voice vote. It has now been considered by the Committee on Public Lands and Mark Dunnell of Minnesota has been instructed to report favorably to the House. If the Committee were on call it would be reported." Hawley looked straight at Dunnell.

Dunnell took the cue and sprang to his feet. "Yes, I was instructed by the Committee to ask the House to pass H.R. 764. It's exactly like the bill passed by the Senate last month. I have examined the matter with great care and am satisfied that the law ought to be passed."

Dawes stood a second time slowly. He looked around the room before he said, "This bill should be passed as soon as possible to ensure that deprivations in that country will be stopped."

"May I please hear the bill once again," asked a representative.

After the reading, Dawes said that the bill followed the analogy of the one passed by Congress six or eight years ago to set apart the Yosemite Valley and the big tree country for the public. "The former bills granted jurisdiction to the state of California," added Dawes. "This bill reserves control to the United States."

Without waiting for argument, Dawes repeated his reasoning for the bill. He added that it had the ardent support of the legislature of the Montana Territory and of the Montana Territory delegate himself, who unfortunately was absent. "We interfere only with the exposure of that country to those who are attracted by the wonderful description and are going there to plunder this wonderful manifestation of nature."

"If I may ask, Senator, does this not interfere with the treaty regarding the Sioux reservation?" The question came from the rear of the chamber.

"Both the House and the Senate have acted on the theory that all the treaties made by the Indian Commission are simple acts of legislation," said Dawes.

"That doesn't answer my question about the rights of settlers to go upon the land. If that land is a part of the treaty, no one has the right to go into the country between the Big Horn Mountains and the Missouri River except for the Indian tribes."

"That may be," said Dawes, "but the Indians can no more live there than they can upon the slopes of the Yosemite Valley."

"I call the previous question," said Representative Scofield. The motion was seconded and a two-thirds majority vote determined that the bill should be read again. The Democratic minority leader of the House, George Morgan of Ohio, asked for a roll call of yeas and nays. When support for this decisive action was counted, Morgan was relieved to see that he had the necessary votes. Now the House would have to take a final vote on the bill.

As one might expect, the yeas and nays followed party lines. Supporters of the bill included Oakes Ames of the Union Pacific Railroad, Speaker of the House James A. Garfield, Henry L. Dawes, everyone on the Committee of Public Lands, and most of the congressmen from New York, Illinois, Maine, and Maryland. Of the one hundred fifteen yeas, ninety-seven were Republicans, eighteen were Democrats. Sixty-five said nay. Sixty abstained.

President Ulysses S. Grant signed the Yellowstone National Park bill on March first. Compared to the other bills that came across his desk for signing, this was a minor one. The media did not make much of a fuss over it. The most vocal were Montana newspapers and a few editorials like the one in *Scribner's* magazine, which also ran an article on the Yellowstone.

When Hayden heard that the bill had passed, his office took the afternoon off. The next day he inserted a note about the bill's passage into his article on the great geyser basin for the *American Journal of Science and Arts*. He gave a brief history of the bill and included a map of the Yellowstone. Then, feeling entitled to play the role of leading scientist, he added: *At a time when public opinion is so strong against appropriating the public domain for any purpose, however laudable, that our legislators should reserve for the benefit and instruction of the people, a tract of three thousand five hundred and seventy-five square miles, is an act that should cause universal satisfaction through the land. This noble deed may be regarded as a tribute from our legislators to science, and the gratitude of the nation, and of men of science in all parts of the world, is due to them for the munificent donation.*

PART 3: NEW ROADS, OLD ROADS

1) Celebrations

"A toast to our noble congressman William Kelly," said Samuel Wilkeson, raising his glass of champagne. "To the Judge!"

"To the Judge!" responded other voices.

"Hear, hear!" said Jay Cooke. "Too bad he can't be with us today."

"To be honest, I didn't think it could be done," said Nettleton to Nathaniel Langford at the edge of the gathering. "I suspect the day the judge told me about his idea, the incredulity on my face exposed me for a skeptic. Perhaps that is the difference between a publicist like myself and a politician like the judge. Congressman Kelly saw the long-range benefits for the Yellowstone and for the railroad."

"Some day," said Jay Cooke, who had walked toward the two men, "you will sit me down and tell me how all that came about." He shook his head as a waiter offered him a tray of food.

"My pleasure," said Nettleton with a small bow.

"At the same time, you can advise me of what plans you have to promote the park, in terms of our railroad, of course. The spur line to the park should pay handsomely. And now that the public knows we are promoting the accessibility of the Yellowstone, that in itself should increase the salability of our bonds."

"We're counting on it," said Nettleton, "but we're not out of the woods yet."

"We will be," said Cooke.

For Cooke, 1871 had been an anxious, aggravating year. The collapse of his enterprise seemed more and more likely. Cooke still cared, desperately, but he'd lost his passion, and the Northern Pacific struggle was now more enervating than energizing.

Cooke knew that graft and corruption had permeated the construction offices in Minnesota. Gregory Smith had spent more than five million dollars on contracts, general expenses, and rolling stock. Against Cooke's advice, he had also let contracts for a year in advance of the need. He had also given an incredible amount of patronage to politicians and paper generals.

Cooke tried to focus on the positive. He saw smiles on his partners' faces. Of course; commissions on bond sales had made it a profitable year for Jay Cooke and Co. Both the New York and the Philadelphia houses had declared dividends and together divided more than a million dollars in profit. But these figures belied the firm's unstable position. Cooke knew it, but he refused to acknowledge it in conversation. To do so was to confirm that he was vulnerable. He had placed his faith in the expansion and prosperity of America and he would not retreat now. Soon, the people would understand the magnitude of the patriotic gesture he was making and rally to his side, as they had done during the Civil War.

"The spread of new ideas and the awareness of potential take time," continued Cooke in a forced but positive tone. "The Yellowstone is a perfect example. Wilkeson has been much more aware of the Yellowstone as a draw for the railroad for several years. My interest was not elevated until I had the opportunity to talk to Mr. Langford." Cooke shook a finger at Langford in lighthearted admonishment. "It was your intrepid expedition that piqued my mind, Mr. Langford. Upon his return," said Cooke to the others, "he furnished me a summary of his talk. I convinced him to speak at Ogontz."

Nettleton turned to Langford. "As a promoter, you turned in an inspired performance, Mr. Langford. The Northern Pacific and Mr. Cooke are indebted to you."

"I enjoyed the challenge," said Langford. "And you, Mr. Cooke, were correct about keeping the Northern Pacific in the background. A few congressmen harbored suspicions that not everything was on the table. We might have lost considerable support had they known you had hired me. On the other hand, many congressmen I reached were friendly to you, Mr. Cooke, and I'm certain they knew of my mission before I spoke. Your connections and influence with Congress made the difference."

"No amount of quiet lobbying would have made any difference had not Professor Hayden taken hold as he did," said Cooke thoughtfully.

Langford nodded. "He was the man of the hour." Then Langford laughed. "One thing about Professor Hayden, if you introduce to him an idea that he can support and ask his assistance, you may soon hear that it was his idea to begin with."

"That's just the way we would like to keep it," said Cooke, "even though passage of the bill by Congress is, I believe, a clear vote in favor of our interest in the Northwest."

"Has anyone read the *Times*?" asked Wilkeson. He held up a handful of newspaper notices. Marshall reached for one. "No, not that one, that's the *St. Louis Times*. The one behind it is from the *Daily Rocky Mountain News*. They're all supportive editorials, but read the *New York Times*."

Marshall scanned the editorial, said "Ah!" at one point, and began to read out loud. "It is far from unlikely that within a few years the Yellowstone will become the Hamburg of America, and strangers from all over the world will flock to drink of its waters and gaze on picturesque splendors in the heart of America."

"Hey, hey," said Wilkeson loudly with a big smile, "that's what we like to hear. And listen to this from the *Helena Herald*. ". . . and few seasons will pass before excursion trains will daily be sweeping into this great park thousands of the curious from all parts of the world."

The men in the room applauded the notices. Cooke then called for silence. "We need to identify everyone who sided with us in the passage of this bill and let them know that neither Jay Cooke nor the Northern Pacific forgets."

"Well said," added Marshall. "We pulled in a lot of favors."

"And got the job done," added Nettleton, "which is what counts."

"I think some form of special thanks should go to several friends," said Cooke. "Schuyler Colfax, for one. The vice president was well acquainted with the Yosemite bill and had a vested interest in the notion of public parks."

"Certainly James Garfield, who supported Hayden," said Langford.

"Add Henry Dawes, Samuel Pomeroy, Mark Dunnell, and members of the Committee on Public Lands of both the House and Senate," advised Marshall.

"Perhaps you'll take charge to ensure we don't forget anyone, Bill," said Cooke as he shook Marshall's hand on the steps.

"Count on it," said Marshall.

As his associates left Ogontz in the barouche, Cooke returned to his library, took out a sheet of Jay Cooke and Co. stationery, and penned a letter to the secretary of the interior.

Dear Mr. Delano: Now that the Yellowstone has been set aside for the public, I'm sure you have begun to address the need for a park director, someone who is familiar with the land and its unique attributes, who supported the park bill, and who is well known for his integrity.

I would like to recommend that you seriously take under consideration Mr. Nathaniel Langford for the position. I base my recommendation on his background as an explorer and politician, his record of public service, and his proximity to the park as a resident of the territory of Montana. I also believe that his selection will find favor among the majority of Congress, particularly those who have been proponents of the park.

Cooke always believed what he said, but he also knew that it would be nice to work with someone knowledgeable and friendly to his objectives. Whoever influenced the direction of the new park would be an important asset to him and the Northern Pacific.

Having finished work for the day, Cooke took dinner alone. The euphoria of having learned that the park bill passed began to fade. His house was quiet without Lizzie. He missed her. He took in the details of the room and its furnishings with the anxiety of one who knew that nothing lasts forever. His financial empire was crumbling. He had been in finance too long not to recognize the malignancy that stemmed from having too much money tied up in investments and too little cash to conduct operations. He had tried everything he knew. His heart told him that it was not enough.

In the lull that followed the celebration of the park bill, Jackson reappeared at the survey office. His eyes were dull and he moved as though he was not fully in control of his muscles. He smiled listlessly at the offers of coffee, words of condolence, and the occasional pat.

No one asked him whether he planned to stay with the survey; his presence was answer enough. In deference to his feelings, the others toned down their voices. The slightly madcap banter between members of the survey faded. Everyone walked softly. After several days, Hayden decided that work might do Jackson good. He called him over and gave him a series of assignments. "I expect the work done on time, Bill," he said paternally. Jackson nodded, hollow-eyed, and disappeared into the darkroom.

Hayden looked to Jim Stevenson to confirm that he'd done the right thing. Stevenson nodded. "It's the worst thing that has happened to anyone I know," Stevenson said. "Not only was he robbed of the two people he cared most about, but the passage of the bill, when it came, was meaningless to him. And he worked as hard, if not harder, than all of us."

"He has a New Englander's mettle," said Hayden, gazing at the darkroom door. "And we need him."

"Mr. Jackson knows that you need him," said Emma to her husband that evening. She had taken the train to Washington, to celebrate the passage of the park bill. Now she was returning to Philadelphia. It wasn't the best living arrangement for a newly married couple, and Emma missed Hayden, but she didn't complain. Besides, she had to admit that she enjoyed her time alone; the mix of being married and still an independent, working woman suited her temperament.

"I believe that he will remain with the survey," she continued. "Now that his wife and child are gone, he has nothing else to stabilize him, or to give him a sense of direction."

"Is this the new psychology or feminine intuition?" asked Hayden with a small smile.

"Men are all alike and not that difficult to figure out, my dear," said Emma with her own small smile. She squeezed her husband's elbow. "You love your sense of freedom, but once you have known a woman's touch, you are forever changed."

"Oh, is that right?" said Hayden with a cheek-raising grin. "Do you have examples for me personally?"

"Of course, Ferdie," she continued straight-faced. "You never would have considered taking a woman into the field, not even Mrs. Jackson, until we were married and I reminded you of your pledge."

Hayden put on a manufactured scowl. "I can still change my mind, you know."

She leaned toward him and kissed him tenderly. "And miss all that married life can bring . . . even in the field?" she asked teasingly.

"Blackmail," Hayden replied.

On the way to the train station, Emma remained ebullient. "Oh, Ferdie, it will be so grand to see this captivating western world that has held you for so many years. In many ways, I'm jealous of her."

"Don't be. I will be the first to admit that she has her own charm and beauty. But she's a cold soul. She cares not a whit about my comings and goings, and she lacks your enthusiasm, your wit, and," he whispered, "your tenderness."

Emma looked with pride and love at the man she had married. In her trunk she kept a collection of the notices and editorials from all of the newspapers. In her heart, she carried memories of all the messages of congratulations and goodwill which her husband had received since Congress approved the park bill. Newspapers were calling the Yellowstone the first national park.

Emma felt lucky to have Ferdinand Hayden in her life: he was a prominent geologist, the author of nationally known reports, an explorer, and a most sought-after scientist. She had kept track of the organizations in which he was an active and honorary member until the list reached fifty, then she stopped.

She had read his "Geysers of the Yellowstone" when it made its appearance in the *American Journal of Science and Arts*. With a flush of girlish pride, she noted that the editor said that the act was in good part due to the interest and devotion of Dr. F. V. Hayden.

"Isn't it nice to see that Congress finally understands the importance of your survey and the measure of your successes? It's so rewarding to see you get the funding you deserve."

Hayden smiled. The almost constant twitch in his stomach that normally appeared when he thought of appropriations had faded. Hayden had remained nervous about his request for an appropriation for the coming summer until he received a note from James A. Garfield a week ago that said the Appropriations Committee had responded favorably to his request for seventy-five thousand dollars for the coming year. *The second letter from the secretary of the interior assumed the responsibility for a definite recommendation and that has greatly aided me in carrying it successfully*, wrote Garfield.

The committee's approval was as good as a signature on the check. And then, beyond his best expectations, Hayden learned that Congress had passed not only the full amount of his request but had allotted him an additional ten thousand dollars to illustrate his publications.

He was returning to the Yellowstone, this time with double the amount of funds he had had the prior year. He would extend his explorations into the little-known mountainous region surrounding the Yellowstone basin, the source of the most remarkable watersheds on the continent. In one magnificent summer he would examine and map the headwaters of the Yellowstone, the three forks of the Missouri, the Snake River which flowed into the Columbia, and the Green which flowed into the Gulf of California. He would also pinpoint the sources of the Wind River, which became the Big Horn before it joined the Missouri. An incredible opportunity!

Hayden celebrated the appropriation by discussing the next survey with Stevenson. They decided they would mount two separate parties. That meant a dramatic increase in the number of personnel. Hayden planned to bring in experts from all fields. "One big difference this time, Jim; we don't have to palm off the issue of payment. Each man will be paid according to his ability."

"What about Thomas Moran?" asked Stevenson.

Hayden shook his head. "He's been absorbed by his great painting of the Yellowstone and will not speak of anything else. I have no idea whether I can get him to return." Hayden looked worried. "When I last heard from him, he said he had been engaged by *Aldine* to make a half dozen large drawings, but had not even started them. He said he was too busy with his picture of the canyon and the falls. I should think it would have been completed by now, but he's said nothing about when he will be finished."

"How long has he been working on it?"

"More than a month. Here's his last letter. It mentions you."

Stevenson always enjoyed reading letters from former field companions. He was especially respectful of Thomas Moran, who had defied the odds by adjusting so quickly to the vagaries of the wild. As far as Stevenson was concerned, Moran had taken to the wilderness like a colt to a new pasture.

Now he read about Moran's passion for his work. *It has been heretofore deemed next to impossible to make good pictures of strange and wild scenes in nature*, wrote Moran, *and that the most that could be done with such material was to give topographic or geological character. But I have always held that the grandest most beautiful or wonderful in nature would, in capable hands, make the grandest, most beautiful or wonderful picture. And that, of course, is the business of a great painter.*

Moran apologized for having done nothing on the picture he had promised Hayden or on the one he had promised Stevenson, but he was consumed with his painting. *I cast all my claims to being an artist into this one picture of the Grand Canyon, and am willing to abide by the judgment of it.*

Stevenson handed the letter back to Hayden. "Moran's gamble on one little painting is risky, isn't it?"

"Perhaps, but I got the impression that it isn't little by any measure. He asked me to send him a portrait of myself. I think he's planning to place me in the picture somewhere."

"That's nice," said Stevenson.

Hayden's gesture was dismissive. "I suppose. He also wants me to come to New York to inspect the painting, to tell him whether it is sound geologically." Hayden looked at his watch. "Don't you think it's time we were going?"

Stevenson looked at his employer blankly.

"Today *is* the day you're getting married, isn't it?"

"Oh," said Stevenson. "True, true."

Hayden shook his head. Half the survey team had gathered at the Washington train station to accompany Stevenson and Hayden to Philadelphia. Everyone wanted to attend Stevenson's wedding and to meet his new wife, Matilda Coxe Evans.

When Emma met her weeks ago, her first comment to Hayden was, "Isn't she something?" Miss Evans was a feisty-eyed little Texas girl who had attended Miss Annabel's school in Philadelphia. According to Emma, she was not afraid to stand up for herself.

After the ceremony at the church, Jim Stevenson was happy to just stand there and let her have the spotlight. Henry Elliott created a most memorable moment when he presented Stevenson and Matilda with the painting he had started in the Yellowstone. In a bouquet of greens, blues, and browns, Elliott had captured the river outlet near Yellowstone Lake, a scene that included Stevenson Island and the *Anna* floating near the shore. Against the background of the Absaroka Mountains, a single deer grazed in the foreground; steam rose from nearby geysers and hot springs. Two birds flew beneath cumulus clouds colored by the late afternoon sun.

While his bride was chatting with members of the survey, Stevenson sought out Ferdinand Hayden. "You know I'm going to have to take her into the field," he said. "She won't stay home once she finds out that Emma is going."

"That's all right," said Hayden. "She and Emma can keep each other company."

"She wants to bring two Saratoga trunks," said Stevenson.

Hayden didn't bat an eye. "Then she'd better be able to paint as well as Thomas Moran."

"I'll tell her to work on her technique," said Stevenson. "See you in the Yellowstone, Professor." And he walked toward his waiting bride.

EPILOGUE

Toward the end of August 1871, Thomas Moran had hurried home from the Yellowstone via coach and train with a portfolio full of sketches. He had captured form, color, and subject matter that exceeded his wildest expectations. He had indeed been to the land of "grand nature." While the train passed scenery that had mesmerized him three months ago, Moran kept his head buried in his sketchpads. Forms and scenes in the Yellowstone permeated his every thought. The iridescent colors of his visions made his fingers twitch with eagerness to finish what he had started. He added notes here and there and mentally considered colors. He sharpened and strengthened a few lines in one or two sketches, made adjustments to a few compositions, and edited the notes he had taken about form and tint. He took special pains to describe little details while the scenes were still crystal clear. Not that he had to worry about forgetting detail: he'd disciplined himself to recall color and form.

Upon his arrival, he rushed into his house to embrace his wife and children. Emotionally exhausted but bursting with energy, he opened his sketchbook and with wild, sparkling eyes told stories about his adventures in the hidden wonderlands of the Yellowstone. Even as he talked, Moran wanted to draw: scenes of hot springs, waterfalls, canyons, and geysers, each with its own unique array of colors. The scenes had the same vividness as they had the day he looked into the Absaroka Range from the trail to Mystic Lake.

"Incredible!" shouted Moran as he entered the *Scribner's* offices several days later. "I have found the secret lair of hundreds of scenes of grand nature! Richard! Look at these sketches. I tell you, with these, I can create fifty woodcuts." He rapped his knuckles

on the cover of the pad, tossed his cloak onto a chair, and stuck his
sketchbooks in Richard Gilder's face.

Gilder chuckled as he shook Moran's hand to welcome him
back. "Thomas, that's great, but we'll probably have to start with
the first half dozen. We can't afford fifty."

Moran filled the first week of his return to New York with two
large illustrations for *Harper's Weekly*, one of the Grand Canyon of
the Yellowstone, and one of the valley as seen from the lower canyon. Two months later, the illustrations remained incomplete, but
they told him what kind of a series he wanted to do for *Scribner's*. In
January, he and Gilder decided which sketches they would use in
conjunction with Hayden's article. Moran began the first series of
woodcuts. Somehow, he also found time to begin a series of drawings for *Aldine*.

Moran transformed his studio into a miniature Yellowstone.
The room was adorned with pencil sketches, watercolor field
sketches, and photographs that Jackson had given him before he
left the Yellowstone. Moran worked ceaselessly, yet he still found
time to laugh, hug his wife, and share stories of his travels with his
curious, affectionate children. During this highly creative period,
Moran exuded a manic joy and infectious excitement about the
Yellowstone. He was the ultimate artist, consumed with the process of bringing his vision to the world.

A week before his illustrations for "The Wonders of the
Yellowstone" appeared with Hayden's article in the February issue
of *Scribner's*, Moran began painting his Grand Canyon of the
Yellowstone. There was no vacillation when he decided to paint in
oils. Moran had exhibited his oil paintings at the Pennsylvania
Academy of Fine Arts as early as 1858. Since then, watercolors
had held his interest, especially while so much of his time was
devoted to wood engravings. Most of his Yellowstone sketches were
in watercolors. He wasn't abandoning one medium for another; a
painting as large as the one he planned to do simply required oils.
He envisioned his masterpiece to be seven feet tall and fifteen feet
wide.

Nor did he hesitate in his selection of his theme. While he constructed the huge reinforced frame, and stretched twelve square yards of canvas, he could see the Grand Canyon of the Yellowstone. He pushed the finished frame upright. Just for an instant, the finished work seemed to flash across the canvas.

Moran attacked the huge white surface with long sweeps of charcoal. First, his eyes would race across his sketches. Then, with a clear vision, his body said "Yes!" as he created another massive form with the powdery stick.

"Every formation will be correct in the way it is seen," he said to himself as he worked. "But this is my picture, my image, so who cares if the relationships between the parts is not exact. Hah!" He erased a long line and replaced it with three shorter strokes. The horizon jumped into place. "Nor should it be," he grunted. He stepped away from the canvas again, glanced at two sketches he had pinned to the frame, then ran back and added more outlines. "This is *my* reality, and that's what counts."

Moran tied triangular compositions to the "V" of the canyon and falls. He elevated the horizon to force a deeper sense of space and depth. For the viewer, the panoramic scene was wrapped around a vantage point in the foreground, a small exploring party that included Hayden, Stevenson, and the fictional but symbolic form of an American Indian.

The hours rushed by. Day after day, week after week, Moran loaded his palette with chromes, raw sienna, burnt sienna, yellow ochre, and bright reds. In a semicircle, he squeezed out gobs of cobalt blue, rose madder, zinc green, and black asphaltum. He shook off the feeling that his colors were too ethereal, too unrealistic. No one on the East Coast had ever seen anything like the Yellowstone. He was not about to dilute the power of his vision.

As the huge painting took shape, Moran remained acutely aware of positive and negative space, of the power of the massive western forms, and the need to use texture for movement, all the time subordinating detail which could weaken the power of the finished work. "Detail does not control my image," hissed Moran to himself. "I do." He held a paintbrush in his mouth as he added a dash of chrome.

Towards the end of April, Mary Moran stuck her head into the studio. "Thomas, there are some gentlemen to see you."

Moran turned as Ab Nettleton walked in. "Hope we're not interrupting you, Mr. Moran," he said, "but several of our Northern Pacific Railroad board members arrived in town and they wanted to see your painting." And with that, R. D. Rice and Vermont Congressman Worthington C. Smith walked into the room.

"You're most welcome," said Moran. He had paint on both hands plus a few smears on one arm and a cheek. He ushered the men to the far end of the studio so they could see the painting from a distance. "I am nearly finished," said Moran. As he picked up a corner of the cloth that covered the painting, he added, "And I must say, it is all that I ever expected to make of it."

On the evening of May second, Levitt's gallery in New York City's Clinton Hall was jammed with people curious to see Thomas Moran's painting, *The Grand Canyon of the Yellowstone*. It was not like most recent artistic "happenings." No one had arranged for birds in cages, huge bouquets of flowers, fancy drapery, or delicately printed programs. None of these adornments was needed. Moran's creation trumpeted truth, sublimity, and beauty in mesmerizing color, size, and form.

The Grand Canyon of the Yellowstone loomed like a doorway to the forge of nature. Flashing cataracts bracketed by a phalanx of gothic cliffs assaulted the observer, drawing him closer to the image. The magnetic force of nature was made less alien by the presence of a small party of explorers. They rested in the foreground in shadows cast by gnarled pines. They were at ease, yet they were clearly tiny in the gigantic world around them. The scene was the epitome of grandeur, an inspirational portrayal of the sublime.

Hayden was one of the viewers. He'd had little choice. "You *must* be there," Gilder had written him. "The Northern Pacific people, the press, literati, artists, the rich, all will be out in force. We want to make a big strike, and we want you there to answer questions. Why not bring Mrs. Hayden and make a grand spree of it?"

Once Moran knew Hayden was there, he rushed to his side. "Well, what do you think?" he asked.

"You have a large turnout. Isn't that a good sign?"

"No, no, Professor Hayden. I meant the painting. What do you think of the painting?"

"Well, I suppose I should see it before I say anything. I've been unable to get close enough to examine it because of the crowd."

The crowd was moved back to permit Dr. Hayden to examine the painting. He walked closer, and appeared to examine details in most of the rock formations. As he spoke, the crowd quieted. Hayden's remarks underlined the artist's devotion to fact, his attention to color, and the truth of his use of space, form, and proportion. Hayden answered a few questions for the press and was introduced to several members of the Northern Pacific Railroad board. Everyone was there but Jay Cooke.

Now Richard Gilder drew the throng's attention. His voice carried well, so he immediately became the center of attention. "I am reminded," he said, "that Emile Zola was moved to say, 'art is nature seen through a temperament. It is the artist's business to produce the impression produced by nature on himself.' As an artist who shares the American landscape with Thomas Cole, Asher B. Durand, Fitz Hugh Lane, Frederick Church, and Thomas Doughty, Thomas Moran has expressed his love of nature. He has imbued his work with a dazzling display of luminous light and color.

"I was privileged to watch this creation emerge, ladies and gentlemen; had M. Zola been present, he, too, would have seen his vision of art come to life." The audience applauded.

"Watching this painting take on form and detail was like watching the creation of the earth. Mr. Moran threw the outline across the canvas in one day. I saw great streaks of meaningless color appear in apparently random sectors of the canvas. To me it seemed hopeless chaos. By and by the sky appeared, then delicate indications of clouds, mist, mountains, rocks, and trees crept down the canvas, slowly gathering body and tone, till at last the artist's full, glorious idea shone perfect in every point."

"Why is it so large?" asked a reporter.

"Is not size the trend today?" responded Gilder. "And is not

Mr. Moran competing with the works of Cole and Bierstadt? I do believe so. But when I think of him carrying that image around in his head, I wonder he didn't have to go through the door sideways." The crowd laughed. Reporters' pencils squiggled quickly across their notepads.

The Grand Canyon of the Yellowstone was a sensation. The *New York Times* said that next to Mr. Church's *Niagara*, the painting was the finest historical work in the country. The renowned art critic Clarence Cook announced that the composition had been handled with masterly finesse. He wrote poetically of the "sapphire river that swept with all its garnered sunshine down to the bottom of the world."

Every reviewer who attended the show found the subject ideal for an artist of the Romantic era. They claimed that Moran's approach to nature was a masterful presentation of the pre-Raphaelites' posture on painting.

Newspaper articles claimed that *The Grand Canyon of the Yellowstone* had opened the eyes of America to the beauty and splendor of her own backyard. It had awakened the country to the extravagances of nature so well exemplified in the West. No longer would America have to look to Europe for the standards of elegance and awe. Now America had her own in the Yellowstone.

With a sigh of relief, Hayden and Emma boarded the train for Denver. Emma was excited because Hayden was keeping his promise to let her experience his mysterious and captivating West. Hayden was relieved to get going again. He had been attending to all the little details that never seemed to stay done. In the midst of those last-minute items, he'd received an anxious letter from Thomas Moran. He had moved his painting, which had hung in the Smithsonian Institution, to the House of Representatives. He was certain that Congress would purchase the painting, if the idea was presented in the correct form.

We need to get a proposition entered in form of a resolution, Moran wrote Hayden. *Dawes says that we stand a good chance. Your influence would be most helpful here. Will you try to get Dawes and Garfield to bring the matter to the right committee? Little of the session remains. I need help now.*

Moran had turned down Hayden's request that he return to the Yellowstone that summer. Moran decided instead to go to the Grand Canyon with John Wesley Powell, who was planning a second excursion into the remote region. But Moran saw no reason why he should not ask Hayden for help with the sale of *The Grand Canyon of the Yellowstone.*

The artist's sense of urgency reminded Hayden of the times when he desperately needed help. He pulled out two fresh sheets of paper and penned notes to Representative Garfield and to Moran. He would miss Moran this summer, but he still had Jackson. He would also have the company of Mr. Langford, who had recently been appointed the first superintendent of the park. And, of course, he would have Emma.

As Hayden's train pulled away from the Philadelphia station, Harris C. Fahnestock stepped on to the platform from a train that had just arrived from New York City. He strode towards the entrance where Cooke's coach waited. He'd telegraphed Cooke from New York: they urgently needed to talk about the firm's financial situation. He didn't have to say that he believed the firm was headed for disaster; Cooke knew his feelings. Fahnestock sensed that the time for talk was drawing to a close. If the fundamental relationship between Jay Cooke and Co. and the Northern Pacific Railroad was not altered, he was certain they could lose everything.

The trip to Ogontz was pleasant and restful, but Fahnestock resisted the balm of late spring's offerings. It was bad enough that he had agreed to talk to Cooke at Ogontz where he would be Cooke's guest. He knew what he had to do, but he still did not know Cooke's posture. Was he ready to face facts? The Northern Pacific Railroad Company's latest financial statement disclosed that they had spent $11,481,000 to date. As the responsible financial agent for the railroad, Jay Cooke and Co. owed nearly $2,000,000 in outstanding bills plus $17,500,000 in bonds. The figures did not show their problems with income. They were strung as tight as a violin string.

Any small contingency or unforeseen problem could break the firm.

Fahnestock had not altered his position since the day he learned that Cooke had taken on the Northern Pacific. The firm had tackled a project that was simply too enormous. Never had one house or one man been entirely responsible for an enterprise of such magnitude. It was more than unwise; it was foolhardy to stake the reputation, perhaps the existence, of the firm on the success or failure of an enterprise that was essentially an experiment. Fahnestock had told his partner just that, many times.

Fahnestock wanted Jay Cooke and Co. to tackle the job like Fisk and Hatch had tackled the Union Pacific, to be responsible solely for the finances. Let others build the road. If Fisk and Hatch had left the Union Pacific, the work on the line would have continued. But Jay Cooke *was* the Northern Pacific. He had the responsibility not only of finance but also of the trusteeship. That position made him morally liable to every man and woman who held bonds, for the application of all moneys received and verification of all the statements in the railroad's publications. He had pledged that the bonds were the best and safest securities for widows and orphans. He had assured them of the integrity, the honesty, and the economy of management. Harris Fahnestock was convinced that Jay Cooke had lied. Knowingly.

The coach rolled over the Germantown hills. Fahnestock felt his muscles getting tight. The lands of the Northern Pacific were touted as being of unparalleled quality, yet everyone in the firm knew that hundreds of square miles between Lake Superior and the Mississippi were practically worthless. Cooke had depended too heavily on his promoters. He had placed too little emphasis on practical considerations which governed the public's assessment of government securities.

God, the man was stubborn. Stubborn? No, blind. If the bonds had been offered at a price that reflected the experimental nature of the railroad, they would have been picked up by monied men, but Cooke had fallen back on his old pattern of selling exclusively to people who relied on his personal recommendation. What he didn't seem to realize was that this class and its money were limited.

But then, Cooke was not a banker. He was a promoter. Fahnestock felt responsible for not having pressed the issue earlier. The firm was indebted to Cooke's enthusiasm and personal dynamics for most of its accomplishments, but the general public had almost quit buying the bonds. The price was too high, too many other railroad projects were in trouble, and Jay Cooke and Co. had not been able to secure assistance from abroad.

Those qualities of Jay Cooke that Fahnestock most admired, that had drawn him to work with Cooke, were the ones he would have to monitor carefully. He had failed to stand up to Cooke when a firm "No" was needed. Now both the railroad and Jay Cooke and Co. were at risk. God help us if anything else interrupts the sale of bonds, thought Fahnestock. It will stop all work. Then we'll have the responsibility to save the company from default.

The carriage drew up to the entrance of Cooke's forest hideaway. Fahnestock stepped out, knowing that he had to force Cooke to recognize that radical means were needed to save the company.

The following afternoon, Cooke's black covered carriage took Fahnestock back to the Philadelphia railroad station.

Fahnestock was in shock. Nothing had changed. Cooke readily acknowledged the problems, but . . . but what? Cooke said he'd spoken harshly to Smith, told him that he was spending money for the fun of running a railroad without receipts. Against all logic, Smith had purchased a steamboat on the Missouri when the tracks were nowhere near there. He had also purchased controlling interest in the Oregon Steamboat Navigation Company, which operated steamboats on the Columbia, Willamette, and Snake rivers and on Puget Sound and portages along the Columbia.

Although Cooke promised Fahnestock that he would oust Smith and his Vermont cronies, he failed to project a sense of immediate action. Nothing in his language suggested that he was about to abandon the project. Fahnestock wondered whether Cooke had some blind faith that God would somehow take over when failure was imminent.

The passenger car jerked as it began its journey. A depressed but resolved Harris Fahnestock returned to New York City, knowing that if the situation did not improve, he would be forced to make the first move.

Eighteen hundred seventy-two proved to be a pivotal year for a number of people. Hayden received approval to return to the Yellowstone. Thomas Moran sold his *Grand Canyon of the Yellowstone* to Congress for ten thousand dollars, and William Henry Jackson's career as a master photographer of the West was all but assured.

And for the Northern Pacific Railroad and the firm of Jay Cooke and Co., 1872 pushed them beyond the fail-safe point. That June, when President Grant opened his reelection campaign at the Philadelphia Academy of Music in June, the first Northern Pacific train was crossing the Red River into Dakota territory. A month later, Cooke wrote every member of the Northern Pacific board. In one paragraph he told them of recent progress, and in the next paragraph told them that they had to pledge their shares in the five-million-dollar pool to keep the enterprise afloat.

That fall, Gregory Smith and General Spaulding offered their resignations, and the Minnesota clique, which had diverted Northern Pacific resources into their own pockets, were sent packing. But overdrafts pushed the railroad deeper into the red. When payments to contractors were delayed, Cooke turned over construction to General George W. Cass, who had managed the Pittsburgh, Chicago, and Fort Wayne Railroad for twenty-five years.

The tracks plunged deeper into the empty Northwest, one hundred thirty miles west of the new town of Fargo. Five hundred men and thirty teams made grade and laid track, but past delays lost the company its credit standing in Minnesota.

Strangely coincidental to the struggle of the Northern Pacific was the epidemic that crippled or killed most of the horses in Philadelphia. The disease, referred to in the newspapers as epizooty, paralyzed local transportation companies. It became a common sight to see people pulling and pushing loaded carts and wagons by hand. But Cooke was more attuned to the editorials that appeared in the

Public Ledger. Drexel had gotten wind of the Northern Pacific's financial problems and denounced the company, calling the grants corrupt and stating that the entire project was in advance of the country's needs.

Just before Christmas, 1872, General Cass asked Cooke whether the company could meet its financial obligations. Jay Cooke and Co. had sold less than thirty million dollars in bonds since the initiation of work. Cooke responded that there was no doubt. He said he had every confidence in General Cass's management and he felt that prosperity would attend the enterprise.

The first two hundred and twenty-eight miles of track laid by the Northern Pacific west of Duluth were examined by the railroad commission and found satisfactory. The track was well located and well laid, with good curves, inclination, and ballast. The company's rolling stock was of good quality, the engineering houses adequate, and the passenger and freight stations neat and tasteful in appearance. The immigration houses that the railroad had constructed at Brainerd, Glyndon, and Duluth were being furnished with cooking stoves and furniture for free use by those intending to settle on company or government land.

The government released one half million acres of land for sale by the Northern Pacific. At the same time, Mother Nature dumped record snows across the plains, leaving all twelve hundred souls in the little railroad community of Bismarck snowbound until April.

In Washington, D.C., winter faded early. Congress tore into the Credit Mobilier, the construction company of the Union Pacific that was owned by the railroad's directors. The investigating committee's final report hit Congress like a falling brick wall. Although no one could determine the extent of fraud, profits, or loss, the investigators said that the amount lay somewhere between ten and forty million dollars.

In New York, Fahnestock read a long proposal from Cooke, who wanted to refinance the Northern Pacific. He recommended reducing the current bond offer. In its place, he would create another railroad syndicate that would issue another bond series. The adjustment in the rates would enable the railroad to develop a reserve fund to pay off the bonds. Jay Cooke and Co would surrender the land grant to the government. The grant could then be sold by the secretary of the interior. Cooke would also turn over net earnings semi-annually.

Fahnestock covered his desk with figures and shook his head. Once again, Cooke had put together a plan that had no slack. Fahnestock pounded the table in frustration. Cooke resolutely refused to acknowledge that the world was not always a sunny place. His plan was far too late and millions short to cover outstanding debt, operating expenses, and the additional cost of advertising the new bonds.

Fahnestock watched Cooke's proposal wither outside the doors of Congress. After the Credit Mobilier scandal, it made no difference what the financier was willing to do. Congress had been badly burned by the Union Pacific. It would not touch another joint railroad venture. As if to underline its position, Congress voted to withhold interest payment on the Union Pacific's coupons. That single move nearly destroyed the railroad bond market. By September, cash was tight, interest was climbing fast, and rumors flew to all corners of the country about a possible stock market panic.

By the middle of September 1873, the tracks of the Northern Pacific Railroad had reached the mouth of Glendive Creek on the Yellowstone River. The anticipated cost of the next two hundred miles was only twenty thousand dollars per mile. Surveys had been completed from Puget Sound to Lake Superior, and trains were running the four hundred fifty miles from Lake Superior to the Missouri River.

The country had been expanding at an unprecedented rate for the past eight years, yet the signs of stability and growth remained positive. Great new steel and petroleum industries had arisen. Mass production had been organized in the shoe, clothing, and meatpacking industries. Cattle ranches were replacing the buffalo on the plains. Mills were running at capacity. Immigration was brisk. Wages were making much-needed gains, and nearly everyone was employed.

On the morning of September 17, Jay Cooke and President Ulysses S. Grant walked together down the front steps of Ogontz. The president stepped into Cooke's waiting carriage. He had taken Cooke's recommendation and enrolled his son, Jessie, in a private school in Chelton Hills near Ogontz. Cooke had invited the president to stay the night.

President Grant was in a good mood. It had been nice to get away from the White House, to be with a friend in whom he had confidence. Grant had great respect for Jay Cooke, not only as a financier and patriot, but also as an entrepreneur. But on this visit, he sensed that something was very wrong. Every time the president tried to lighten the conversation, he received silence or a half-hearted response. His friend was preoccupied with grave problems.

They talked of inconsequentials for a while. Then President Grant looked across the seat to where Cooke sat. "We've been friends a long time, Jay," he said paternally. "You've assisted my office in ways I will never be able to repay. And the services you have provided the country have left the nation in your debt. But since my arrival yesterday afternoon, I have seen a deeply troubled man. You are not the vigorous and optimistic friend I used to know. I sense that you are wrestling some inner demon."

The president looked away to soften his words. "I normally keep my questions to myself, Jay, but this morning my sense of friendship begs me to ask you what is so bothersome."

Cooke seemed to brace himself before he spoke, but the president raised his hand. "If I should not ask, you will tell me, and that will be as it will, but do not forget the power of my office and my willingness to assist you in any way I can."

The carriage stopped at the train station. The president got out. Cooke shook Grant's hand. "My apologies, Mr. President. I have been preoccupied. Your offer is most generous, but everything is under control. God has always been with me and the situation will resolve itself in the course of events."

"Then Godspeed, Jay."

"Mr. President."

Following his routine, Cooke went to work the next day. But nothing was normal, certainly not according to the telegram he

440   David M. Delo

clutched in his hand. At his office he waited, and at ten o'clock, he
received what the first telegram had predicted, a second telegram.
They were both from Fahnestock. The second telegram said: *Jay.
After having conferred with a group of bankers, I have closed the
doors of the Jay Cooke and Co. New York banking house. I had no
choice. Fahnestock.*

Cooke remained in his chair for about five minutes, then got
up and walked into the lobby. To his manager, he said calmly, "As
soon as the lobby is clear, Albert, please close and lock the doors."
In response to Albert's look of total disbelief, Cooke added, "The
New York house closed its doors an hour ago. We must follow suit."

The news spread and pandemonium filled the financial districts of New York, Boston, Philadelphia, and Washington. Brokers
surged out of the Stock Exchange, tumbling over one another pell-
mell to reach their offices. In downtown New York, hundreds rushed
to their brokers with orders to sell. The bear clique was already
selling the market down. Prices across the board were in fast decline.

Early that afternoon, Fahnestock faced reporters with a prepared statement. *The immediate cause of suspension of Jay Cooke
and Co. was the large drawing by the Philadelphia house and their
depositors during the prior fortnight. Both houses had suffered a
large draw by their depositors in consequence of the uneasy feeling
which has recently prevailed and which has affected more or less all
houses closely connected with railroad enterprises. The Philadelphia house had previously been weakened by large cash advances to
the Northern Pacific Railroad of which they are the financial agents.*

*The business of Jay Cooke and McCullough in London is en-
tirely distinct and perfectly solvent and will be able to meet all claims
without inconveniences to travelers and have a large cash surplus to
apply to the American house of that firm. Also, the members of Jay
Cooke and Co. have large amounts of real and personal property
upon which however they cannot immediately realize. They are confident that all depositors will be paid in full.*

The reporters all shouted at once. "What amount has been
withdrawn to supply the Philadelphia house?" asked one.

"I cannot say at the moment and I do not care to speculate."

"Did the run on the bank result from a lack of confidence in the house?"

"Yes," said Fahnestock. "We had that feeling."

"Are most of the depositors in the bank salaried persons?" asked another.

"No such thing. Almost all the depositors in New York were banks or bankers. Our failure is distributed all over the country, and if any losses are sustained by them it will fall on those who can afford them."

"What amount of the bonds has been placed?"

"About twenty-five million."

"What was behind the failure of the Philadelphia house?" asked a reporter from the *Herald*.

"Advances to the Northern Pacific," said Fahnestock without hesitation.

"And how long has the house anticipated the current failure?"

Fahnestock opened his mouth, then paused. How long had he known? How long had Cooke ignored it? "About two years," he said, "but the righting of affairs is only a matter of time."

The domino effect swept across the financial world. Fisk and Hatch, who promoted the Union Pacific Company, failed, then the First National Bank of Washington failed, and then Enoch Clarke and Co. followed suit. Vanderbilt investments, including the New York Central, Lake Shore, and Harlem, were caught by falling prices. Representatives of Jay Gould and Vanderbilt pleaded that immense reserves in stock and ready cash were available, but self-preservation was the rule. Everyone wanted to close out of the market.

When Western Union gave way, the whole market slumped, and soon every house in good standing was under attack. At the corner of Broad Street Exchange, a wild crowd of moneylenders and borrowers collected and tried, unsuccessfully, to fix a rate for loans. Gold took a sudden start in prices because the government declined to make any awards of the one and one half million it said would be sold the day before. The mayhem was greater than the panic of 1857, when the Ohio Trust Company had failed.

In Philadelphia, a newsboy hawked, "Extra! Extra! Learn all about the failure of Jay Cooke."

"Hey," said a policeman, grabbing the lad by the shirt collar. "You should know better than to yell things like that. You'll spend a night in the pokey, you will." And he dragged the protesting lad towards his wagon.

By midafternoon, several hundred people had gathered in front of Jay Cooke and Co. Shouts rang out from the crowd. "When are you going to pay us?" "I want my money." "Jay Cooke is a crook!" "You have robbed the people."

Each time someone shouted, the crowd became more agitated. Police arrived to keep them from the doors. The crowd sensed that they were being denied their rights. They shouted and yelled and pushed back. Fighting and swearing, the police used their clubs, but the crowd remained loud and threatening until after five that evening.

When analysis began to replace panic, the major newspapers ran editorials. A few referred to the historical echoes of former financial panics. Some talked about Cooke's long, successful record in banking.

One editor summarized cause and effect succinctly. *The storm has come and the whole scheme has come down. Its good effects in developing the Northwest will remain, but for the unfortunate holders of its securities we are sure there is only disaster. Mr. Cooke forgot he was a banker and became too much of a promoter.*

The Gilded Age took its place in American history as a time when great men made bold moves to gain wealth, power, and reputation. It is nice to remember that together with its scandals, this period also gave America its greatest cultural symbol, the Yellowstone National Park!

END

Bibliographic Guide

Biographies of Thomas Moran and Ferdinand Hayden may be found in most libraries, as can the autobiography of William H. Jackson. There are two books on Jay Cooke's financial dealings, but copies are not widespread. No biography yet exists for Nathaniel Langford. His life is described in articles published by the historical societies of Minnesota and Montana. He also wrote a book about the Washburn Expedition.

A solid biography of Ferdinand Hayden was recently published and should be easy to find. Manuscript collections at the University of Wyoming and Federal Archives microfilm also shed light on the life and character of Ferdinand Hayden. The letters of Jay Cooke that I located in Philadelphia were irreplaceable. Most of William H. Jackson's photographs are at the Federal Information Center in Denver.

I read a number of general histories on the Gilded Age, the American West, the Hudson River School of art, and Washington, D.C. during the time of Grant's administration. Books and articles gave me needed information about the Smithsonian Institution, America's banking system in the mid-1800s, and the histories of Helena, Montana, and South Pass and Fort Bridger, Wyoming.

Books by Aubrey Haines and Richard Bartlett on the history of Yellowstone National Park were very important, as was the array of publications on the exploration of the Yellowstone— the Cooke-Peterson exploration of 1869, the Washburn Expedition of 1870, and Hayden's 1871 and 1872 geological surveys. I also collected the majority of articles written by and about Ferdinand Hayden.

Congressional documents on the process by which the Yellowstone became a national park were most revealing, as were books on the history of the development of the Northern Pacific Railroad and attendant personalities.

About David M. Delo and Kingfisher Books

David Michael Delo (1938 ,) is a Renaissance man who has earned praise in every field of his endeavors. As an intelligence agent assigned to NATO, he was awarded the Commendation Medal. At Levi Strauss & Co., a Fortune 500 firm in San Francisco, he was awarded a Vice Presidency. And for his first non-fiction book of American history, *Peddlers and Post Traders*, he received unrestrained praise from his reviewers.

Five years ago, while he was conducting research on 19th century government geologist Ferdinand Hayden, Delo discovered that the careers of three noted figures of American history emerged from the same time and place. The three were Ferdinand Hayden, artist Thomas Moran, and photographer William Henry Jackson. The place was the Yellowstone!

Delo had been educated as a geologist. He had been an artist since birth, and had photographed portions of the great West with his own view camera. The coincidences were too great to ignore. The resulting 450-page book weaves the ambitions and personal problems of these men into the story of how America acquired its first national park.

Beginning in 1999, Delo's new publishing company, Kingfisher Books, will reprint a paperback version of his 1992 book on military post traders. He will then publish a second historical novel of the West, and the first four books in his action-adventure series about a photojournalist in San Francisco named Touch. Delo's goal is to make Kingfisher Books known as the Rocky Mountain publisher that produces Rocky Mountain books for Rocky Mountain people.

For the past six years, Delo has been a resident of Helena, Montana. In the spring, summer, and fall, he may be found in the Rocky Mountains, hawking his books and his pen and ink notecards.

ORDER FORM

for

The Yellowstone, Forever!

$15.00

Tear off this order form and mail to:

Kingfisher Books
POB 4628
Helena, MT 59604

If you send this form with your order no
later than June 1, 1998 you will save
$3.00 shipping and handling.

**This book carries a money-back guarantee of quality
from the Rocky Mountain company that publishes Rocky
Mountain books for Rocky Mountain people.**

ORDER FORM

for

The Yellowstone, Forever!

$15.00

Tear off this order form and mail to:

Kingfisher Books
POB 4628
Helena, MT 59604

If you send this form with your order no
later than June 1, 1998 you will save
$3.00 shipping and handling.

**This book carries a money-back guarantee of quality
from the Rocky Mountain company that publishes Rocky
Mountain books for Rocky Mountain people.**